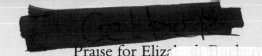

Praise for Elizabeth Buchan

Wives Behaving Badly

"Hats off to a title that titillate . . . *Wives Behaving Badly* . . . smartly lives up to its name. An unusually tasty morsel of Brit chick lit." —*O, The Oprah Magazine*

"Hard to put down." —*The Seattle Times*

"Wickedly entertaining . . . This polished novel is about a slippery second marriage, but first and fifth ones will recognize the conjugal territory that Buchan so glitteringly explores." —*Timesonline.uk*

Revenge of the Middle-Aged Woman

"A thoughtful, intelligent, funny, coming-of-middle-age story." —*The Boston Globe*

"Wise and wonderful" —*USA Today*

"Revenge may be sweet, but *Revenge* is not, thank goodness." —*The Wall Street Journal*

"A sophisticated and satisfying novel . . . Buchan opts for a more believable examination of one intelligent woman's coming-of-age." —*Publishers Weekly* (starred review)

"Middle-aged or not, readers will find this book funny and sad, serious and light. Bottom line: Get *Revenge*." —*People*

"What I like most about this novel is everything." —Elizabeth Berg

Everything She <u>Thought</u> She Wanted

The Good Wife Strikes Back

PENGUIN BOOKS

WIVES BEHAVING BADLY

Elizabeth Buchan is the author of ten novels, including the bestselling and prize-winning *Consider the Lily* and the bestselling *Revenge of the Middle-Aged Woman*. She lives in London.

Wives Behaving Badly

Elizabeth Buchan

PENGUIN BOOKS

PENGUIN BOOKS

Published by the Penguin Group
Penguin Group (USA) Inc., 375 Hudson Street, New York, New York 10014, U.S.A.
Penguin Group (Canada), 90 Eglinton Avenue East, Suite 700, Toronto,
Ontario, Canada M4P 2Y3 (a division of Pearson Penguin Canada Inc.)
Penguin Books Ltd, 80 Strand, London WC2R 0RL, England
Penguin Ireland, 25 St Stephen's Green, Dublin 2, Ireland (a division of Penguin Books Ltd)
Penguin Group (Australia), 250 Camberwell Road, Camberwell,
Victoria 3124, Australia (a division of Pearson Australia Group Pty Ltd)
Penguin Books India Pvt Ltd, 11 Community Centre,
Panchsheel Park, New Delhi – 110 017, India
Penguin Group (NZ), 67 Apollo Drive, Rosedale, North Shore 0745,
Auckland, New Zealand (a division of Pearson New Zealand Ltd)
Penguin Books (South Africa) (Pty) Ltd, 24 Sturdee Avenue,
Rosebank, Johannesburg 2196, South Africa

Penguin Books Ltd, Registered Offices:
80 Strand, London WC2R 0RL, England

First published in the United States of America by Viking Penguin,
a member of Penguin Group (USA) Inc. 2006
Published in Penguin Books 2007

1 3 5 7 9 10 8 6 4 2

PUBLISHER'S NOTE
This is a work of fiction. Names, characters, places, and incidents either are the product
of the author's imagination or are used fictitiously, and any resemblance to actual persons,
living or dead, business establishments, events, or locales is entirely coincidental.

ISBN 0-670-034886 (hc.)
ISBN 978-0-14-311218-1 (pbk.)
CIP data available

Printed in the United States of America
Set in Bembo
Designed by Spring Hoteling

For Marika

"We will now discuss in a little more detail the struggle for existence."

—Charles Darwin, *The Origin of Species*

Acknowledgments

I owe many people for generously giving me their time and expertise. In particular I owe a huge debt of gratitude to Clive Sydall, Antony Mair, and Sebastian Leathlean. Any mistakes are mine. I would also like to thank Janet Buck, Lucy Floyd, William Gill, Pamela Norris, Diana Stephenson, Belinda Taylor, and many other friends, who, as ever, gave rocklike support. I would like to include here the many friends I have made through the book clubs and, in particular, Angela, Emily, Gail, Jo, Linda, Theresa, and the Ami Machi Monday Reading Group in Japan. To my wonderful editor, Pamela Dorman, and her assistant, Katherine Carlson, my copy editor, Noirin Lucas, and the brilliant team at Viking Penguin, Mark Lucas, my agent, and lastly my husband and children a big thank-you.

Wives Behaving Badly

How It Began

On my wedding day, I got dressed in a full red silk skirt and a black jacket to hide my ten-week pregnant figure. For a considerable time, I hovered in front of the mirror in the cramped bedroom of my flat, fiddling with the lie of the skirt, adjusting my makeup and wishing I could wear high heels, but pregnancy made my feet hurt. I think I was trying to persuade myself of my imminent status. "Mrs Lloyd." The mirror reflected my lips shaping the words—but, of course, what I saw was the distortion. What I really, truly saw in the mirror was "the second Mrs Lloyd."

Nathan hailed a taxi and we sailed off to the registry office. He had chosen his dark gray office suit, and had cut his hair too short, which I disliked. It made him appear unfinished, and not the worldly sophisticated man that I rated, and since he had lost weight, underfed. He did not seem particularly happy.

"You could look a *little* pleased," I remarked from my side of the taxi.

To his credit, his face cleared. "Sorry darling, I was thinking of something else."

I watched a cyclist weaving suicidally in and out of the traffic. "We're on our way to our wedding and you are thinking of something else."

"Hey." Nathan reached over and captured one of my hands, which were permanently hot—another little pregnancy joke. "There's no need to worry, I promise."

I believed him but I wanted to drive the point home. "This is our special day."

He gave me one of his strongman smiles. "Everything is fine. And I promise I'm thinking of you."

I nipped the flesh of his palm between my fingers. "Well, here's a shock. The bridegroom is thinking about the bride."

Nathan had specified "casual" to the guests, who were eight altogether. No fuss, he said. No fireworks. He had been anxious not to make a big deal of the day. "You *do* understand?" he asked me more than once, which irritated me. On the other hand, since I was pregnant and, as it turned out, without a job, my negotiating position was limited.

When we arrived, Nathan seemed transfixed by the ugly stone office block which housed the registry. Inside, there was an anteroom adorned with fake paneling, crude gilding, and a stand of plastic flowers in hideous pinks and blues that no one had dusted.

As we filed in, Paige rushed up behind us. She was still working at the bank then and wore a beige suit and white blouse. There was a lick of grime on the lapel. "You look great, Minty." She hefted a briefcase that bulged with papers from one hand to the other. "You did say not to dress up and I've just dashed out of a meeting."

"Yes . . ."

She peered at me. "Oh my God, you did want me to dress up."

I could only stare back at her, mute and uncomprehending. For, so help me, I did. I wanted Paige to be in her best Alexander McQueen and a hat that shrieked "occasion." After all, and after everything, I craved silk and tulle, a flash of diamonds in the ear, the hiss of champagne, the scent of expensive flowers, and the welling up of emotion and excitement—of the kind that stirs the guests to stand on metaphorical tiptoe, united for a moment by unselfish kindness and by the yearning to start all over again themselves.

Paige frowned. "Where's your bouquet, Minty?"

"I don't have one."

"Right," said Paige, and you could not fault her. "Hold on." She thrust her briefcase into my hand and disappeared.

Nathan beckoned me to a group in which his eldest children, Sam and Poppy, and their spouses, Jilly and Richard, were talking to Peter and Carolyne Shaker. Poppy was in black and Jilly was markedly pregnant in a demin smock that needed a press. Only Carolyne had made an effort in a glaringly bright red dress and a white jacket.

Sam did not quite meet my eye. "Hallo, Minty."

Jilly made more of an effort and pecked at my cheek. Her long, silky hair brushed against my cheek; it smelled of shampoo and wholesome things. "How are you feeling?" she whispered meaningfully, one pregnant woman to another.

"Fine. Very little different. Apart from very hot hands, and feet that hurt."

Her eyes raked over me. "You hardly show, you lucky thing."

Jilly meant the opposite. Every line of her body with out-thrust belly proclaimed her delight in being so obviously fecund. She leaned against Sam. "You wait. Sore feet is only the start," she said contentedly.

Paige burst back into the room. "Here's your bouquet, Minty. It's terrible, but it will have to do." She thrust into my hand a bunch of red roses, the kind that were sold on street corners by oppressed immigrant workers. They were tightly furled and only half alive.

The registrar cleared his throat. "Are we ready . . . ?"

"The cellophane," Paige hissed. I ripped it off, squashed it into a ball, and left it on the table.

"Oh Minty," Nathan said. "I forgot you should have flowers."

In the restaurant afterward we were joined by Aunt Ann, Nathan's last remaining relative, and there was a great deal of fussing and rearranging of chairs to accommodate her wheelchair.

I observed the guests at the table. Their expressions were fixed, as if they were struggling collectively to find a way through the experience. Jilly drank ostentatiously from a glass of water. Sam draped his arm around his wife. Poppy chattered and fluttered, her Thai silk scarf flashing scarlet and gold. Every so often, she touched Richard's shoulder or his arm. Once, she pressed her lips to his cheek. None of them looked in my direction. There was comment about my first name being Susan, a fact revealed by the registrar. For most of my life I had hated the name and had refused to use it since I was fifteen, but I went to its defense. "What's so funny about Susan?"

Jilly and Poppy put their heads on one side. "It's just that you're so *Minty*," Jilly explained.

"I'm sorry you haven't got any family here," Sam remarked as we ate Dover sole and scallops.

"My father vanished when I was small, my mother is dead, and I don't have any siblings or cousins."

"I'm sorry."

"I don't miss what I've never had," I added stubbornly, insistently. "It's not so terrible."

Sam might have said: we are your family now. But he didn't.

At the end of the meal I watched Nathan proffer his platinum credit card to pay the bill, and thought with relief that I would not have to worry about money any more. I went to say good-bye to Aunt Ann, stooping over the wheelchair and inhaling face powder and dust from her hat with a black feather. "Goodbye. Thank you so much for coming."

She raised a startlingly thin hand blotched with liver spots, on which rattled a platinum wedding ring and diamond solitaire, and touched my cheek. "So nice," she murmured, and I felt a rush of unexpected tears. They say cynics are the only true romantics. I was marrying Nathan without any of the true and proper feelings, only nonfeelings, but I was doing it all the same. And Aunt Ann's touch was worth more than it was possible to describe.

Poppy was hovering. "Aunt Ann. We must take you home. I promised that I would not let you overdo things."

Her exhaustion and confusion obvious, Aunt Ann groped for her words. "Good-bye, Rose," she said.

Chapter One

I have found that for me, it is wise to have a few rules tucked up inside my head, and the ones currently governing my life are:

Rule number one: there is no justice.

Rule number two: contrary to a husband's hopes, a second wife does not have *The Kama Sutra* nestling in her handbag. It is more likely to be aspirin.

Rule number three: never complain, particularly if you have been instrumental in demonstrating rule number one, which I have been.

Rule number four: never serve liver or tofu.

Nathan and I were wrestling over the guest list for the dinner party.

"Why do we need to give one?" he demanded from the sofa. It was a Sunday afternoon in early November, and he was sleepy after a lunch of roast chicken with tarragon. Newspapers paved the floor and the room was stuffy with winter and central heating. In their bedroom directly above the sitting room, the twins played at airports, taking off and landing with excruciating thumps.

I informed Nathan that it was necessary for his position at Vistemax to *keep going,* that I had already compiled a list composed of key Vistemax couples, and it would be smart to mix them up with friends.

Nathan leaned his head against the back of the sofa, closed his eyes, and contemplated the maneuvers necessary to keep a career afloat. "Been there, Minty."

He meant with Rose.

There it was. Despite having left his first wife, Rose, for me, Nathan still measured his life against that first marriage. Holidays, house decoration, even the choice of a new jumper were accomplished beneath the arid rain shadow of the past. Worse, Nathan punished himself for what he perceived as his and my transgressions. It was a bad habit, and I had failed to nip it in the bud. In this marriage, the quality of mercy proved to be in short supply and, during our seven years together, it had been thinned, strained, and darkened, like varnish on an old painting.

My gaze drifted past the figure on the sofa to the perfectly normal London view outside Number 7 Lakey Street. The trees seemed weighed down with grime, and the pile of rubbish outside Mrs. Austen's flat opposite more than usually noxious. This type of exchange between Nathan and me had become commonplace. What kept me in a state of perpetual astonishment, bewilderment, even, was how I had miscalculated in having gotten myself into this position in the first place.

Never complain. "What about the Frosts?"

Sue and Jack were Nathan's very special friends. They were also Rose's very special friends but they were *not* my special friends. The reverse, in fact, for I was (Sue had been heard to say) a husband snatcher and a home breaker.

I could not deny either.

As a result, Nathan was frequently invited to their house a couple of streets away to cozy evenings but I was not. What they talked about I don't know, and I never inquired. (Sometimes I amused myself by imagining the conversational hole around which these special friends tiptoed.) Was Nathan disloyal? No, he needed to see his old friends but nobody, *nobody,* appeared to note the irony in the situation: both Frosts were on their second marriage.

"Would they come do you think?"

The hissing noise that meant "I don't think so" issued from Nathan and his eyes flicked to the painting above the mantelpiece. It was of Priac Bay in Cornwall, by a local artist, and rather dull. But Nathan liked it, and frequently I caught him peering into the turquoise-paint depths of the sea at the base of the cliffs.

"No," he said.

The outlook on the friend front was grim. "What about the Lockharts?" The Lockharts were also friends of Nathan and Rose.

Nathan sprang to his feet and removed a fleck of something from the bottom right-hand corner of the painting. "Minty. It's no use flogging dead horses. They feel strongly . . ." He did not have to finish the sentence.

I glanced down at the list of guests that, so far, was composed only of work colleagues. "Did I mention that I met Sue Frost the other day in the supermarket and I tried to sort things out?"

"Actually, she told me," Nathan confessed, "but she didn't go into detail."

I found myself inscribing two heavy underlinings on the list. "Well, I will go into detail, Nathan. I asked Sue why, since she and Jack were both on their second marriages, I am banished from their court. What makes me different from them?"

Sue Frost had tapped her pink suede loafer on the ground and peered over a trolley stacked with vegetables and cleaning aids. Her cheeks had flamed in her pretty, but obstinate, face, as she replied, "I would have thought it obvious. I am not the one who left my first husband. I wasn't the party who broke up a marriage."

"So . . ." Nathan shoved his hands into his trouser pockets. He put on the face he used for tricky business meetings: hugely unreadable. "What did you say?"

"I said I wanted to get the situation absolutely straight as she saw it. As a second wife, Sue was okay because her husband had had the midlife crisis and left. While I, as the second wife and the object of the midlife crisis was not? But I wanted to know what it meant if Sue had *driven* her first husband away . . . ?"

That succeeded in amusing Nathan. He stopped looking haunted and relaxed back into the kind, intelligent man he was—the man who beat his chest and imitated gorilla noises to make the twins laugh, and the man who had recently persuaded the Vistemax board to rethink their position on the future of newspapers. As an able man he could do both.

"And?"

"She vanished into the frozen-fish section."

Nathan uttered a short, barking laugh. "You won that round, Minty."

"What I really wanted to ask her is why I'm a home breaker, and you're not."

Nathan met my eyes steadily. In his lay the detritus of painful history. "I'm blamed too, Minty."

"No, you're not. That's the point."

His gaze drifted toward the painting, as if he were seeking reassurance in the shimmer of water, rock, and cliff.

"In Sue's eyes you are still married to Rose. There is nothing I can do about that. In the complicated hierarchies of marital morality, Sue gets a tick, Rose gets sainthood, and I get the cross."

Any trace of amusement vanished from Nathan's features. "Would you prefer it if I didn't see the Frosts any more?"

In *Successful Relationships,* a manual that in the past I had studied diligently, it says that to bind a partner you must release him. I am a great believer in the self-help manual—although lately I have found myself wondering if they only add to the confusion by suggesting problems you did not know you possessed. However, mindful of *Successful Relationship*'s teachings, I said, "Nathan, I insist you see Sue and Jack Frost."

I offered up the unfinished guest list which was composed of Nathan's boss and his wife, Roger and Gisela Gard, and my boss and his wife, Barry and Lucy Helm. "We haven't got very far."

Before I married Nathan, I had pictured my situation so differently. Who did not dream of a fine, harmonious household in which friends and family gathered? "It's no use asking

Poppy and Richard, I suppose? And Sam and Jilly are too far away."

As always, Nathan brightened at the mention of his elder children. "Poppy *is* very busy," he said carefully. "And I don't think Sam's due up in town for some time. And he would probably go and see . . . his mother."

If I had to choose one overarching objective in this marriage between Nathan and me, it would be: get rid of Rose.

Scrape her away from the surfaces of this house, then dig deep, as she had once dug the garden, to exhume the Rose roots that were threatening to throttle us. She was everywhere, I was in no doubt of that, and her power lay in my victory and her suffering.

"Minty . . ." Nathan disliked it when I ignored him, which was one of my weapons. "I'm still here."

I turned my head. "Don't mention Rose, then. Don't. *Don't.*"

He came over and hauled me to my feet. "I wasn't thinking." He placed his hands on my shoulders and looked into my eyes.

"We have to try," I murmured. Robotically.

"Course we do."

He smelled of Vetivier and—faintly—of tarragon and garlic. Whatever went on in Nathan's head was only half my business but there were times when I could not face even a tiny percentage of the mixture of disappointment and fatigue that I suspected churned within him. I craned my head back and took a good look, and it struck me he was very pale. Nothing a useful dinner party would not put right. I reached for another of my weapons and slid my arms around his neck. "Come here."

After a while, Nathan saw the point, which I knew he would. "Sometimes, Minty . . ." he played with my fingers, "you can be so sweet. And sometimes . . ."

"And sometimes . . . ?"

"Not."

He wanted to say more, but he would never get it out in a month of Sundays, and there was no point wasting more time. I placed a finger on his mouth. "Hush."

I returned to my labors over the guest list and to my private thoughts—not least, why was it that in such an apparently godless world when anything went and everything possible was done, I was the object of such censure?

Later, getting ready for bed, I discovered a yellow Post-it note stuck to the back of my hairbrush. On it, Nathan had written "sorry."

At seven fifteen A.M. on the day of the dinner party, I picked up the phone to Five-Star Caterers. "This is to check that everything is okay for this evening."

A voice reeled off. "Ten twice-baked cheese soufflés, chicken with ginger in soy and sherry sauce. Bitter cherries in maraschino served with a frangipane and *paté sablé* tart."

I had toyed with having menus printed because I so relished the names of the dishes, but Paige put her foot down. "Nope, not the thing."

The "not the thing" was annoying, but I bit my lip. Paige was a neighbor and also a good friend. She had never met Rose, so her relationship with me held the extra sweetness of the untainted. Paige knew what was what and, during her years as an international investment banker, she had been on the receiving end of many dinners like this one. I needed guidance through the pitfalls. Paige provided it. Enough said.

Paige had also given the thumbs-down to sticking taffeta bows on the chair backs which, I reckoned, would be the finishing touch. "Finish the guests off, more like." She hooted with amusement. "For goodness' sake, you're not a brothel."

Yes, someone had to tell me what was what. I knew that much.

I am a fast learner, but as the taffeta bows incident indicated, there were gaps in what I knew, and what I understood— puzzling and slippery points of taste and appropriateness. Those are the one with which I struggle.

Knives, forks, wineglasses . . . I checked the place settings on the dining table which I had laid at six-thirty that morning, that is, before the twins were up. Only the flowers for the center of the table, which I had ordered to be an exact match of the one I had seen in *Vogue,* were missing. Hovering in the doorway, I gave the *mise-en-scène* a final sweep and concluded that there was nothing to embarrass, and everything to enhance, Nathan's reputation.

I nipped back to the table, and adjusted the angle of a knife.

My watch said seven-twenty A.M. Say good-bye to twins, before racing to hairdresser and on to work.

Eve—twenty-two, Romanian, and not a threat—was bathing the boys when I arrived home at six-fifteen.

As I let myself in, the draft made the cat flap in the back door (long since unused) open and shut with a bang and, for the hundredth time, I cursed it.

"It's Mum . . ." Lucas's high-pitched call sounded out. I stopped and waited. Sure enough, Felix echoed. "It's Mum." I had not clocked in until I heard the echo that meant everything was fine.

Upstairs, I snatched up my shower cap. I had not spent all that money at the hairdresser to have the results ruined in a steamy bathroom.

Eve raised a moisture-licked face from her position kneeling against the bath. "They have so much energy, Minty." Her eyes ranged disapprovingly over the shower cap—which I did not mind. As long as Eve did her job, she could think of me what she liked. "Lucas fell down this afternoon." She informed me in her awkward English.

On cue, Lucas shot a grimy knee up from the water for me to inspect. The graze had puckered around the edges, and was pretty businesslike. "I was braver than Superman, Mum."

"I'm sure you were, Lucas."

At the plug end, Felix scowled. "Lucas cried a lot."

"Eve, did you disinfect it?"

The briskness of Eve's nod made it clear she considered the question redundant. She knew her job. Lucas was always knocking himself about. He hurled himself at life as if its obstacles—stairs, curbs, walls—were there to be conquered. Felix was different. He watched, waited, and then made his move.

The slippery bodies heaved around in the scummy water. They chattered away, releasing snippets from their day.

"You look so funny, Mum." Lucas poked Felix's leg with a foot. "Funny, funny."

"Out," I ordered. "Eve is waiting."

Eve sat on the stool with the cork seat and Lucas clambered onto the towel spread in her lap. Felix was instantly riveted by his red plastic boat. He did not look at me. Reluctantly, I reached for a second towel and spread it over my Nicole Farhi trousers. "Okay, Felix." A wave of water hit the sides as he ejected, bulletlike, out of the bath. "Careful."

He paid no attention and buried his head in my shoulder, nuzzling and whinnying like the ponies he loved to read about. "I've got Mum."

Instantly, Lucas abandoned Eve and forced his way onto my lap too. "Get *off*," he ordered his brother.

Eve was watching. She liked to ticket and docket my behavior and imagined I did not notice. It gave her material to share with her friends, and she liked it best when I did not rise to her strict notions of good mothering because then she had plenty to discuss.

What did Eve know?

Nathan and I had created the squirming bodies competing for space on my lap . . . the skinny limbs, the raucous bellows of laughter or distress, the endless craving for warmth and reassurance. They had been a logical consequence of my longing for that fine, harmonious household.

Yet even Eve could sense that the story required fleshing out. She knew that when I was tired or low, I recoiled from the *urgency* of the twins. I found it impossible to reconcile myself with their kidnapping of time and energy, their need to creep inside my mind. Then I was back in the box from which there was no exit. *Then* I took refuge in imposing strict routines, making lists, in striving for perfection.

In the peace of my own bedroom, I removed the shower cap and inspected my face and hair in the mirror—the twice daily patrol along the border between (to quote Paige) the wife and mother who was still "pretty sexy" and the woman who "looked good for her age." There was a difference.

I ran a bath. One of my first acts after the twins were born was to insist we build a separate bathroom for Nathan and me, which entailed Nathan sacrificing his wardrobe and knocking a hole in the wall.

Nathan had been appalled. "We can't," he said.

"Why not? Are walls sacred?" It was five-thirty in the morning, and the twins had not slept much. "We must have somewhere that we smell nice."

Nathan sat up in bed with Felix over his shoulder. "We always managed before."

We. I ignored the small word that carried such weight. I leaned over and kissed Felix and then Nathan. The gesture pleased him. "Okay," he conceded. "New bathroom it is."

If he was truthful, Nathan loved the new bathroom—the marble, the honey travertine tiles, the glint of mirror and stainless steel, his separate basin. "See?" I teased him.

"I take pleasure in small things." He was smiling.

"In that case, I'll give you plenty of small things in which to take pleasure. Carpets, curtains . . ."

But I had gone too far, too fast, and the smile was quenched. "We must be careful, Minty. Things are a bit tight."

I kissed his mouth lingeringly. A Judas kiss. "I promise."

It had taken me four years, inch by inch, stealthy infiltration by sly addition to redecorate the house—a bedroom painted in pretty yellow here, a chair recovered there—to achieve the transformation of Nathan and Rose's house into Nathan and Minty's house.

In the days when Rose and I had been friends—when she was my boss and editor of the books section of the *Weekend*

Digest and I was her deputy—she beguiled me with her domestic tales. I can see her now: head bent over a book or a piece of copy, hugging a mug of coffee to her chest, dropping those details into an atmosphere that snapped and crackled with other considerations. *Parsley caught a mouse. Nathan bought me a white penstemon and I planted it by the lavender. The washing machine flooded.*

I pictured the gray scum running over the kitchen floor, the scramble to mop it up, the penstemons nodding in the breeze. I eavesdropped on the family exchanges, with all their coded allusions and easy shorthand. Poppy's challenge to her brother. "When were you born, then?" And clever Sam's riposte. "Before you, you dag."

Rose's family portrait was a chocolate box, framed by comfortable, warm words. Then it had been foreign to me, that pretty picture. I do not have a family and it does not bother me, I told Rose. Nor did I want children. Why hang a millstone around your neck?

Looking back, I should have insisted that she tell me what she had left out. But when I asked, Rose laughed, all apology and sweetness. "There's nothing to leave out."

How would she couch her reply today?

I will never know. Never again will I hustle her into a coffee shop, or accompany her on the walks she liked so much. Or pick up the phone and demand, "What do you think?" Never again will I observe her huddled over a pile of books, sifting through them with the greed of a child let loose in the pick'n'mix.

Between us lies the deepest and darkest of silences, sinister in its composition of pain and betrayal. And absolutely appropriate.

Chapter Two

Dinner was going well. (The timetable was stuck to the fridge. "8:15, Guests arrive. 9:00, Serve." A schedule was crucial to my peace of mind.)

We were ten in all, a number than ensured separate conversations could be conducted and thus mask any awkward little silences. The final guest list was mostly Vistemax but, in view of my *keep going* philosophy, not wasted.

The Hurleys arrived at precisely eleven minutes past eight. When I opened the front door, Martin pushed Paige, seven months pregnant and large, into the hall. "Thought you could do with some early back up," he murmured as Nathan unwrapped Paige from her coat. "And Paige wanted to check out what you were wearing."

I flushed. "Will I do?"

Martin studied my green wraparound dress approvingly. "Sure. You look great." He touched my arm in a gesture of support and I felt as if I had been given a million dollars.

But a little later, with the Shakers and Barry and Lucy

Helm still to arrive, Paige lumbered over and hissed, "The dress is too tight."

I pushed a plate of miniature blinis and caviar in the direction of her bump. "Your dress is just as bad. Besides, your husband approves."

"My husband wouldn't recognize taste if it sat in his lap." She flicked a glance in his direction, and it was not an affectionate one. "Look, you fool, this evening depends on the wives, not the husbands. You're thinking like a singleton. The wives will have taken stock of the dress. It outlines your nipples and reveals that you're wearing stockings." She lifted a finger and waggled it at her temple. "They will be thinking, *This woman is not safe with husbands.* In the car on the way back home, the assaults will begin. Remember, husbands listen to their wives, even if they hate them."

"I wouldn't touch any of them with a barge pole."

"Try telling the wives that."

Every so often, I glanced at Nathan from my end of the table. These days, candlelight suited him. It lent his eyes a sparkle and disguised his pallor. I liked that. And myself in the candlelight? A woman in a green dress (hastily loosened over the bust), a trifle anxious but masking it competently. Granted there was a string of fatigue strung behind the back of my eyes and, every so often, an unseen hand tugged at it. I raised my wine glass and willed Nathan to look up at me across the silver and crystal. I wanted him to register pleasure in the scene and to know that he was pleased with my creation.

Gisela Gard sat on his right. Married to Roger, chairman of Vistemax, her little black dress, Chanel corsage, and hefty sprinkling of grade E diamonds advertised his status. Roger was sixty-five to Gisela's forty-three and gossip reported that it was *his* money that lured *her* into his den. "Of course it was his money," Gisela was also reported to have said. "But in return, I look after Roger beautifully."

On Nathan's left sat Carolyne Shaker, married to his colleague Peter. She had chosen a royal blue dress—a mistake from whichever way you looked at it—and bright gold earrings, and was listening to Gisela and Nathan. As a general rule, Carolyne left conversation to others, and wore her silence with an expression that suggested she knew her limitations. Not by so much as a flicker did she suggest she minded that she did not shine on these occasions. Carolyne knew where her strengths lay—in the home—and I learned from that too.

Nathan said something to Gisela and turned, courteously, to Carolyne, who seemed a bit sleepy. He whispered something in her ear that made her laugh.

On Gisela's right, Peter Shaker was talking to Barry's wife, Lucy. On arrival Lucy, who was dressed in a complicated version of Boho, had seemed nervous and I'd whisked her over to the reliable, kind Carolyne. The latter had obviously done the trick, because Lucy was responding animatedly.

"The cherries are good." Beside me, Roger dipped his spoon into the bittersweet juice. "I like tough skins."

On the other side of me, Barry nodded. He had been pleased, as I had calculated, to dine with a man as powerful as Roger, and Barry's pleasure took the form of agreeing with everything Roger said. A dedicated foodie ("You should hear the fuss if I don't buy Hunza dried apricots for his cereal," Gisela told me), Roger kept up the food bulletins throughout the meal. Did I know the best cherries came from a valley in Burgundy? Or now that they were eating more meat, the Japanese were growing taller? So practiced was his conversation that it could almost have been dubbed automatic, except that Roger was too clever to let that happen. His party trick was to gaze directly at whomever he was speaking to, and the listener enjoyed the illusion that they were the only person in the world. The magic was working beautifully until he let fall, "I remember the best salmon was at Zeffano's. It was when Nathan was still married to Rose . . ."

There followed a tiny pause. My smile did not waver. "Yes, Roger . . ."

Barry's radar locked on to the telltale flicker of tension. "And . . . ?" he encouraged.

"It was years ago, but I remember that salmon so well . . ." Roger steered past the minefield. "Nathan was less enthusiastic . . . but we won him round."

Reminded of my place, my pleasure in the evening was now spiked with resentment. Rose sat at the end of the polished, laden table, not I. Rose had chosen the flower centerpiece from *Vogue* and brought these people together. Rose's ability to soothe, her love and concern, were what the majority of the guests at my table remembered.

In these situations, it is no use looking hopeless or weighed down by the burden of being wife number two. The best thing, I find, is to trade through, thus emphasizing how sensible and mature everyone involved is being. I maintained my shiny smile. "Isn't it wonderful how Rose's career as a travel writer has taken off?"

"Yes," agreed Roger. "I saw a very good article she'd written on China in the *Financial Times,* I think it was."

Barry was amused. I could sense him piecing together a history—first wife, a minx, old dogs, new tricks, etc., etc.—

and making so thorough a job of it that there was a good chance he would think it correct. He muttered: "You're Nathan's second wife?"

"Yes, aren't I lucky? Not the first, but definitely the last." The words tripped off my tongue and I made sure I included Barry in my next remark to Roger. "Nathan and I must visit the cherry valley. I'll make him take me."

Roger tapped a cigarette packet. "Is it permitted?" He exhaled a plume of smoke. "You must be the only person in the world who can make Nathan do anything. We have to work hard to convince him sometimes to come on board. It's one of his strengths."

Suddenly, shockingly, I scented danger. "Vistemax has had an exceptional year," I explained to Barry. "They've wiped the floor with the opposition." I pushed an ashtray in Roger's direction. "You must be so pleased. Nathan is."

Before Roger could respond, we were interrupted by a cry from the doorway. It was Lucas in his teddy bear pajamas, hopping from one foot to the other. "I can't sleep . . ."

The red mark on his cheek suggested otherwise. Nathan turned round. "Lukey . . ." He smiled and Lucas tumbled toward him, arms outstretched. Nathan pushed back his chair, scooped him up, and settled him on his lap. "What are you doing up, you naughty boy?"

"Naughty boy." Lucas agreed and settled himself against his father's shoulder for the duration. He reckoned that he was in with a chance and, judging by the way Nathan held him close, he was right.

The clatter of forks and spoons acted as a counterpoint to Lucas's high, childish voice and Nathan's deep tones. This had not been included on the timetable stuck to the fridge. My gaze slid to Roger who was observing this tender little scene with an expression that did not necessarily bode well for Nathan. This is the way the wind blows, he was thinking. This is why a man loses his edge.

Gisela touched the red patch on Lucas's cheek. "Wide awake, eh?"

Lucas grinned at Gisela, and I rose to my feet. "Come on, Lucas."

But Lucas had no intention of budging. I bent down and scooped him up. "No bed, no bed," he wailed.

I whispered in his ear and Lucas screeched. "Mummy, don't smack me."

"Minty . . ." Nathan threw down his napkin, shot to his feet, and wrested Lucas away. "I'll deal."

He and Lucas vanished upstairs and we heard Lucas's chuckle. My cheeks flamed, and Roger and I exchanged a long, measured look. "Nathan's quite a hands-on father," he commented.

"Oh, not really," I said. "An on-and-off sort of father, depending on how available he is." I switched subjects. "Are you planning more changes this year? A new launch?"

"Sadly, even if I was, I could not tell you, Minty."

Roger enjoyed his business secrets. And why not? "Of course, Roger," I said and urged Barry to elaborate on one of Paradox Pictures' more recent successes. When a somewhat tousled Nathan returned, I rose (nb 10:45, serve coffee) and suggested we adjourn to the sitting room.

Paige grimaced. She and I had debated whether to have coffee at the table or in the sitting room. I was never *quite* sure. Paige maintained it gave you an escape route if you had been bored and I said stiffly that I was not planning on anyone's being bored. *"Ayez pitié de moi,"* begged Paige, who sometimes fell back on her international past. "I can't move. In my present condition I'd rather be bored silly than have to move, and anyway with my legs under the table no one can spot my varicose veins."

I sacrificed Paige.

I showed Gisela upstairs to the guests' bathroom, a haven of brilliant white towels, Jo Malone essences, and French soap in the shape of a mermaid.

"The house looks very nice." Gisela bent forward to peer into the mirror. Her voice was warm and pleasant, and I had a feeling that she had marked me out for more serious acquaintanceship.

I adjusted the angle of a towel. "It took a bit of time and persuasion. Nathan's not exactly receptive to change." Then it struck me the latter was not a sensible remark to make to the wife of your husband's boss and I added, "Over matters of paint."

"Men . . ." Gisela smoothed back her hair. She did not mean it, for she was, undoubtedly, too intelligent to fall into a gender trap. "Nathan's looking a tiny bit haggard . . ." the manicured fingers continued to pat and adjust. "Is he quite well?"

"He caught a bug from the twins. It was a women-have-colds-men-have-flu sort of thing."

She turned her head to check her profile. "Even so, he's looking a little worn."

Once upon a time, I had been twenty-nine, slender, glossy. I had celebrated this condition by dressing in tight tops and kitten heels. I squinted down at my chest to check the neckline of my dress. "Don't we all?"

Gisela picked up the soap mermaid. "Charming." The mermaid was returned to its soapdish. "Carolyne really shouldn't wear velvet hairbands. And Minty . . . it's a lovely dress, but I wonder if blue isn't more your color?" The charm and lightness of Gisela's smile neutralized the criticism. She put her head on one side and exhaled thoughtfully. "It isn't easy being the second wife . . . or the third."

"Was it awful?"

Gisela searched for her lipstick in her tiny evening bag and applied it. "Nicholas was very old, and I had to do a lot of nursing. It was lonely, and the children hated me. Richmond wasn't quite so old, and his children not quite so bad. In fact, we quite liked each other . . . until Richmond died." She pursed her lips and the color stained them. "All hell broke loose over the will. We lived in Savannah in the family house. So I came over here and met Roger and . . . *poof* . . . everything was fine." She made it sound easy, but I dare swear it was anything but. "Don't get me wrong, Minty. I chose to do what I did."

I ran a rapid life review through the internal projector. The resulting picture was not exactly romantic, being more practical and calculating, but that *was* life. "So did I."

As we trod downstairs together, Gisela surprised me by saying, "Don't you think we are realists?"

"Do you mean that we look after ourselves?"

Gisela tucked a hand under my elbow. "That's exactly what I mean."

I carried the coffee into the sitting room and Martin helped me set it down on the side table. "We'll be off in a minute," he said. "Paige needs her sleep."

Martin was fair-haired but had strongly marked dark eyebrows that gave him a permanently questioning look. If he was the slightest bit cross, they snapped together and suggested a thunderous temper that must have helped him in the job of deputy chairman at the bank where he had met Paige. "You're sweet to her. Are you ready for the new arrival?"

"Paige is," he replied. "She's got it organized down to the last contraction."

I gave Roger his coffee, and he took a sip. "Very good." He replaced the cup on the saucer and his eye fell on Barry, who had cornered Gisela. "Did Nathan protest when you returned to work after the twins?"

This was not a conversation that I wished to conduct at this moment for I had been thinking about changes. "The twins were three, and it was only part time. So, no, not at all," I added. "At the moment."

"Of course not," said Roger. "He made that mistake with Rose."

I slept badly. The cold had crept into me, and I searched my mind for sources of warmth. I pictured myself as a void, filled with echoes from the past. I did not mind very much how others judged me, but I needed to make sense of my life, some connection, somewhere, somehow.

Beside me, Nathan was breathing deeply and a little laboriously, the price of a rich meal and good wine. I stroked his cheek. A gossamer touch. He stirred and moved away. My hand fell back to my side.

Around four-thirty, I slipped out of bed, went down to the kitchen, and made myself a mug of mint tea. When I returned upstairs, I poked my head around the door of the twins'

bedroom. Felix was flat on his back, making puppyish, whuf-
fling noises. Lucas was curled into a ball, and I could just make
out the contour of his spine. This was sweet, innocent sleep,
such as I could never have.

Cradling the tea, I took myself up a further flight of stairs.
The twins now occupied the original spare room, and its replacement, next door to Eve's bedroom, was much smaller
with sloping eaves. There was scarcely room in it for one person, which suited me as I did not wish to encourage guests.

The bed was slotted under the eave, and over it hung a
painting of white roses in a pewter vase of which Nathan was
also especially fond, but like the Cornish picture, I could never
see much in it. I did not come up here very often, but since
the advent of the new bathroom, Nathan had used the cupboard to store his clothes. A pile of his ironed shirts lay folded
on the bed. I lifted them and stowed them on a shelf. As I did
so, my fingers encountered a hard object. It was a notebook,
black and bound in hardboard, and held shut by a rubber band
now slack from age and use. I slid the band off, and opened
the book up. Inside ruled pages were filled with the distinctive slope of Nathan's left-handed writing. Notes for the office? Financial plans? (Nathan was careful with his money.)
Private things?

Of course they were private. I got into the bed, cradled the
mug, and felt its heat trickle into my cold joints. I drank the tea
before I picked up the notebook and began to read it. It was
some sort of diary, and began shortly after we had married.

"Jan. 5. Minty angry . . ." The scope for my anger was as
great as anyone's, and its sources just as forgettable. What had
I been angry about? True, the list of things had been accumu-

lating. Married things. Nathan's habit of leaving cufflinks in his dirty shirts. Small change dropped from his trousers that clogged the Hoover. His inability to tell me what he wanted for Christmas or birthdays.

I leafed back through time. "March 17th . . . Felix and Lucas arrived. They are beautiful. Minty took it well . . ."

Did I? I hated pregnancy. I hated labor. "Look at your babies," cooed the midwife, and invited me to peer through a plastic incubator at two tiny frogs. I remember being surprised at the precision of my response. I had expected to be tipped into a maelstrom of passionate feeling, only to experience nothing, *absolutely nothing,* like that, only the sharp pain of my cesarean wound scar.

"July 20. Twins thriving. Exhausted. What can I do to make Minty's life easier?"

If Nathan had asked me, I could have told him. He could have helped me search for the tenderness, the physical desire for my babies that eluded me. That would have made my life easier.

I leafed forward. "June 6" (Two years ago.) "I would give almost anything to be walking the path above Priac, smelling the salt and feeling the wind in my face. A healing solitude."

Then I read, "Feb. 21" (of this year) ". . . disappointment with oneself is a fact of life. It is something one must try to come to terms with."

I looked up from the notebook and through the window where the darkness was just lifting over the city. How was I going to deal with this discovery? I was conscious of irritation at the revelation of Nathan's hidden inner life, and the forensic manner in which he was analyzing us. I was aware that I should consider how to square this circle, and puzzle away at Nathan's mind-set in order to *understand* him, but I only possessed so much energy.

"October 30 . . ." This year. "I read somewhere that most people have a secret grief. That seems right."

A secret grief. And yet, and yet, I minded about Nathan's secret grief. Its existence, its confirmation in writing, was to point to a wound and a failure. The words spelled out the ridiculousness of our ambition to be happy and its defeat.

Here was the deal. I had seen Nathan and taken him. He had talked a lot about new beginnings and freedom and climbing out of a box and that had made it all very exciting. Rose had wept and grieved and gone away, leaving me to run her house and produce more children for Nathan. Before I knew it, that had constituted the main business between Nathan and me: bringing up the children and running the house—or was it the other way around? Instead of climbing out of his box, we had climbed back as fast as possible into it.

I made to shut the notebook and its revelations. As I did so, I noticed a document tucked into the pouch at the back and pulled it out. It was a professional drawing of a small garden—ten meters by fifteen meters, according to the plan— and the compass indicated it was southwest facing. An arrow pointed to a line of trees that bisected the space reading "pleached olive." Other arrows pointed to plants: *humulus, ficus, verbena.* . . . Typed in at the bottom of the diagram were the words: "Height. Route. Rest." At the top of the diagram was scribbled, "This is it. What do you think? Why don't you talk it over with Minty?"

The handwriting was Rose's.

Downstairs, Nathan was sleeping on his back. He murmured as I climbed back into the bed and took him in my arms. "Wake up, Nathan."

After a second or two, his protests died, and I helped myself to my husband's body, as angry with him as I had ever been.

Chapter Three

At nine-fifteen precisely, hair brushing cleanly across my cheeks and smelling of almond shampoo, I walked up the Shepherds' Bush Road, past two—hitherto unreconstructed and raucous—Irish pubs undergoing rebirth as gastropubs, and past the recently repaved green. THE BUSH IS THE NEW GATE, read the graffito on a brick wall.

Once upon a time, the old United Kingdom Provincial Insurance building used to be what its name suggested. These days, United Kingdom Provincial Insurance operated entirely from Bombay and the building was home to seven start-up enterprises. Each of these shared reception, coffee facilities, and conversations conducted on stairwells that centered chiefly on the inequities of the rent.

Some things are eternal but not, as I have discovered, the obvious candidates. It is the stained nylon carpets and the smell of plastic and paper in offices that never change. Yet I had never been so glad to inhale a deep, plastic-filled breath as I was when I returned to work after three years at home with the twins. It notched up my pulse rate from lackluster to viable. Nathan's response to my exhilaration, I remember, had been a little sour. The office—he stabbed the air to emphasize the point—isn't all that it's cracked up to be. For all the fuss he made, you might have concluded that it was I, not he, who worked from eight to eight five days a week, rather than the three on which he and I had compromised.

Paradox Pictures was one of the numerous small independent television production companies clustering in Shepherds' Bush. "Dirt cheap rents and easy access to the Beeb and Channel 4," confided Barry, chief executive and executive producer, when he interviewed me over lunch at Balzac's. (In the covering letter with my application, I pointed out we had both taken degrees at Leeds University, a sliver of research that probably earned me the interview.) He cast an eye round the crowded restaurant. "I'd say most of the Beeb are here at the trough right now. I got the sack for being a naughty boy." His lived-in features slackened with nostalgia. "She was *very* beautiful. Anyway, Auntie and the then-Mrs. Helm took a dim view, and I had to take off to the States for a time where I made *Spouse Exchange*. When I came back there had been the Thatcherite decree that the BBC was to use independents. I met Lucy. So here we are." He held up both hands, palms toward me. "No longer a naughty boy."

There was a pause while we drank the wine and mourned the death of naughty boys and, by implication, naughty girls. Barry then came to the point. "I need ideas. The more bizarre the better. We need to reach younger audiences. We need to think big and *interactive*. I need someone who knows people, who has a hinterland."

The pleasure of being perceived as possessing a fertile hin-

terland was immense. "My husband," I told him, "is chief executive of Vistemax. We entertain all the time."

That did the trick too.

So, three days a week, I schmoozed with journalists, au-
thors, and agents and kept tabs on anniversaries and big public
events. I watched television, listened to radio, read books,
magazines, and newspapers. I learned rapidly that far from being scarce, ideas were ten a penny, but their implementation
was a different matter. Ideas fluttered around the office on
gauzy wings but few, oh so few, soared into flight.

Now, when anyone asked what I did, I replied, "I'm a
deputy development producer with Paradox Pictures," which
took a little time to articulate but was all the better for that.
Certainly, it took longer to say than "I'm at home with twins."

"Morning," said Syriol, the receptionist, who spoke four
languages. She was studiedly casual in Sass & Bide jeans and
striped plimsolls and was eating a bowl of granola with one
hand and sorting the post with other. The script she was trying
to write in her spare time was flickering on her screen. Thrift-
ily, she had based it on life in a television company.

"Morning," I echoed, picked up the stack of newspapers,
and headed for my office where I dumped them to read later.

Friday was the weekly ideas meeting day and, armed with
a file, I took myself off to the meeting room. This was an oblong box with natural light and a coffee machine that emitted
a smell that scraped the back of the throat. Barry was already in
situ and, today, he was dressed in a white linen suit and a black
shirt that suggested he was in an executive frame of mind.
Deb, the current development producer, in combat trousers
and a denim jacket, was logging his every move.

"You seem a bit pale." Barry looked up from the enormous Filofax that he favored over his electronic diary. He complained that it was so heavy that it gave him tennis elbow but he couldn't help it if he was an old-fashioned bloke at heart.

I took the chair next to Deb. "It's the excitement."

Barry grinned at me over Deb's head. As a boss, he was tough, but nice, the sort of person who refuses to allow the everyday exasperations of a production company get to him. "She gives cracking dinner. She is a wife and mother. She looks good. For God's sake, she *reads*."

From this I deduced Barry had gained something at our table. Yet there was the tiniest suggestion of a bared fang buried in the praise. Barry expected his employees to give their pound of flesh.

"Easy when you know how, Barry. Ask your wife," I said, cucumber cool.

Idea number one was taken from a book, *Vanishing Rural Crafts*. "It would make a great series." (Plus point: more money could be extracted from the television companies for a series than a one-off.) "It would be a valuable social document with archive footage." (Minus point: If it includes black and white film, it is likely to be ghettoized in a late-night slot). I cited an example of a rush-basket business on the Somerset Levels. For generations the Bruton family had passed on their expertise from son to son (nb no daughters). A Bruton basket lasted a lifetime, which might have been a self-limiting market but for the success of their increasingly popular willow coffins. The quote from John Bruton was lovely: "My job is my life. The two are bound together. Like this landscape and the water which makes the willows grow." I had scribbled in the margin a potential title: *From the Cradle to the Grave?*

Barry did not take the bait. "Sounds a bit regional telly. You might get some local funding, but no foreign deals. Pass. Anything else?"

Women Between the Wars: A Lost Generation.

The homework on this had produced: "In 1921, there were 19,803,022 females in England and Wales, nine and a half million of them of childbearing age. There were 18,082,220 men of whom fewer than eight and a half million were in the marrying age band. Thus, the women were not so much lost as surplus to requirements and it resulted in depression, low self-esteem, poverty, and emigration." I looked at Barry. "It was a terrible collective experience of loss. Loss of expectation and ideals, not to mention a comfortable future."

Barry shrugged. "Maybe. Who are you targeting?"

"Ben Pryce at History is planning a two-week season around the first World War. He says he's run out of Nazi stories and needs material. But the main target must be Channel 4."

Barry gestured at Deb. "Pour us a coffee."

I knew then it was nonrunner but I ploughed on. "One of these women, a Maud Watson, set up the Feline Rescue Association." I read out a quote from Maud. "'I was an old maid and a useless one for I could never have been a doctor or a lawyer. Men were stupid enough to kill themselves on the battlefield and I could not stop them, but I could save cats . . .'"

Mistake. I should have been talking about a signature director, foreign sales, and hourly rates.

Barry stirred the tarlike coffee. "Half of today's audience won't have heard of the First World War." He exchanged a glance with Deb that excluded me.

Barry's assistant, Gabrielle, appeared in the doorway. Her Lycra top strained over her breasts and the waistband of her jeans marched across the dangerous area between her belly button and her groin. "Barry . . . chop, chop."

She bit a glossy lip, her teeth nesting on the pink platform, and looked important. "The meeting," she explained to the now five-year-old Barry. "With Controller 2. You are due at the restaurant in five minutes."

"I'd forgotten." Barry jackknifed to his feet. "Deb, I'll hear what you have to say this afternoon."

And that was that.

Deb swept up the plastic cups, dumped them in the bin, and rubbed a tissue over the tabletop. "No green lights today. We'd better have a chat, Minty. Tomorrow." She checked herself. "Oh, but you're not here tomorrow, are you? You're not in till next week." Her expression was quite nasty and she had scrubbed so hard that the table was dotted with balls of wet tissue.

"So . . ." Gisela arched her eyebrows. "Rose and Nathan are in touch." Gisela was giving me lunch at the Café Noire as a thank-you for the dinner. We had talked long and hard, and that long, hard talk gave birth to confidences in which I had not intended to indulge, and thus it was I found myself explaining to Gisela how I discovered that Rose and Nathan were in contact. Gisela's eyes sparkled. "Did you read the diary?"

Some loyalty was owed to Nathan. "No."

Gisela did not believe me. "Have you talked to him about Rose?"

It had been a relief to confide in her. "No, but I will." I reached for my water, so stuffed with ice I had difficulty drinking it. "It's complicated. Nathan and I have not gotten to the stage where we are each other's best friends. Perhaps that is where Rose fits in?"

"Perhaps not," Gisela sounded a warning note. "Perhaps not, Minty."

The ice clinked my teeth and sent an unpleasant frisson through the enamel. "Technically, can one commit adultery with one's ex-spouse?"

"So you think it's like that?"

"No," I denied quickly. "No." I changed the subject. "I'm thinking of going back to work full time." I recollected Deb's nasty expression. "There are tensions when you work part time, and I never feel I am giving it my full attention."

"I admire your working in an office. I could never do it. Have never done it."

"You entertain, run the houses. That's not hard work? I think it is."

Gisela spread out her hand, nails sculptured and polished, skin creamed. "Remember, I have time to concentrate on one thing. I don't have children or a job, so I can give my all to the husband of the day. Nice and simple." She closed her eyes briefly. "But tiring from time to time."

Her mobile shrilled. Gisela gestured toward it apologetically. "Do you mind . . . ? It will be Roger. He likes to check up on arrangements about this time." No one could accuse Gisela of shirking her duties. She ran through Roger's schedule. "Meeting at two-thirty tomorrow. Three-thirty-five you are seeing Mr. Evans in Harley Street. Remember Annabel's birthday . . . and Roger, the guests are arriving at seven o'clock sharp." There was more in this vein, so much so that I had finished my apricot and arugula salad by the end of the call.

"Minty, I'm sorry it's such bad manners but if I'm not on tap for Roger he gets into a state." She did not, I noticed, turn off the phone.

I twirled my glass. "Can I ask you something? How did you cope with Richmond's first wife?"

"Ah," Gisela tapped my hand. "I didn't think about her, Minty. That was the trick. There's no safety in thinking. If one harps on all the difficult things, and I acknowledge that there are many, then you put yourself at a disadvantage. Her name was Myra, and she rescued Richmond when he was down on his luck, and they built up the business together. But she made a mistake. She forgot to treat him as a husband. So . . ." Gisela looked thoughtful. "It was simple for me." After a moment, she added, "Richmond wanted me. Yes, he did. Elderly as he was. So you see . . ."

The phone rang for a second time. Gisela picked it up. "Roger," she sounded sharp. "I *am* having lunch." To my astonishment, a flush flamed up into her cheeks. "Marcus? Where are you? No. Not tonight. I'm entertaining." She swiveled away from me. "I'm having lunch with a friend. No. Yes. Soon."

Now, she did switch off the phone. "Would you like some coffee?" The color still danced in her cheeks, and she made a show of dabbing her mouth with her napkin, and then an eye. "Bit of mascara," she declared, and consulted her handbag mirror.

"Is everything all right?" I watched Gisela smooth the tiniest of lines at the corner of her eye. "Is Marcus one of the hostile family?"

"Marcus . . ." Gisela dropped the mirror back into her bag. She fixed her eyes on me thoughtfully, and it was evident some kind of calculation was being made. "I've known Marcus all my life. He sort of . . . fits in between my marriages. Some people do, you know. You can't get rid of them."

"*Between* marriages? Are you between marriages?"

She played with the diamond on her left hand. "No. But there is work, and there is play. Tonight at the dinner Roger and I will give, there is a good chance I will be a little bored by the person sitting next to me. But not by so much as a flicker will I suggest it, and I will make that person feel good about himself, and it will benefit Roger." She glanced down at the coffee, which had arrived. "I never confuse work and play."

Gisela had been exceptionally indiscreet and I was curious to know why. Across the table, I observed the expertly tinted lids mask the knowing eyes and the equation was solved. It was a simple one, even for one whose mathematical skill was limited. Gisela knew perfectly well that her secret was safe with me because her husband was my husband's boss.

By mutual consent we moved on to safer subjects—the Gard house in France, Roger's clutch of directorships, and the rumor that Vistemax was being eyed by a German conglomerate. The Chelsea house was in the process of redecoration and Gisela was fretting over the color schemes. "Did I tell you that Maddy Kington, who is advising me, has run off with a builder on the last house she worked on? She's now living in a bungalow in Reading. A case of *l'amour du cottage*. What do you think the *cottage* is like?"

I returned to the office knowing that under Gisela's Chloe suit and the matching Bulgari jewelry, was a woman who had worked out to the last flutter of those tinted and mascaraed eyelashes what was necessary for her survival.

———

I let myself in through the front door of Number 7 and braced myself.

Sure enough, Lucas appeared at the top of the stairs, half in and half out of his trousers. I put down my bag and went up as he launched himself at me. I picked him up and carried him into the bedroom where Eve was battling for supremacy. Lucas nuzzled my neck, damp little lips nibbling away. Then he wriggled until I put him down and he dived toward Eve, who seized the moment to haul off his trousers.

A fully dressed Felix was standing by the window that overlooked the street. He turned around. "Mummy, there's a poor cat out there. I think he wants a home."

I went over to inspect the scene. "That's not a poor cat, Felix. That's Tigger. He belongs to the Blakes; you know that."

"But he *looks* lost." For some time now, Felix had been begging for a kitten. "If he was lost and came here, Mum, he would sit on your knee. You would like that and he could go out of his special door."

I stroked the thin, little shoulders. "I don't like cats, Felix."

He fixed a bright blue gaze on me. "Daddy says we can have one."

"Did he? When?"

"Last night."

"You were asleep when Daddy came home last night."

Felix discovered that discretion was the better part of valor. He dropped his trousers and stepped out of them. "It *seemed* like last night."

I sighed.

Half an hour later, they were settled on either side of me as I read their bedtime story. "Once upon a time, there was a big jungle where it was very hot . . ." Felix's thumb had sneaked into his mouth, and I removed it. The illustrator had gone to town. There were scarlet and blue parrots, and pale beige monkeys in the trees. On the ground, he had drawn in a scurry of ants, an anteater with a long, businesslike snout and, tucked into the left-hand corner, the sinister coils of a boa constrictor.

Lucas pointed to a monkey. "His eyes are as big as yours, Mummy."

"The ants were very good at keeping house," I read. "But along came the anteater and ate them all up." The illustrator provided graphic detail and the boys shrieked. "Afterward he became very sleepy and forgot to look around."

"Oh . . ." Felix drew the word out. "The snake is squeez-ing him."

Downstairs, the front door opened and shut. Nathan's briefcase hit the tiles with a clunk. Eve ran up to her bedroom and the sound of radio music began to float from it.

On the final page, there was a swoop of striped fur and a glint of bared fangs as the tiger leaped onto the boa constrictor.

"Mummy," asked Felix. "Does everybody always eat every-body else?"

"Yes . . ." Lucas bared his teeth. "Like this . . ." He sank his teeth into his brother's arm.

Nathan arrived into the melee and roared for order, and I fled downstairs where I extracted a ready-made dish of chicken breasts and mushrooms from the fridge, shoved it in the oven, and set the timer. Eve had done the laundry and I picked up the basket and took it upstairs to the landing where I had set up the ironing board.

Unless Eve stepped in, Nathan did his own shirts and was

frequently sighted on the landing. He burned himself once, sought me out, and held out a hand on which glowed a strip. "What do I do?"

I held his hand under cold water, made him a cup of tea, and asked every hour or so if he was feeling better. For days afterward, I caught him examining it and eavesdropped on his phone conversation to Poppy. "It could have been very nasty." In due course, the scab fell away leaving a scimitar scar. "Poppy tells me," Nathan was pleased with the information, "that this kind of burn is listened in medical textbooks as housewife's syndrome."

I scrutinized my own unscarred wrists. "What does that make you, Nathan?"

"Experienced at ironing," he replied evenly.

I returned downstairs. Nathan was not in the study, and I looked into the sitting room. He had drawn a chair up by the French window. He was staring out through the dark in the direction of the lilac tree and was quite, quite still.

The hairs on the back of my neck prickled. In the kitchen, the timer shrilled. I took a step into the room. "Nathan?"

He sighed, stirred. "Yes . . ." He looked at me. "What do you want?"

After supper Nathan rolled up his shirtsleeves and tackled the glasses too delicate for the dishwasher. It was late, the heating had gone off, and gooseflesh colonized my arms.

He worked in his usual methodical way, running fresh hot water into each glass and setting it on the draining board. I tipped the hot water back into the sink, rubbed them with a cloth, and put them away.

"Nathan, what would you say if I went back to work full time?"

"*That* again," said Nathan.

"That again," I echoed.

Seven years ago Timon, my boss, had called me into his office at Vistemax. On the door, there was a plaque that read EDITOR, WEEKEND DIGEST. I remember in particular the emphatic curve of the D. Timon, who modeled himself on Gordon Gekko, was in full pinstriped suit and braces. "Look, we want you to take over from Rose." Timon never bothered much with preliminaries.

My skirt was short, the skin of my legs was buffed, creamed, and polished. My heels were high, my hair lustrous with youth. With the aid of kohl and gray eye shadow, my eyes were darkly inviting. I had dreams of domination: not the sexual kind, but of being able to manage my life effortlessly. "Are you sacking Rose, Timon?"

He sent me his best Gekko look. "You know perfectly well that is what you have been angling for."

The previous evening, Nathan had slipped into my bed, shuddering with emotion. He had left Rose. "This is a new beginning." At that point, he had no intention of marrying me but he craved the transcendence of the love affair. He gazed so deeply into my eyes that he was in danger of x-raying my skull, and I grew uncomfortable with the intensity. Nathan was funny, tender, and much politer than I was used to in my lovers. "Do you mind?" "May I?" As we moved this way and that on my cheap, inadequate double bed, sealing his arrival, I told myself that Rose did not deserve to keep him.

Timon drew a perfect circle on his notepad. "Six months' probation. Yes or no?"

"Yes."

I quit his office high-wired with nerves and exhilaration. Abraham Maslow had been correct when he drew up his pyramid and formulated an individual's hierarchies of need. Once food, warmth, safety, and sex were more or less seen to, then it was vital to have the respect of colleagues. And respect for oneself, of course.

Six months later, I received one of those letters. "Your probationary period has now run to its close. While we have appreciated your efforts on the Books Pages, we have decided not to appoint you. Perhaps you will consider the alternatives. . . ." and so on.

This time, Timon did not bother to call me into the office.

It took me a while to decide where to file this record of my failure. Eventually, I slotted it into "Family History" in Nathan's immaculate files, fitting it between—chronologically—the photographs of Poppy's surprise wedding in Thailand, and the christening of Jilly and Sam's Frieda. Nathan demanded to know why I had put it there, and I told him there was no point in not facing up to the fact that I had been sacked. He lost his temper, cursed Vistemax, and raged around the room. I watched him with my heart galloping under my pregnant bump. For Nathan, life was no longer obedient and tidy, and his family had lost its shape, and I knew, I knew then, that his regrets were for that loss of symmetry as much as his guilt at having cut it into bits.

Nathan placed the penultimate glass on the draining board. Foam flecked his forearms, and his fingers were pink. "Your timing, Minty. It's late." Pause. "Why?"

Again, I recollected Deb's nasty expression. "I don't think part-time works."

He pulled out the plug. Greasy and cold, the water drained away. "I know it doesn't, but the boys need you. It seems to me that you have a good balance with what you have got."

"I *need* to work and I think I would do better at Paradox if I was full time."

He nodded, and wiped down the draining board with a cloth. "You see that as your priority?"

"I do. It will be okay, Nathan. I promise. It's not so difficult. Thousands of women do it." I slid my arms around his waist and made him turn around to face me. "Surely, you're not surprised?"

"No." He moved out of my reach. "I had an idea you might be thinking along those lines."

Why hadn't he *said* something? "Don't make me sound like a monster who abandons her children. I need to do something properly. You do see?" I thought of the ideas landing in my lap. I would nurture them, make them grow, and watch them fly.

"Don't you put your heart and soul into your sons?" Nathan gave me a long, slow appraisal, and all our differences were reflected in that scrutiny. "I'm tired." He rubbed his eyes. "Let's go to bed."

I stared at him, trying to read beyond the set look on his face. What could I say to dissolve those differences? Somewhere—and I could not place my finger on it—I had lost my hold on the essential Nathan, the one who had tumbled so willingly into my grasp.

One by one, I turned off the lights, and the kitchen slid into darkness. "I have decided, Nathan."

"Well, then," he said from the doorway. "You have decided."

"Oh, for God's sake," I said. "*Don't* sound as if I plan to murder you all."

With that he swung back to me. "And you . . ." his anger broke through the fatigue, "are never satisfied." He checked himself and when he spoke again it was with a low, wooing voice. "Minty, why can't you just get on with what we've got? It's good enough, isn't it?" He pulled me to him, and buried his face in my hair. "Let's not quarrel over this."

Quarreling spelled another sleepless night. It meant what the self-help manuals called a session to settle the issues. It meant the whole question of my work spiraling from a minor problem into a nuclear disaster. I kissed Nathan's cheek. "Let's not."

Chapter Four

Last night Rose was on television. Granted it was one of the lesser-known digital channels, but on television nonetheless.

Nathan was at a Vistemax dinner, one of the many in the run-up to Christmas. On these occasions, he rolled home smelling of cigars and brandy, often with a chocolate mint secreted in his pocket. "Mints for Minty." And, tender and pleased with himself, he would urge me to devour this fruit dropping from the tree of corporate life.

In the interim, I sat on the sofa with a tray on my lap and the opening credits of *Rose Lloyd's Wonders of the World* for company. The twins were asleep, and Eve had gone out.

I had known about the program. Poppy had made the point of informing me about it when she phoned up to ask us to Sunday lunch. "It's so exciting. Mum put up this idea of presenting her *Seven Wonders of the World,* and they gave her more or less free rein." Knowing what I did about television production companies, this was an exaggeration, but you could never accuse Poppy of forgetting whose side she was on. "She's been all over. It's amazing."

There was a pause and I said, "That's wonderful."

Poppy weighed and measured my sincerity and, evidently, found it acceptable and rattled on. "Lunch then. It's our anniversary so we thought . . . It's great being married, don't you think?" Realizing she had fallen into the verbal equivalent of quicksand, Poppy changed the subject and inquired about Felix's recent stomach upset. She ended the conversation by saying, "One o'clock. But Minty, if you feel you want some time to yourself, which I am sure you do, just send Dad and the twins over."

I had not intended to watch Rose's program. No, really. But here I was eyeing the opening credits over a plate of grated carrots, sliced tomatoes, and ultra nonfat salad dressing.

How long was it since I had seen Rose? Two years? Three? No matter, for in my case, *seeing* was irrelevant. You don't have to see someone to know they are there, and Rose and her shadow were sewn to me as securely as Peter Pan's.

Unable to make up my mind if I wished her withered and bony, thus adding to my guilt, or flourishing, as she appeared now, I scrutinized every inch of her. Rose looked wonderful, and like a woman in charge of her life, and totally unencumbered, which, if irritating to anyone struggling with encumbrances, let me off the hook. If Rose could look *that* good, then she was not suffering, and—perhaps—the odds had evened out a trifle. On the other hand, I reminded myself, this was the woman who was discussing garden plans with her ex-husband who happened to be married to me.

Rose's first wonder turned out to be hidden in a Polish salt mine. Dressed in combat trousers and a thick jacket, she led the viewer down a tunnel, and every so often, the camera panned over the figures and animals carved by the miners into the walls. "This unicorn is fourteenth-century," Rose said in a voice-over. "And this is a bas-relief of a church and was probably done as a record during a period when churches were being destroyed. In making these carvings, the miners found relief from boredom and fear. They also gave themselves something beautiful to look at." She went on to describe that the carvings were made by lamplight and with the crudest of tools. Apparently, the rock crystal possessed special molecular qualities that helped preserve the images, and each carving had accrued its own set of stories and myths. Obediently, the camera settled on a figure in a long coat and hood. "This is the Butcher of Kransk, who lured maidens into his shop." The focus switched to a figure on a horse. "This is the knight who reputedly haunts the local forest and whose horn is heard on summer nights."

Rose always preferred fiction to nonfiction. "Novels contain the real truths," she once argued in the calm way that used to annoy me because it was so *settled*. I could never budge her from that position—and now? Now, I never will. For myself, I stick to those self-help and makeover manuals (which, when I first met him, Nathan said was *so touching*). Nathan couldn't be bothered with fiction either. I don't think Nathan had read a novel for, oh, fifteen years or so.

I pushed the tray aside, slipped off my shoes, and tucked my feet up on the sofa.

The camera panned onto Rose's face now cast into shadow. But she still looked wonderful. "The real treasure of the salt mine, the one I have come for, lies farther down this corridor . . ." I followed her progress down the passage and into a vault whose walls reflected pinpricks of light. "Here"—her excitement about her *Wonder* infected even me—"is the Madonna of the Salt. Work began on her in the fifteenth century, and legend has it that she was based on a nun from the convent of St. Caterina who died after experiencing visions of Mary, the mother of Christ. Each year, the community celebrates the statue's reputation for protecting mothers with an underground candlelit procession, and women, who are not normally allowed inside the mine, come with their babies to be blessed . . ."

She gestured with her right hand, and the large gold ring she wore slipped down her finger. "The Madonna of the Salt may be out of sight but she is very much a presence in the town. She is referred to as the hidden mother. Incidentally, the phrase 'hidden mother' is also used for brides. For obvious reasons, no one is permitted to touch the Madonna, but as I stand here in front of her, I'm finding it difficult not to reach out as she is so very lifelike . . ."

That was enough. More than enough. I reached for the remote and switched Rose off.

That Poppy had never accepted me and, doubtless, never would bothered me not a jot. Well, not much. That Poppy had only to pout her red lips and Nathan went running did concern me. "She's a good girl," he made a point of telling me (more than once). "Her heart is absolutely right."

Nathan did not tolerate criticism of his children. Not one word—however tactfully I went about it, which I considered misguided. We all could do with a little, especially children, but when it came to Poppy and Sam, Nathan retreated to a locked and soundproofed chamber, and no amount of knocking would make him open the door.

Poppy's heart might have been made of the best-tempered steel, but she was often *wrong*. For instance, it had been unkind to wear black at our wedding, and to persist in making her feelings about me so clear after seven years was divisive. When Nathan left Rose for me, Poppy spat defiance at her father. "I never want to see you . . . or that woman, again. *Ever.*" Floating on a tide of moral certainty, she had reduced him to shivering and weeping. "She called me an old goat," he confessed to me. "An *old goat.*"

Poppy and Richard had made the transition from flat to large house in a disgustingly short period of time. Richard had made a lot of money in "strategy" and Poppy spent it. The house was Edwardian, spacious, and newly refurbished. The windows and paintwork were pristine. The front garden had been designed by a professional. It featured box and carefully graded gray stone. An olive tree in a blue ceramic pot stood in the center.

The door was flung open and there was Poppy. "Dad," she cried, interposing herself between Nathan and me. "How lovely."

Father and daughter were very alike. They had the same coloring, and facial structure. Naturally, Poppy was modeled more delicately—her waist was tiny and I found myself pulling my pink cardigan edged with ribbon down over my hips. Underneath, I wore a lacy half-cup bra that was digging into my flesh. Before the twins, a half-cup bra fit like a second skin but these days, I was bothered by its secret chafe. No longer the student, Poppy was groomed and highlighted and, unlike when I first met her, she never wore glasses, only contact lenses. Yet she had not lost her shortsighted habit of peering at you, nor her quickness, nor her tendency to outbursts. She grabbed her father's hand and carried it to her cheek. "It's been ages. I've missed you, Dad."

Nathan put his arm around his daughter and glowed. "Hallo, Minty," Poppy said at last. Her gaze veered past my shoulder. She broke into a huge smile, and flung wide her arms. "Twins, I have been counting the minutes," and she swooped down and drew them close.

"I've got red socks," Lucas informed his big half sister.

"And I've got blue ones," Felix brought up the rear.

"I'm wearing socks too." Poppy hoicked up her trouser leg. "They've got spots on them. Now boys, I have an important question to ask you."

Felix knew exactly what was coming. "No," he said. "I haven't."

Poppy held them tight and pushed her head between theirs. "How naughty have you been? Tell me everything."

There was much whispering and muttering, and Poppy giggled and said, "Felix, you're tickling my ear." Eventually, she pronounced. "Is that all?" Then she said gravely, "I can be *much* naughtier than that."

Lunch was a gigot of lamb cooked with flageolet beans and garlic. Nb: flageolet beans are a useful, sophisticated vegetable. Halfway through, I glanced at Nathan. He was talking about oil prices, but there was an abstraction about him, a suggestion of discomfort for, every so often, his eyes squeezed shut.

Did Poppy notice? While she talked, she fiddled with her expensive crystal necklace—the leather thongs, feathers, and beads she loved to wear when I first met her had been long banished. It was beautiful and she caressed it with reverence. When she thought no one was watching, her gaze rested on her husband and there was no doubt of her adoration.

Richard appeared unconscious of his wife. He had settled in to enjoy himself—which he showed every indication of doing. He and Nathan had moved on to a detailed discussion of hedge funds, the twins were concentrating on their ice cream, and I was behaving myself.

Poppy seemed restless and had disappeared more than once into the kitchen. She jumped up to refill my water glass. "Daddy and Richard are boring for England." Her eyes rested indulgently on them as she cast around for some point of contact between us. "How are your friends, Minty?"

"My friends? Oh, Paige is fine. About to have her third baby."

Poppy replaced the jug on the mat and wiped away a minute spot of water from the table. "She gave up her very high-powered job, didn't she, to look after the children?"

"She made the sacrifice." I spoke lightly.

Poppy's long eyelashes beat down over her eyes. "Women just don't know which way to go."

"Isn't that just sloppy thinking? All we have to do is to choose."

"But it's so *complicated*."

True, but I was reluctant to yield a point to Poppy. Furthermore, she was spoiling for a confrontation. Nathan was watching me. *Please,* he begged silently. *No arguments.* Why Poppy should escape censure for some of her sillier statements, I would never fathom, but I did the right thing and, conversationally, ducked. "How are things at work?"

Poppy used to work in publishing but recently had astonished her family by taking a job in a firm that imported exotic candles from China and sold them through up-market shops. "Fine, fine, fine. The mad Christmas push is still going on. So mad, sometimes, I have to help with the packing." Poppy sketched an imaginary box with her hands. "I like that. I like physically handling something, and the colors and scents of some of the candles are exquisite." She added, "As a culture, we are not hands-on enough. We don't like to get dirty."

Richard had been conscripted into telling the twins a story. Lucas was snorting with laughter, but Felix was puzzled. I knew that look. It meant that he was questioning what he was hearing. "The big brown bear," said Richard, crooking his fingers and placing them on either side of his head, "gobbled up the wizard."

"Wizards don't get gobbled," said Felix flatly, and I rejoiced in his capacity not to be taken in.

Richard lowered his hands. "I can't make you believe me."

Lucas shouted. "I believe you. I believe you, don't I, Mummy?"

I was about to reply, "Of course you do," when I encountered Felix's anxious gaze, and realized that he was terrified of being shown up. Nathan sent me the tiniest shake of his head. "You can believe what you wish, both of you," I said.

"Of course you can," said Richard, all good humor but with the slight uneasiness of someone who was not truly at home with children.

Felix slid down from his chair and flung himself against me. I ran my fingers through his hair, relishing the texture of his tufty curls. His breath was scented with garlic, his body pressing against mine. Whether I liked it or not, the connection between him and me flowed up through my fingers.

After a few seconds, Lucas climbed down from his chair and leaned against Nathan in imitation of his brother.

"Twins," Poppy reproved them. "We haven't quite finished."

"Leave them," said their indulgent father.

"But you mustn't let them be spoiled." Poppy laid a hand on her father's shoulder. "Not even a teeny bit." She shook her head and the crystal necklace glinted very satisfactorily indeed. "You mustn't spoil them, Dad."

"They are *not* spoiled," I said crossly. "Far from it."

For a second or two conversation was suspended. Richard threw in a diversionary tactic. "Are you going on holiday this year?" He managed to sound so interested that the tension was broken.

Grateful to him, I sipped the remainder of my wine and assessed the room. To her credit, Poppy had gotten it right. A striped wallpaper in old rose and gold, comfortable chairs, flowers. The effect was simple and muted and I set to wondering if I had overdone the decor in the dining room at Lakey Street. Was the effect too crowded? Had I tried too hard? I decided that the Chinese figurines should go.

Later, I went up the freshly painted and carpeted staircase to the bathroom and passed a shelf of photographs, all framed in the same way. And there was Rose. *Of course.* Dressed in shorts and thin-strapped sandals, she was sitting at a café table in what seemed to be a Mediterranean port. The sun was shining, and the scene exuded a shimmering iridescence. Leaning back in the chair, she was inclining her face to the camera, a trustful pose, and a smile played on her lips. One hand held a coffee cup, the other rested in her lap. There was tenderness evident in the composition of the photograph by the unseen eye. From the bottom of my heart, I envied Rose her ease, and the sensation of bright, hot sun on her arms and legs.

Coming up behind me on the stairs, Poppy said, "That one was taken of Mum last year in Paxos."

"I saw the program the other night. It was very good."

"Yes, Mum is quite, quite brilliant." Poppy was poised between a challenge and the good manners she imposed on herself as the hostess, and the latter got the better of her. "Which bathroom do you want to use?"

I murmured that I did not mind, and as she led me to the second guests' bathroom, we passed a small room in which a computer terminal was switched on. The screen saver showed a lot of brightly colored fish darting over it.

When I returned from the bathroom, someone had evidently been in there for the screen now read, "Poker Online. Game Five."

Before we left, I sought out Poppy, who was stacking china in the kitchen. "Thank you so much for lunch," I said and then, surprising myself, "Is everything all right?"

She cast a look over the piles of crockery, and her lips tightened. We did not say a word, but she knew that I had seen the online poker on the screen. Poppy fixed me with defiant eyes. "Absolutely," she said. "Couldn't be better."

As we drove home in the late afternoon, Nathan touched my thigh. "I know you have tried with Poppy." I must have given a visible start, for he added, "Am I such a pig? Do you think I don't notice?"

"No. I don't think you are a pig." I looked out of the window, unsure of how to respond. I had grown used to saying nothing. Anyway, the silences that characterized Nathan's and my life together were deceptive, for they were noisy with the unsaid. The London streets rolled past my vision revealing their Sunday aspect: serviceable acres of tarmac and city trees that struggled to survive.

The interior of the SUV required a cleaning and smelled of the cranberry juice one of the boys had spilled in the back. *Nb: put on the list for Eve.* I searched in my bag for a tissue. "Poppy and I rub along."

Nathan's hand tightened on my thigh. "I didn't marry you to get on with Poppy."

It was a small concession, but I felt a sudden comfort and pleasure in the ratification of my place in Nathan's hierarchy. Deep in my handbag, my fingers encountered a half-sucked boiled sweet that Felix had discarded and I had rescued from the car seat. Its awful stickiness and the fact that it was in my handbag, which I liked to keep immaculate, instantly banished the feel-good factor, and I said more sharply than I intended, "You married me because you thought you would be happy. I don't think you are. And I don't know what I can do about it."

Nathan stared straight ahead. "You read my notebook, didn't you?"

"Yes."

"You shouldn't have."

"Perhaps not." I could hear the sound of many doors banging shut in Nathan's head. "Nathan, we should make time to have a discussion."

I cannot pretend that I uttered this with utmost urgency and conviction, but I thought I should try.

"Not here." He jerked his head at the back where the boys were making favorite aircraft noises.

"Of course not here."

We halted at traffic lights, and the occupant of a small Fiat shook his fist and pointed to the poster on his back windscreen. SUVS ARE FUVS. The lights changed and Nathan nosed the car into Lakey Street and parked. "Minty, the notebook was private." He rubbed his forehead. All the same, I detected a frisson of . . . what I felt was relief. "I cannot trust you not to pry."

"What, Mummy?" interrupted Lucas. "*What,* Mummy."

"Maybe you can't." I left it like that, swung out of the car, released the twins from captivity, and exhumed spare clothes, toys, and the books that Felix never went anywhere without. Thus burdened I trod up the path behind my husband and sons.

A little later, Nathan said, "I need some exercise." He had changed into a pair of worn corduroys and a plaid shirt with frayed cuffs.

I was unpacking the twins' toys and working out what to give them for supper. "A walk? Take the boys, will you?"

"I think I'll have a go at digging the garden."

"Dig the garden!" Wooden engine in hand, I whirled around. "You haven't done that for years."

"All the same"—Nathan stuck his hands in his pockets— "I think I will."

The twins' football sessions had turned the lawn into a Slough of Despond. I watched Nathan pick his way across it and haul a fork out of the garden shed. From the set of his shoulders, he was perfectly happy, and it was a fair bet he was whistling. He began to dig under the lilac tree and, after a while, a pile of earth stacked up beside him.

Half an hour later, I ferried out a mug of tea. The dark was galloping in, it was growing chilly, and Nathan's shirt was damp with sweat under his arms. He wiped his hands on his trousers. "Good girl."

"Why the interest in the garden, all of a sudden?" The question was redundant because I already knew the answer.

He drank some tea. "It used to be beautiful."

"You've been thinking of Rose," I accused him. "Haven't you? You've been talking to her. That diagram I found in your diary. Was it for this garden?" I gestured toward the broken fence, the tangle of grass, the leafless lilac. 'Height. Route. Rest.' Was it for here?"

"*Don't*, Minty," Nathan said heavily. "We don't discuss Rose. Remember?"

"About the diary . . ."

"Forget it. It's mine, *private*." His brows twitched together.

"Are you all right?"

"Fine, fine." His finger beat a tattoo on his chest. "Bit of a pain. I ate too much."

In chapter three of *Coping with Life Strategies* (currently beside my bed), the author recommends cognitive behavioral therapy for tricky problems. If a bad thought recurs to the point of damaging one's well-being, then it is best to avoid it and employ thought evasion techniques. Weary to the bone, I bent down and plucked a white root from the dug earth, and dangled it from my fingers.

I thought hard of Paradox's Monday agenda. I conjured the picture of Chinese figurines whose days were numbered in the dining room. I thought about the fish fingers I had extracted from the freezer for the twins' supper.

Failure. I turned back to Nathan. "Why on earth did I believe you when you said you came to me with the sheet wiped clean?"

I should have kissed him and prevented him answering. Regrets are a waste of energy, I should have pointed out, stopping his mouth with that ungiven kiss. I should have talked about anything but this.

Nathan wiped his upper lip with the back of his hand, leaving an earth moustache. "There is no point fighting over something you can do nothing about, Minty."

I gave up. Memories do not obey commands. You cannot ever pronounce that the past is in the past. It is there, dug in.

I left him to it. I went inside, fed the children, and put them to bed. Then I gathered together my notes and files and went up. On the kitchen table, I left a Post-it note on which I had written, "Get your own supper."

Chapter Five

"Hey, Minty." Barry's summons was issued via the internal phone. "We need you."

I was flicking through the daily papers, the phone squeezed between shoulder and neck, a pose I found useful for suggesting that I was engaged in top-whack activity. Lately, I had noticed that my shoulder and upper arm were stiff and aching. Nathan laughed when I explained the reason why and murmured that he had missed a trick all these years.

"Can you wait while I get this call, Barry?"

"No," he said. "Okay."

When I arrived at his office, Gabrielle and Deb were ensconced on the supersized sofa, wedged so far back that their feet were in danger of leaving the ground. From his desk, Barry loomed a telling couple of feet over them. He was dressed in a leather blouson jacket and chinos. He also wore a white silk evening scarf draped around his neck and, when he raised his arm, a red kabbalah wristband was prominent on his wrist. But his eyes were sharp and intelligent. He held up a green plastic envelope and kicked off with "There's a mass of stuff in here about middle age. What is it? Who is it? The girls . . ."—"girls" was emphasized—". . . agree that this is worth a look at but it needs work to see if it can pull together." Without a mitigating shred of irony, he handed the dossier to me. "The consensus is, Minty, that this one is yours."

Gabrielle and Deb exchanged looks. "Gabrielle and I don't feel we know enough," Deb pointed out.

A small, but significant note sounded in my head. "And I do?"

I could choose any number of metaphors to explain the transition from imagining you are one of the girls to knowing that you are not. Depending on my mood, they would make me laugh or weep accordingly. In this case, I would decide which later.

Deb shook back the mass of her wavy hair—very North London, pre-Raphaelite hair—and the gesture suggested (and was intended to) unfettered vision and youthful boldness that knew *exactly* where it was heading. Gabrielle focused on Barry and, as usual, he was pretending not to notice.

"I do sense possibilities here." Barry was passing me the baton. "I think you could deal nicely, Minty."

I skimmed the first paragraph of an article from the *New Statesman*. "The social and cultural emphasis of youth has resulted in a neglect of the middle years. We have more than sufficient cultural and financial data on youth and, to an extent, on the old. But what do we know about the important phase in between the two?"

An urgent phone call took Gabrielle out of the room, which released Barry for proper thought and the "creative" discussion that followed. Was middle age defined by behavioral habits? (Avoiding danger? Inability to sleep in? Caffeine intolerance? Regular checking of the bank balance?)

Deb tapped her pen on her clipboard. "I wouldn't know."

Barry dropped a small rocket into the room. "Or is it when people discover, or rediscover, faith?"

"Good heavens." Deb sounded appalled. "Really?"

Barry retracted. "Perhaps not. Maybe middle aged is defined financially. When the mortgage is paid off."

Deb swept back her hair and anchored it with a hand, exposing her smooth, unlined forehead. "Middle age is forty?"

"Fifty." Barry was firm.

"Oh? Okay." Deb sounded as though she had never heard of fifty. "You think?"

Never once during this exchange did either Barry or Deb look fully at me.

"Minty, have a word with your friends." Barry brought the meeting to a close. "People who know. What do they think about middle age?"

"I've hunted out a few statistics that might help," Deb said kindly. She handed over a sheaf of papers, and her hair mimicked the pliant, supple movements of her body. "Maybe you could go over them during your days at home?"

The following morning, I came in early when I knew Barry would be in the office and presented him with a memo delineating why Paradox Pictures would benefit by hiring me full time. I had dressed carefully in linen trousers, a camisole that exposed a hint of cleavage, and a tight denim jacket.

At home, his wife's thank-you postcard of a Matisse silhouette in brilliant blue was still pinned to the kitchen notice board. "Barry and I thought the dinner excellent. . . . P.S. Could I have the recipe for the chicken?"

Barry listened to what I had to say. Then he tapped his finger on his Filofax and spoke pleasantly and reasonably. "Not sure, Minty."

Any minute now the phones would go mad, and Barry's focus would be lost. I had always believed in being straight. "I have everything you need."

"Yeess . . ." Barry was still reasonable. "Don't take this the wrong way, darling, and I would like to help, truly I would." To show willingness, he skimmed the main points of the memo. "You do have a lot on your plate."

"I know."

"There are plenty of smart women like you, and unencumbered, if you see what I mean." This was thin ice, and he switched tack. "I have to consider the dynamics. It would put Deb's nose out of joint." He added with ironic inflection, "Budgets, you know."

Under the camisole donned so hopefully, the half-cup bra itched. "At least consider my suggestion."

Barry's smile was catlike. He would so much rather not have to deal with my request. "I'll do that. We'll talk after Christmas. Okay?"

He never so much as glanced at my cleavage.

Mindful of Barry's warning about Deb, I sought her out at the end of the day. "Have you got a moment?"

"Hi." She was gathering up her stuff into a leopard-print tote bag. She worked efficiently, and I noticed that she handled the papers with a kind of reverence. She listened without comment to the outline of my plans in which I made sure she understood that I posed no threat to her position. Eventually, without looking into a mirror, she dabbed lip gloss onto her mouth. "It really doesn't matter one way or the other, Minty. We take it as it comes." Mobile phone in hand, she hovered in the doorway. "You're not in tomorrow, are you? See you the day after."

"So?" Paige maneuvered herself onto the car seat like a ship's container into berth. The baby was due late January, but during this final trimester she was finding it difficult to walk, and I was ferrying her to the shops to do some Christmas shopping. "Why do we *need* categories of age or behavior?"

"We don't. Or rather, sensible people don't. It's business and marketing that require handholds."

Paige considered. "You'd better watch that Deborah. Take it from me." This was not light advice. Paige knew whereof she spoke. She had survived coups and countercoups. "By the time she got home after you talked to her, she would have worked out several scenarios as to why no one else was needed full time at Paradox, all of which spell bad news for your plans, especially when Barry consults her—which he will."

I absorbed the advice. "After Nathan left Rose, and she was sacked, I wrote to her, saying it was my turn now."

"You didn't?"

"I did. I regret it. At the time, I wanted to explain. To show why things had turned out the way they had."

After a moment, Paige said. "Some going."

I eyed her bulk. "How is it going?"

"*It's* fine."

This was not the former Paige—all hustle, smartness, and gloss—who had featured in the photographs that adorned the Hurley household. That Paige had been a top banker. No, this Paige had given it all up when Jackson (eight) followed by Lara (six) arrived. There was no choice, I overheard her telling Nathan (who lapped it up). Children cannot flourish at home without a mother. *Period*.

This Paige was deeply fatigued with her third pregnancy. Her lipstick had been carelessly applied, leaving a rim round the pale interior of her stubborn lower lip, while a smudge of mascara adorned the papery skin under her left eye.

"You look tired."

"So?" She shrugged and still managed to convey . . . excitement and commitment. "You know, despite feeling like the largest sack of potatoes on the planet, if I could make a wish, I would have started earlier."

"Your energy is ferocious. You should be working in a bank."

"Ha."

We drove past the common. Paige eased herself back in the seat and gazed hungrily out of the window. "Do I look like a prisoner offered an hour's exercise in the yard?"

"The sacking smock gives you away."

The dog walkers were out in force, some of whom were struggling with as many as six or eight charges. "Look at them." Paige sighed. "That's how I feel."

Winter had snapped its jaws shut. The trees were stripped bare and, since the autumn rains, the grass had returned to its proper color. The shops glowed with Christmas lights. Suddenly, Paige asked. "What if I die with this one? Women do die sometimes."

Startled, I replied, "You won't."

"If I do, will you insist that I have 'Mother' somewhere on the tombstone?" Paige laughed as she spoke, but it was not a happy sound.

"Don't you mean 'Wife and Mother'?"

She shook her head, and there was the suggestion of new flesh settling under her chin. "Sort of excessive, don't you think?"

"Paige, what's going on?" In my book, Paige and Martin were a *happy* couple. They represented all that was stalwart in the tough battle to preserve family values. All of a sudden, I had a disconcerting flash that I had been looking at the wrong picture.

"Nothing, sweetie. Nothing at all. Husbands are tiring, that's all." There was a pause. "Hey, did I tell you about Lara? I've got her into Partingtons, the ballet school. Lara's been aching to go and the list was this long . . ." Paige sketched a gesture that fishermen frequently employ when discussing their catches. "Anyway, I collared Mary Streatham at the book club. She's a board member, and we understand each other, and she said she would see what she could do. No favors, mind. But . . . and no favors, mind . . . apparently a donation to the new studio fund would not go unnoticed. Martin isn't so pleased with his bit."

I snorted. "I smell a similarity to Nathan's taking paper suppliers to Paris for a long weekend for a cultural adventure."

"Whatever you say." You could cut Paige's smugness with a knife.

Back at Paige's kitchen—complete with a pink Aga and copper *batterie de cuisine*—I unpacked and hid various packages while Paige instructed me from a chair into which she had lowered herself with a groan. The table had already been laid with a full complement of china, glasses, and napkins by Linda, the au pair. One of Paige's nostrums, one of the many to which I helped myself, was that children should be made to eat properly at the table with adults.

"Does Martin get home in time?" I asked.

Paige sighed. "What do you think?"

A big, blond child, Jackson, bounded into the kitchen. "Mum, where have you been?"

The effect was of an electric switch being tripped. Paige jerked out of her torpor. "Darling. How was your day? Say hallo to Mrs. Lloyd."

Jackson was full of his news. "Guess, Mummy . . ." but he could not wait for Paige to run through the options. "I came in second in the spelling test."

Even I knew my duty. "That's wonderful, Jackson."

Paige cupped her son's chin in her hand. "Only *second*, darling." So gentle she sounded, and so inexorable. "What went wrong?"

I drove back from Paige's, parked, and let myself into the house. All over the country parents were hurrying home to scoop up their offspring. Parents who, laden with briefcases and last-minute shopping, kicked open the front door and cried: I'm home. That species of parent sank gratefully into a welter of flesh, warmth, and children's muddle, and ambition was laid aside as they embraced their children.

According to the list in the kitchen, the twins were at Millie Rowe's for tea. I checked the post, which included a volume of poems by the feminist poet Ellen Black, whom I had schmoozed at a party. It was entitled *Origin of a New Species*.

One of Lucas's red socks lay on the stairs. I picked it up and smoothed it absently. It was a very little sock with the suggestion of a hole in the toe. Soon I would have to think about supper and endless more meals. Then there was the twins' Christmas party. On the list I had written "sausages, pizzas, red jelly in the shape of a cat, and pirate hats," and I knew that for days afterward, I would be picking up bits of sausage and crisps that had been trodden into the floors and carpets.

The front door opened and the boys did their windmill act—arms outstretched and flailing—toward me. "Here's Mummy," Lucas's cry rang with a note of pure joy. His shirt was hanging out and encrusted with chocolate biscuits. Felix had green paint splodges on his cheek. Laden with stuff, Eve bought up the rear.

Felix tugged at my hand. "You are my real mummy, aren't you?"

"Of course I am."

He looked important. "Lucas says Eve is our real mummy."

"*Lucas . . .*" I glanced at Eve, who shook her head.

Lucas seemed shifty. "Millie says her nanny is her real mummy . . ."

Millie was a recently acquired friend. The only child of divorced parents, her life was spent shuttling between two tight-lipped adults. She had the bewilderment—and the malice—of a child at sea. The boys needed reassurance, and I thought rapidly and inventively. "Why don't we invite Millie to tea, and she can see who the real mummy is?"

Nathan arrived home, pale and shivering, and I ordered him to bed. Later, I took him up a tray with scrambled eggs laced with smoked salmon and cranberry juice. "You've been overdoing the parties." I pummeled his pillows, patted the duvet straight and checked over the bedroom, which was in apple-pie order.

"There's a bad flu going around." He placed a finger on his pulse, and squinted up at me with a grin. "It's galloping."

I grinned back. "Probably terminal."

I sat down at the end of the bed and studied him. True, Nathan did not look quite in the pink, but his hair was thick, in good condition, and attractively gray-streaked. Thank goodness he was not coarse or lumpy or hairy. Nor had he run to fat, and the veins in his hands and legs were still decently buried beneath the skin. Thank goodness too he was not the sort of man who smelled, a roaring masculine presence whose limbs and noise invaded every space, for there was a delicacy and proportion about his appearance. "*Should* you have a checkup?"

He forked up egg. "I might."

"I insist."

"Bully." He spoke without rancor. "I'd prefer a holiday in Cornwall. How about it, Minty?" The old spark flickered in his eyes. "It would be fun. The boys would love it. It would do us all good. It would be like old times."

Outside, a car door slammed, and rain spattered the window, but in the bedroom it was warm and peaceful.

I sidestepped Cornwall. "Talking of the boys . . . about the nativity play."

"What about it?"

"Mrs. Jenkins promised Lucas could be a wise man." Nathan raised a questioning eyebrow. "I'm afraid she said Felix could be a sheep."

"What!" Nathan pulled himself upright. "And you didn't *do* anything?"

"Nathan, there was nothing I could do." I rescued the tray and set it down on the chest. "There's no need for drama. I'm sure that next year Felix will be a wise man." I cast around wildly. "*Joseph,* even."

"Minty . . . come here." I obeyed and he caught my hand in a grip so fierce that I cried out. "Don't you understand anything about your sons? Can't you remember anything of what it's like to be a child? Don't you *see* . . . how Felix will mind? How that fragile little bit of confidence, which is all he has, will be shot to pieces? God knows, we have to learn about suffering and exclusion and mistakes, but not yet for our two. Not yet . . . if I have anything to do with it."

I stared down at the figure in the bed. The warm, peaceful atmosphere had vanished. "You're hurting me, Nathan." At once he released me. "Don't you think Felix should learn that the world isn't fair?"

"At *five,* Minty. Are you totally without mercy?"

"Almost six," I heard myself say.

Felix was the youngest by ten minutes. It was nothing, and everything. Ten minutes appeared to have ensured that Lucas was apportioned the greater percentage of confidence and attention.

"So what do you want to do, Nathan? Tell Lucas he can't be a wise man?"

"If I ever see that woman, I'll wring her neck."

"Why? She's only doing her job."

There was a long silence, and Nathan whistled under his breath. "Well, the boys can count on their mother, then?"

That hurt. "I see things differently, Nathan." I picked up the tray and prepared to leave the room. "While we are on the subject of loyalty and support, are you coming to see them in the play?"

Nathan rubbed his earlobe, and I glimpsed a bone-deep weariness that frightened me a little. He was only fifty-five. "As it happens the fifteenth is a bad day. Big meeting scheduled, but I'll talk to Roger."

I had a lightning change of heart. "Actually, Nathan. I'm not sure that is a good idea. Don't mention it to Roger. Trust me. Just *don't.*"

"Do you know something?" he asked sharply.

"No, just instinct."

"Hum," he said. "Your instincts are usually sound." He moved restlessly and the once neat bed was a muddle. "You think I'm not up to it anymore?"

"I didn't say that."

"But you think it."

The question went through my mind: *how would Rose have handled this?* Nathan's flash of neediness left me cold and unsympathetic—and I knew I was failing to grapple with the uncertainties and strains of his life. Instead, I asked, "Nathan . . . do you want some coffee or tea?"

"Can't drink coffee in the evening anymore." He pushed the tray aside. "Come back, Minty."

Something of the old, decisive Nathan made me melt, and I knelt beside the bed and laid my head on his chest. He stroked my hair. In our particular story, there had been no time nor room for gradual wooing. No leisurely drinks or dinners. No trips to the zoo or meanders in the park. I had sent out the message: *I would like you.* Nathan received it and he turned up at my flat, and came straight to the point. "I want to sleep with you." He was trembling, and I was struck by the gap between the man I observed at his work, and the manner of this request. It touched me and filled me with exhilaration.

Sleeping with Nathan had been the easy part. It was all the rest that had been difficult.

"How do we manage to misunderstand each other?" he asked.

His fingers moved onto my face, softly stroking my neck and cheek. Between us was a cessation of darkness and hostility and, in its place, was warmth, communion, and peace.

I willed these precious moments to expand, to cradle, and to buoy us up for the hours, and the days, and the years ahead.

By the time the nativity play had come and gone and Christmas arrived, I had overdosed on lists. There was one for presents, another for food and menus, yet another for events.

"Events" read initially, "Sam and Jilly to us?" This had been crossed out and "Sunday before Christmas to Sam and Jilly" substituted. When I rang Jilly and proposed that they come to us in London for Christmas lunch, she said that she was frightfully sorry but they had already arranged lunch to be with them. When I suggested that we join them, Jilly had been acutely embarrassed. "It's not that you're not welcome, Minty. Of *course* you are, but we are pretty booked up. Poppy and Richard are coming, my parents and . . . Rose, actually."

We agreed that Nathan, the boys, and I would drive down to Winchcombe on the Sunday before Christmas and arrange a separate meal with Poppy and Richard. Into this settled plan, Poppy inserted a spoke. She rang up. "Could you come over to us on the Sunday before Christmas? Otherwise, we won't have a chance to see Dad and the boys because Richard and I are nipping off to Verbier on Boxing Day." I explained we were going to Sam and Jilly's. "Oh well," said Poppy, and there was only faint regret. "We'll pop in to you on Christmas Eve on the way down to them."

We drove to Winchcombe through lashing rain and arrived on the dot of one o'clock. Jilly greeted us at the front door, dressed in a pair of old jeans and a baggy sweater. This put us all on the back foot. Nathan was in his suit and I was in my best green dress and high-heeled boots. Furthermore, I insisted Nathan stop at the service station before we left the motorway and the boys were spruced to a fault with washed faces and brushed hair.

"Goodness," said Jilly. "Don't you all look smart." She led us into the kitchen where Sam was sitting in muddied gardening clothes with his feet up on the table. "Here they are," she sang out, and a look passed between husband and wife. A slight widening of the eyes which indicated: we have been caught out.

Eaten in the kitchen, lunch had been hamburgers for the children and stew for the adults. "I meant," Jilly said, as she dished up the latter—and again, there was a silent exchange between her and Sam—"to cook something special. But . . . getting ready for Christmas takes up so much time. You know how it is."

No, I don't, I wanted to say, outraged by the lack of ceremony. I thought of the goose stuffed with raisins that I would have ordered, the crackers in their box, the silver candles and gauze ribbon that would have adorned my table.

Nathan reached over and picked up a fork that Frieda had dropped onto the floor. "This is lovely," he said quietly. "No need for a fuss."

Jilly sat down and gazed at her plate of stew. "The important thing is that we are all together."

"Absolutely," said Sam.

On the way back in the car, I mentioned to Nathan, "They didn't go to much trouble."

Nathan paid keen attention to his driving. "No fatted calf, certainly," he said lightly enough, but his lips tightened.

On Christmas Eve, Poppy and Richard arrived in a rush, their car stacked with luggage and presents. It was raining hard and Poppy stood in the hallway, shaking her wet head, and demanded, "Where's the Christmas tree? It's always in the hall." I explained that this year, for a change, it was in the sitting room. "Oh, what a pity." She flung her coat on a chair and swept past me. "Dad? Where are you?" She hugged Nathan. "How are you?" She swooped round to kiss Felix. "Have you been a good boy? No? I thought not. No pressy for you." Felix raised stricken eyes, and Poppy sank to her knees beside him. "Darling Felix. Don't look like that. Of course, I've got you a present. A big one."

"How big?" Felix was (rightly) suspicious.

Poppy sketched an air square. "That big." Felix looked marginally reassured and went off to tell his brother. Poppy got gracefully to her feet. "Sweet." She turned to Nathan. "We can only stay for half an hour. Otherwise, we won't get to Sam's in time for dinner."

"Oh, no," said Nathan. "I thought you could stay for a bit."

"We'd better eat then," I said.

In the dining room, I had laid up the table with a dazzling white cloth, and set out a plate of cucumber sandwiches. There were also tiny sausages roasted in honey and mustard, slices of pizza for the boys, and a Christmas cake (thank you, Self-ridges) that had a tiny skiing scene on it, including a twinkly ski lift.

I made to light the candles and Poppy exclaimed, "Don't on our account. We'll have to go any minute." She surveyed the laden table. "Goodness, you have gone to a lot of trouble." Nathan offered her a sandwich. "I'm not that hungry, Daddy, and I don't want to spoil dinner."

Richard was kinder, accepted two sandwiches and ate his way steadily through them. Lucas climbed onto a chair and strained for the nearest cracker. Nathan picked him up and settled him on his lap. "Hang on, young man. We'll pull them in a minute."

Poppy addressed me in a low voice. "Jilly told me how smart you all were when you went down to see them. She was a little worried that you might have been offended because they were so disorganized. I said *of course* you wouldn't. You knew perfectly well that she had to concentrate her energies on Christmas Day." She stopped, looked down at the empty plate in front of her and, as a great concession, said, "Maybe I will have *one* sandwich. Actually, Jilly doesn't need to worry. Mum will take over cooking the lunch. She does it so brilliantly."

I sneaked a glance at Nathan. He was still cuddling Lucas and talking away to Richard, but I detected a wary, whipped look in his eye. There were not many occasions when I felt protective, but Poppy's words triggered a novel rush of fury. Nathan was hurt, and would continue to be hurt, by these women, his daughter and daughter-in-law.

My amended "Events" list read: Christmas at Number 7. Turkey, roast potatoes, Christmas pudding for 4.

Chapter Six

On the way to work, I met Martin Hurley. It was Monday, January, very cold and I was still recovering from Christmas. Unusually for Martin, he was mooching along, weighed down by his briefcase. We stopped to chat outside Mrs. Austen's front garden where a frost was smeared over the jumble of flowerpots and yogurt cartons that typically lurked on the windowsill. Mrs. Austen was a fanatical gardener but, as she lived in the first-floor flat of the multitenant house, she had no proper space to indulge her passion. It was lacks in a life such as Mrs. Austen's that turned a man or a woman sharp-tongued, nosy, and tart as a lemon and, on cue, she appeared at the window.

"Not your usual style, is it?" Martin was normally seen stepping into a chauffeur-driven car.

"Broken down." He made a mischievous face. "Actually, I feel as if I've been let off school. Big meeting today, and I wouldn't mind escaping. I keep thinking, I could go AWOL traveling the District Line."

I smiled. We both knew that Martin would not miss the meeting for the world. His meetings, as with so many people who worked, ratified his professional existence. "I doubt if you'd think Ealing or Hainault a destination resort. And after two seconds on the tube, you'll be begging for a fleet of cars. Trust me."

"I do trust you," he said, which was nice and also unexpected. It would have been wrong to dismiss Martin as a one-dimensional man, focused only on meetings. Martin possessed discrimination and was generous about many things. Even money. Plus, he was nice about his wife, which not every husband was. From time to time, when Nathan and I were chez Hurley, I caught Martin observing Paige in a careful, serious manner. It was a version of paying attention to the fine details that made him such a success at work.

Snooping from the window was not yielding enough rewards and Mrs. Austen emerged onto the front step in order to edge closer to this interesting street theater. I waved at her. "Paige okay?"

"So-so. Pregnancy is an exclusive business. Unlike the conception."

"You are looking forward to number three?"

Martin did not reply immediately and when he did he sounded a little troubled. "It's very crowded. Life, I mean."

That worried me a little. "Too cryptic at this time of the morning, Martin."

"I feel cryptic, Minty. Never mind. Now, for the meeting." He dropped a kiss on my cheek. "See you." He raised his briefcase in salute to the watchful Mrs. Austen, and we went our separate ways.

Sandwiched between bodies on a packed train, I began to

wonder in earnest about Paige and Martin. *I am practically the only mother in the world prepared to put her children first,* Paige maintained, and she was not entirely joking. It's lonely. If we go on like this, there'll be no population in the Western hemisphere. Look at Italy. Look at Germany. Child-free countries. Paige's zeal was both heartbreaking and infuriating; a missionary among the heathens. Yet there was something reassuring about the straightforward outlook that did not involve any of the watering-down "if's and buts," those dependent clauses that draw the sting out of rules and regulations.

Barry sauntered into my office, but his greeting was sharp. "What kept you?"

I cursed inwardly and flushed, for I was twenty minutes late. "Sorry Barry. The tube."

He glanced at his Rolex. "You can make it up later."

Barry was only half joking. He threw himself down into a chair. "I've got a tricky day. We need the green light for the AIDS film, so say your prayers." He was dressed in a dark Armani suit and red tie that meant big meeting and probably explained the sharpness. He smelled of aftershave, and a hint of claret from the night before.

Again he checked his watch. "Five minutes to go, and I'm going to waste them with you."

"What's up with Gabrielle?" hovered on the tip of my tongue, but I resisted. On closer inspection, Barry looked tired, and his collar points were not quite adjusted. Then I understood that he did not, at this moment, require the diversions of a superb body and a sexy giggle. What Barry needed was an adult, sensible, grounding conversation before he went into a big meeting.

As we talked, I was unsure whether to cry because I no longer occupied the pretty and diverting category or to laugh because I had been elevated into the category of serious.

Barry departed, and I was left to beat the working day into shape. I went through my in-tray and sorted into urgent and pending. Rose had taught me the tricks and procedures of an office, and the lessons remained with me. Funny, that: She had handed me professionalism and her husband on a plate. I wrote a report, made phone calls. I read scripts until my eyes blurred.

Eventually, I pulled the file marked Middle Age toward me. I had definitely been avoiding it. I opened my notebook and wrote: 1) *What* is the story? 2) *Why* are we proposing it? 3) *Who* will make it? 4) Likely costs?

What was there to say? Wasn't middle age a furtive, secretive stage? When I bought my first bra, there was nobody I did not buttonhole with the news. Ask the spirit of my dead, unsympathetic mother. But I would rather die than reveal the existence of a varicose vein in my leg. (Thank you, twins.) I had no desire to discuss my body's slippage. The first blows of age. That was akin to tourists' tramping around a ruin. And which of us would volunteer to examine the mistakes, guilt, regret, or banalities of working, nurturing, and fretting? Who wished to acknowledge the loneliness of growing older?

"When middle age creeps up on a woman, she discovers that younger women are also wolves, as much as men," one newspaper pundit was quoted in the cuttings that Deb had handed over. On that point I conceded I was the expert.

I remembered playing the wolf . . .

Nathan tracked me down in Bonne Tartine. He must have followed me from the Vistemax offices. He slid into the opposite seat and nodded at my coffee and the plate on which sat a tiny, uneaten croissant. He seemed inordinately pleased with himself. "Is that just there for temptation?"

"How did you know I was here?"

"I watched and waited."

I swallowed the uneven lump of excitement and apprehension, for now that I had gotten to this point, some questions needed to be asked. "What about Rose?"

Very carefully, Nathan cut the croissant into pieces. "Rose is busy with her own life." He paused. "All things considered, I don't think Rose would mind. I've never been her first concern . . ." He leaned forward and began to feed me the croissant. The sweet crumbling texture dissolved in my mouth and I thought: Rose must be mad or stupid to be so blind.

"Why did you do it?" asked the forty-two-year-old Rose of me, after I had taken Nathan. "We were friends."

Yes, we had been friends. Sweet, sweet friends.

"You look busy." Deb sashayed into my office. "Anything I should know about?" Uninvited, she perched on the edge of my desk, and I suppressed the desire to push her off.

"Okay." I sat back. "Do women feel middle age more acutely than men?"

"God, I don't know," Deb gave an exaggerated shudder. "Isn't it all over for the middle aged, whichever sex?" Her eyes drifted past me to reception in case anyone significant was waiting.

"I think my husband feels it."

Deb transferred her attention back to me. "Barry says you're a second wife. Is he a lot older? Is he nice?"

"He's very nice," I said flatly. "That's why I married him."

"How much older?"

"Twenty years."

The corners of Deb's mouth went down, registering dis-taste. "How . . . very brave," she said, after a few awkward seconds. Then she said, "I wish . . ."

"You wish?" Deb might be wishing for a new body, a new life? Or maybe, she was just wishing she could fall in love, in which case I might warn her off it. Apart from anything else, love is aging. As I say, you fetch up with twins, varicose veins and being hated by a clan.

"Did I tell you I'm going mad with my flat? It's above a curry restaurant and it reeks of it. I reek of curry. And the landlord won't do anything about the ventilation and is threat-ening to raise the rent." She spread her hands. "I long to live in a clean, white palace high above the trees. I long to be dif-ferent. But at the moment, the future doesn't look bright." She paused. "Did you know that Barry is taking on another producer? You *didn't?* He's brilliant apparently."

Annoyance with Barry clocked in. No doubt, he had his reasons for not mentioning it when I talked to him earlier, which only went to show one should never forget the boss always has a hidden agenda. I closed my notebook with a snap. Perhaps things were not going to work out with Paradox. I experienced mild regret at the thought, but there were other production companies, and I would allow Nathan to indulge in an I-told-you-so conversation.

Deb stood up and stretched, and a junction between her cargos and T-shirt revealed gooseflesh. I nearly said, *I so nearly said,* "You'll catch cold if you're not careful."

I returned home in good time to take over from Eve, who

was going out. "Thanks, Mrs. Lloyd." A rare, pale smile stretched her mouth. "This is big night."

Best not to inquire. From the window of the boys' bedroom, I watched her clatter down the street on a cheap pair of high heels. She looked released, happy, her hair loosened from its customary prison wardress's clamp, and it occurred to me that I must never forget that Eve was entitled to an off-duty life.

"You are a busy mummy." Lucas's fair hair—which was beginning to darken—was tumbled and mussed, and he looked the image of his father.

The Thomas the Tank Engine clock clicked on the chest of drawers. Two pairs of socks, two T-shirts, and two pairs of underpants dripped off the chair stenciled with dragons. Under their duvets, I could see the boys had a long way to grow before they reached anywhere near the end of the bed. Years and years, in fact.

"Never too busy for you two." I tried to remember whose bed I had sat on the previous evening, and chose the opposite. Felix smiled shyly, his gaze flicking up to a point above the bed where he had stuck a drawing onto the wall. I was about to expostulate "Felix, the wallpaper" when it dawned on me that Felix's drawing was of a large cat with black and white stripes. Underneath it he had written "My Lost Cat" in blue crayon.

When they were asleep—Felix curled up on his right side, Lucas spread-eagled over the entire bed—I turned on the nightlight and left them to dream.

Then it was I found myself slipping upstairs to the spare room, where the white roses in the painting appeared to leap out of their dark background. There I searched through Nathan's shirts for his notebook.

On January 21, three days ago, he had written. "Is it better not to care?" Yesterday, he wrote. "I feel that I don't really exist. I look in the mirror and I am not sure who I am looking at."

I closed the notebook and only then, saw the yellow Post-it note stuck to the front. "Private," it said in Nathan's handwriting.

That made me smile. If the notebook was that private why did he not hide it more securely? Answer: he wished me to read it. It was a challenge and I took it up. I went downstairs, found a pen, and wrote underneath, "Talk to me, Nathan?"

The candles I had placed on the table guttered. Nathan ate the salmon with mushrooms slowly. "Not bad."

Not bad? Every mouthful had cost a fortune. I swallowed the final piece on the plate as if it were gold dust and said. "One day I will learn to cook."

Nathan uttered a snort midway between laughter and derision. "It's not you, Minty."

Upstairs, there was an eruption. Despite the direst warnings, the twins were swapping beds, as they did most nights. Nathan cocked an ear. "It's fine," I reassured him. "Tell me what's happening at Vistemax. I talked to Gisela yesterday and she mentioned that Roger is ultrapreoccupied. I thought you had had a good year?"

Food half eaten, Nathan pushed away his plate. "A big libel suit," he confessed. "It was an article in *Weekend Digest* about bribes for football managers. It is likely to cost Vistemax and it happened on my watch."

"But not your fault."

"Not directly. My responsibility, though."

"You should have told me." The kitchen was quiet. "Journalists," I murmured. Since leaving Vistemax, I had lost my bearings as to what went on in the company. Nathan, however, swam with ease though the sea of numbers and strategy. "You should have said something," I repeated.

Nathan shrugged.

The silence had become that of two people who were not communicating on the same level. On this point, *Successful Relationships* was firm and clear: it was a situation that should be sorted.

"I've bought you these," I heard myself saying and handed over the bottle of multivitamins I had bought in my lunch hour.

That amused him. He tossed the bottle from one hand to the other. "Thank you, Mother Minty."

He changed into an old shirt in a washed-out blue that he had had since the dawn of time and refused to throw away. In the candlelight, the color deepened. My own deep black skirt now gleamed a bluish black. One of the candles flickered and went out, and Nathan leaned forward, nipped the wick between his fingers, and said with regret, "Minty, you should not be spending your life watching me."

"It *has* been a bad day."

He blew on smoked fingers. "Yes, it has."

"Nathan . . ." The words trembled on my tongue. What is your "secret grief." But they failed to materialize for I already knew the answer, and it was useless information. Nathan's secret grief was Rose and the past . . . and so was mine.

"Take one of those vitamins," I reached for the bottle and unscrewed the lid. "I'll take one too." I held a pill between my thumb and finger. "Be a good boy."

Nathan observed it for a second or two. "Later," he said.

I should have pressed onward: let's discuss your diary. Let us, together, sort out what is making you unhappy but the expression that had settled on Nathan's face meant that my words were stillborn. It was not so much impatience and distaste, although they were mirrored in his face—and whether they were directed at himself or directed at me, I was unsure. It was his obvious—and disturbing—detachment. Nathan had removed himself from the kitchen, and I had no idea where to.

I tried again. "Nathan, I know I should not read what you wrote, but we must talk about it."

"What?" With an effort, Nathan refocused on me. "Actually . . ." He stopped.

"Nathan, I want to talk to you about . . . the diary. About what I read."

"No . . ." Nathan cut me off. "No, I don't want to discuss it. It is silly and very private."

"But . . ." The obvious question was: why did you leave it for me to read? But I had learned that most things, in this relationship at any rate, were not straightforward. It was a question of picking through the maze.

"I said I didn't want to discuss it."

"If you feel like that . . ." Suddenly, I had lost interest in exploring my husband's psyche. I shoved the chair back and got to my feet. If I had three magic wishes all three would go on summoning back the old Nathan. I could never have the young one, but I would dearly like to reclaim the version who had swashbuckled into my life and said, "Let's escape."

"Nathan, can you pass me that saucepan?" I busied myself running the hot water and swishing in the detergent.

"Sure." If he was surprised at my change of mood, he was not going to remark on it, "but there is something . . ."

The sound of the doorbell shot through the house. Nathan started visibly. "This is what I should have mentioned."

I stiffened but said coolly enough. "You'd better go and answer the door then. Hope it hasn't woken the boys."

"But . . ." Nathan was alight with an excitement and dread that I could not place. Then he shrugged. "Okay."

He went into the hall, and I heard voices, then the front door closing.

Nathan led the visitor into the sitting room, and I wiped my hands, tucked my hair behind my ears, and went to see who it was. Nathan whipped around at my entrance and there was curious smile hovering at the corners of his mouth. "Look who's here."

But a sixth sense had already told me.

Rose.

This was the encounter that provided material for any late-night demons, any restless dreams, for the chill of a dawn catechism when I asked myself what I had done. My first impulse was to laugh: for it was ridiculous that Rose should be standing here. Then my knees drained of strength.

"Rose," I held the back of a chair for support.

"Hallo, Minty." She held out a hand. "You are looking well."

She was dressed simply but expensively, in jeans and a tweed jacket nipped in at the waist, and was slimmer than she appeared on television. She was tan and her hair was glorious: long, highlighted, and silky. Barely recognizable was the woman I had first encountered in the office, dressed in a gray skirt and black jumper that bagged in all the wrong places. "Literature, Minty . . ." I pictured her saying as she did in those days, "is full of stories of the tensions between servant and master." Her hair would have been bundled up any old how, and her lipstick was always too pink. "There's a short story about a pair of sisters who were so in awe of Cook that they never dared to go into their own kitchen. They spent most of their lives fearful and thirsty."

Then, Rose had hovered between wryness and laughter. This Rose did too. There was no hint of bitterness, only a polite interest as she took in the changes to the sitting room.

Terrific, I thought. We end up where we began. Where once I had observed this room through Rose's eyes—painted in pale dove gray, the sofa and chairs arranged close to the window—Rose was now observing it through my eyes: a cream-yellow paint wash, the sofa and chairs pulled closer to the fireplace. She was probably concluding, as I had done all those years ago: that woman does not *understand* this room.

"What are you doing here, Rose?"

Her gaze swung between me and Nathan. "Didn't Nathan tell you . . . ?" Her eyes gleamed as she took in the situation. "Nathan, you didn't *tell* Minty. That's bad of you. I wanted to talk to Nathan, and he suggested that I drop in since I was going to be in the area. Sooner or later, we'd have to meet, wouldn't we, Minty? Is it okay?"

"I didn't know," I said. "I'm not prepared."

Rose could have said: *nothing prepared me for your taking Nathan away.* She considered. "I don't think either of us has anything to be afraid of, Minty. Not anymore."

I missed her. What I mean is that I missed the kind, soft

Rose, the wife to Nathan who brimmed with a desire to help and who said things such as, "Tell me what's wrong, Minty." Or, "You're *not* to worry." Not surprisingly, that Rose had vanished from my life.

She shifted a bag with fashionable buckles and straps from one shoulder to the other. Her love of handbags had not changed. The smile she directed at Nathan was friendly and well disposed, and I swear he winced. "Nathan, about Sam . . ."

I raised an eyebrow at Nathan, who looked utterly helpless. He ran his hand through his hair. "Sam has a bit of a problem, and Rose wanted to discuss it . . ."

"Ah," I said. But I did not add: *why didn't you tell me?*

"Dad . . ." There was a cry from the top of the stairs and Nathan went out of the room and hissed. "Get back into bed, Lukey. Now."

Rose said. "I'm really sorry, Minty. I would not have come if I had known Nathan hadn't cleared it with you. I should have realized he would have ducked it." I gave a little laugh, and she added. "I remember your laugh. It is distinctive, and I could always tell where you were."

For some reason, that made me feel both angry and sad. "Do you still see Hal?" I asked. "How is he?"

Her eyes narrowed, but she answered politely. "We still see each other. Of course. Quite a lot. It is a great . . . a great friendship. I'm lucky in that."

"I've always wondered."

Nathan returned and pressed on Rose drinks, coffee, whatever she would like. "Some wine," she conceded.

"I'll check on the twins," I said. "You'd better get on with your conversation. Don't mind me."

Nathan sent me a look that meant: please don't be like that. I sent him one back: give me a good reason why I should not be like that.

"The twins. How are they? I hear a lot about them." Rose could only summon a polite interest in two children she had never seen. "I gather Frieda . . . Sam's Frieda, gets on well with them."

"I know who Frieda is, Rose."

"Minty . . ." Nathan sounded a warning note.

Rose merely replied. "How stupid of me. Of course you do." She turned back to Nathan. "As for our son . . ."

"Our." It dropped from Rose's mouth with all her rights to its usage.

I fled the room, and up the stairs. Lucas had settled and both of them were sleeping calmly enough—in the wrong beds. Felix was hunched under the duvet. Lucas had thrown his off, and I tucked it over him, adjusted the night-light and found myself by the ironing board on the landing.

Downstairs, the voices murmured. I heard Nathan laugh and say "No . . ." in the way he did when he was particularly amused. The construction and timbre of that no seemed expressly designed to exclude me.

I snatched up one of his ironed shirts and began to fold it this way and that. In the perfect syllogism, the logic flows without a hitch from proposition A to proposition B, which results in the only possible conclusion. For example: husband leaves first wife because he is unhappy. He marries second wife who he—to quote—"knows" will make him happy and she believes him. They are happy.

Perfect syllogism. Imperfect world.

I was clutching Nathan's shirt so tightly that my hands hurt. I dropped it on the floor, stepped over it, and crept downstairs like the thief I was.

Light spilled out into the hall from the sitting room. The door was half closed, but sufficiently open for me to watch the scene inside.

Chapter Seven

Nathan and Rose were ensconced on the sofa. Rose was toying with her glass, fingers curling and uncurling around its stem. The big gold ring she wore on her right hand caught my eye, so bright it hurt. Nathan was leaning back against the cushions, one hand spread along the top of the sofa. It was a pose suggesting relaxation and ease. Every so often, his gaze fixed on his first wife and settled like a starving dog on a bone.

"They never last . . ." Rose was saying, all indulgence and affection, which meant she could only be talking about her daughter. "How many times, Nathan, have we seen that?" Nathan hung on Rose's every syllable. "All the same, I am a little worried about Poppy. I detect a certain, well, a restlessness. . . . I asked her if she and Richard were getting on all right, and she said she'd never been happier. But you know how it is, Nathan? You can sense there's something not quite right."

Nathan lifted the hand that rested on the back of the sofa in agreement. "Can't be money, surely?"

Rose said affectionately, "*No*, Nathan, it's not money. At least, I don't think so. It can't be. Richard earns such a lot."

"Someone has to think about money." He smiled at her, complicit and gentle in a way he never was with me.

I could have enlightened them both as to what Poppy was failing to tell her mother. Almost certainly, it had to do with the online poker games. I could have said to both of them: do you realize that Poppy is probably gambling and she is probably losing? And the more she loses, the more she will play. It is the nature of the beast. Then they could have seized the chance to act in concert and asked: how much and how deep in debt? They could have gone in tandem to have it out with Poppy. *You can tell us, we are your parents. We love you.* But I held my silence. I did not hold any loyalty for Poppy, but what was her business was her business.

Nathan now put his elbows on his knees and leaned forward. It was a favorite pose that emulated Rodin's *The Thinker*. "About Sam. Will Jilly be happy if he takes the job?"

Rose tucked a leg up under her. "That's what I wanted to discuss. Jilly is furious at the idea of leaving Winchcombe. Apparently, she's threatening to stay behind. She says she *hates* America. And Texas in particular."

"Jilly has never been to Texas and she won't stay behind. She's not that kind of woman. She knows that it is a big step up for Sam, and it is important."

Rose clicked her tongue against her teeth, but it was not an impatient or angry sound. It was a marker that formed part of the discussion. It meant that she was considering what she would say next—and my husband, my foolish husband, waited, a smile on his lips that was doting to the point of being offensive. "Difficult, Nathan. Jilly's very settled in the village. Parish council and book clubs, and the school is perfect. . . ." Rose turned to Nathan and her hair tumbled over her shoulders. Nathan . . . Nathan reached over and tucked a tendril behind her ear.

"It's uncanny," he said in a low voice. "Frieda looks more like you each day."

Rose ignored the gesture but she was pleased. "Do you think? She's very special. Has she told you about the pink bike? Last time I went down, she and I conducted a ballet class. We leaped off armchairs and pointed our toes very, very hard." She drank some wine.

He said, "Savor the merlot," in a Russian accent, which made Rose laugh.

"Don't remind me of *him*," she said, and I had no idea who she meant. She tapped the glass. "This is nice, though. Did you buy it at the usual place?"

I had an impression that I was gazing into one of those fairground mirrors that, by their curvature, invert what they reflect. In theory, it should have been me sitting on the sofa all cozy and intimate and Nathan's hand resting behind my shoulder, and Rose should have been peering through the door like a prize snooper.

I must have moved, for they swung round. Immediately, Nathan looked tense and reared back against the sofa, but Rose stayed where she was. I advanced into the room. "Since you ask, darling, the twins are fine." I sat down in the chair opposite them. "Have you sorted out whatever it was?"

Rose got to her feet and smoothed her jacket. "Yes and no. I am sure Nathan will tell you about it."

The "tell you about it" was irritating but, under the circumstances, I had to ignore it. "I enjoyed the television program, Rose. It was very good."

"Yes," she replied simply. "It was, wasn't it? We had a lot of fun making it. It came about by serendipity. I was mulling over the idea and Hal introduced me to a producer. It took a lot of haggling and I had to persuade them I was the right person to front it, but we got there." She made a rueful moue of her mouth, which invited me to enter into a solidarity with her. "Camera adds ten pounds, though. Not that one should mind."

I was trying not to stare too obviously. But I could not avoid the conclusion that the woman standing before me was the model I had gone to a lot of trouble to copy. Rose had worked through the messy bits of her life, and there she was, furnished and burnished with the electricity I was supposed to possess. Yet here I was, weighed down by minutiae, my lists, my children . . . and my husband. Then it occurred to me that hundreds of thousands of second wives had been faced with encounters such as this one, only to realize that what they had suspected was true: they had volunteered for the predicament of the younger sibling who would never, ever catch up with the dazzling elder.

"There might be a follow-up series," she was saying. "I had no idea . . . until . . ." There was a frozen little silence. "Until I . . . I mean I have only just discovered how vast, diverse, and wonderful the world is."

Nathan pulled himself to his feet and moved a fraction closer to Rose. "Don't feel you have to go."

Rose knew Nathan. I knew Nathan. We both knew he was making a bad job of concealing that he ached with regret.

If I had truly loved Nathan . . . if I truly *had* . . . this imperfect, humiliating pretense would have cut my heart in two.

"Let us know," I said. "We'll make a point of watching."

Rose picked up the fashionable handbag and searched inside it. "Did I leave the keys in my coat? I shouldn't do that, they're always falling out. No, here they are." She managed to convey a sense of charming disorder that would not, nevertheless, inconvenience anyone.

Nathan was spellbound. He gazed down at Rose from his height. "I'll ring Sam tomorrow." He touched her arm. "And I'll find out if he's serious about this Texan job."

"I'm off to Italy tomorrow. Last minute, spur of the moment. Long weekend. Then I have a couple of pieces to write that will take lots of research, but they should be fun."

There was so much more about Rose that she could have told us. She had walked into Number 7 carrying a new history about which Nathan and I were largely ignorant. She could have told us about her intriguing new life. *I live here. I work there. I had dinner with so and so.* If I had been prepared, I could have dealt with it. I would even have wanted to hear it because I would have been able to make realistic comparisons, instead of the reverse.

She placed her hands on Nathan's shoulders and leaned forward and gave a light kiss on the cheek. "I'll give you a ring next week. And . . . Nathan about that other idea . . ." The light caught the gloss on her hair and the sheen on her jacket. "Let's talk about that too."

Nathan's hands clenched. "Yup . . ." he cut Rose off. He stuffed his hands into his pockets and rocked back on his heels. Suddenly, I glimpsed the younger Nathan—the one who had swept Rose up from her disaster with Hal Thorne, married her, and given her children and a domain that she had guarded until I came along.

The light in the sitting room was a flattering one—which it should have been for I had gone to a lot of trouble to make it so. Rose seemed so fresh, so mysterious in her intentions and busyness, but mysterious with what? I struggled to understand precisely what I was up against.

The answer seemed to be that Rose had become powerful because it was impossible any longer to pin her down.

Nathan led Rose into the hall: there they had a further conversation lasting five minutes or so, and I heard him say, "Tell Frieda I'll be looking out for her pointy toes when I come down."

The front door closed, and he came into the kitchen to face the inevitable scene.

I had taken refuge in checking the store cupboard in readiness for Eve's weekly shopping trip and lucky I did so. The cupboard was practically bare.

He was braced for a major explosion and knocked his clenched fist on the table. Deliberately, I kept my back to him. "I'm sure you didn't mean to make me feel uncomfortable or humiliate me, Nathan." I kept my anger in check and turned around. "Anyway, why would you wish to do that?"

He was shocked, and took a step toward me. "Of course I didn't want to humiliate you. Of course not. Rose was going to be in the area and she wanted to talk to me."

"It might have suited Rose, Nathan. But was it the best thing for us?" I strove to keep calm.

"Oh, come on," he said, but he was on the defensive.

"Look at us both," I pointed out. "All churned up."

Nathan fished the whiskey bottle out of the cupboard and poured himself a slug. "It's not much to ask you to be a little flexible and civilized about it."

My anger escaped the leash. "I don't hold with this be-nice-at-any-price thing, Nathan. Even if she doesn't show it, Rose hates me, and rightly so. And I hate her."

"Why *hate* her? She's done nothing to you."

We glare at each other, and the adrenaline pumped through me, drained away, and left me shaky and weak. Of their own volition, my hands continued to rifle through the contents of the store cupboard. "If you don't understand, then I can't explain." My fingers encountered a stray pasta shell, and I knew—I knew—that I was walking into a darkness of the spirit and I was going to say things I would regret. "It's not rational, what I feel about Rose. I hate her because . . . I've wronged her. Can't you see that, you stupid man? It's to do with the battle for possession, but I don't think you wish to see it, let alone acknowledge it. Plus, you want it both ways." I emptied the remainder of a rice packet (wild) into a glass jar. "You want to have me and to see Rose. You want us all to be friends."

Nathan sat down at the kitchen table and put his head in his hands. "Wouldn't you like to be friends with her? You were once."

I kept myself busy with the rice packet because I could not bear to see his unhappiness. "You can't have two wives. Not in this country, at least."

I heard him swallow more whiskey. "I can't talk to you about this, Minty. It's like trying to have a conversation in a foreign language or with a total stranger."

That was more than enough. It was far, far too much.

"Okay, Nathan, let's talk plain English. I think you're hiding behind the let's-be-nice mask because what you really want is to stop feeling guilty."

He made an indeterminate gesture with his hands, which, if I needed it, provided proof. "And I have tried with you, and your family who loathe me. If you remember, you were the one who felt imprisoned in your marriage with Rose. *You* said, not me, that it was dull and void. That's why you left her. You convinced me, and I believed you."

Nathan went white with fury, for I had pricked his vulnerable area: he was never a man who liked to be thought of badly. "Could I point out that you fell over yourself to believe me? You couldn't get enough of how Rose had failed."

"Times change, don't they? For two pins you would go back to her. If it wasn't for the twins . . ."

"*Someone* had to put their interests first," he cried.

A long, dangerous silence ensued. "I will forget you said that, Nathan."

Another mouthful of whiskey went down.

"Don't," I said sharply, alarmed at his pallor. "It's not good for you."

"Shut up."

"Look at me, Nathan. Look at me." Reluctantly, he did so. "Tell me the truth. You want to see Rose. You miss her. Your find this marriage less than satisfactory. Disappointing? Is that plain enough for you?"

"Stop it."

"Rose is more your age, Nathan."

"*Stop* it."

"Coward."

Nathan snatched up his glass and left the kitchen. The study door banged shut.

"Rice," I wrote on Eve's list. "Spaghetti shapes."

I crept up to the boys' bedroom and peered through the door. There was a pillow on the floor, and Lucas had flung his teddy bear to the other side of the room. The shade on the nightlight had been knocked askew. My fingers twitched to put everything back into order.

I leaned against the door jamb, closed my eyes, and imagined a future that featured hundreds of objects to pick up. And hundreds of shopping expeditions: tins of baked beans, cartons of orange juice.

Every year, I would have to buy larger clothes for the twins. They would demand to play cricket and football. *Football!* Maybe Felix would prefer to learn the violin or the piano. That would cost money. Where would it come from? Barely a week went by without Nathan saying: we have to be careful. Our funds aren't limitless. What he meant was that he was still paying off Rose when he bought her share of Number 7 Lakey Street. Nathan might get ill. He was at the age when a body began to slow up. He would demand more peace and quiet. Where was *that* to come from?

That night, I slept in the spare room. Rattled and miserable, I dipped into the poems in *Origin of a New Species* that Ellen had sent me. The publisher had been generous—or rash—and had bound them in stiff board with facsimiles of her writing on the endpapers. The titles ranged from the epic "Men's Lament" to the domestic "The Object in the Fridge" to the eponymous poem "Origin of a New Species."

"At forty-seven, I have reached the age of reason/No longer female, but no man either/Triumph?"

Two pieces of news here. The narrator had a decade on me, and the outlook was not all bad. Throughout, the language was littered with references to "banging," "clacking," "clashing," and "the rush of dark tides"—enough to keep a small orchestra busy—and its noise permeated my sleep.

Sometime during the night, one of the boys cried out, and I heard Nathan moving around their bedroom, his voice low and hushed, soothing whichever one it was.

In the early morning, Nathan slid into the bed, dragging me up from the long, slow depths. He was cold and needy. He spooned himself around me, and placed his mouth on my bare shoulder. "Why didn't you come back? You should have come back, Minty. We should not have gone to sleep on our anger."

"Because . . ." I murmured. "Officially, I hate you."

"I was wrong, Minty, not to say anything. Okay."

I felt the cold, cold chill of not getting anywhere much and the sadness that descends after a major quarrel. "Okay."

He smelled of sleep, his breath of whiskey. "What happens today, Minty?"

Ellen's poems were still racketing around my head. "I don't know what happens today . . ." Then I remembered. "It's parents' evening at the school. Are you coming?"

"Yes." His reply was barely audible. "But probably late."

I was suddenly alert. "Do you need to tell Roger?"

Nathan chuckled in my ear. "Roger is not my keeper. But if he asks, I'm seeing the lawyer." Nathan's fingers walked across my shoulder. "I don't like the lying. Much. But I have an idea you may be right."

The sheet had bunched uncomfortably between us. They were not the best sheets. Too large a percentage of man-made fiber in the cotton but, for that reason, they were ideal easy-wash guest sheets. "You and I 'worked late' most evenings. Remember?"

Nathan pressed the nervy point between my shoulder blade and spine. "I didn't feel it was lying then. Isn't that strange?"

Those days had been made up of what, precisely? Episodes when a pitching stomach, unreliable knees, and the beating heart of the clichés featured? Yes and no. Certainly, I had been dazzled and mesmerized by my own power. "Get over it, Nathan. Most working mothers lie every day." I added, "A checkup is a *good* idea." His body was warming up. "Are you feeling okay?"

"Fine. Don't fuss."

If I had been more collected, I might have pointed out that I was only fussing as he had been acting like a hundred and ten lately. Furthermore, I reckoned we could alter our routines a little bit, do things in a different way perhaps, exercise more. For a start, the twins would love him to take them bowling. Or to play football on the common.

"As a matter of interest, have you ever considered that Roger is nearing retirement? Well, if you haven't and I bet you have, why don't you think about who his successor will be? They might get rid of Roger sooner rather than later."

Nathan poked my hip. "A little tasteless?"

"Yes, and?"

He changed the subject. "Has Barry said any more about going full time?"

"He's still thinking about it."

There was a small silence.

"About Rose, Minty."

The sigh came from a black and bitter place. I was sick, so heartily sick of Rose. "What about her?"

"Why don't you remember sometimes that you were friends? Good friends."

Mornings in the Vistemax office that smelled of bad coffee and photocopying and Rose saying, "Here, take these," and passing over a parcel of manuals on Low-Fat/No-Fat/Outer Mongolian cuisine, or Five Hundred Ways to Thinner Thighs. "You deal." Coming in once, and finding her weeping, her too pink lipstick smudged and the ends of her hair damp with rain. "It's Sam," she confessed. "He's having a hard time with his girlfriend, and I can't bear it for him." I had put my arm around her and kissed her cheek.

"Nathan. Please shut up."

Their shared history, their shared children, their past—all mixed in together. "Nathan, Rose said there was something else you had to discuss . . ."

"Nothing," he said. "It was nothing."

"What was it?"

There was a pause. "Nothing worth bothering about."

You know what they say? When the mistress marries her lover, a vacancy is created.

He moved even closer, and his hand snaked between my thighs. His stubble was grazing over my skin. "Minty, about what we said last night . . ."

Nathan probed even farther and I bit my lip. He was hot

now, and urgent. In our bedroom downstairs, my skirt and jacket were waiting on a chair. I had sufficient change in my purse for the morning's journey and a cappuccino. The bag containing my documents was zipped and ready to go. By my reckoning, I had precisely an hour to get the twins and myself up, breakfasted, and ready to go.

So much in life is about timing. Truly it is.

His voice echoed in my ear. "About last night . . ." And then I realized what Nathan was doing.

"Oh my God, Nathan . . ."

His fingers dug into the soft part of my arm. "Minty . . . I'm sorry about not warning you. She looked good, didn't she? Rose seemed in charge. Happy. That's good, isn't it? I had never seen her hair that long before . . ."

He turned his face to me, and his eyes burned with a fever that was not of my making.

With all my strength, I pushed him away. "I'm not . . . Rose. Do you understand? I'm not Rose."

Chapter Eight

The following week Barry called me into the office. "Hey," he said. "I'm sorry I've taken so long to get back to you about the job."

How lucky that I had made an effort that morning and dressed up (floating floral skirt and belted black jacket).

Barry eyed me in a detached fashion and a sliver of apprehension flickered. Maybe things would not go to plan. "You know the AIDS series has been green lit?"

"Yes. Congratulations."

"Charles at Channel 4 is very excited about it." Barry ticked off the points. "Big money. Big foreign sales. And Kevin Stone to direct. Fantastic package." Again the speculative appraisal. "You know, Minty, you started me thinking."

Generally speaking, when bosses begin to think, it is bad for someone.

"I reckon this is how it is for Paradox. I've been looking to expand the output and I need plenty of ideas. You can come full time on a probationary basis. Six months. Then I'll take a raincheck and see what is working, and what isn't. We will discuss money and everything later."

I noted that Barry was not keen to go over the "and everything." "I'm delighted. Thank you."

He leaned forward. "No problems with child care?" I raised an eyebrow and he added hastily, "I'm asking as a friend."

"All taken care of."

"Six months, then."

The joke that darted like marsh gas through the offices when I left Vistemax really had been quite funny. At other times, I would have savored and dissected its delicious taste of schadenfreude. The joke? Which board director uniquely has two wives sacked from the same job? Answer: Nathan Lloyd. *What a sap that makes me, Nathan pointed out. Was he blaming me for my failure? And what a fool me, I flashed back.*

"Fine."

Barry tipped back his chair. "Also . . ." The word was elongated. "Also Chris Sharpe will be joining Paradox as a producer. He used to work for me at the BBC. Bright. Sharp as his name. You'll be working together. He doesn't suffer fools gladly."

I smelled gladiatorial combat but I snapped my fingers in a bullish manner. "Then he'll thrive here, won't he?"

We were introduced to Chris Sharpe at the Friday meeting. He turned out to be slight of build, brown haired and hazel eyed, and dressed entirely in black Armani. All the same, he was not that noticeable. Barry ushered him into the room. "Say hallo, girls." Deb and I obediently smiled a welcome.

Chris raised a finger in greeting and sat down, and Deb presented a proposal for a six-part series on gardening, *Dig for Victory.* "Each program will be fronted by a different celebrity gardener and deal with different topics. The format of each program will be general overview of the topic, plus two related features. In city garden editions, we will discuss a couple of city gardens, one established, one in makeover, and focus on window boxes . . . the pensioner window box, the window box for children . . ."

"Won't you need to put in something like the bachelor's window box . . . ?" Chris Sharpe interjected. "Otherwise, a little unbalanced . . . ?" His confident hazel gaze shifted around the table, tabulating and assessing. Evident was a feline quality, a subtle and determined sniffing out of motive and opportunity. "And should you stick to UK gardens? If we want to sell in Europe?"

Her certainty punctured, Deb pushed back her north London hair. "Sure," she said. She retrieved the initiative. "I would have come to that."

Barry muttered about the costs, and Chris totted down a column of figures. "You might have to increase the unit cost initially, but with anticipated wider subsidiary sales your margins are better."

Barry looked pleased. "Nice."

Next up was *Middle Age: End or Beginning?* Nb ran the memo to myself: assurance and fluidity. "I see this as a two parter. One, defining what middle age is. Two, following a selected group and showing how it affects them. The conclusion being: it is a desirable place." I went on to show how the programs would touch on affluence, diet, exercise, plastic surgery, and spiritual regrowth. My commentary flowed over the rocks and pools of statistics and attitude, consumer practices and personal histories. Barry pressed his pen up and down between his fingers. Chris cupped his chin in his hand, observed me carefully, and, every so often, took notes.

Deb got up and poured out the coffee. She slid a cup in my direction and Barry's hand hovered over the biscuit plate. "I shouldn't. I shouldn't." The hand dived toward the Jammy Dodger. "Middle age sounds like a destination resort," he commented, without a trace of irony. A spray of crumbs accompanied the remark and Deb extracted a tissue from her bag and gave the table a furtive wipe.

"We should emphasize to the controllers the spending power of this group," I continued, "which is underestimated according to some experts. The gray pound is huge and people who are middle-aged will want to watch this. Particularly if we tell them good things."

Chris scribbled away.

Barry ate a second biscuit and reflected.

Chris looked up from his notes. "It's an interesting subject, but it's lacking"—the cat's eyes closed briefly—"sharper orientation. . . . Shouldn't we be asking, 'Are you, the thirty or forty something, irrelevant because you are middle-aged?'"

Paige's eyebrows climbed Everest, and then again. I enjoyed the effect.

"Rose just turned up out of the blue? Outrageous." Propped up on some evilly uncomfortable-looking pillows and knitting, she begged for every detail. It sounded simple— Rose came, she and Nathan talked, I snooped, Rose went. But it wasn't.

After a couple of false alarms, Paige had been admitted into the People's Hospital and I dropped in to see her on the way home from Paradox. The People's Hospital was the size of an airport and it had been billed as the latest and finest in state-of-the-art medicine. State of the art or not, someone had failed to grapple with temperature control, and it was far too hot. Plus, it had taken me the entire reservoir of my patience to find my way to the Nelson Mandela maternity ward.

Paige listened, her needles emitting little clicks. When I finished, she commented, "You must not read too much into it." Then she laughed. "You've just described the perfect triangle." She finished the row with a flourish. "With Rose at the top."

"I've realized something. Nathan didn't leave Rose because he was tired of her. He left her because he was tired of himself."

"Maybe so." She began a new row.

Paige's one-woman craft industry was a revelation. "I didn't know you could knit."

The crying of newborns punctuated our conversation. Reedy little sounds from lungs that were still learning how to function.

"There's nothing I won't do for my babies." Paige counted the stitches. "I like to think of them wrapped tight and warm in something I have made."

"You could buy a shawl."

"Not the point. But putting myself out for them is . . . ten . . . twelve . . . fourteen."

A woman with long fair hair shuffled past the bed, hauling a drip after her like a suitcase, with the other hand clasped to her stomach. Folds of flesh bulged on either side of her fingers.

Now that I had embarked on the subject, it was difficult to

stop. "Perhaps she had been thinking about Nathan and the old days. Perhaps she was missing him. I don't know. They seemed so cozy together, Paige. It was as if the conversation between them had continued all these years."

Paige was not a natural knitter and she had trouble looping a stitch back onto the needle. "Think yourself lucky it is just an occasional encounter. In the old stories, Rose would have died of grief, or killed herself, and returned to haunt you."

"She does that without having gone to the bother of dying."

"What a pity you don't write or paint. It's a good subject and your experience *is* firsthand." Paige carefully placed her needles together, wrapped the work in progress around them, and stowed the package in a bag.

"Ah," I cried. "That's the trouble . . ." The only too-well-remembered sounds of new babies in their plastic cots provided a counterpoint to my cry. "That's the point. Everything I do is second . . . secondhand. Everything has been seen and done before. Nathan set up home before. He had children before. He had friends before . . ." Oh yes, the frosty Frosts, the disapproving Lockharts . . . "A whole raft of them. Lined up in rows. And Nathan has family. Boy, does he have family—that was set in stone before I arrived, and it has no intention of unsetting itself." I paused. "And then there is Rose."

That blew the lid off the jar of maggots in my brain and they were crawling everywhere. Soon, I must catch them and put them back. I contemplated my hands. "I'm not complaining, or anything," I said. "Just telling."

"Well, you are complaining," Paige pointed out. "But that's fine. You can complain to me. And I can tell you that Rose is nothing. You've built her up for no good reason."

"I'm sorry," I said. "I didn't mean to give you an earful. We should be discussing your bump."

"Aren't you forgetting one thing?" Paige placed a hand on her abdomen. "No one else had the twins, did they? That's not secondhand. Or am I missing something here?"

"Yes," I conceded.

"By the way, you are godmother to the new arrival."

"Oh . . ." Godmother meant acceptance. Godmother meant a settled role, a place in the hierarchy. "Thank you, Paige."

When Sam and Jilly's Frieda was born, Nathan went around in a grandfatherly glow. He wanted to know her weight, how well she slept and fed, and was she wearing the darling Babygro he had picked out?

Pregnant myself, I listened to this with only half an ear. I had never reckoned on Nathan's being thrown into such a fuss, but he was and that was that. However, there was no fuss whatsoever over the question of the seating arrangements at Frieda's christening, and that was that too.

"I'm sorry, darling," Nathan apologized, awkward and out of his depth. "Sam and Jilly feel it would be best if you did not sit with the family."

It did not take two wits to picture the kind of conversation that had taken place behind my back.

I grabbed his wrist. "Did you stick up for me, Nathan? Did you fight at all?"

He hunkered down beside the chair I was sitting in. "Of course I did, Minty. I would fight a lion for you. But it is a difficult situation."

Not that difficult. Divorce and remarriage are not unknown. "Is it that you are ashamed of me?" The question is-sued from between clenched teeth.

"No. *No.*"

But I knew the question struck a note of truth and, what was more, Nathan was ashamed of himself.

"And where will you be sitting?"

"In front."

"With Rose, you mean."

He said stiffly. "She is the grandmother."

There are not many good things about being pregnant. In fact, there is nothing good about being pregnant—except for one thing. If you are disposed to weep, and I was, then the disposition could be employed to advantage. I turned my face to his, and tears drifted down my cheeks. I whispered. "I know your family *hates* me."

Deposited by Nathan on a back pew in Winchcombe's village church near Bath, and given a couple of cushions to prop me up, I knew that I was the focus of many eyes—some of whom longed for me to fall to my knees (impossible at thirty weeks) and to declare: *I beg pardon for my sins.* Everyone would have felt much better, including any sinners.

But I was tempted to rise to my feet and to declare in ring-ing tones, *Listen, Nathan was not happy with Rose. He told me, again and again. Listen, I rescued him.*

My reflections were interrupted. "Minty," Poppy's Rich-ard edged past me and sat down on the empty seat on my left. "Nathan thought you might like company, and I'd like to pro-vide it."

There was sufficient flirtatiousness in his manner to cheer me up. I smiled at him. "That was nice of you."

He smiled back, sympathetic and not unfriendly. "Confession time. Being married to a Lloyd is rather exhausting, don't you think?"

After the main bit of the ceremony was over, and Frieda had shrieked in the approved manner, Nathan trod back down the aisle. What it cost him, I dared not reckon. But that was the bargain I struck with my tears. He slid into the seat on my right and took my hand. "Hi," he said.

At the point of doing—for example, stealing a husband who belongs to a woman you rather love (but not enough)—the exhilaration of the doing and taking is what matters. Only afterward, during the cold, reflective nights, does the enormity of what had happened assume its true shape.

Nathan stuck the photographs of Frieda's christening into the album covered with red leather that he had bought specially. Photograph number one showed Jilly, Sam, and Frieda in a lace gown that had serviced several generations of Lloyds. Frieda's mouth had dropped open and there was a milk blister on her upper lip. Photograph number two featured Nathan and Rose. Dressed in her favorite olive, a proud Rose was holding Frieda in an irritatingly competent way, and Frieda's tiny fingers curled round one of hers. But there was a clue to how she had been feeling for she had inclined her head to the left. "Left is my best profile," she had told me once. Nathan had his arms by his sides, but in a way that suggested he wished to put them around Rose. Photograph number three was the formal group one. In an old-fashioned hat, Jilly posed with the baby in the center, and Sam stood protectively beside her. Nathan, Rose, and Jilly's parents, plus godparents, siblings, and cousins, fanned out from this nexus.

I was not in the photograph . . .

Nor did I speak to Rose during the whole affair. But I caught her looking at me. Many times. I knew this because I had been looking at her . . .

I seized Paige's hand, which was slick with sweat. "How can I kill Rose off, in my mind, I mean? How can I stop her haunting this marriage?"

Paige sent me a look filled with pity. "I'm surprised at you. It's simple. Just think of your children."

I dug in my bag for the magazines I had bought to amuse her and handed them over to Paige. "Is there anything I can do?"

"Linda is in charge, and Martin takes over in the evening." Paige frowned. "I have a funny feeling that Linda is thinking of quitting, which she absolutely cannot do." She bared her teeth. "If she does, I'll throw the book at her. Being here is a big nuisance. I wanted to be at Jackson's school play. I had planned a huge tea party with all the works and invited his teachers. This baby is not scheduled to arrive for two weeks. I've been telling it off, very severely, and you know what? It's not listening to me." Filaments of wool clung to the front of her nightdress, and I picked them off and threw them away. "Thanks." She raised herself gingerly farther up the pillows and settled back with a tiny shriek. "Ouch. That's my sciatic nerve. Martin's temper has not improved. He didn't really want this one. He says we won't have time to breath." She raised her eyes to mine. "Did I mention I tricked him into it? It wasn't pretty, but it was the only way—" She was arrested midsentence. "It's starting to act up again." She patted her stomach. "Stop it."

"Paige, I'll drop over to the house and check things out. Is there anything you would like?"

"Actually, yes. A huge big bloody steak with a plate of fries."

A group of male and female nurses was conferring by the nurses' station. One of the men in a pretty blue uniform headed for Paige's bed. "Hi, I'm Mike. Just making sure you're not worried about anything, Mrs. Hurley."

"Nothing at all, except the small matter of heaving a huge baby into the world."

He patted the bedclothes. "You've done it before."

"Precisely, Mike," said Paige.

He consulted his clipboard. "I thought we'd run over a few things in order to give you a timetable. At midnight tonight, we will give you . . ."

Unwilling to listen to these intimacies, I moved away, only to be confronted by more intense ones: mothers feeding, changing their babies, groaning as they shifted in their beds. Some seemed bewildered, an emotion I recollected perfectly. There was an almost sinister quality to the hopefulness of the others and their visitors who clustered round the cots. Each time a baby was placed in one, it was assumed that a good, successful, loving life lay in store.

I glanced at Paige. Mike was writing on his clipboard, and Paige was talking at him, and arguing in a decided way. I found myself smiling. How very like Paige to try to organize the ultimately unorganizable such as birth . . . or, for that matter, death.

Mike bustled away and Paige beckoned me back. "I rather like being asked by nice men if there's anything I'm worried about."

Dodging the drugs trolley that was progressing down the ward, I bent over to kiss her goodbye. "I must go as it will take me *hours* to find my way out of here." There was an unmistakable smell coming from Paige, the milky odor of giving birth. "What made you decide your children should come before your career?"

Not an iota of doubt clouded Paige's serenity. "Simple. When Jackson was a baby, he cried at night and I was the only person who could shut him up. He needed me, and only me."

Nathan was already home when I returned and was reading to the twins, who were tucked up beside him. Number 7 was warm and hushed; Eve had put a stew into the oven; Nathan, Felix, and Lucas presented a tangled, contented tableau, and I halted in the doorway to savor the moment, to allow the color and shapes to flow over me.

I inspected the boys. Damp, soap smelling, and pretty tousled. "Lucas, have you put on your cream?"

Lucas had a rash, but resisted every attempt to make it better. From beneath his father's arm, he shook his head. I fetched the tube. "Come on, Lucas." Reluctantly, he tilted his head, and I dabbed cream on the red patches by his ears. Beneath my fingers, his skin was both dry and soft, softer than anything else I had known.

Nathan rubbed his knee. "That's sore." He spoke lightly. "Falling apart."

"Poor you." I sat on the bed and buttoned up Felix's pajamas and smoothed his hair. "Maybe you need some exercise."

"Too tired for that."

I glanced up as a spasm darkened Nathan's expression and I knew what my husband was thinking. If I had been Rose, I would have gone upstairs, searched out embrocation, and insisted on rubbing it into Nathan's stiffening muscles.

Secret grief.

I could picture this intimacy—the collusion—to the last detail. No, I could *feel* it: a warm coziness, with no specter of the past to cast a chill. Nathan and Rose had acted in tandem. Which school for the children? Did the hall require painting? Hey! They addressed each other over breakfast, after a night of passion that left them with burning eyes and aching flesh. We can take it.

Was Rose aware of how lucky she had been? She had helped herself to the young, strong Nathan, the one who had carried a laden breakfast tray up to her in bed with the ease of toting thistledown—the one who had balanced job, wife, and children in his palm with the skill of the juggler. *Look, I'm not tired. Look, I cannot fail.*

I switched off the light and both of us stood for a moment in the doorway as the twins settled under their duvets.

"What are you thinking?" I asked.

Nathan slipped his arm round my shoulder and dropped a kiss on the top of my head. "Nothing very much," he said.

Chapter Nine

Early the next morning, shrieks of protest from twins, abandoned bowls of cornflakes, mad hunts for reading primers, a flustered Eve, a preoccupied Nathan—the phone rang. It was Martin.

"Minty, Minty . . . listen. We have another son. He arrived late last night. Isn't that great? He's big; he's beautiful. He's perfect. He's even textbook weight."

"Oh, that's lovely. Congratulations." I cocked an eye at Nathan departing out of the door. "We're thrilled." Nathan sent me a thumbs-up sign and disappeared.

Tiny baby in a cot. All four limbs and ten digits accounted for. Clean and sweet after the traumas of its arrival.

A good, happy, successful life.

There was traffic noise in the background. Martin was clearly on his way to work. "Did you get any sleep? Shouldn't you take the morning off?"

"I had more sleep than I bargained for."

"Oh, was it that fast?"

"Ask the mother. Paige kicked me out at the final stages. She said it was her business, not mine." Martin's tone altered to convey a touch of anger and disappointment. "But both are doing well." After a pause, he added, "I'm told."

I cast around for a safe comment. "Did Paige manage to finish her shawl before it all happened?"

Martin was at his very, very driest. "Paige finished her shawl. She put the final touches to it during the second stage."

"Grief, Martin. She is made of iron."

"That's rather a good description," he said, and again, anger crept into his tone.

"Martin, I'll go to see her over the weekend. From next week I'm working full time."

"I know," he said. "She disapproves. She thinks it's frivolous to work full time when you don't have to."

Paige's disapproval hung over me as I organized a delivery of organic yogurt and fruit to her and settled down to sorting out final arrangements. Preparing to go back to full-time work was full-time work. Nathan had had fun teasing me about it. "You're not going to war, you know." Then a little later. "How's the supply train?" Or, "Do remember the general requires a slap-up meal." The joke ran and ran.

I pinned Eve's reconfigured timetable to the kitchen notice board and considered the logistics of provisioning, school runs, recorder lessons, and swimming practice and felt a sneaky but shameful admiration for Mussolini's making the Italian trains run on time.

I ran my finger over the blocks marking off the days and hours. There was no going back. Come to that, there was a theory that the First World War had happened not because of

the shots at Sarajevo—an archduke or two were expendable—
but because the Russians had mobilized their trains. Once that
happened, it was impossible to cry halt.

Eve had driven the twins to school and, to my astonishment, had volunteered to take them for a session in the park
afterward. Already I felt differently: I had waved them off,
pleased that all concerned in this household had reached another milestone. Again, I ran over my timetable. It was im-
pressively severe in its just-in-time scheduling, with no margin
for slack.

I ploughed on. Wardrobe checks. Nathan required new
socks, and the twins had grown out of their dungarees. Equip-
ment: "Frying pan," I jotted on the shopping list. Food: menus
for the following two weeks.

The phone rang. "Minty," Poppy dispensed with preliminaries. "Can I ask you something? Do you think you could
speak to Jilly?"

This was entirely unexpected. "Why on earth?"

She was full of importance. "I don't know if Dad mentioned it but she's refusing to go to the States with Sam, who
has been offered this fantastic job. Well, you know what that
means. Sam will be the target of every predatory female in the
state. And did you know that he has bumped into Alice? You
remember her? His girlfriend before he married Jilly? She was
very cut up when he went off with Jilly. Personally, I think
Alice maneuvered it. She's never gotten over losing Sam. Anyway, he talked about her last time I saw him, and it set alarm
bells ringing." I knew Poppy well enough to know that it was
a matter of a short wait before all became clear. "Minty. I'm
sorry, but there's no two ways to put it and I'll have to be
rude. But could you talk to Jilly and explain that the Other

Woman seizes her chance? No, no, I shouldn't put it like that but if Sam goes off by himself, then . . . who knows what damage Alice will do, or someone like Alice. She'll believe it if *you* talk to her."

My intake of breath brought Poppy to a halt. I did not waste time saying emollient things such as: "Sam would never do that." I did not point out that it was hardly likely that Jilly would appreciate anything I had to say and there was a good chance that she would be very, very angry. Or I might be very, very angry. Or that I had no wish to interfere. Or even, it might be Jilly who found someone else. Instead, in simple acknowledgment of my Other Womanness, I said, "I'll see what I can do."

"Would you? *Would you?*" Poppy was surprised by her own success. "You don't mind . . . ?" She rattled on. "I know it's a long shot but I couldn't think of anyone else. Or rather, you seemed the best person."

"How are the poker games?" I asked. "Are you winning?"

It was Poppy's turn to fall silent. "I thought you might have forgotten. . . . Does Dad know?"

"No," I said. "I've said nothing. It isn't my business. But he and your mother are worried about you."

Poppy uttered a little gasp and began to cry and I could not make out what she was saying. Eventually, I heard, "I'm going to have to ask Dad for money. I've had a bit of bad patch . . ."

"No, you're not," I flashed back. "He worries enough about money as it is. You know he does. Can't you ask Richard?"

"No." Poppy sounded terrified. "I can't do that."

"I can't let you bother your father."

Poppy stopped crying and her voice switched to the icy cold. "You know, this is none of your business."

"Maybe." I rolled Poppy's dislike of me around my head. "But it does not alter the situation."

We said good-bye, more or less politely and, almost immediately, Deb came on the line. "Deb, you sound very cheerful. Have you won an Oscar or something?"

The words almost choked Deb, so anxious was she to spill them. "Actually, I spent the evening hooked up with Chris Sharpe. Quite by chance. He's *really* fascinating. Done lots of things."

I supposed—correctly—this information was the real point of Deb's call. "Chris is your new best friend." I tried to make it sound like a question, not a statement.

"My new best . . . yes, friend. What I was calling about is *Middle Age* . . ." Deb's incredulous lilt, yet again, underlined how remote it was from her own situation. "Some new statistics have come in. One of which gives a rather shocking percentage of widows living below the poverty line. Might be something you should build in?"

"Sure. Thanks."

"By the way," Deb added, "does the name Rose Lloyd register with you?"

"No," I said. *No, no, no.* "I mean yes. She's my husband's first wife."

There was a small silence. When it was clear I was not going to elaborate further, Deb said, "Someone mentioned her as a possible presenter for the slot on city gardens. Apparently, she's considered good news. I think I might pursue it."

"I thought the idea had gotten the thumbs down."

Deb said stubbornly. "*I'm* not giving up on it."

When the phone rang yet again around one o'clock, I pushed aside my notes with resignation.

"This is Sam."

"And what can I do for you, Sam?" If my voice was a trifle hysterical, it was to be expected.

He was taken aback. "Are you all right? You sound a bit odd. Is Dad home? I'm trying to track him down, and the office said he was on a personal lunch but his mobile is turned off."

"He isn't here, Sam." I said cheerfully enough, but unease and suspicion were running fingers down my spine.

"Oh well, not to worry. He'll be somewhere." Sam sounded very positive. "Did Dad tell you about my new job? It's a big leap, but I have an idea it will work out. Jilly is not so happy but I reckon if I can get her out there, she will settle. If not, then we will just have to improvise . . . or maybe Jilly can come out every six months. We'll miss each other, of course. . . ."

"Sam . . . do you think that is wise?"

His tone cooled. "We'll manage, but thank you for your concern. Are you sure you don't know where Dad is?"

But I was no longer listening. As soon as possible, I terminated the conversation. I was aware, of course, that old habits had a way of sticking. That is how addiction clinics make most of their profits. On the warm summer evening when Rose bought me back to Number 7 to meet Nathan for the first time, the three of us had discussed loyalty, and Nathan had said, "You end up being loyal simply because you've known someone a long time."

Rose and Nathan had known each other forever and ever and there was nothing I could do about it.

I really imagined I had cracked the problem of the future when I offered Nathan the alternatives to habit of a glossy body, hot blood, excitement, and (to quote Rose) a comforting gaze. I pictured our life together like postcards: firelight winter scenes with snow outside; sunny uplands, with fragrant hay baled in neat lines. I had imagined, too, that tenderness and laughter lasted.

I snatched up my bag and keys and found myself in the car, driving down the street, telling myself I had no idea where I heading.

I lied.

As I approached the river, I lowered the window and smelled the slime and sludge of low water. The city unraveled before me: dirty, assured and industrious, new buildings springing up like dragon's teeth in every empty inch. This was the city I admired and melted into. It hustled and bustled: unsentimental, indifferent, surviving the knocks. It did not crave love.

There was a parking place outside Rose's flat, and I slid the car into it. Turning off the engine, I dropped my head into my hands. I considered what I was doing. I considered switching the engine back on and driving away. I considered how badly spies were rated in the food chain.

After a while, I raised my head. The building on which I was focused was a tiny, pretty flat-fronted Georgian house with large, very clean windows.

And there was Rose. Framed in the window of what appeared to be the bedroom of her ground-floor flat talking to someone out of sight. She was dressed to go out somewhere smart, in a black linen skirt and tiny jacket to which was attached a fake camellia corsage.

She picked up her brush, ran it through her hair, and the sun caught a glint of diamonds in her ears. Then she shook her head in an impatient gesture, ran her fingers through her hair. She looked grave, and the exchange between her and the unseen person appeared to be intense.

Just discernible in the corner of the window, the bed was covered with a blue and white vintage quilt. Very pretty, very Rose. Rose sat down on it.

Had Nathan occupied that bed? Had he sneaked away from the office, with a bottle of champagne? Had he drawn his first wife down onto the blue and white expanse and placed his lips on her bare shoulder as he had on mine? Had he propped himself up on his elbow and asked "Can you forgive me, Rose, for what I did to you?" Or had he murmured, "I can't live without you"?

Was he sitting there now, out of sight?

I turned my head away, so roughly that my neck protested. Rose could have been beaten by the circumstances of her life but, plain as day, she was not. I don't know quite what I had envisaged—that Rose should live out her life on some prison ship with hard labor? I have no idea why I thought that someone to whom I had done such wrong should suffer more. But I did.

I could taste my hatred and despair, as I could smell the musky odor of sweat springing under my arms in the heated car. I turned back to look through Rose's sparkling windows and I was peering into my mind's secret mirror with all its reflected darkness and turbulence.

A man bearing a bouquet of spring flowers—beautiful, whites and yellows and pale greens—crossed the road and let himself into Rose's front garden. He was tall, with sun-bleached hair, and wearing scruffy trousers and a brown jacket with leather patches at the elbow. I knew him well from photographs.

He rang the doorbell. It took Rose a minute or so to open the door. A minute when she would have said to the hidden Nathan. *What is your story?* And Nathan would reply. *There's no point in concealing it any longer.*

Rose appeared on the doorstep. "Hal . . ." I heard her say. "Oh, good. Oh, *good.*" She reached up and kissed him, and his arm snaked round her. Then I drew a sharp breath, as Rose called over her shoulder, "Mazarine. He's here," and a smartly dressed woman emerged.

The three of them chatted for a while. Mazarine was a small woman with carefully dyed hair, who gesticulated a lot. Hal was less vocal, but amused, his arm around Rose's shoulders. When he smiled the lines on his face were etched deep. And Rose? Rose was radiant, her happiness almost palpable and living—a feeling she woke up to each day and defined the seconds and minutes as they slipped past.

Those time-tested loyalties stretched between the three. Even if I had not known who they were, it was clear they were old friends But I did know who they were, and years ago Rose and I had sat over salad lunches and discussed most things, including their friendship.

Nose buried in the flowers, Rose went inside and re-emerged to lock the door. Hal linked arms with both women and they walked into the street. They were too busy talking to notice me. As they passed, I heard Rose's friend say, "*C'est la bêtise, Rose. Tu sais.* Hal is impossible . . ." Rose turned her head and looked at Hal.

Together they crossed the street, turned in the opposite direction, and disappeared.

When I got home, I went up into the spare room and searched for Nathan's notebook. It was no longer there. Up on the wall, the painting of the white roses presented its challenge. The bruised, dying petals scattered at the base of the vase sent a mocking message. *It was all so brief.*

Downstairs in Nathan's study, my shameful search continued. I scanned the bookshelf, opened drawers, rifled through the filing trays.

Nothing.

Was I going mad with suspicion and supposition? Possibly. I glanced up and caught a blurred reflection of myself in the window. There was a woman in danger of being suffocated by hatreds and guilt, and there was no kind surgeon's scalpel to drain the poison.

After a while, I had to accept defeat. Nathan had withdrawn from the conversation. He was covering his tracks and denying me the tiny glimpse he had given of himself.

Perhaps if I had remained silent in true, repressed English silence, then it would have been different. Perhaps if he had known that I knew but had not tried to turn into words, then it would have satisfied him? Nb. No marks here to *Successful Relationships.*

A Scarlet Woman possessed the virtue at least of being useful. We need sinners in order to feel superior. To be the Other Woman, as Poppy had indicated, also had its uses. The role of the Second Wife trailed way behind in interest and excitement. But that was what I was left with. No doubt the moralists would rejoice, and I was prepared to allow them—having first insisted on having my say. *Nathan was unhappy with Rose.*

Downstairs in Nathan's study, I picked up the Post-it pad, and scrawled onto the top one. *Don't go.*

I stuck it on the filing cabinet.

Chapter Ten

Nathan never mentioned whether or not he found the Post-it note.

I did not refer to it either. But I did say in passing. "You're not letting things slip at Vistemax?"

Nathan had never been a fool. "Do you know something?"

A nerve flickered in my cheek. "I don't *know* anything. But it's a jungle out there and you have to keep up."

"Has Gisela said something?"

"No. But I don't trust Roger."

"Shall I tell you something? Nor do I." He placed a finger on my shoulder and pressed down. "Let's hope nothing happens. Otherwise . . . well, a lot of things but money will be a problem."

His finger hurt. I thought of Nathan's steering a path through the rough jungle. He would need all the help possible. I gave him what I had. "Gisela has a lover, Nathan. "

Nathan went very, very still. "Why are you telling me?"

"I promised I wouldn't. But I thought you should know. It might help. You're my husband, and we share things and I know which side I am on. He, the lover, wants Gisela to leave. But I don't think she will."

Nathan removed his finger. "You never know what people are capable of doing."

No, one was never sure. I looked up at him. "Really?" I replied, but what I really meant to say was: will you being seeing Rose again?

Gisela rang me in the office. "How's the new routine?" I told her that two weeks in, it was going fine, and she asked if we could have lunch. "I know it's last minute," she said. "But I do have something to discuss."

I scribbled "Dance? Series?" on the article I was reading about ballerinas in *Harpers Magazine* and agreed I was free, and it was arranged that she pick me up at twelve forty-five.

She was in Roger's Vistemax company car. The interior had been sprayed with a manufactured flower scent that made one long for the smell of tarmac or manure even, anything more real. Its leather and upholstered comforts provided insulation from the real world—which, presumably, was why company executives favored them.

My head was full of ideas, the ones aching to take flight. "What do you think about a television series on modern dance? Salsa, tango . . ." I rattled on until I noticed that Gisela was not paying attention. "What do you want to talk to me about?"

"Several things," she replied enigmatically. "Vistemax for one thing. But let's enjoy ourselves first."

"How is Roger?"

"A bit gloomy. A lot of boardroom activity . . . There's

talk of selling off the *Digest* and launching a free newspaper. Apparently, the younger generation doesn't read newspapers and the advertisers have spotted this. But Roger is capable of dealing . . ." Gisela checked herself and pointed out of the car window. "Did you see those shoes?"

I pictured the scene. Nathan and Roger in shirtsleeves at the gleaming boardroom table, mineral water, crystal glasses, biscuits, and a plate of fruit—untouched exotic stuff like pawpaw or star fruit, the chef's fantasy, which no red-blooded male would dream of eating.

Gisela said dreamily, "Roger gives me a nice life, you know. And he's promised me a merry widowhood. Don't look shocked, Minty. Roger and I have discussed it many times."

The car slid along Piccadilly and turned left into one of the smaller streets off Bond Street and stopped in front of a gallery with a bowl window and discreet gold lettering that read: SHIPLEY FINE ART.

Gisela thanked the driver, instructed him to return in a couple of hours, and swung gracefully out of the car. She was wrapped in a leather jacket, so supple it was like silk, so well cut that not one wrinkle marred the line across the shoulders. "Come."

The gallery was a rectangular room, painted cream with antique stained floorboards. At one end there was a desk with a flower arrangement in pink and white and a couple of spindly chairs. There was no evidence to suggest that money changed hands, no paperwork, only a stack of catalogs.

Two men stood by a large painting at the end of the room. It depicted three boxes of differing sizes suspended in a night sky dotted with stars and planets. The boxes looked as though they should fit into each other, but on each an attachment made it impossible. The first, painted red, had a chain looping over the sides from which hung a ball that read POVERTY. Dozens of naked babies clung onto the sides of the second, so numerous that—shockingly—a couple had let go and were falling through space. A tree grew out of the third, a pretty arching shape with withered leaves. The painting was entitled *Slow Apocalypse*.

"So good," Gisela breathed in my ear.

"*Is* it?"

She smiled. "We shall have to educate your eye."

No doubt this was an oblique—and unflattering—reference to Nathan's taste in Cornish pictures. Gisela's eyes widened a little but, even if I had been in complete sympathy with her, I was not going to drop Nathan into the black hole of flawed taste.

She smoothed the sleeve of her jacket and my uneducated eye noted that her hands were trembling. "That's Marcus." She indicated the taller of the two men.

Everything fell into place. My main reaction was surprise. This was the man with whom Gisela had a special friendship, whom she probably loved, and there was nothing out of the ordinary to single him out. Marcus wore a linen suit (rather rumpled) with a gold watch chain. He had thick, unruly hair, smallish but nice eyes, and a pleasant expression. He gestured a lot and talked fluently. "Simple to ship . . . a couple of weeks. Insurance . . ." And so on. He acknowledged our presence by raising a hand.

"Okay." The client was American and expensively dressed. "I'll phone you with the details."

Politely, Marcus ushered him out of the gallery and

whipped around. "Hallo." He touched Gisela's arm. "This must be Minty." We shook hands. "Forgive me, I was just finalizing a sale that had been a long time cooking." The pleasure of the sale shone in his eyes, and his voice was surprisingly deep. "Good, eh? I've only just opened here, and the rent has to be paid." He lifted his shoulders in a gesture designed to include me in his despair at the iniquity of landlords. "Shiftaka is an extraordinary painter. I hope you'll take a look at the rest of the exhibition."

There was sufficient suggestion that I was extraneous, and I took the hint and moved away. But not before I saw Marcus draw Gisela close.

For a second or two, Gisela relaxed against him. "How are you, Marcus?"

"You know exactly how well I am." The "exactly" was inflected.

"I wouldn't have come if I had known you were going to be difficult."

"Don't bother with games, Gisela."

And Gisela (cool, determined Gisela) still trembled visibly. "Sorry."

In the back room, I studied an oblong painting entitled *Submission*. It featured a series of broad horizontal stripes running through the red palette, from brick to the palest pink. The eye longed to remain anchored to the red at the top of the canvas, and it took a conscious effort to pull it down through the spectrum, which, I suppose, was the point. It was only after examining the bottom section of the picture that I realized the pale pink contained a misty outline of Africa. The link between the pretty pink and the implication that Africa had been bled dry of its lifeblood was intended to shock, and it did.

In the other room, the murmur of voices was punctuated by Marcus raising his. "Haven't we muddled around for too long?"

Gisela said something unintelligible, and Marcus added, "End of the road, Gisela."

I edged back into the main gallery. Marcus was leaning against the desk, inspecting his shoes. Gisela was flushed and upset and she was fingering the necklace of Persian coral round her neck.

"I think I should go," I told them.

"I'm coming, too." Gisela grabbed her bag.

Marcus rolled his eyes, and levered himself upright. "Okay."

Gisela snapped open her bag, extracted a mirror, and, in a now familiar gesture, dabbed at the area below her eyes. "Give me a minute."

I turned to Marcus. "The artist? Tell me about him."

Without a blink, Marcus shifted into another gear. "Abandoned on the streets of Kyoto, he was fostered by a retired geisha. He's a political painter . . ."

His gaze slid past my shoulder and rested angrily on Gisela.

As we left, Marcus placed his hand on Gisela's chin and forced her to look up at him. "Dinner tomorrow. You owe me that."

Yearning was printed all over Gisela's porcelain perfection. She seemed docile, obedient even. "Tomorrow, then."

But outside in the street, she slid back into her normal self. "Did you like him?"

"Very much. But forgive me, he does not seem your type."

She tucked a hand under my elbow. "He isn't. That's the point. Isn't life funny?"

We skirted a pile of rubbish spilling out of a black plastic bag and stepped into the road. "Surely, . . ." I hesitated, "Roger knows? How do you get to see Marcus?"

"Oh, details." Gisela was impatient. "One can always arrange them. How did you get to see Nathan? But Roger does not know and he never will. Okay?" She squeezed my elbow. "Okay?"

I crossed my fingers. "Okay."

We reached the opposite side of the street, and Gisela said, "I met Marcus when I was eighteen and already married to Nicholas, who was my godfather, you know. Nicholas was fifty, but well-off, concerned, generous. Marcus came to catalog his collection of paintings and he's been in and out of my life ever since."

"Why didn't you marry him after Nicholas died?"

Gisela swiveled to a halt and flicked her finger in the direction of the Hermès shop window on the corner of the street. Framed reverently in it, on a bed of flowing silk, was a beige Birkin bag. "You get used to certain things, and Marcus was very, very poor in those days. He says I'm a gold digger. He's right. I am."

We continued our progress up the street toward the restaurant where Gisela was taking me for lunch, traffic wailing in the road, the shop windows crammed with desirable objects.

"Marcus and I would have worn each other out," she said at last. "I didn't want that, Minty." She pushed me toward a door that looked expensive. "I want to give you a good lunch."

As I was being helped off with my coat in the plush, hushed restaurant, my mobile rang. "Yes."

"Minty." I felt the hairs on my arms rise. "It's Rose."

Maybe Rose had seen me outside her flat after all and she was ringing to say: please don't do that again. Or, what do you think you are playing at?

I stiffened with dismay. "Rose, this is not a good moment. Can I call you back?"

Rose's voice veered uncharacteristically from its normal modulations. She sucked in her breath with an evident effort. "Minty, is there anyone there with you? . . . I am afraid . . . you must prepare yourself. Minty . . . Minty . . . Nathan." She collected herself. "Minty, I think you must come at once. Nathan isn't very well, and it would be best if you came . . ."

"Where?" I said and, alarmed by my tone, Gisela laid a hand on my arm. "*Where* should I come?"

"My flat. As soon as you can."

Gisela asked, almost shrill. "What's happened?"

"It's Nathan, something's wrong. That was Rose. He's at her flat."

"Oh, my God . . . I hadn't imagined . . ." she checked herself. "Right. It will be quicker to get a taxi and I'm coming with you."

"What's he doing with her? Gisela, what do you think has happened?"

"Let's get the taxi" was Gisela's reply.

I cannot remember much about what happened next apart from staring hard at a set of traffic lights. Then there was the motorcyclist who edged so close to us that the driver shouted at him.

"You shouldn't have come," I said to Gisela. "There's no need."

Gisela was matter-of-fact. "It did sound urgent but it's

probably nothing. Anyway, I would like to meet this famous Rose."

"Gisela," I repeated. "What is Nathan doing at Rose's?"

She did not meet my eye. "There's probably a very good reason."

I stared out the window. *Nathan and Rose. Old times.*

Keeping one hand on my leg to anchor me, Gisela hunched forward on the seat and issued instructions to the driver. Once, she asked me for more precise details, and I heard myself giving them. "It's left at the bottom of the street, then right . . ."

Was Nathan really ill? He had rung me that morning on my way to work. It had been a relaxed, easy conversation, almost intimate.

"Lost my glasses."

"I saw you put them in your briefcase."

"Ah."

"What have you got on today?"

"Roger wants to see me about something. Probably something to do with the supplement on Africa we're planning for the autumn. How we can help it without inflicting Western values at the expense of indigenous ones . . . that sort of stuff. Doesn't stand a prayer of enlightening anyone because it will be so politically correct it will be utter rubbish."

I had laughed and now, in the speeding taxi, with anxiety beating a rising crescendo in my ears, I wondered if he'd heard that laugh.

Surely there could be nothing wrong with Nathan? But perhaps there was. Perhaps Nathan so missed the nice, loving things that happy couples say to each other that he had gone to Rose and said, "Let's go back to what we were," and the effort had made him ill.

He had been pale lately.

When we arrived at Rose's gleaming-windowed flat, Gisela gathered up her handbag, and I searched in mine for the fare. "I think I should stay with you, Minty. It might be that Nathan's had a shock."

My eyes narrowed. "Gisela, what do you know?"

She pushed aside the notes in my hand. "I'll pay."

The front door to the flat appeared to open of its own volition and Rose appeared on the doorstep. She was white, whiter than a ghost. I had never seen anyone quite so drained of color, and there were black streaks on her cheeks. She looked from Gisela to me, and back to Gisela. "You'd better bring Minty inside."

I stepped into small hallway painted in mushroom and white, with sanded floorboards. It flashed through my mind that this was a place I would like to be.

"I have something to tell you," said Rose, directing a warning look at Gisela. She took both my hands in hers. Her touch burned. "Minty, will you come and sit down in the kitchen. Please."

I snatched my hands away. "Where is Nathan?" Rose was silent, and anxiety changed into fear. "What's he doing here?"

"Please, Minty," said Rose. "C . . . come and sit down." Awkward and stammering, she seemed completely at a loss. Then she pulled herself together. "Come into the kitchen." Again she looked at Gisela. "Could you help me, please?"

I cried out, sharply. "Has Nathan gone? Is that it? Tell me."

Rose shivered. "I am trying to explain to you, Minty, and I'm not sure how to do it."

"Something *has* happened to him."

"Yes," she said and, again, she took possession of my hand. Her fingers pressed into mine. "Yes, yes, it has."

"But *what?*"

"Has Nathan complained of feeling ill lately?"

"No . . . yes. I've been a bit worried."

Rose was drawing me toward the kitchen. "I must talk to you before . . . anything . . ." She glanced at Gisela as if for help. "I am afraid I don't know your name, but could you persuade Minty to come and sit down?"

But I dug my heels in. "Just say whatever it is, Rose. Have you got something to confess?" I paused and threw out the first thing in my head even though I knew it would not delay whatever was making her so ghost-white and shaky. "What are you two up to?" I turned toward a door opening off the hall. "Is he in there? Nathan," I called. "Nathan, are you there?"

"Don't . . . don't go in. Not yet." Rose placed her two hands on my shoulders. "Minty, you must prepare yourself."

Various explanations presented themselves. *Nathan had left me. A doctor had given him bad news. Nathan had gone back to Rose.* I was frightened, and angry that my husband should have shared the news with Rose. I tried to push past her, but she caught my arm so hard that I winced.

"Minty . . . listen . . . *listen* to me. . . . I'm sorry, but Nathan is dead."

Gisela gasped. Dazed, confused, I shook my head and did not reply. Eventually, my head cleared and I said, "Don't be silly," in a conversational tone. "I was talking to him earlier. He wanted to know where his glasses were. He couldn't find them . . ." Gisela's hand was at the small of my back, propping me up. The words slithered into silence, and I thought: *the boys.*

I was not prepared. It was not as though Nathan and I had had a long run-up to this moment. I hadn't written a list. *Get used to idea. Read manual on bereavement* . . . There had been no doctor saying, "I'm so sorry, but . . ." No Nathan saying, "Minty, we have to face it . . ."

Painting and literature were stuffed full of farewell scenes. Wives knelt beside the bed—not always weeping. Children were generally at the foot and wept enough for the wives. Black-clad relatives waited outside death chambers. This primary rite of passage, this moment when the strings were so tightly drawn that the merest touch would produce a note of exquisite beauty and sadness, had been rehearsed down the ages and everyone in these scenes knew their role.

An arm went around my shoulder, and I was enveloped in a jasmine scent. Rose's. But the arm was awkward. I muttered, "This isn't a joke, is it, Rose?"

"A *joke?*"

I disengaged myself so abruptly that Gisela reached out to steady me. "When . . . ?"

"An hour ago. I don't know. It was . . . quick. Very quick. One minute Nathan was here. The next, he wasn't. He gave a little sigh. That was all."

I examined my hands in detail. Snagged cuticle on fourth left finger and a thumbnail that required filing.

Shocked and clearly agitated, Gisela leaned forward and touched my cheek. "What can I do, Minty? Tell me."

"Go," I replied. "It's best."

Gisela shrugged the unwrinkled leather jacket closer round her shoulders. "Of course." The front door clicked shut.

I raised my head from the detailed observation of my hands. "I need to sit down."

I allowed myself to be led into the kitchen and put into a chair. "You must take your time." Rose was so gentle, oh so gentle. She placed a glass of water in front of me and I stared at it. *Nathan is dead.*

After a while, I asked, "Can I see him?"

"Of course. They haven't moved him. It was too late by the time the ambulance came. He hasn't been disturbed. There is nothing to be frightened of, Minty, I promise you." Rose's voice beat on my eardrums. "The doctor will be here in a minute. Death certificate. I'm afraid it's necessary."

"Yes." I managed a sip of water—it's nontaste on my tongue, the accompaniment to my slide from wife to widow. I buried my face in my hands. How was I going to tell the boys? Lucas had felt sick this morning. Had he been sick? "Rose, I must phone home."

"I'll do that for you," said Rose. "I'll explain that you will be home later, but I won't go into detail." She bent over me. "Is that best? I think so."

After I had drunk the glass of water, Rose helped me upright and led me to the door of the sitting room. She stepped back. "He's in there."

Chapter Eleven

The room had magnolia walls, a chair by an open window upholstered in faded china blue, several pictures, and a photo on the small table by the sofa.

The air coming through the window was cool and damp—the type that frizzes the hair. It held a promise, though, of spring, for it brought with it the tiniest drift of flower scent from the shrub blooming beneath the window.

My feet did not seem to be connecting with the floor and a pulse thudded in my ear. The details of the room accumulated. If I had been cross-examined in court, I could have told you everything about it. *How useful she is,* the judge might think. *How indispensable.*

I turned back to the blue chair and concentrated on a cushion. This was made from a mushroom shot silk, looked old and there was a surprising variety of texture and color.

We're planning a supplement on Africa in the autumn, I heard Nathan say. *Shouldn't you have kept Lucas at home?*

He was sitting well back in it, his body folded in a natural position, his face turned toward the door as if he was listening out for something, someone. A lock of his hair had fallen over his forehead, just tinged with gray. His mouth was slightly open. Had he been speaking to Rose when his heart shuddered, jumped, and declared "enough"? His left arm was tucked by his side, palm up, fingers curled a fraction.

He was still Nathan—he was still evident in the bone structure, the angle of the chin, the width of the forehead. Yet he had become remote. Between one heartbeat and the nonarrival of the next, he had weighed anchor and rowed far away. He had sped past his children, past his life with me, toward a horizon of which I had no knowledge.

"Nathan . . ." I reached over and smoothed back the lock of hair. Tidying him as I knew he liked. His skin held scintillas of warmth and hope flared that I could run from the room shouting, "He's not dead, only asleep."

I touched one of the fingers, willing it to curl round mine. What was there left to read in his face, with the blind closed eyes? There was no distress as far as I could make out, only surprise . . . and a suggestion of . . . release?

In the other room, I could hear the murmur of Rose's voice.

Had she traced the line from nose to chin, as I did in the gentlest of gestures? Had she bent over to be quite, quite sure that no rogue breath soughed from his mouth, as I was doing? Had she sunk to her knees and whispered, "I don't believe you're dead, Nathan," as I was now doing?

I shed no tears. Shock I think. No easy relief then. Again, I searched Nathan's face for the clues. "Why did you not call me, Nathan?" I begged the still figure, as I knelt in front of him like a penitent. I knew—I feared—that Nathan had struggled on feeling ill and alone. "You should have called me. I would have come. Of course I would have come."

How *was* I going to tell his . . . our children?

Which would be the right words? My toes cramped under my weight, but I welcomed the discomfort.

In the end, the pain was too acute. I got to my feet and went in search of Rose. She was in the kitchen, sitting at the table with her head in her hands. At my entrance, she looked up. "Are you all right?"

"What do you think?"

"I don't think anything, Minty."

I pushed myself into a chair. "I was thinking how unfair it was on Nathan. He did not *deserve* this."

Rose got up, went to a cupboard, took out a bottle, and presented me with a drink. "Brandy. We'd better have some."

The glass was heavy, with a pattern incised into it. It felt weighty and expensive. I recognized it. We had two exactly the same in Lakey Street. "We divided things," Nathan reported when he and Rose divorced. "Straight down the line. I owed her half of everything." He had been so pleased with his fairness and generosity that I had snapped shut my lips and forborne to point out that two matching glasses out of four were not *that* useful and half a set of silver-plated cutlery limited one's options.

Obediently, I drank. Rose asked, "Were there any clues that Nathan's heart was giving him problems?"

"No. But then I had not been looking for any."

She accepted this. "I was concerned about him. Don't ask me why, I had not seen much of him. But even so . . ."—she was too upset to bother with tact—"even so, there was always the connection between us and I felt, well, when things were not right. I did try to ask him about his health but you know Nathan . . ." She wrapped both hands around her glass and lifted it to her lips. "How like him, how very like Nathan to say nothing."

I could not face talking about his death. The subject and the situation were too big and unknown, too fearsome and desperate. "Did you talk to Eve?"

"Yes. She will manage, so you are not to worry. I talked to her very carefully."

Before I could stop myself, I lashed out. "Did you talk to Nathan very carefully?"

"Stop it, Minty." Rose raised a white countenance. "Don't."

"Sorry." I groped for clues to the puzzle. "He had a checkup a couple of months ago. There were episodes when he said he was feeling really tired. But that was it."

There elapsed another of those pauses that were impossible to describe, only endure. I gulped the brandy as if it were orange juice. They say men wounded in battle do not, at first, feel anything. Then they do. The brandy was a precaution.

Nathan had not often mentioned death. Not to me, anyway. We were too busy negotiating life. When he did talk about death, it was to wag a metaphorical finger. "As long as it doesn't come too soon."

What had Nathan been doing in Rose's flat?

I felt cold and faint. I struggled to reach past myself, to think of Felix and Lucas. They would not understand, perhaps not for a long time. I tried too to consider Sam and Poppy.

And Rose.

And yet, out of all the suppositions and shocks, the one

question that forced itself past my lips was, "Rose, what was Nathan doing here?" I stared at the brandy in the glass and waited for the answer. "I must know."

Rose positioned her glass with care on the table and got to her feet. Slowly and deliberately, she walked around to where I sat, bent down, and wrapped her arms around me. It was a gesture we both suffered and endured. Rose needed to make it because it was in her nature. I had to accept it because I craved the comfort of contact, even from her. She gave a jagged sigh. "Poor Minty, what you must think."

"Yes," I echoed bitterly. "What I must think."

Her cheek was against mine. "Nathan was here for a reason. Had he told you what happened . . . ?"

It was pitiful to utter lies with Nathan dead in the next room, but a yes slipped through my lips. I did not know what she was talking about but hated to admit it.

"Then you will know that Vistemax . . ." Rose's face was close to mine, her arms a circle in which I was trapped.

"Yes . . ."

My mendacity had a false, brassy note but I clung to it. A tap dripped and the fridge emitted a muted electrical choke. We both knew that I was not telling the truth, and Rose was debating how to handle my ignorance of something that was, clearly, important.

Rose released me. "That's why."

Wasn't death supposed to be a cleansing agent? A blow so huge and pulverizing that all the petty emotions and subterfuges and secrets were smashed?

"Oh, for goodness' sake," I braced myself. "I *don't* know, Rose. Tell me."

But the phone rang and Rose answered it. She said, "Yes,

his wife is here. Yes, we're waiting." She was cool and in control, the sort of person who was practiced at formalities and procedures. "That was the doctor." She kept her hand clamped around the receiver. "He will be here any minute."

Impatient to know, I laid both my hands flat on the table. "What has happened? And why did Nathan come to . . . you?" My knuckles whitened with the pressure. "Why here?"

Still clutching the phone, Rose told me the truth. "Roger sacked him this morning."

"Sacked!" The news was brutal enough to bring the blood rushing into my face. I pressed my hands against my cheeks. "Poor Nathan." Rose put down the phone. "So they got him in the end," I said. "They always do."

"Vistemax is hardly the gulag." Rose leaned against the sink. "And Nathan had a good run with them."

"You always did see the best in things." Still I clung to the inconsequential, curious as to how Rose's generosity could survive just now. "I often wondered if it was a strength or weakness."

Rose gave a short laugh. "I leave you to decide. I don't think Nathan expected it. Do you?"

"Nathan did not confide in me" would have been a truthful answer. "He had been there a long time and he knew the form." But clearly, he had neither known, or cared enough, to guard himself against the consequences of Roger's cynical appraisals. "He was in his fifties . . . and there is a sell-by date for all of us. There was probably somebody else coming up fast, and you know how they operate at Vistemax. . . ."

"Yes," answered Rose flatly. "Funnily enough, I do."

"Roger would have dressed it up to Nathan. He would

have said, 'Change is happening faster than ever and we must harness our energies to keep up.' As sacking formulas go, it does pretty well for most people."

Rose completed the narrative. "By the end of the session, Nathan would have been persuaded into thinking his was a necessary martyrdom."

Rose was talking about her own sacking, as I had been talking about mine. "No," I had to defend him because I wanted to get it right. "He wasn't that sentimental. He knew his worth. He would have fought. He would have been angry . . . very angry, so angry his heart couldn't stand it."

Rose turned away.

My gaze lit on objects around the kitchen. A white jug. A wicker shopping basket by the door into which plastic bags had been stuffed.

"Nathan had his vulnerabilities," Rose offered. "Everyone does. Roger would have known which button to press."

The picture assembled of Nathan listening to the delicately phrased insults of the sacking. I knew, *I knew,* that Roger's careful cruelty would have smashed his pride. It was then Nathan must have felt the first intimations that his heart was faltering. Did he register then the choke and stutter of his blood, the pain of the squeezed muscle, and refuse to call out? God help us, Nathan preferred to die (and did) rather than ask the man who had just sacked him for help.

Rose added, "Peter Shaker is taking over."

"Well, that would have killed him if nothing else did."

Rose's lips curved in wry amusement. "Yes, it probably did."

Later, I thought, I will force myself to believe that Roger

chose Peter over Nathan for a *good* reason. After all his years at Vistemax, Nathan deserved that at the very least. Dull Peter and his good-hearted Carolyne in the navy blue suit and gold buttons—both of them, not so long ago, had eaten twice-baked cheese soufflé, chicken in ginger, and bitter maraschino cherries at our table. On Nathan's behalf, I felt a black, killer rage dig in for the duration.

Rose choked and made a sound like a small animal in distress. She heaved herself round, placed both hands on the edge of the sink and, retching, leaned over it. I got up, filled a glass with water, and handed it to her.

She wiped her mouth with the back of her hand. "One should never drink brandy too fast."

Now it was my turn to slide a hand around her shoulders and press her into a chair. "Rose, are you getting drunk?"

A bit of color crept back into her cheeks. "Nathan had only been here fifteen minutes or so. He said he wanted to talk over what had happened, and how he was going to manage the changes. He wanted to sound me out." She must have registered my instinctive flinch because she added, "He would have talked to you, Minty."

That was unanswerable and none of Rose's business. "Don't say that."

She was taken aback and struggled with her answer. "After the doctor and the undertakers have been, you must go."

I left Rose in the kitchen and fled back to the cold sitting room, the smell of spring, and Nathan. "Why didn't you ring me," I demanded of the still figure.

"You married me because . . ." went the stupid, dangerous game we sometimes played in the early days, and there was only one rule.

All the answers were to be a tease. "I married you, Nathan, because you drove a Lexus."

"And? What else, Minty? My looks, my wit . . . ?"

"Naturally, your serious bank account. And, Nathan, you married me because?"

"Oh, I married you, Minty, because you were pregnant."

In his hour of need, Nathan had not defected to Rose because he wished to talk over his options or to block out a new future. He would have done that with me and I would have given him better advice. No. No, Nathan had turned to Rose because he craved her comfort, the long history, her sweetness in his hour of deepest trial, her reassurance.

Behind me, Rose entered the room and closed the window. She had gotten herself under control and spoke calmly. "I opened it to allow his spirit to go. I think . . . I believe it's customary." She clicked the catch into place, and I had an almost irresistible urge to laugh at the notion. Rose fiddled with the curtain, a calico thickly interlined and expensive, and I imagined Nathan's spirit forcing his way past it and up into the dark somewhere.

"When the undertakers arrive, we shall have to make some decisions." Rose nerved herself visibly because once this quiet interlude was over a process would begin. "When I've spoken to Sam and Poppy." She turned to me, as if appealing for help with such an appalling task, and I tasted fear at what lay ahead of me too. "I dread that. They will be devastated."

"Decisions?"

"All of us must decide what we want. We must try to think of what he would have wanted. Poppy and Sam will have views."

"Rose. *My* decisions, I think."

She shook her head, and a strand of hair worked loose. "That can't be, Minty. We are all in this. We are his family."

"And I am his widow."

"How will you tell Felix and Lucas? Will you need help?" Rose adopted the voice I sometimes heard in the office when either Sam or Poppy rang up. It was ultrasoothing. I used to think it rather silly and false until, after I had had the twins, I realized it was a means of staving off panic.

"No." My rejection of the idea was instant. I did not want her softness and comfort stealing my children.

I glanced at my watch. Incredibly, I had been here only three quarters of an hour or so. I wondered (courtesy of Gisela) who else knew and was even now telephoning others, or the florist to order flowers. *With deepest sympathy.* I wondered if the clocks would stop. Who would cry genuine tears, and who would not. I wondered if Nathan had been a tiny bit ready, whether he had thought about his death at all. Or if he was circling up there, cursing.

"Why don't we sit with him?" Rose suggested. "He won't be here for much longer."

I chose a chair close to the body. Already Nathan was drawing further away, much as his body must be stiffening. "Your children had their childhood with him." I was fierce with the unfairness for my boys. "Mine won't."

Rose sat down on the sofa and her eyes met mine. "Yes, Minty, there was that."

After a moment or two, Rose began to talk about the old days when she was married to Nathan. Every year, they had gone on holiday to Priac Bay in Cornwall, always to the same cottage. She described the slap of the water on the sides of the clinker fishing boat, the hiss and heave of the sea, the oily smell and texture of mackerel.

"The thing I remember most is the rain. Sometimes it was hard and slanted in from the west. At others, it was as soft as a caress and seeped into your clothing. However carefully we put away the mackerel lines at home, they were always knotted when we got them out of the cupboard the next year. Nathan was impatient and demanded that we buy new ones, but I said no and I made it my business to make him laugh. It was an effort but I learned the routines. I planned we had a good meal on the first night, and I bought a heater to ensure we weren't cold. By day two, he seemed always to breathe easier and he slept differently. More quietly. When he picked up the book I'd chosen for him, I knew the best part of the holiday was beginning. It was a sort of healing from the frazzle of the year. I don't think we would have survived so long without Cornwall."

"I never let him go to Cornwall," I said. "What was the point? It was your territory. I thought it would be good for him to look at different things. I thought a little Greek or Italian sun would work magic, but he never liked the heat. You knew that. And the boys were too young. The heat made them fretful and difficult to manage."

"But I was tired too, always so tired," Rose said. "Until the children were older. I didn't realize, and it wasn't a question of accepting the tiredness, I just thought that was the way things were until I began to feel better. Really better. By then, it was too late and Nathan had looked elsewhere."

When the doctor arrived, he examined Nathan. "It looks very much as if it was a heart attack," he told us, writing notes and organizing the paperwork. "The postmortem will confirm." He was a busy man, and overworked, and did not stay long.

The undertakers also arrived, three burly men, and the dimensions of the flat seemed to shrink.

Rose took Nathan's hand, kissed his cheek, and stepped back.

"Please, could I say good-bye privately?" I asked Rose and the men shuffled away, leaving me with my husband. "I'm sorry," I whispered, bent over, and adjusted his tie, and pulled his jacket straight. Just as he liked it. "I'm so sorry."

It seemed to me that the flesh was already vanishing beneath my lips as I kissed him good-bye.

I retreated to the kitchen where Rose and I helped ourselves to more brandy.

Eventually, there was a knock on the door, and one of the undertakers, an older man who introduced himself as Keith, addressed a series of questions to Rose. It was clear that he regarded her as the widow.

"Excuse me," I interjected. "I am the current Mrs. Lloyd."

Keith's gaze slid between us. There was a modicum of embarrassment but little surprise. "Then I'll await your instructions, Mrs. Lloyd. Your husband's body will have to go to the mortuary for the postmortem, but after it is released we can discuss the details."

I cast around in my mind. "There's a church near us. I'll find out who the vicar is . . ."

"Oh, no," said Rose. "Nathan would have wanted to be buried at Altringham, Minty. Where his parents are . . ."

"Altringham? That's too far away," I cried.

Keith stepped delicately around this one. "Perhaps it will be specified in the will. It always takes a little time to make these decisions. And as I say, we are at the end of a phone."

Rose busied herself folding a tea towel, first one way, then another. Finally, she placed it on the table. "Of course."

They left, taking Nathan away. The front door clicked shut, leaving a stony silence between us.

I broke it. "I am his wife, Rose."

Rose sighed. "So am I. In a way." She shrugged. "So help me. In a strange way."

"For God's sake . . ."

"It doesn't matter. Listen, Minty, listen to me, we *can't* leave him where no one will know about him. We can't leave him where he will be alone."

I hated myself for minding that Rose had got it right, and usually did. "I will decide where Nathan is buried, Rose."

She whirled round. "Go, Minty." And she pushed me out of the kitchen and into the hall. "I'll take you home in the taxi. Then I must . . . I want to see my own children." She turned an anguished face to mine. "I *must* see them . . ."

Chapter Twelve

The dark has never held any real terrors for me. It was the time in which hot, pleasurable things were accomplished. It was the moment to dream, to plan, to sleep: to touch a warm sleeping body, and marvel at its beauty, or its power, or to realize that you hated it.

But when I went to bed that night I was afraid.

There were scattered clues that I had come home and gone through the motions but I cannot remember much. A waterfall of socks, underpants, and trousers flowed out of the boys' linen basket. In the bathroom, my face flannel was damp. In the bedroom, my shoes had been put away in the cupboard. In the kitchen, the dishwasher had been switched on and was ready to unload and a half-eaten tin of tuna from the boys' supper was wedged between the cheese and bacon in the fridge.

Eve and I had whispered to each other while the boys romped upstairs. "So dreadful, Minty." Her complexion combined an agitated red and white, and she had brushed her hair flat. "Poor, poor Nathan." She sketched the sign of the cross on her breast. Not once, but twice and I suppressed a hysterical desire to hiss. "That won't help him now."

"Eve, we won't tell the boys until tomorrow . . . after school." She looked skeptical and, wearily, I summoned the energy to persuade her. "It will be easier for me. It will give me time to do some things before I concentrate on them. I can make arrangements . . ."

"Okay."

I knew I should be doing things, but what things exactly? There were procedures, but unknown ones. Then there were questions to be answered.

I rang Theo, Nathan's lawyer, and was forced to repeat that "Nathan is dead" because even überprofessional Theo could not believe it. "Will you help me?" I begged him. I was frightened that Vistemax would not honor Nathan's severance package. "Don't worry." Theo was swift with reassurance. He clicked his tongue. "Hear that? That's the sound of the bit clinking into place between my teeth. They'll *pay*."

I rang Barry to tell him. "This is so awful." His voice oozed genuine concern. "Awful. You are not to think of setting foot in the office for the time being. We will see to everything. I'll brief Chris."

Chris would steal my ideas.

But I had already forgotten Chris Sharpe when I rang Paige. A similar species of words filtered down the telephone— it was the stockpile on which we drew in moments of blackness and emergency. "So awful." Paige was stuttering with shock. "Terrible. Terrible, Minty. Can you manage? I'm so sorry I can't help at the moment. Linda can come and take the boys."

"I haven't told them yet. I'm waiting for the right moment."

Paige could not, and did not, resist this challenge. "Won't they guess something is up?"

"I'm good at pretending."

There was a small silence. "Yes, I suppose you are."

In between these conversations, I did my best to make a list. But it proved beyond my powers. I struggled with words such as "probate," "death registration," and "newspaper announcement," but they refused to slot into their places.

"Mum," Lucas ran into the house, and hurled himself at me. "Mum, read me a story." He was glowing with exercise, and looked so winning and wholesome that any film director who happened to be passing would have scooped him up.

A hand slipped into mine. "Hallo, Mummy." It was Felix. "You look sad. Are you sad, Mummy?"

I bent down and scooped them both into a hug. Their small hard heads butted into my chest. They were now my entire responsibility.

Nathan was with me throughout that fear-filled night. We were in the sitting room. The clock ticked on the half-moon table by the window and we were arguing about it. Nathan thought it would be safer on the mantelpiece. "Please do as I wish, Minty." I looked up from a card of paint samples and heard myself say, "Do you think Eastern Beige would look right in here?" "Eastern Beige," he retorted. "Compost, more like."

Nathan was in the garden, in his brown corduroys, favorite blue shirt, and a pair of Wellingtons, digging under the lilac tree. On the landing, I was struggling to iron a shirt that, however skilfully I stroked and stretched it, would not lose its creases.

Nathan pushed the fork into the earth, reached into the ground with both hands, and extracted a bundle wrapped in a white wool shawl. "This is my secret grief, Minty," I heard him say in that restless, half-conscious interlude.

The bedroom was airless, sucked dry of its oxygen, and I alternated between sweating and shivering, which, I supposed, was shock. *Could I have done more? Answer: yes, I could. Was Nathan so unhappy? Answer: yes, he was* . . . I fled upstairs to the spare bedroom. The bed was not made up but I slipped into it between the bare mattress and folded duvet and stared into the darkness.

I could not see the rose painting on the wall above me in the dark, but with an internal eye, I traced those roses. I calculated their dimensions, the arrangement of the shapes on the canvas. I struck up an intimate acquaintance with each shade and tint, ticking them off on my fingers: chalk white, clotted cream, weak tea, and the blood brown of the darkening petals scattered at the base of the vase.

When I could bear it no longer, I slid out of bed, reached up, and turned the painting to the wall.

There. They had gone.

A little later—how long?—I found myself in Nathan's study. I opened his filing cabinet to reveal the sections neatly labeled in black ink. "Insurance" (an orange file). "House" (a blue file). "Lawyer" (red). "Health" (yellow).

Why had he chosen yellow for health? It was not a good

color. Yellow was dispiriting and suggested disease. Yellow fever. Dengue fever. Malaria. Jaundice. I flipped it open at the back, then rifled through the documents from the bottom up.

There were assorted letters from doctors with addresses in Harley Street. One reported the results of an eye test. Another a blood test. All routine, all normal, negative, nonthreatening. The top letter on the pile was different. It read: "Dear Mr. Lloyd. As we agreed at our consultation, I have made arrangements for you to see my colleague, Mr Oxford, at the London Heart Hospital. I have explained my concerns—blood pressure, murmur, etcetera, and he will proceed with the investigation. If you would kindly get in touch with him directly . . ."

The letter was dated six months ago.

I reread the polite sentences. Behind the bland "concerns" was hidden a coded allusion. Nathan, the consultant was suggesting, displayed a cluster of symptoms and was required to do something about it.

Nathan had failed to do so.

Angrily, I snatched up the letter. Why? And why had he not told me?

It would have been so easy to manage. We could have attended the appointment together. I would have sat meek as a mouse reading *Country Life* or dog-eared copies of *Hallo!* while the highways and byways of his arteries and the chambers of his heart were flagged up on a screen. As we listened to the verdict of what was wrong, I know I would have reached out and taken his hand.

Nathan would only have had to say, "I'm having problems

with my heart," for me to swing into action. It would have been a field day for lists. *Low-cholesterol spread, green vegetables, vitamins, an exercise bike.* And for timetables, which I was good at too. *Exercise, 7:00–7:30 A.M. Breakfast, 7:45 . . .*

The enormity of Nathan's silence was an excruciating reminder of how silent we had been during his life. I had failed to comfort him. I had not stroked his cheek. We had not waited stoically together in a doctor's waiting room.

Nor had my phone rung this morning, and I had not picked it up to hear him say: "Minty, I've got something to tell you . . . it will be a shock."

So he never got to hear my reply. "Vistemax sucks. Have you rung the lawyer? Nathan, this is not personal, you know . . ." Especially, Nathan never heard me say. "Nathan, hold on. I'm coming over to get you and we'll talk this through . . ."

Nathan had chosen to bury his anguish in silence and then, to seek out Rose.

But Nathan was dead.

I fell to my knees by the filing cabinet, placed my hands on the open drawer, for it held the facts, the hard facts of which I was so fond, of Nathan's life.

I bowed my head and, finally, I wept.

It was three-thirty in the morning, on the first day of my widowhood.

At nine A.M. the following morning, I sat at Nathan's desk in his study. The boys had already gone to school and Eve was vacuuming the next-door room. The noise drilled into my skull.

The phone rang. "I don't know what to say."

"You don't have to say anything, Roger."

"I assume it was his heart."

I put down the phone, which rang back almost immediately. "If there is anything we can do, it shall be done," said Roger. "Please, will you let us know when the funeral is? Minty, I recognize that this is the most tragic, intolerable situation."

Was this the moment to point out that Roger had made *such* a mistake in dismissing Nathan's accumulation of experience for the sake of change? Should I also mention that he had almost certainly driven Nathan to his death?

"I know you will have mixed feelings . . ."

"No, Roger. Not *mixed* feelings. Very straightforward feelings."

"We were doing what was best for Vistemax."

"Peter Shaker? Really?"

There was nothing more to add. Roger was a businessman, and I was a widow and, however much I might long to connect, there was no chance. Again, I terminated the conversation and took the phone off the hook. Not a moment too soon, for it was almost too much. And I could not let go. Not yet. Perhaps never?

The vacuuming drilled into my skull. I called out, "Eve, could you stop that?"

She appeared out of the sitting room. "You need clean house, Minty. People will come."

Would they?

"You look bad, Minty. I get you cup of tea."

I sat at Nathan's desk, holding the cup and wondering how long my fingers could stand the pain. That was easy to

deal with—unlike the pain I must inflict on Lucas and Felix. Should I call an expert who could tell me what to say?
Experts had formulas at their fingertips. Daddy has gone on a
long journey and won't be coming back. Would that do?
Or . . . Daddy is watching over you but he can't actually be
here.

The doorbell rang, and there was instant, welcome peace.
Eve clattered out into the hall.

It was Mrs. Austen: the crabby Mrs. Austen. "Eve. We've
just heard. Here is soup. My tomatoes. Feed it to them."

Ten minutes later, the doorbell sounded again. This time
it was Kate Winsom from across the road. "This is so awful,"
I heard her say as I cowered in the study. "Look, I'm off to the
supermarket. Can I do the shopping? Tell Minty I will be in
touch at a more . . . at a more appropriate time. Unfortunately,
I have to fly now. The children . . ."

For the tenth time, I attempted to make a list. But what
good was that?

The doorbell—oh, that doorbell—rang and I pressed my
face hard into my fingers. The next thing I felt was a light
touch on my shoulder. Gisela said, "I came as soon as I could."

I reared my head. "You knew what Roger was going to
do and you didn't tell me."

"Would you have expected me to? What would you have
done? But I was going to drop a hint at lunch . . ." She slid a
finger onto my pulse and felt it. "Have you slept? And when
did you last eat?"

My hair felt hot and heavy, and I pushed it back. "Cup of
tea. I don't know, Gisela."

She bent over me and spoke with an urgency I had never
heard before. "You will need your strength, Minty. You have

the twins to think about. I am going to get you some more tea and some toast."

She led me into the sitting room, and eased me down onto the sofa. "Sit there until I come back."

The morning light streaming into the room was so bright it hurt my eyes. I looked out of the French window. The lilac tree was unfurling its first buds and, in the neighboring garden to my right, a magnolia had unleashed tiers of porcelain-cup blossoms.

"Spring is cruel," I said.

"Yes." Gisela had returned with a tray. She put it down on the coffee table, reached into her handbag, and switched off her mobile.

"Goodness," I said. "It must be serious."

The sun lit a patch of carpet that years of exposure had changed from dark gray into a lighter shade. I heard Nathan, so clearly, so very clearly: *no, we can't afford a new carpet.*

"Minty . . ." Gisela picked up a finger of toast spread with butter and marmite. "Eat."

"I never touch butter, Gisela. Waistline."

"You do today."

I took the toast and chewed. The tang of marmite was not disagreeable, and the tea was hot and strong. Gisela sipped from a second mug. "Terrible tea. What is it?"

"Ordinary stuff. I don't know."

"Lapsang is better."

Cross out "ordinary stuff" on weekly shopping list, and substitute "Lapsang."

From her vantage point, Gisela appeared wise and Buddha-like. She was filled with substance and purpose while overnight, I had shrunk into a depleted figure huddled on the sofa. "Minty. About Rose."

That piece of information was a gold mine for clacking tongues. *Do you know where he died? With first wife.* It was unlikely to remain secret.

"Roger has talked to Rose. He rang her after he spoke to you. He's going to see her this afternoon."

"But not coming here?"

"I'm here." She reached over to put her mug on the tray. "You know cutting Roger off is not going to raise Nathan from the dead."

"No." This exchange was superfluous because at that point Nathan did not seem to be dead. He was there, in the sitting room, because I could feel him very strongly.

Gisela continued. "Let me advise you. Don't ignore Roger's offer of help. You will need it."

The remaining marmite soldier sat an angle on the plate, and I adjusted it. "Nathan was the reliable one. He was a man who tried to be the person who never left you in the lurch. But it was all too much for him. Leaving Rose, marrying me. Vistemax. He couldn't keep the bandwagon rolling. His body protested." I was beginning to feel very odd in the region behind my eyes. "Am I making sense?"

Gisela was wearing one of her blindingly white blouses, with three-quarter-length sleeves and tucking across the breast. It was French and of exquisite cut. A rope of large pearls circled her throat and matching ones were in her ears. She was hunched forward on the chair, her body language spelling pity, pity. "I don't expect you to make sense." She pulled a notebook out of her bag, wrote something, and tore out the page.

"I can't do much for you, Minty, except help with the small things. Here's the name of a good florist. Just tell them what you want for Nathan, and they'll understand."

Florist? "Thank you." My lips were trembling. "Did Roger say how Nathan was yesterday?" Gisela made a play of stowing the notebook back in her bag. "I'd like to know what he said and how he looked."

"All right." Gisela seemed to have been expecting my question. "Roger was dreading the meeting. Nathan was a friend. No, don't look like that, Minty. You *know* it, as well as I do. Roger gave the news to him straight. At first, Nathan did not say much." Gisela paused. "Roger said he walked over to the window and turned his back on him. It was shock, he said, and he needed a minute or two. Then he went on the attack and told Roger the decision was crazy and wrong. Furthermore, Vistemax did not need destabilizing at the moment."

"Nathan fought back." To those who knew him intimately, the signs would have been readable. When he tightened his mouth, things were not good for the opposition. If he dug a hand into a trouser pocket, the strategy had been worked out.

"I have never seen Roger so sad, so rattled. At the . . . prospect of doing it," Gisela offered. "And Nathan gave him a very, very hard time."

"Gisela. Nathan was about to lose everything."

"Not everything. He had you and the boys. That was one of the points. Roger reckoned that he might be quite glad of a period at home to see more of the twins."

Astonished, I stared at Gisela. "Nathan was sacked because Roger thought he'd make a good nanny?"

Gisela's lips barely moved. "Nathan had had good innings."

"Let's hope Roger can be philosophical when it's his turn to head back to the pavillion."

With a touch of panic, Gisela said, "There's no need, Minty . . ."

"Roger really concluded that Peter Shaker was a better man than Nathan?"

Gisela smoothed the cuff of her dazzling shirt. "Is this the right time to discuss all this? It's impossible to be rational."

"Oh, rationality," I said. "It's overrated."

I got up and went to the half-moon table. Very gently, I lifted the clock and placed it on the mantelpiece in the space that Nathan had always intended for it.

Gisela picked up her bag. "I must go. But remember, Roger will help if he can. I will help all I can with the arrangements. If you like."

I heard myself cry, "Why did Roger do it?"

Gisela put down her bag again, placed her hands on my shoulders, and looked deeply into my eyes. "That is the way it is. Nathan did it to others, remember."

"But it killed him."

The pressure on my shoulders increased. "Nathan liked his whiskey, he had a stressful job. He had a . . . busy . . . home life. A large family. Those things contribute. No, it wasn't getting the sack, Minty. Nathan's *heart condition* killed him."

The doorbell continued to ring, but I let Eve deal with it. Each time, she returned bearing something. A bottle of wine with a label that read "Condolences." A paperback entitled *Wills and Probate*. The front cover was coffee stained and many of the pages were dog-eared. In the section entitled, 14.4.3, "Fair Division Between Parties," someone had scribbled violently in the margin, "I should be so lucky." Who sent it? I inquired of Eve. But she said she had not recognized the woman.

Wills and Probate lay on the kitchen table in front of me. I supposed the rest of the world was carrying on very nicely without Nathan. Chris Sharpe had, in all probability, enjoyed a good day. Peter Shaker's would not have been too bad either, except, perhaps, for the odd jab of conscience. I felt sorry for Carolyne, who would be caught between loyalty to her husband and her strict notions of what was correct. Booting Nathan out in favor of Peter would not come under her heading of the latter.

Someone walked into the kitchen. "Martin."

He placed a cling-wrapped Pyrex dish on the table and bent over to kiss my cheek. "I came as soon as I could and I've brought a macaroni and cheese."

I cast around for the polite response. *Any* response. "Lucas loves macaroni and cheese."

He sat beside me and took both my hands in his. "Paige asked Linda to make it." There was a pause. "This is terrible, Minty, but you will survive. That's what I've come to tell you. It might seem that you won't, but you *will*."

His grasp was cool and firm, and I was grateful for it. "Keep telling me that, Martin."

"I have every intention of doing so."

The macaroni and cheese had been made to perfection with a crisp crust on top. "I'm not sure what to do first."

Martin let go of my hands, and extracted a piece of paper from his breast pocket. "I've made a list," he said. "Cobbled together from what I remember when my parents died. Funeral arrangements . . ."

"A list!" I exclaimed. "You made a list when you have so many other things to do."

"That's what friends are for . . ." Martin handed it over. "It helps to have something concrete to think about."

"How are Paige and the baby?"

He frowned a trifle. "They're fine. I'm not sure how much rest Paige is getting."

"Are the nights bad?"

"I'm in the spare room at the moment."

It was getting dark, and the lights needed to be turned on, but I did nothing about it. Martin and I sat in the kitchen while dusk crept in, and I was grateful, oh so grateful, for his presence.

"No story tonight," I said to the boys. "I want to talk you." They were scrubbed, shining, hopeful. "It's about Daddy."

Two trusting pairs of eyes fixed on me. I patted Felix's bed. "Come and sit beside me."

Felix settled on my right, Lucas on my left. I put my arms round them and held on tight. Felix wriggled free, slid down from the bed, and fetched *The Very Hungry Caterpillar*. He held it out to me with both hands. I shook my head. "No story tonight, Felix."

"Daddy . . ." I faltered and stopped. "He . . ." I was searching for the right words, the best possible ones. I was searching for control. That I *must* exert. I was searching to help them travel through a grief-stricken future.

"Daddy . . ." Lucas was confident and giggly. "Our daddy?"

"Yes, your daddy . . ."

Felix picked up Blanky, hauled it on board, and climbed back into a position against me: a warm, surprisingly solid weight for his size.

"Daddy loved you very much," I said, and drew them closer. "And he will always be with us, but I am afraid something happened to him . . ." I found myself choking, and struggled to continue. "He got very ill, and his heart could not beat any longer, and he died. He's gone away and he won't be coming back."

Lucas burst into tears. "Daddy promised to come to the football."

I experienced an overwhelming sense of heaviness and defeat. "Lucas, Daddy can't come to the football." I took his little hand and stroked it. "He would come if he could."

"Where's he gone *to?*" Lucas's sobs were panicky.

"He's gone up into the sky. He can probably see us, and he'll think about you all the time. I'm going to take care of you, and we shall be together. But we shall think about him a lot, won't we, boys?"

Felix wriggled out of my embrace and went over to the window. "*Naughty* Daddy," he said angrily.

"Daddy's not naughty, Felix," I said. "He can't help it."

"Naughty, naughty," Felix repeated. Then he said, "There's Tigger in the road."

"Come back, Felix."

But he shook his head and remained stubbornly by the window. Lucas sighed and looked up at me. "Does that mean we'll be getting a new daddy to drive the car?"

Chapter Thirteen

Felix climbed into my bed and woke me. "Mummy. Where's Daddy?"

It was six o'clock. I had just fallen into a heavy sleep, but his question sent a shock through me. Through stiff lips, I murmured, "Do you remember we talked about it last night, Felix? Daddy's gone away where he is very happy and peaceful."

The voice in my ear was insistent and anxious. "Are you going away too?"

I reached over and wrapped him in my arms, and we raveled into a knot of limbs under the duvet. "No, I'm not."

"Promise." Felix wound his leg around my torso and pressed his head into my chest. Bolted together in that innocent, sad embrace, I pictured the river of DNA that flowed through me into him. I was him. He was Nathan. He was me. Never before had I chosen my words with such care. "I have no intention of going away, Felix. I've got you both to look after."

Felix's grip loosened. "Daddy is naughty to go away."

Nathan had had no choice. He had not wanted to go. Either of those statements would have been true. Yet even a child could spot how hopeless and insecure they made the world appear, and the point of being a parent was to persuade your children that they were safe.

After a while, Felix relaxed. His body grew heavy and his breathing regular. I lay with my arms still around him as the sounds of the day outside multiplied and I knew I had to get up and face it.

The boys and I got dressed together. "I bet I can put my trousers on quicker than you can put your socks on." I held up a red pair and a blue one.

"Quick," said Lucas, and hauled off his pajamas, revealing a bottom that had a picture of a cat on it drawn in black pen.

"What on earth have you two been doing?"

At the breakfast table, I said, "If you eat all your cereal, you can have an ice cream for supper and an extra long story at bedtime."

In that way, with stops and starts, little bribes and games, we got through that early morning and breakfast. That was how it would be for a good while: games, subterfuges, and stratagems to make the days pass.

After Eve had taken them to school, I cleared the table and tidied the kitchen. *I am a widow,* I thought, as I swished water around the sink.

As I went upstairs to make the beds, the letter box in the front door rattled. The flap was lifted and a magnified eye peered through. I recognized that eye and opened the door.

"There's a perfectly good bell," I said to Poppy's stooping figure.

"Minty." Poppy levitated upright smartly. "I wasn't sure about coming here. But Mum sent me. There are things we need to go over."

Clad from head to toe in black, her eyes red and swollen, she looked frail and devastated. Pity for her and Sam, pity for the boys, pity for myself swamped the nooks and crannies of my tired mind. "I don't know what to say, Poppy, except that I'm so sorry."

"Sorry." She experimented with the word. "I didn't see him last week as usual. I canceled because . . . well, because . . . something came up." She grimaced. "Isn't that typical of Fate, or whoever . . . just so cruel."

"Yes, it is."

Richard had been parking the car and joined us. He was dressed for the office. He gave me a quick hug. "Minty. Are you all right?"

"You'd better both come in." I stepped aside. Richard placed an arm around Poppy's waist and guided his wife inside. Poppy's eye fell on Nathan's coat, which was hanging on its peg, and she stopped in her tracks. "That's his. Oh, Dad."

Richard maneuvered Poppy past the coat and into the kitchen. "Poppy hasn't been too well since she heard the news." He eased her into a chair and brushed the hair off her forehead. "Not surprisingly." He turned to me. "I hope someone has been looking after you, Minty."

A hand squeezed my throat without compunction. The only person who was likely to take care of me was dead. "Eve and the neighbors have been very good."

Poppy's haunted gaze roved restlessly over the objects in the kitchen. "Everything will change, won't it?" She glanced at Richard. "I woke up this morning, and it seemed fine. Then it wasn't. Can you afford to stay here? You won't have to sell the house?"

"I don't know. I'll have to find out. I'm still trying to take everything in."

"Sorry," said Poppy. "That was stupid of me. Unfeeling." Her frailness was emphasized by the thin wrist that she raised to her forehead. "I'm sure Dad will have provided . . ."—there was a tiny pause—"for everyone."

Occasionally, very occasionally, during the past seven years, I had wondered if Poppy and I could skirt past Rose and become friends. Everyone benefited from an alliance within the family on which they could call at times when the chips were down. In this case, Poppy and I might have achieved something rather wonderful—a transformation where none had seemed possible.

But we had not.

"Where are the boys? How are they? At least . . . they are so young. Maybe it helps if you're that age. Maybe you don't feel . . . quite . . . in the same way, I mean."

"It's a nice theory," I said.

Richard positioned himself behind his wife and laid a hand on her shoulder. "It will take time," he said, in his practical way. "But they need normality, not you weeping over them."

"That's not fair," Poppy jerked away from him.

I seized on his lead. "The boys are at school. Their break starts on Friday. We're trying to keep the routines as usual.

They are bewildered, but okay. So far. I tried to tell them the best way I could, but I'm not sure they've taken it in. How could they? They're so little."

Poppy made an inarticulate noise and covered her eyes with both hands. Richard cleared his throat and said very nicely, "Would you like us to have them for a day or so? Poppy and I could take them for the weekend? Rose said she'd help."

I had a sudden and terrible premonition of what life would be like without them. "No, please *no* . . ." I had not intended to be so confrontational but I could not bear the idea. "They stay here. You mustn't steal them."

"Minty . . ." Poppy sat up straight. "We didn't want to steal them. We only wanted to help. We thought it might be best for them while you get on with arrangements."

Richard was appalled. "The offer wasn't meant in that way, Minty, believe me."

I felt my way into a chair. "I'm sorry. Of course you did not mean it that way. Things are a bit odd at the moment, and I'm not sure what I'm saying." Richard looked as though he might understand. "It was kind of you, but I don't think they'd want to be taken away from home by strangers."

"We're not strangers," countered Poppy. "I'm their half sister."

I licked my lips. "Rose is a stranger."

"Okay. Okay. We're not going to steal the twins. But the offer still stands, whenever you want to take it up." Poppy pushed herself awkwardly to her feet. She hesitated. "Was it . . . was it heart failure as Mum thought?"

"Probably. We won't know until after the postmortem."

"How typical." Poppy let out a passionate wail. "There was Dad just slogging on, providing for everyone. He must have been so worried, and he had no one to confide in."

"Poppy . . ." Richard sounded a warning note. "We don't know yet."

She twitched a fold of her black skirt, which had caught on the chair and said more quietly. "Now we are all saying things we don't mean. Sorry. None of us is ourselves." She crossed to the wooden dresser ranged along the wall, and ran a finger along a shelf. "He liked this, didn't he? And he loved this blue and white plate with cabbage roses. I was with him when he bought it."

"Yes, he did."

Richard interposed himself deftly between me and his wife. "I want to reiterate that if you need help with anything, Minty, you have only to ask." He shone with youth and afflu-ence. The results of an organic diet and money were evident in his skin, the crocodile watch strap, and the polished leather shoes. Once upon a time, Nathan would have shone with a similar health and energy.

Poppy turned her attention to the back garden. She went over to the window. "Poor Mum," she murmured. "She's devastated."

"And Minty is too," said Richard. If there was ever an order of honor for kind, nice husbands with powers of re-straint, Richard belonged at the head of it.

"The garden needs work." Poppy shielded her eyes against the morning sun, which was sliding toward the lilac tree. "I suppose if Dad's heart was playing up he didn't feel like gar-dening and, of course, he had no help."

There was a clatter by the front door, the hissed admonition, "That is not the action of a well-behaved person," and Paige shuffled bulkily into the kitchen holding Lara's hand and carrying the baby in a sling. "Minty, Minty, I came as soon as I could manage." She abandoned Lara. The baby bumped between us as Paige crushed her face to mine. "What can I say?" Her cool flesh introduced a note of sanity, and I had never been so glad to see anyone in my life. "I used my key to get in." She held it up. "But I see you have company. I can always come back."

Dear Paige. It must have been such an effort to get over here. "You remember Paige." I made the introductions to Richard and Poppy. "She's just had a baby. And this is Lara."

Lara was wearing a smocked blue dress and woollen cardigan. She looked cross and uncomfortable. The baby snuffled. Paige cupped a hand over his head. "Shush, Charlie," she murmured. "I'm so sorry about your father," she said to Poppy. "He was such a fine man. He will be missed."

"He was wonderful, wasn't he?" Poppy cried.

The grief in her outburst made us wince. Richard put his arm around his wife. "Perhaps we should go," he said.

Poppy ignored him. "Minty, we need to ask you something"—she shot a look at Paige—"but it's private. Family private. Some things need to be decided."

Paige took the hint. "Lara, darling, why don't we find some of Lucas and Felix's toys for you to play with?" She cocked an eyebrow in my direction, which meant call if you want reinforcements, and disappeared. "Come along, Lara," we heard her say.

Poppy took a deep breath. "About where Dad is buried.

I . . . *we* . . . feel strongly that Dad would wish to be at Altringham where he was brought up. He told Mum he would. He did. Ask her."

All this was foreign territory, and Poppy's declaration knocked the wind out my chest. "He lived in London for most of his life, Poppy. And what about the boys? They will want to visit his grave and it should be easy for them to do so."

"You *can't* want him in some grim, municipal cemetery. All that disgusting soil and traffic. I know he lived here, but he now belongs where he was brought up. Everyone does. It's a sweet churchyard, all calm and peaceful."

"No," I said. "*No*. He must be near the boys."

Poppy planted herself foursquare in front of me. "Please, Minty. I beg you. I know we don't see eye to eye, but we should be united on this . . ." She clasped her hands, and added what she obviously considered the clincher. "It would help Mum." Her chest heaved and the kitchen was filled with a cold, terrible sadness.

There was a movement behind me, and Paige came back into the kitchen. She had taken off the sling and draped a muslin square with the baby over her shoulder. "Is it okay if Lara plays with . . . ?" She abandoned pretence. "I couldn't help overhearing and I know I'm interfering," she said, "but don't you think Minty has a point? It's important for Felix and Lucas."

"Please." Poppy sounded dangerously overwrought. "I don't want to be rude to you. Please don't interfere."

"The boys would want him here," I repeated stubbornly. "*I* want him here, in London."

Poppy's pupils enlarged so violently that I thought she

was about to faint. "You never did think of anyone except yourself."

The baby shrieked. Paige ignored him and went into battle for me. "Minty has every right as Nathan's wife to decide where he's buried. I'm sure that, when you've thought about it, you will agree." It was the calm, reasonable voice she used for negotiations in the days when she led the team.

My immediate concern was not to cry. I would have died rather than show my guilt and, yes, shame. Weakness too. Poppy turned to Richard. "It's no use."

Over the head of his wife, Richard sent me a look that suggested he would deal with Poppy in private.

"Richard," I said. "I'm not being difficult for the sake of it."

"No wonder," Poppy spoke slowly and quietly. "No wonder Dad's heart wore out. It was worn out by *you*."

"That is *outrageous*," said Paige.

"I will forget you said that, Poppy." To Richard I added, "But you must both go, now."

They left behind the bitter residue of the things said and thought. Paige dumped the baby in my arms and shuffled painfully around the kitchen—"The episiotomy waltz, Minty"—and made yet another pot of tea. She wrapped my fingers around the mug and kissed me. I held on to the baby, whose tiny face was crumpled with the effort of being alive. "You know what I said about secondhand experience? Well, this isn't."

"No," said Paige. "It can't be." She sat herself down with a groan and reached for the baby. "Sorry about butting in. I phoned you and phoned you, Minty, but you never answered."

I passed a hand over my face. "There were so many calls. I couldn't cope with them."

"That's why I'm here to help."

"That's nice, Paige."

"How are you feeling?"

"My husband has died."

"Not all bad then," escaped from Paige's lips, and was followed by, "Sorry. *Unforgivable.*"

Thus it was that I found myself sitting at the kitchen table rocking with hysterical laughter at Paige's unforgivable joke. Charlie burped and regurgitated a stream of milk, and she dabbed at his mouth.

"My husband is for sale," she remarked. "Any offers?"

The post brought a copy of the postmortem. I sat at the kitchen table and deciphered it word by word . . . decoding the medical terminology in order to understand the precise nature of Nathan's heart, lungs, and brain.

The brain was fine. I could have told them that. Any fool (which included Roger) knew that. Snap, snap. The messages in that brain zipped unerringly from synapse to synapse. One of those messages had been a simple one: I must provide for my family. Another: let me get on with my job.

Nathan's lungs? For a man of his age, in excellent condition.

The arteries? If it could be put this way, they had been Nathan's Achilles' heel.

How often had I observed his outer casing? Hundreds of times. He was a man who looked good for his age. (*nb.* A label that is quite different in meaning when applied to the male.) He looked *right* in his old blue shirt at home, or on the beach, tousled and windblown. In his favorite gray office suit, he seemed substantial and capable of action. Yet as it turned out, that pleasing outer casing was host to a network of those highways and byways that had hidden treacherous blockages.

Yet as I pondered and deciphered, I saw so clearly that we are the architects of our own deaths. Nathan's brain and lungs belonged to the successful, upright man. But layers of his secret grief had been laid down in his arteries, and they killed him.

I abandoned the postmortem on the kitchen table, unlocked the door to the garden, and went out into the bright sunlight.

It was spring.

Early in our affair, during one of the lunchtime sessions at my flat, Nathan gave me a valentine. It was large, vulgar, and had a padded pink satin heart at the center (his idea of a joke). Inside he wrote: "In spring, thoughts turn to love."

"Love," he said dreamily, propped on an elbow. "I wish I could describe what it feels like . . ." With his other hand, he ran his fingers up and down my bare shoulder, a whispered caress. "I had forgotten how perfect it is."

Back in the office at Vistemax, a mini production crisis was brewing. While I was illicitly kissing her husband, Rose was snatching a sandwich lunch at her desk and dealing with it.

"You will forgive me . . ."—Nathan's finger rested on my breast—"if I'm rusty on the subject."

"Of course," I answered. Now that the sex was over, I was impatient to be back in the office to see what was going on.

He lay back on the pillows. "I feel you've rescued me, Minty. Given me back a sense of purpose."

"Do you never talk to Rose about this sort of thing?"

He grimaced. "It's easy to tell you have never been married."

"You must have done once."

"It gets buried, Minty. Under the everyday." He held up a hand and ticked off on his fingers. "Bills. Traveling to and from work. Endless discussions about the children. House maintenance."

I remember feeling outraged on Rose's behalf. That was to my credit, at least. "She only bore your children, kept house, warmed your bed, and, no doubt, sorted your socks. All to make your life easy."

"I can't deny it." Nathan pushed me down and kissed me, his mouth hot and lazy with spent passion.

Had Nathan, when he was married to me, purchased a bottle of good champagne and stolen a lunch hour with Rose? Had he drawn her down onto the blue and white quilt, kissed *her* bare shoulders and afterward, propped himself up for the delights of elbow talk? Would he have confided to his ex-wife: "Minty and I only discuss bills and house maintenance but you, you, Rose, offer me love more perfect that I imagined"?

I wish, I wish I had told Nathan then, over the padded satin heart, that I loved him, because it would have made him happy.

The lawn was ragged, and the boys had trampled the worm casts into the grass. Very soon I would have to think about mowing it, which I had never done. That had been Nathan's department. Felix's football had been abandoned by the door; I picked it up, and flakes of dried mud dusted my fingers.

I was ravenous, but food nauseated me. I choked when I bit into a piece of bread or tried a mouthful of omelette between my lips. Yet hunger was making me shaky and weak. I held up my hands and examined them. The fingers were trembling. One of my thumbnails had torn on the lock, and a tiny pearl of blood was drying on the cuticle. I sucked at it. The metallic taste made me retch.

I halted by the lilac tree—such a perfect resting point in the route around the garden. (Rose knew that.) I looked up into it. A few leaves in a bright, trashy green had shaken themselves loose. The colors hurt my eyes; the sounds and scents of new growth were unbearable.

The young and pretty, one of Rose's friends had said (and Poppy had told me) in order to comfort her when Nathan left her, could be pretty wicked. But they only got away with it for a short time.

Seven years, to be precise.

"Nathan," I murmured into that fresh, sparkling morning. "What would you want?" Do you want to lie in a peaceful churchyard under the yews? Or would you rather be where you had lived, fought, hustled, and made your children?

My eyes filled. Definitely, I would have to mow the lawn, and I hadn't a clue how to set about it. But it could not be that difficult.

Chapter Fourteen

Rose telephoned as I was planning the order of service. She asked me how I was, had I managed to sleep, then went straight to the point. "Minty, I would like to give an address at the funeral."

"Do wives give addresses?"

"I am not his wife, remember. I'm a . . . well, friend-wife."

"I thought only people who didn't care too much gave the address, otherwise you break down."

"It's my last gift to him. The children would like it."

"*Your* children."

"Nathan's children." She sounded very far away.

"Where are you?"

"Romania. A trip that had been planned for months and I couldn't get out of. But I'm cutting it short. Is it agreed? Only five minutes, but I don't trust . . ."

"Trust," my voice echoed feebly.

"Anyone else to give the real Nathan."

Was the real Nathan the man who color-coded his files? Who said: we have to be careful with money. The man who longed to put on a worn pair of jeans and battered boots and walk the cliffs above Priac Bay? Or was he the man who propped himself on his elbow and searched unsuccessfully for the words to explain how happy he felt?

"Rose. I've made a decision. Nathan will be buried in Altringham. I thought it better he be somewhere where he was known. Where he won't be alone."

"Oh, Minty," Rose was almost inaudible. "*Thank* you."

Barely a half hour later, Poppy was on the phone. She was hostile and cold and I no less so. "About the hymns, Minty. Dad's favorite was 'Immortal, Invisible.' We should start with that. He was very particular about hymns."

"Was he?"

"You wouldn't know, perhaps. You didn't need hymns when he married you. And 'Love, Divine, All Loves Excelling' to finish with."

I groped for a dim memory of various weddings I had attended with Nathan when those hymns had been sung. "I don't think he liked either of them. He thought they were boring."

But Poppy had appointed herself keeper of her father's flame, and in this matter she was not to be denied. Her voice trembled. "I think we're the ones to know what Dad liked or disliked . . ."

During the first verse of "Immortal, Invisible," Sam bent his head and wept. Jilly slid her hand unobtrusively under his elbow and pressed closer. He edged away from her and blew his nose. Jilly dropped her hand and stared straight ahead.

Across the aisle, seated on either side of me, Felix and Lucas shifted uneasily at the sight of their big brother's grief. For the hundredth time, I questioned if they should be at the service. Both had gone missing as we were due to leave Lakey Street, and after an increasingly tense search, Eve discovered them in Nathan's cupboard. I bribed them out with a bag of (normally forbidden) Tangfastics. As Felix got into the car, he asked, "If we put Daddy in the ground does that mean he will grow again?"

In the pew directly behind, elegant and somber in black, Gisela's voice was a pleasant alto, "God Only Wise." Beside her, Roger sang bass rather badly. Gisela had been as good as her word and had kept in constant touch. "Ask me anything," she said. "I'm a professional widow, I know what to do."

I held Felix's and Lucas's hands in my gloved ones and sang the hymn chosen by Rose, Sam, and Poppy. I rarely wore gloves, and the weather was warmer, but they seemed *necessary* at a funeral, as necessary as this rite of passage, and I had longed for the funeral to arrive. The dead are always with us runs the truism, and truisms have a knack of being true. Everyone is accompanied by a crocodile of ghosts, trailing fore and aft. I sensed that Nathan was hovering over us, seeking permission to leave.

The church at Altringham was as pretty and ancient as Poppy had vowed, and every pew was taken, which, considering Altringham was more than an hour's journey from London, was a tribute to Nathan. The nave was filled with the scent of narcissi and lilies that had been placed in the window niches in huge bowls. More were massed on the altar and beside the coffin, which was made of bamboo—Nathan was going to his grave with impeccable green credentials. There were two flower arrangements on top of the coffin. The first was a bouquet of pink and white camellias whose label read: "Nathan and Daddy with love." The second, white roses woven with laurel leaves and ferns, read: "From Rose, Sam, and Poppy with all our love."

The scent was dense, almost solid. I pressed my gloved fingers to my mouth. Forever after, I would associate this light, sweet, *unbearable* perfume with death.

Earlier, before the service, I left the boys in Eve's charge and sneaked into the then-empty church. The porch was cluttered with leaflets, service manuals, and postcards whose edges were curling. Have I got it right? I wanted to ask the presence in the coffin, that was not quite body and not quite spirit. Do you like the flowers? Gisela's florist had proved more than helpful. "Just leave it to me, Mrs. Lloyd," she had said. "I'll make sure I get what you and he would want."

Would the wine to be served at the funeral wake at the local hotel be drinkable, the tea and sandwiches acceptable? The rules of this ritual were as mysterious to me as those that governed my faltering marriage had been. I had a nagging feeling that a good funeral lasted longer in the memory than a wedding. If nothing else, Nathan was owed a long memory.

Hymns . . . undertakers . . . tea for the twins . . . there was a hint of hysteria as I ticked off the mental list while I walked down the aisle. There had been so many to work through, and so much advice, most of which I could not remember—except that offered by Mrs. Jenkins at the school. Glasses positioned at the end of her nose, a gesture designed to ward off too intimate a contact, she had said that Felix and Lucas should go to their father's funeral because it offered closure.

I approached the coffin, craving the moment of silence and calm in which I would try to talk to Nathan for the last time.

I planned to tell him again: *I am sorry*.

My heels clacked on the uneven tiles and a woman sitting in the front pew swiveled around. "I thought it would be you," said Rose. Her hair twisted into a chignon, she wore an exquisitely cut linen dress and jacket (French, no doubt). A bouquet of white roses, laurel, and ferns lay on her lap. She was pale but, all in all, she presented herself with distinction as the not-quite-but-almost-widow.

I slipped into the pew beside her. I raised my eyes and looked into the face that was bent toward me. Like my own skin and bones, Rose was impossible to eradicate. I could never, ever scrape her away. Nathan had lived with her first, had his first children with her, died with her. On that last day, stricken and beaten, he had fumbled his way to Rose.

She was to blame for everything and nothing.

In the window embrasures, the bowls of flowers seemed to be floating, poised on the boundaries of this world and some spectral realm. "Do you think the flowers will do? The florist was uncanny. She seemed to know," I said.

Rose hesitated. "I hope you don't mind, but I had a word with her, and told her what Nathan preferred." She touched one of the roses in the bouquet on her lap. They were creamy white, on the edge of full bloom, perfect, as flowers chosen by Rose would be. "I thought that I wouldn't be treading on your toes. You'd want what Nathan liked?"

"You should have asked me."

At that, she colored. "Perhaps, but you were busy and I know you want to keep contact between us to a minimum.

I thought you would agree that it was Nathan who was important."

We looked at each other and, for the thousandth time, I asked myself why I had chosen to use Rose, of all people, in the way that I had.

She pointed to the bouquet. "I'm going to put this on the coffin with your flowers. It's from us, the family."

"Ah . . ." The sound slid away from me.

"You can't *possibly* say no."

Anything was *possible*. "Please," I said, and gestured toward the coffin. But I had the curious sensation that my years with Nathan had disappeared pulverized in the fierce, implacable determination of his first family.

Rose got to her feet and her linen dress fell into place as it should. The heavy gold ring gleamed on her finger. She placed the flowers beside mine on the coffin and rested her hand briefly on it. "For you Nathan," she said to the coffin. "They're the best I could get."

She turned round. "Are the twins coming today?"

"Yes. I wasn't sure about subjecting them, but they are here."

"There you are." Poppy rustled up, pale and hollow eyed. "I got here early to help out." She slipped a hand under her mother's elbow and peered into her face. "Are you okay?" she inquired anxiously. "Will you get through?" Poppy wanted—*needed*—Rose to be bowed down with grief. "You're doing brilliantly, Mum. I'll look after you later."

Mother and daughter exchanged a glance of perfect understanding. Without being told, Rose knew that Poppy was terrified yet elated by the drama of her sorrow and Poppy understood that her mother's courage was stretched taut.

"Minty, I'm glad you agreed to let Dad be buried here," Poppy looked round the church. "It would have been wrong to have him elsewhere. What made you change your mind?"

Rose stroked Poppy's hand. "Shush. This is not the time."

Above in the organ loft, the organist unlocked his instrument and settled himself into place. The pipes released a series of groans and sighs, some distinctly digestive. My lips twitched.

Poppy had not finished with me. "It would have been awful if, in the future, you married again and went to live, oh, I don't know, in Spain or somewhere, and he would have been alone in London."

"Poppy," Rose was sharp. "Enough."

At that moment, I admired Poppy for her truculence and rudeness, and her fine line in insult. "Listen to me, I would *never* live in Marbella."

Organ and congregation stumbled to the end of the hymn. Out of the corner of my eye, I caught the flutter of several white handkerchiefs. In a dark suit and black tie, Roger approached the lectern. He cleared his throat. At that moment, the sun came out and a multicolored refraction of light from the window spread over the floor of the nave. "I knew Nathan for twenty years, many of them as a colleague," he began. "He was a company man, through and through. We fought many battles together, and rejoiced when we won."

Had Nathan been a company man? I supposed so. Roger smiled just enough not to fool us into levity, but to suggest the recollected joys of the companionship that he had shared with Nathan in pursuit of the company's welfare. We live a life of false smiles. It is one of the prices we pay for civilization—

bared teeth and stretched lips, unholy thoughts teeming be-hind them. I bet Roger couldn't remember anything *truly* significant about Nathan.

"Loyalty is what distinguished Nathan. He was loyal to colleagues, to his work, ultraloyal to the company."

I bit my lip and blanked out the rest of Roger's speech.

The service wore on. Richard read an extract from Walt Whitman's "Leaves of Grass." Afterward, Rose took her place at the lectern. "This may seem strange," she addressed the congregation, "but Nathan discussed his funeral with me more than once."

Rose was disingenuous. There was nothing strange about people who had lived with each for a long time, and presum-ably loved each other, discussing their finale. It was those who got stuck in the intricacies of the second act who never got round to it. For the record, Nathan and I had never touched on the subject.

There was a rustle, part embarrassment, part anticipation. The light fell over Rose. She was past coltish prettiness and she had never been sexy, but there was beauty. If a face truly mir-rored the inner being, Rose was offering hers for inspection, boldly and without pretense.

Poppy's hand flew to her mouth. Roger stared straight ahead, and Felix whimpered. I bent over him. "Listen, Felix," I whispered, "it's about Daddy."

Rose went on. "Nathan loved his family. He loved potter-ing in boats, mackerel fishing . . ." She told her story, decon-structing the bland company man whom Roger had presented. Rose's Nathan was a man who strove to think and to feel.

She could have added . . . "the Nathan who shouted out the answers to a radio quiz program, who disliked broccoli, who sat utterly still when he was thinking." She could have described Nathan's cradling one or other of the twins and his struggle to find words . . .

"He loved the poem I'm about to read. It was one of John Donne's, and Nathan felt . . . Nathan honored humor. A man of strong feelings, he sometimes found it difficult to see the funny side of things. I know he wouldn't mind me saying that, and I know he would want me to tell you that he admired people who could find humor in difficult moments." She paused and peered at the paper from which she was to read the poem. "Print's a bit small," she said, and elicited a laugh.

> Sweetest love, I do not go
> For weariness of thee,
> Nor in hope the world can show
> A fitter Love for me;
> But since that I
> Must die at last, 'tis best
> To use my self in jest.

She read it in a husky but unwavering voice. This, indeed, was her gift to Nathan, the husband who had left her for me.

Then we got to our feet and sang the hymn I was sure Nathan had hated.

The sandwiches were excellent, with just the right amount of filling and interest when chewed. The wine—Sam's choice—was also good, a fact tacitly acknowledged by the guests who were swallowing it in large quantities.

My former colleagues from Vistemax clustered round me. Rose's former colleagues clustered round her. In between, there was a no-man's-land of relatives and friends who were not quite sure to which camp they should be seen to belong. The twins veered between the two, and I lost count of how many times someone reached out and almost absently placed a hand on one or other of their heads.

A combination of shock, grief, the excellent wine—you could take your pick—loosened tongues. I negotiated past Maeve Otley with a plate of sandwiches, just as she was confiding to Carolyne Shaker, "Of course, he was a nice man but he wasn't *exactly* loyal to his family . . ."

Carolyne, dull, sweet Carolyne trussed up in a too-tight navy blue suit, replied, "Well, he was loyal in his way."

Nathan's cousin Clive collared me. "You must remember me. We met at Poppy and Richard's wedding party."

"Clive, of course." Clive-the-expert-on-wind-turbines, arguably the most boring subject on earth.

Clutching his wine, he edged closer and I noticed that his black tie was stained and his shirt was fraying at the cuff. "What did the old boy die of?" He seemed anxious and unsettled. "He wasn't . . . you know . . ." Clive tapped his nose. "Someone mentioned he was . . . er, in bed."

There and then, I abandoned Clive and made my way over to Sam. Glass in hand, he swung around. "Minty . . ." he searched for something to say. "You've done this well."

That was something. "I want to say how sorry I am." Emotions had never been Sam's strong point, and he looked uneasy. But I persisted. "He talked about you a lot. I know he wanted to talk to you about America."

Sam's grasp tightened on his glass. "Actually, I've accepted the job, and I'm off to Austin in September."

"And Jilly?"

"She hasn't made up her mind, but I'm hoping to persuade her." His gaze shifted away to his wife. Evidently some telepathy was working, for at that moment, Jilly turned round from a group that included Carolyne Shaker and Rose to look at her husband and the exchange was neither sweet nor happy.

"I'll commute for the first few months," he said. Then added miserably, "I'll miss Dad."

Many of the guests did not stay long. Those who spoke to me edged over and proffered an excuse: a meeting, a train to catch *and you know what the trains are like*. Carolyne and Peter Shaker were among the first to go. Peter held out his hand. After a second or two, I decided to take it.

"This is difficult, I know," said Peter, "but Nathan was, despite everything, a friend."

"Well, yes. A friend." My inflection of "friend" was intended to convey irony. "No doubt you have a meeting to go to."

"As a matter of fact, I do."

"A meeting that Nathan might have attended? If he hadn't been sacked?"

Carolyne flushed and stuffed a hand under her husband's elbow. On closer inspection, there were signs that Peter's elevation had had an effect. Her hair had been cut expertly and the flashy gold earrings had been replaced with diamond studs. "There's no need to be like that, Minty."

The Shakers dematerialized as Martin came up. "Must go. The car is waiting. But we will be in touch, as you know, Minty."

"There must be a fleet of company cars outside. Don't get in the wrong one."

He smiled. "It was a good service, Minty. Good for Nathan. I will remember it."

"That's what I wanted," I said.

The room emptied, leaving a whiff of tobacco smoke from a rebel smoker, spilled wine, and egg and cress sandwiches squashed onto plates. Some time ago, Eve had borne the pro-testing twins back to London, which, I promised them, would be much nicer than being bored by all the grown-ups. Now only the family and Theo, the solicitor, remained. He gestured for us to gather around. "Why don't you all sit down," he suggested.

Theo leaned back against the table on which were stacked the wine bottles and dirty glasses, and explained what was in Nathan's will. "The estate is to be divided as follows. The arrangements are quite complicated and involve the appointment of trustees. I'll come back to that in a minute. But briefly, the arrangements cover first, the house at Lakey Street and its contents, and second, Nathan's investments and cash. Minty has a life interest in the house at Lakey Street, subject to her occupying it. If she chooses to live elsewhere or if she dies, it is to be sold and the proceeds divided equally between the twins. If that happens before they are twenty-one, the trustees are to invest the money until they reach that age. The contents of the house are left to Minty absolutely, except a vase and two paintings, which Nathan specifically wanted to pass to Rose, Sam, and Poppy, plus the dining room table and chairs, and an inlaid half-moon table that he particularly wished the twins to inherit, although Minty will have the right to look after them until the twins come of age. That leaves the investments and cash. Here the trustees are instructed to realize everything and first to pay any money outstanding to Rose under the divorce arrangements, then a specified amount to Minty. The remainder is to be divided as follows: one third each is to go to Sam and Poppy, and one third to be divided between Lucas and Felix when they come of age. Until that time it will be invested by the trustees. Nathan's only other asset was his pension, and he had already made arrangements to the effect that in the event of his death, Minty would be entitled to a widow's annuity. As you will appreciate, these are quite detailed arrangements, and Nathan appointed his financial adviser and me as trustees to ensure that his instructions would be carried out."

My hands twisted in my lap. At least, I would not be destitute. But with the parceling out of his capital, Nathan had ensured that I had to go back to work. Just as I had wished.

"One final point . . ." Theo held up a hand. "There is a codicil that Nathan added a couple of months ago. It concerns the guardianship of the twins. In the event of anything happening to him and to Minty, and the twins are still under age, he wished Rose to be their guardian and hoped that Minty would agree."

"Surely he meant us?" Poppy's surprised interjection sounded very loud in the astonished silence.

Jilly leaned over and muttered in Sam's ear. "That can't be right," Sam said.

Theo shook his dark head. "No mistake."

Rose was deathly pale. "Did you know about this?" I demanded.

"No. Yes. He asked me in a roundabout fashion. I said it wasn't possible, but he insisted."

"Over my dead body."

"Don't, Minty."

"Nathan wouldn't do that," I said.

But Nathan would do that. He *had* done that.

Theo took off his glasses. "The fine details can wait for another day. If each of you would care to contact me, I will explain probate, and so on."

"Mum . . ." Poppy rushed over to Rose. "Let's not talk about anything now. Later, when we've all calmed down. When you feel better. Go and get your bag, and we'll take you home."

She pushed her mother toward the cloakroom and addressed me more or less politely. "Thank you for . . ." she seemed near breaking point, "giving him a good funeral."

Sam and Jilly were talking to Theo and comparing diaries. The waiters were moving around the room clearing up plates and tea cups. An end had been reached, and an end was in sight. "I wanted to do the best I could for your father."

This provoked a strange reaction. Poppy narrowed the shortsighted eyes. "I want you to know that your extravagance got to my father. It worried him sick."

Her cruelty acted like a lash. "Oh? And how would you know?"

"You stupid, stupid woman . . ." Poppy's self-control collapsed entirely and she began to shake. "He told me."

But of course. I pictured him talking to his daughter, she listening with her chin resting on her hands. *Minty wants a new bathroom, carpet . . . but we can't afford it.*

Seasoned poker hands play aggressively when they reckon

they hold options, and I was not going to let Poppy get away with it. "Actually, he worried about you too."

"Did he?"

"You know he did. I told him nothing, but I know he thought you were in some kind of trouble." I laid a hand on Poppy's arm. "Going off tilt? Isn't that the term for poker players when luck has packed its bag?"

Rose emerged from the cloakroom, and Poppy looked me in the eye, "Thank God we don't have to see each other again," she said.

Thank God hovered on my own lips. Once uttered, there would be a sundering, a clean one, and it would suit both of us. But as the words formed, I remembered my boys. The casual manner in which Poppy was ready to abandon them was as wounding as anything I had ever felt. They *loved* their big half sister. *Naughty, naughty* Poppy. She offered them laughter, fun, exoticism.

Poppy was their family. The family might be a nest of vipers, but the vipers were their vipers, unlike the vipers elsewhere.

I swallowed, and felt exhaustion clamp down hard. "Nathan would have wanted us to be polite, at least. And it would distress your mother."

"My mother . . ." Rose was walking toward us. "My mother is the best. *The best.*"

Theo packed up his briefcase. I gestured to the half-eaten plates of sandwiches, dirty glasses and empty wine bottles. "We're the only ones left."

Theo surveyed the empty room. "Who's taking you back to London?"

My list hadn't specified that. I had forgotten to think about it. "I don't know."

He glanced at his watch. "I'll give you a lift."

"Thank you."

And that was that. We had buried Nathan.

Chapter Fifteen

Instinct told me to dress smartly to go in to Paradox and I chose black trousers, green TSE cashmere, and Stephanie Kelian high-heeled boots, and pulled my hair into a ponytail.

At my entrance, Syriol jumped up. "We didn't expect you. Should you be here?"

Her raised voice brought Deb into reception. "Minty? How . . ." Deb had cut her hair in a different way and looked radiant. "How *are* you? We didn't think . . ."

Chris Sharpe (in total black) opened his office door and stuck out his head. "Deb, when you have a moment."

At her name, Deb gave a self-conscious little jerk of her head which made her hair swing seductively. "I'm just talking to Minty, Chris. Won't be a moment."

"Oh, Minty." Chris emerged from the office and held out his hand. "I want to say how sorry I am. We are all deeply, deeply sorry."

Deb was not to be outdone. She said in low voice. "We are all *so* upset. And those poor little boys."

Chris raised an eyebrow. "Isn't it a little soon to be in?"

I explained I wanted to talk to Barry and to check up on my projects.

"You needn't worry about them," Deb said quickly. "We have them under control."

Barry was somber but helpful. "It was good of you, Minty, to come in. We appreciate it."

I opened my diary and spread it in front of him. The pages were mostly clean and white. "I plan to take the boys away for a short break and then I need to sort out Nathan's affairs with the lawyer. If it is all right with you, I'll come back in three weeks?"

"Three weeks?" Barry twirled his mobile thoughtfully between his fingers. "Are you sure that's long enough for you to get back on your feet?"

"Best to hit the ground running." Both of us were resorting to clichés, but I had noticed that at pivotal moments, such as the giving and telling of bad news, or making sure that my career survived in the face of a stealthy takeover by predatory colleagues, they did the job.

Barry looked extra thoughtful. "Let's tease this out, Minty. I assume you still want the full-time position, but I wondered, given your new circumstances, if you shouldn't be thinking part time."

This time my answer was certified cliché free. "I can think all I like about part time, Barry, but it won't do any good. It has to be full time."

"If that's the case . . ."

"About my projects . . ."

Barry leaned over and placed a hand on my arm. "You're not to worry about them. Chris will take over. He knows your thinking. You must concentrate on getting yourself through." His voice was rough with sympathy, and his genuine concern almost masked the fact that it made no difference to him whether I was in the office or not.

"I'm afraid there's gossip," said Paige. "There always is. But . . ." She straightened up from the laundry basket. "You have to admit it's not entirely unjustified. Why *was* Nathan at Rose's flat? Gossipwise, Minty, it's the equivalent of throwing a juicy Christian to the lions."

To reward myself for struggling through a morning of paperwork and Theo, I had dispatched the twins to the park with Eve and come over to Paige's for lunch. We sat in her neat, clean-smelling kitchen with something delicious cooking in the pink Aga. The baby was sleeping upstairs. "I think Nathan went to Rose out of a kind of loyalty."

"Really?" Paige's eyes widened in disbelief.

I pressed my forefingers into the pressure points on my forehead. "Nothing more than that."

Paige was not convinced. "If you say so." She folded the sleeves of a shirt across its breast, like a figure in a church brass. "Linda should be doing this, but I've given her a day off. She doesn't know yet, but it's a bribe because I want her to help me out on the weekend. Bribes work most effectively I find, when they are *post facto*. It's too late then." She picked up a striped yellow and black outfit and inspected a tiny sleeve. "This makes Charlie look like a wasp. How is it at Lakey Street?"

"Deadly quiet."

Nathan had been dead for two weeks and the doorbell no longer rang innumerable times every morning. There were no more deliveries of flowers. The boys, Eve, and I had worked our way through soups and other offerings in unfamiliar containers that at one point clogged up the fridge.

The boys' understanding of the situation fluctuated. "Daddy's gone to a nice place," Lucas announced to Eve. But every so often, their grasp modified and slipped. Several times since Nathan's death, I had woken to discover a pair of unblinking eyes observing me, and one or the other of them burrowed like a velvety mole into the safety of my bed. They seesawed between understanding and bewilderment, and it made them ragged tempered and uncertain. "Where *is* Daddy?" Felix had demanded at breakfast.

Paige hefted the basket into the utility room and checked on the contents of the oven. "You could do with a hot meal," she said. "How does a fish stew grab you?"

I was halfway through a plateful when the storm hit me out of nowhere. Chewing on a fat, pink prawn, I felt sweat break out on the soles of my feet, and a rush of rage, the likes of which I had rarely experienced. "How dare Nathan die?" I dropped my fork and pushed the plate to one side. "I'm so *angry* with him for leaving us. What was he thinking of not seeing to his heart? Was it willfulness? Fatalism?"

"That's better," said Paige. She bent over and wiped away a drop of stew by my plate. "You have a good hate. I always tell the children it is best to get it out of the system." She became deadly serious. "I mean it. You must not bottle it all up."

Paige always favored the get-it-out-of-your-system approach. In her book, a good hate would evacuate the agony of the loss of Nathan's life and the sorrow of the what will never be.

"He *must* have thought about Felix and Lucas, and what it would mean if he wasn't here. How will they manage without him?"

If Nathan came whirling back out of the darkness and the beyond, I would say to him: "Nathan, I will never again ask for a new bathroom. I promise to work at loving you." I would even promise I did not mind that I would be damned forever by his family and friends like the Frosts and the Lockharts.

I would promise to wipe the slate clean and begin again.

I extracted a shred of shrimp shell from the fork. "How am I going to cope, you might ask? The boys, how am I going to help them? Keep them? Maintain a house?"

"Much as you're coping now, I imagine. Adapt."

"I had a dream, Paige. I had been transformed into a wise, hands-on mother, like you. The sort of mother who says on a rainy afternoon: 'Let's make a dinosaur out of a cardboard box.' Or, 'Hell, why don't we write a play about Daddy and I'll run up the costumes.' But it was only a dream."

"Eat," Paige dumped another spoonful of stew onto the plate.

I stared at the mixture of prawns and cod. My anger burned out, leaving only sadness. "Nathan wanted to humiliate me, Paige, by suggesting Rose become a guardian . . . if anything happened. How could he have done that? Gisela says he was thinking clearly. Rose is the only one with time, she's older, and she knows what she's doing. She would put the boys' interests first."

Paige considered. "Gisela's right. But, it's not going to happen. You are in fine health. Maybe, maybe, Minty, he wanted to put things right between you and Rose."

"Well, he hasn't."

Paige ate what was on her plate at top speed with the haste of the new mother. "Charlie will wake up in a minute."

On cue, a noise like a small lawnmower struggling into life drifted from the baby alarm. Paige threw down her fork, and her face lit up. "I'll fetch him."

She returned with a now roaring Charlie and sat down to feed him, supporting him with one hand. With the other, deploying an elaborate movement so that her fork did not pass over Charlie's head, she shoveled food from plate to mouth.

"How's Martin?"

"I barely see him. I booted him into the spare room, which means I have little Charlie to myself." Paige smiled down at Charlie. "Don't I? And it's delicious, isn't it, my tiny little tiger? We have a *lovely* time."

"Don't you miss the bank?" I gestured at the sterilizer, the timetable pinned to the noticeboard, the copper *batterie de cuisine*. "Figures used to be your life."

"Oh, I miss the figures," she said. "I miss their purity, but they are only part of the deal. Most of my time was spent politicking, schmoozing clients, and firefighting trouble or bad press. You could never get a run at the purity."

Whenever Paige mentioned a word like "figures" or "statistics," it was noticeable that her face was suffused with longing, as it was now. If she had been a nun, Paige would have brought the same steely concentration and ferocious will to being the perfect bride of Christ.

She shifted Charlie to the other breast and returned to the original subject. "You are going to have to sort yourself out about Rose. You mustn't let her become an obsession." She caressed Charlie's head, bent over him, and cooed, "Who's my pretty boy? Who's my good boy?" She straightened up and asked in a normal voice. "You don't really think anything was going on between them, do you?"

That question nagged away as I struggled uneasily into sleep at night and it was there when I awoke, still fatigued. Its implications swirled in my brain. "I don't know. All I know is that I don't want to have to think about her at the moment. And Nathan with his ridiculous request made sure that I have to."

"People do strange things, Minty."

I became aware of the pulse beating in my right wrist. "Yes."

"Look, it's not a problem right now." I looked skeptical and she explained patiently. "Don't mind about it."

The fingers of my left hand circled my wrist and pressed down on the errant pulse and I pushed back the thought: history repeats itself. Paige threw a muslin square over her shoulder, draped Charlie over it, and eased herself to her feet, where she performed a circular rocking movement, like some tribal elder. "Helps with the wind." Charlie obliged and, the other hand rubbing her back, Paige gyrated in the opposite direction. "I've sent out a search party for my waist, and it's still out there."

I laughed. "Presumably all your checkups have been okay?"

"Back is a bit dodgy. The ligament had gone into perma-

nent tension. And I'm not so good at sleeping. But then I anticipated not sleeping for a hundred years. Do you want to
come upstairs while I change Charlie?"

Paige was a champion mother. She was also a champion
housekeeper. Her store cupboards were immaculate and none
of her spice jars ever overran their sell-by dates. Each shelf in
the linen cupboard corresponded to a room in the house, and
the clothes in her wardrobe were color coded. You could hate
Paige, unless you loved her.

I trailed up behind her, noting that every shelf was dust
free and the curtains in the children's bedrooms had strips of
transparent cling film sewn along the bottom to preserve them.
When I passed the spare room and glanced inside, though, I
did a double take. It was awash in discarded clothes, books, a
pile of papers on the floor.

"You're looking at the mess? Martin said the deal was that,
if we had the third, which he didn't want, then he would grab
a space where he could live like a pig."

"Ah."

Paige changed and washed Charlie. For all her talk, she
was clearly tired, so I gathered up the discarded baby things
and wiped down the mat.

"You shouldn't do that," she said. "But I'm grateful."

"Have you any idea how I crave to do something ordinary?" I chucked the cotton wool into the bin.

Suddenly Paige sat down on the nursing chair. Her stomach bulged over her skirt, and her thighs had a flabby under-
done look. "What next, Minty? What are you going to do?"

"Go back to work. Keep the boys and myself."

"You wanted to go back."

"I did."

Paige pinched the flesh of one suety thigh and winced. "Well it's a beginning."

A week later, I packed shorts, T-shirts, sweaters, buckets, spades, favorite cereals, teddy bears, and alphabet spaghetti into the car, loaded Eve, a map, and the boys and drove out of London.

We were heading for Priac Bay in Cornwall. To be more specific: we were going to the cottage where Nathan and Rose had holidayed every year. I could not say it had been either an easy or a difficult decision to make, because it had not been a decision in the formal sense. I had never been to Priac Bay—I distrusted the idea of it. "For God's sake," I had protested to Paige in the past when Nathan had brought up the subject of going there. "It's where Nathan took his first family." Paige had been suitably shocked. "Is Nathan stupid? Or very, very limited in the imagination department?" Yet, in his absence, it seemed imperative to take the boys and me to a place where Nathan had been happy, so I had got on the phone and arranged it.

It was raining—a light spume—when three hundred or so murderous miles later, the car jolted down the dirt road that led to the cottage. Stupefied and bored, Felix and Lucas were silent in the back.

The world was drenched. The horizon was wiped out by mist, and the sea roared with white crests. The slate tiles on the cottage roof gleamed, there were damp patches sprouting on the gray walls, and the plants in the garden dripped.

Eve drew the sleeves of her jersey farther down her wrists. "It's cold, Minty."

I too was cold, with apprehension and tiredness. We felt worse when we discovered that two of the bedrooms under the eaves were damp, the plumbing questionable, and the nearest shops several miles away. Eve and I did our best. We made beds, unpacked, and stacked the buckets and spades in the ready position by the front door. We ate a scratch supper of beans and fried eggs, watched the rain sweep across the gray sea, and listened to the gulls.

"Daddy came here," I told the boys. "Lots. For his holidays."

"Daddy," said Felix, and his blue eyes darkened. "Daddy."

After a moment, Lucas asked, "Am I sitting in Daddy's chair?"

"It's possible. It looks as though it's been here for a long time."

Eve chased a bean around her plate.

In the morning, Eve and I led the boys down the steep path to the tiny beach. After the rain, the mud was as sticky as toffee, and the boys squealed with joy. As we slid and slithered down, moisture from the thick clumps of vegetation seeped into our clothes. The air was heavy with salt. The leaves and branches as we brushed past smelled of it and it left its residue on our lips.

Down on the beach, the tide was retreating, leaving dark patches on the stones. Gulls screamed overhead. The boys ran madly up and down, calling to each other. I sat on a rock and watched them.

My feet were wet and, under my jacket, I was shivering almost uncontrollably. Nathan had loved this place. That much I knew, but little else. I had never asked why, or which was his favorite spot, or where the best bay was to swim. I had been silent. Metaphorically, I had turned my back. "You know, Minty, you don't know me very well at all," he had once accused me.

If only I had taken the time to answer him. If only I had sat down, there and then, and said: "Let's talk, Nathan. *Tell me.*"

Finding oneself so ordinarily materialistic and without grace at the mercy of such pain, impotence, and ugliness was bewildering—it was like being dashed this way and that in a tide as strong as the one peeling back the water from the sand.

Eve beckoned to Felix. "Felix, come. There is something here." They huddled together and inspected an object in the sand. Lucas circled them. He looked cross and sang very loudly. "Look at me. Look at me."

Long ago in the Vistemax office, before the sea change had taken place in me, I told Rose, "I don't have a family. Who wants one? I don't have children. Why hang a millstone round your neck?"

Now I had a family, and the intolerable weight and size of the millstone tugged and pulled at every bone and muscle.

"Mum . . ." His white legs flashing under his green shorts, hair pushed back from his forehead by the wind, Felix trod over the shingles toward me with a goosefleshed arm outstretched. "See what I've got."

He unclasped his hand to reveal a perfect spiral shell.

After lunch of bread and cheese, the boys were chased upstairs for half an hour's quiet reading. I left Eve grimly washing up in the sink and complaining of the lack of hot water, got into the car, and went to find provisions.

The nearest supermarket was on the outskirts of Penzance. It was busy and noisy. This was a beginning (as Paige would have it) of the new economy, a different fiscal regime. I chose cut-price jam and chicken breasts, and the least expensive butter, and every store-brand that I could bear to buy.

I drove away slightly nauseated. The wind had dropped, and warmth from the sun had crept into the still air. The sea had turned into a blue, gentle wash. It was a beautiful day and, out at sea, boats of all sizes were scudding across the water.

When I got back, Eve had taken the boys down to the beach, and I could hear their shouts and cries. I unpacked slowly and awkwardly, stowing the cut-price jams, fish fingers, broccoli, and carrots, unable to shake off an overpowering, almost frightening, feeling that Nathan was in the cottage.

In the end, I snatched up my jacket and went outside. The coastal path passed directly in front of the cottage, and I headed toward the point. After a while, I increased my pace until I was almost running, my feet bouncing over the turf and stones. The sun was blinding, and the sea, shallow by the cliffs, a transparent turquoise. The seabirds wheeled and dived to the rocks. As I rounded a corner to the point, the wind hit me and I slithered to a halt.

I smelled sea and turf and the freshness of the air. I faced the bay, where water, rock, and vegetation shimmered, a mysterious and beautiful trinity. I knew that Nathan had been up there. Maybe he had stood exactly where I was now and my feet were planted in the ghostly imprint of his.

I stood and listened to the unfamiliar, wild music made by the wind and the waves. Its chords beat in my ears and unwillingly, suspiciously, then with relief, I gave myself up to it.

With that surrender, I inched closer to understanding my dead husband. I knew then why Nathan had come to Priac Bay. Why he had loved it so.

A week later, we returned to Lakey Street late in the evening, exhausted and dirty, and fell into bed.

I woke to find Lucas on my bed, wrapped in his duvet, which he must have dragged in. Reluctantly, I focused. "Hallo, sweetie. How long have you been there?"

"Ages and ages." His treble voice piped in the silence. "Why didn't you wake up, Mummy?"

"Because I was tired."

"I wanted you to wake up."

I knew Lucas was trying to ask me something but I was unsure what it was. "You'd better come in." I lifted up the edge of the duvet and Lucas, importing the morning chill, climbed in. He snuggled into me, and I smelled sand, salt, and seaweed.

I waited.

"Do you think Daddy can see us?" His voice wavered.

I squinted down at him. He stared back and he was trying so hard to be composed. "Probably." Then I collected my wits. Lucas wanted certainties. "Yes," I said.

"I can't see him." His fair, rather stubby, eyebrows twitched into the frown that was growing habitual.

I stroked the tender skin between his eyes until the frown smoothed away. "We have to believe he is there."

Lucas edged closer to me, and I slipped my arm around him. "Daddy was nice, wasn't he?"

"Very."

"Millie says her daddy is bad. He went away too. Daddies shouldn't go away."

"Sometimes they can't help it, Lukey." *Lukey* . . . that was Nathan's name for him. "Your daddy couldn't help it. You must remember that. It's different for Millie's daddy."

Lucas considered. "Millie's daddy said he couldn't help it."

I pulled Lucas as close as I possibly could. "Lukey, you must listen to what I say. Millie's daddy is different from yours. Yours would never have left you unless . . . unless he had no choice."

I was thankful that neither Poppy nor Sam could hear me.

"Will I get a new daddy?" Lucas asked.

I spooned my body round him. He was tense, and there was a lick of sweat by his hairline. Every one of his bones was so fragile, and I was shaken by terror for his safety. "No, Lucas. You only have one daddy."

Outside the bedroom, the sun made an appearance. Fastened on to me, Lucas relaxed, his breathing slowed and he tumbled into one of those instant childish sleeps.

Cautiously, I eased myself out of bed and went into the boys' room to check on Felix. He wasn't there.

Oh, my God. Where *was* Felix?

Then I spotted him at the bottom of the stairs that faced the front door, sitting bolt upright. He was dressed, sort of, in one blue sock and a T-shirt squashed over his pajama top. His treasured, tatty bit of blanket was scrunched between his knees, and he clasped his teddy bear to his chest.

He was sitting utterly still, with an air of saintlike patience and expectation, of *determination* far beyond his years.

I ran down the stairs and sat beside him, my heart fluttering with pain and anxiety. "What are you doing, Felix?" I pulled him close. "What are you doing? You gave Mummy a fright. I didn't know where you were."

At my touch, Felix stirred and seemed to return from somewhere far away. His eyes were so blue, so trusting, so bright. "I'm waiting for Daddy to show him my treasure," he said, and unfurled his hand in which lay his shell.

Chapter Sixteen

I drove myself into Nathan's study, where a pile of letters had to be read and answered.

"Dear Minty," wrote Jean, Nathan's secretary. "The shock is considerable and I keep asking myself if I could have *done* something. He was so considerate and so kind to me . . ."

Charlie from Vistemax reception wrote. "Mr. Lloyd was never too busy to say 'hallo,' unlike some. He always asked after Sheila and Jody . . ."

To my surprise, Roger had written. "Thank you for the privilege of letting me speak at the funeral. I realize what a hard decision it must have been for you. I meant every word. Nathan was a Titan, big in vision and strong in execution. He was also delightful to know."

Clive-of-the-wind-turbines chose a more direct approach. "Jolly good send-off for the old boy. Very difficult for you. Nathan and I did not always see eye to eye as he was an obstinate old buzzard, but we came from the same stock and that always sorts things out in the end . . ."

A couple of more letters were so adulatory that they were in danger of suggesting that Nathan was one of the great businessmen of our time. Another, from an old school friend, was more modest. "He was a sweet boy . . ."

"Dear Minty," said Sue Frost. "This letter could not be more difficult to write. We do not know each other, and that was of my choosing. But I thought about it and I thought you would want to know that we loved Nathan dearly . . ."

To read these letters was to shuffle a pack of cards. Nathan the businessman. Nathan the friend. Nathan the father.

Each one must be kept. I would buy a scrapbook and paste them in, and one day I would it give to the boys. Perhaps we would read them together. "This letter was from Daddy's boss . . . this one is from the lady Daddy worked with."

To my surprise, Jilly had also written. "Dear Minty. Nathan's funeral went off very well, and I know that Sam was comforted by it. Sam was going to write but he is so busy getting ready to go to the States. Frieda is flourishing, and I hope the boys are not bad. Maybe we should hook up for Christmas . . . ?"

I must have moved awkwardly, for my elbow caught the pile and caused the letters to rain onto the floor. I bent over and picked up the one written in black ink on expensive white paper.

"Dear Minty . . ." The sharp strokes of her *t*'s and *l*'s cut into the paper, and the rounded *d*'s and *n*'s seemed to cradle the words. "I am writing this after the funeral because I am at a loss. I know you will be too. You will be indescribably busy and tired at the moment, and perhaps the shock hasn't really registered. Please take care of yourself. It is important. I also want to say that sometimes you can be very angry with a person who dies. I was when, like Nathan, my father died unexpectedly. Actually, I was more than angry, I was outraged. But I want to say, anger will weaken you, Minty, as it weakened me when Nathan decided our marriage was over. I suspect you might be thinking: *how dare Nathan leave it all to me*. You might be asking yourself how you are going to cope with earning a living and keeping the children . . ."

The word "children" appeared especially black on the white paper.

"You may also be thinking as you read this that I am being indelicate and unsubtle, and interfering. But I thought I would take the risk."

Rose was inviting me to filter my grief through her. I had slept in her bed and now she was sleeping in mine. "But it won't do, Rose," I murmured into the empty study. Above all, and above everything, I owed Nathan direct, undiluted grief. That I must grant him. And I would. I did.

"Welcome back." Barry looked up from the stuffed Filofax. "We've missed you." He was wearing his leather blouson jacket, but he had added to the red kabbalah wristband a couple of others in pastel colors.

He sounded as if he meant it. A lump wedged itself in my throat, but I managed a weak wave in his direction as I disappeared into my office. In my absence, it had been swept and cleaned. Two polite mountains of paper sat on the desk.

"Hallo." Deb walked lightly into the room. "How are you?"

"I hope I'm managing."

"I'm so very sorry, Minty. It must be quite dreadful."

I managed to smile. "So dreadful that I need diversion. Please tell me what you've been doing."

She needed no second invitation. Within five minutes, I had been acquainted with every shudder and sigh that made up her affair with Chris Sharpe. He was, I was reliably informed, the most talented man since Einstein, and fantastic in the sack. Chris had such ambitions for Paradox, and vision that stretched far into the future of the industry and the changes that were likely to take place. "He says that people will compose their own television viewing programs in the not too distant future. . . ." Her voice dipped, swooped, grew dreamy as she released one detail after another. She said things like "To think I could so easily not have met him." And, "Do you think he's good looking?" Listening to the outpourings of the former cool urban hunter now girl-clearly-besotted, I was reminded that other things did exist.

"Is he nice to you, Deb?"

"Oh, sure. Sure. But he doesn't want absolute commitment at the moment. And that's how we're playing it." Deb reached over and flicked on my screen. "He's organizing new software." She fiddled with the keyboard. "It might mean that I have to look for a new job because it's not sensible for us both to work for the same setup."

Alarm bells clanged. "Hang on, Deb. Why should you leave? You like the job, and you've earned your place here." But I could see that whatever I said would make no difference. "Tell me about the projects."

A suggestion of worry traced itself across her glowing features. "That's a bit of a story. I'm afraid we had a clear out after you went off. Chris and Barry have been talking hard about trends. Reality shows, property and things. Chris thinks we will improve the margins that way. There are a couple of good ideas going through the pipeline at the moment."

"And . . . ?"

"You'll have to talk to Barry, but I have a feeling . . ." She paused, then added, "Chris feels we should not get too cultural or earnest. It brings the strike rate right down." She giggled. "Do you know what he's called the middle age proposal?"

"Tell me, Deb."

"*Finished at Forty.*"

Later on, in the editorial meeting, we discussed strike rates, and I heard myself issuing comments that made enough sense to get me through. Not that either Chris or Barry paid me much attention. They were far too busy talking to each other.

"Okay," I said, and my voice sounded rusty and foreign to me. "There's an article I read in *Harper*'s about ballerinas. One of them, Nora Pavane, is quite something, and a defender of the arts. I think we should grab her and ask her to participate in a series on dance."

Chris reflected. "Get her to front even."

"Yup," said Barry. "Sounds good."

"I'll work on the treatment and think about the format," I said. "Ed Golightly at BBC2 might be interested. He's an arts editor, and I met him at a Vistemax do. I could set up the meeting."

"Sounds good," repeated Barry.

On the way home, I sprinted into Theo's office. I wanted to talk over my financial and legal position, and he had suggested that I call in.

Theo sat me down at his desk and ordered up some tea, which arrived in a china pot. "The next few months won't be easy," he said. "Probate will take awhile and then I have to convene several meetings with the trustees to discuss the division. Meanwhile, Vistemax are honoring the severance package . . ."

I let out a sigh of relief.

"And of course there's Nathan's pension. That will be sorted out." Theo paused. "There is the question that Rose might be due a portion." With a steady hand, he poured me a second cup of tea. "Whatever you do receive won't be riches, but it will provide you with a base from which to operate. Add to that the money from your slice of the stocks and shares, and any earnings you may have, and I think you'll be all right, providing you are not extravagant. So if you did lose your job, you wouldn't be entirely destitute, and it would tide you over the worst."

I stared at my tea. "Theo, what was Nathan doing when he suggested Rose as a guardian . . . what was he thinking? He must have known how . . . difficult, impossible, that would be."

"Nathan made it clear that he wanted to put the boys' interests first. He said he had every faith you would understand."

"But I don't," I cried. "I don't. And to make it so public! He should have talked to me."

Theo witnessed many such exchanges in his office. Scenes in which outrage, betrayal, and bitterness burst through the dam of good behavior and politeness. "It's difficult to absorb, perhaps, at the moment. But things change. Why don't you drink that tea?"

Obediently, I took a sip, and Theo showed me the facts and figures of my new life.

"If you marry again or live with someone else," he said, as

I rose to take my leave, "you will be obliged to sell the house and the proceeds will be invested for the twins."

He left me to reflect that since Theo's hourly fees made anyone's eyes water, this had been a very expensive way to learn that celibacy paid.

I climbed onto a bus. At least I knew that in the coming months, I must be vigilant. Extra, extra vigilant. Those months, possibly years, would require energy and attack. At the moment, I was not sure I possessed either. What I did have was an overwhelming sense of panic. That would have to do. In fact, its blackness and sharpness would do very well.

Theo advised me to draw up a list of priorities, plus a financial timetable. "Be ruthless," he had said. "Put together all the facts and figures to see the whole picture. It will make it easier for you."

Fact: There was no one to fall back on.

Fact: I must get used to it.

Fact: A widow with two children was hampered in what she could do to survive.

Fact: After cataclysm, my mind indulged in curious illusions.

Once, early in the morning, I stumbled downstairs and there Nathan was in the kitchen making breakfast. Coffee. Bacon. Toast—all those lovely aromas. He was in his dressing gown, whistling under his breath. "Hallo," I said with a rush of pure delight. "You're up early." Without turning round, he reached back and slipped his arm around me.

Then he was gone.

Yes, my mind skittered about. Concentration lapsed and I

found it hard to read. Sleep was unpredictable, and I asked myself difficult questions. Would Nathan have known as he died what was happening to him? Had it been painful? I prayed not. But perhaps, if he had understood what was happening, he had been granted the chance during the final seconds to think *thank you for a good life.* I can't imagine what it must be like to die with the conclusion *I had an unsatisfactory, woeful, beastly life.*

Did he manage to think about any of us?

The self-help manual *After Life,* which I was now reading, said we cannot possibly comprehend death. Anything we think we know is a fantasy.

I want to know how the author knew.

Sue Frost turned up at the house. At first, I did not recognize the figure in pink cutoffs and matching loafers, for she looked older than the woman whom I had encountered in the supermarket. "Surprised?" she said.

"Well, yes. But no."

Sue held out a bunch of peonies and a couple of leaflets. "For Nathan's sake, I brought you these."

Her eyes filled and so, to my distress, did mine. "Thank you," I managed.

"We will miss him." She was weeping openly now. "We really loved him."

The tears were rolling down my cheeks and I lashed out. "But not enough to recognize me, which would have made him happy?"

Now it was Sue's turn to be surprised. "Yes, well," she wiped her cheeks with her sleeve. "We all do things we regret. The leaflets. I don't you if you know, I'm a trained counselor. In fact I run the operation. If you would like, if you feel you need help . . . if you need . . ."

"Closure," I offered.

"A listening ear . . . just ring this number."

She went away, leaving me with the leaflets.

Scenes from our married life . . . summoned to help me counter the torture of sleeplessness.

"These are for the bride." Nathan returned from his first day back at work after our honeymoon and presented me with a bouquet of such beauty that I cried out with pleasure. "This is to make up for no flowers at the wedding" . . .

"Broccoli needs butter." Nathan stared at the plate when I served him up broccoli into which I had mixed pine nuts and raisins. "Why do we have to gussy up vegetables?" "Because," I said, "it's to make sticks-in-the-mud like you sit up a little. Things are changing, including broccoli." Nathan dropped his head in his hands and groaned. "Nothing is sacred." He added. "I hate broccoli." . . .

In the bedroom, I drew the bustier out of the elegant carrier bag in which it was packed. From the bed, Nathan's eyes flicked over it. "Put it on, Minty. I want to see you in it."

I looked down at it: such a pretty, sexy thing. Into it I would insert a body altered by childbirth and pretend that it wasn't.

"Minty . . ." Nathan was impatient. "Put it on. It will be like . . . it used to be."

That was what Nathan wanted. He craved the sharp, heightened excitement of our affair, the novelty of his willing inventive mistress.

I gave a tiny sigh, and did as he asked and thus accoutred, joined my husband on the bed—but I was no longer willing or inventive for I carried a tally of the past, of routine and fatigue. No bustier would ever mask those. . . .

Oh, we're *absolutely fine,* I heard myself say into the phone to Mrs. Jenkins who had rung up to ask if I needed extra help with the boys. Or, that would be *such fun* when Millie's mother rang up to invite us to a picnic on the common, giving the impression that the boys and I were thoroughly enjoying Nathan's being dead.

I never found Nathan's diary although I searched his drawers and files. I went through the car, his pockets. I went through the bookshelves. At the finish, I was forced to concede I had lost the tussle between us. Nathan had decided to deny me the intimacies revealed on its pages and I grieved for that too.

Yet there was a curious beauty to grief, a haunting, solitary beauty that was hard to describe and more than a little alarming. It was *almost* a pleasure.

Meanwhile, I worked steadily through the letters in the study, determined to reply to them all.

When I got round to sorting out the piles of newspapers that had accumulated since Nathan's death which I had never read, I came across an ad in one of the supplements for the Shiftaka exhibition that Gisela had taken me to see. I examined the painting. A series of free brushstrokes created a forest glade, a mixture of deciduous and pine. Imposed on the mesh of foliage were the lines of trunks and branches so rigid and black they added an air of menace to what should have been a tranquil vista. I showed this to Felix, who said, "Ugh."

"Why ugh, Felix?"

"Because there are nasty things. Look, Mummy."

Felix had seen instantly that the leaves on the trees were withered, and the outcrops on the tree trunks were clumps of insects, not natural growths. Printed at the bottom of the painting was the legend: "Only beetles survive the nuclear winter . . ."

The following Saturday, I cooked sausages and mash for lunch, and the boys and I ate together. Afterward, they demanded to go into the garden and I retreated into Nathan's study. I gave it a good hard appraisal. When it came to his study, Nathan had a tendency to behave like a bear in its den. *Don't touch anything.* It was very much his room, masculine and utilitarian, cluttered with papers and now a little dusty. *Don't touch anything.*

But in getting through a situation such as this one—my personal nuclear winter—I must look over the parapet. *Good girl,* I heard Paige say.

Panting with the effort, I put my shoulder to the desk and prised it, inch by inch, from its berth. *Why did you leave us, Nathan? Why didn't you take more care? Yes, I am angry with you.* I shoved it over to the window and the chair followed. If I sat in here, I could see the garden, where the twins were chasing a squirrel.

Wrong, I thought, rubbing my shoulder. *You're wrong, Rose. Anger makes you strong.*

The study seemed bigger, and unfamiliar, a friendly area on which I would imprint what I wished. Moving the desk had let loose a snowstorm of papers: including a directory of key Vistemax employees which went straight into the bin, invitations, a timetable, and an out-of-date list of golfing fixtures at a club I had never heard of. They went into the bin too.

The doorbell rang. The silence in the house was so pleasant, rather reassuring, in fact, that I was tempted to ignore it. It rang a second time, and I went to see who it was.

Rose was on the doorstep, clasping a long brown paper package. She was wearing jeans and a short, tight jacket. She seemed strained and harassed. Instinctively I made to shut the door, but she placed a foot on the step and prevented me. "Don't, Minty."

"I'm not sure I can take this," I said, with a sour taste rising in my throat. "But thank you for your letter."

"You look awful," she peered at me. "Are you taking care of yourself? You should, you know. Have you seen the doctor?"

"There's no point, Rose. Go away and don't come back. We're not friends anymore."

"That's true." She nodded reflectively. "But you still need someone to check up on you." She added. "I know what it's like."

"Don't you think that's what makes it impossible?"

"In normal circumstances, but these aren't. So . . . here I am."

Several cars roared down the street, followed by a lumbering white van from which blared heavy rock music. Opposite, Mrs. Austen glanced up from her pots. Fork in hand, she stared openly at us.

"Be kind, if only to a dog. Is that it?"

"That's it."

The sourness turned into humiliation. "Kindness to canines apart, there must be some other reason."

She held out the package. "I think this is meant for you. I've opened it. It's from Nathan."

I examined the label. It was addressed to Minty Lloyd but the actual address was Rose's. "The wrong wife."

She smiled wryly. "Maybe Nathan had fallen into the habit of thinking of us as a composite. He always was thrifty."

I thrust the package back at her. "Go away. Don't come back."

Rose should have obeyed. Any reasonable person would have done so. A reasonable person would have seen where the line had been drawn, and that the old loyalties were finally dead.

But she was not prepared to give up. "It's a plant for the garden. He must have ordered it months ago."

"A plant? What on earth for? He rarely went into the garden."

"You know he was thinking of redoing it. In fact, he was quite excited at the idea." She pointed to the package. "It deserves a chance, don't you think?"

"Why?"

"Lots of reasons. Not least that Nathan obviously wanted a rose."

"It's a *rose*?"

"A white one."

The urge to throw back my head and laugh hysterically at this extra twist of the knife was strong. "I don't know anything about plants."

"But I do."

It was ridiculous. Nathan should have been more careful. But then, in conflating his two wives, he was making a point. Or perhaps he had reached a fork in the road where he had been too tired to consult the map. "You want to come in and plant this thing?"

"Well, yes. I don't feel we can waste it, under the circumstances."

I thought of all the reasons why I would not want Rose to come inside the house, bearing this muddled gift from Nathan.

"I haven't much time." She shifted the package to her other hand and checked her watch, a plain square Cartier that rested on a tanned wrist. "So?"

Across the road, Mrs. Austen was entranced by this drama on the doorstep. She put down her fork and wiped her hands on her blue and white apron. Any minute now, and she would cross the road and push herself onto Rose and me.

I stepped aside. "You'd better come in."

Chapter Seventeen

Rose walked into the hall and waited. Her gaze traveled over the unopened post on the table, to the moraine of shoes and jackets at the foot of the stairs and the pile of ironing on the chair.

"Don't look at how untidy it is," I said. "It's been difficult."

"Of course." Up close, Rose had as dark a pair of shadows under her eyes as I did. "Of course, you won't have been able to cope." She fixed on Nathan's coat, still on the peg. "When Nathan left, it was the same. Stuff everywhere. No sense to the day. No shape."

I bristled. "Do we need to rake over old ground?"

"There isn't any point in pretending that what happened didn't." Rose's shrug had changed. It was no longer weary and burdened, as it had been years ago, but a light and sophisticated, an almost Gallic, gesture.

I led her into the kitchen. She placed the package on the kitchen table. "You've made it nice," she said. "Different but nice." Her eyes flicked toward the door. "How are the boys? Are they in?"

Again I bristled. "They are in the garden."

Her eyes drifted past my left shoulder to the back door. "I didn't catch more than a glimpse of them at the funeral. It . . . gave me quite a shock to see how like Nathan they are. Is Felix the one with the slightly fairer hair?"

"No. That's Lucas."

"They seemed big for five-year-olds."

"They're six," I said. "They were six in March."

"Sam was nothing like Nathan until he was eighteen or so. Then he turned into Nathan's clone. I wonder if they're going to be tall like Nathan?"

"I have no idea."

If Rose imagined that she could spread her soft maternal wings over my children, she was wrong, wrong. *I could never fault her as a mother, Nathan said. Never.*

I gestured toward the kettle. "Can I make you some coffee?"

"No, thank you."

The shadows of four children fell over the ensuing hard, cold silence.

I broke it. "The twins are not your business, Rose. I don't know what Nathan was doing when he made that extraordinary . . ."—I dropped my voice—"that *senseless* request. Was he having a huge joke at our expense? If I die or end up paraplegic or mad, my children will be with *you*. What was he thinking of?"

She moved restlessly. "Don't make too big a deal of it, Minty. It's optional and not likely to happen."

"Even so," I said bitterly. "I don't want you involved with them."

"For goodness' sake!" she flashed at me. "Do you think I want to be?" She checked herself. "Sorry."

"I've realized I didn't know Nathan at all."

Rose sighed and said as if it was the most obvious thing in the world, "That's what I thought when he left. It astonished me how little I knew about someone I had lived with for so long. It happens all the time, and it's probably better that you can't pry into every nook and cranny of someone's mind."

"Sometimes, I wonder if Nathan was so bored that he dreamed up the guardian scheme because it gave him something to think about." I knew perfectly well that I was traducing him.

Rose evidently agreed. "If you think Nathan would have been so selfish . . ." She sent me a glance that suggested that no bridge would ever span far or wide enough to connect us. "He was only thinking about the twins." She tapped the package and said, without much enthusiasm, "Shall we get on with this?"

Smarting, I led her into the garden. But if I had been wrong to accuse Nathan of self-gratification, it did not mean that his motives had been entirely pure.

The twins had burrowed out of sight behind the shed. On our return from Cornwall, their heads filled with tales of pirates and rock fortresses, they had set up a camp, which, they had informed me, was very, very private.

"Where are they?" asked Rose.

I pointed to the shed. "In their headquarters. I think it's the Jedi battle command."

"Ah," said Rose. She bent down and tugged at an elderly lavender bush. "You didn't care for my garden. You never did."

Rough moss-infested grass. Shrubs that required pruning. Overgrown flowerbeds. These were the casual outrages, the result of Nathan's and my neglect. "No. I never did."

She straightened up, a sprig of lavender in her fingers. "Funny, that. I imagined that every blade of grass and leaf would be imprinted on my memory. But once you leave a place, you leave. Or rather, it leaves you."

I had devoted not inconsiderable time to imagining Rose's feelings on being banished from her garden. "You mean you *forgot* about it?"

"No, I would never forget about it." She rolled the lavender between her fingers. "It holds the early days . . . of us . . . of me. But it was no longer central . . ."

"Height, route, and rest?" I asked. "Did you build those in?"

"Height? Route . . . ?" Puzzled, she frowned. Then her brow cleared. "You're talking about the plans I sent to Nathan? Did you like them? He asked me for some ideas, and it sort of took off."

"Actually, he never mentioned them. I found them in a notebook."

"Oh." Rose flushed fiery red, and her lips tightened. "If you like, I can send you what I suggested. I have a copy."

"No," I said. *"No."*

After a moment, she added, "I don't think Nathan liked it that I didn't mind doing the plans. I had an idea that he wanted me to say that I'd have nothing to do with it. I think he was surprised that I didn't *mind*. Anyway, that was why he ordered the rose, don't you think?"

"Probably." I flapped a hand at a damaged section of the fence. "The boys. Ball games. It ought to be mended, but I was never interested in it. Nathan isn't . . . I mean, Nathan wasn't. Occasionally, he had a fit of conscience and did a bit of digging. When I moved in here, he said that it had been your thing, not his. I took the implication to be that it was not mine either."

"Poor Minty," said Rose, ultra-dry. "What a lot you had to put up with."

There was a shout from behind the shed, and Felix emerged red faced and wailing. "Mum. He hit me." He flung himself against my knees.

"Shush," I said. "He didn't mean it."

Felix wailed harder, and I shook him gently. "Shush, Felix. Say hallo to Mrs. Lloyd."

But Felix decided that he wanted a scene and upped the decibels. "Don't show me up," I whispered to him at which Felix threw himself down on the lawn and kicked his legs in the air. He looked like an angry insect. Out of the corner of my eye, I caught sight of a grinning Lucas waving a stick to which he had attached Felix's Blanky. I transferred my attention back to the insect, who was now roaring. I tapped his bottom. "Stop it," I said sternly, which had no effect.

Rose said. "Oh dear," in the amused way that onlookers have when they really want to say, "Don't you have any control over your children?" The black rage, with which I was becoming familiar, swept over me. It was an ugly emotion and I manhandled the screaming Felix upright more roughly than I should have done. "Don't you dare say *anything*, Rose."

"Why would I? It's nothing to do with me."

"You know perfectly well why you would."

She hauled a pair of gardening gloves out of her handbag. "May I take a look in the shed?"

I bent over Felix. "Why don't you show Mrs. Lloyd the shed, and I'll talk to Lucas." But Felix refused to cooperate and clung to my hand. As we passed the lilac tree, Rose paused and pulled a branch toward her for inspection. She exclaimed softly at its condition, then allowed it to snap back.

Weakened by neglect, the shed door shuddered when Rose opened it. The interior was festooned in spiders' webs. A garden fork was propped against the wall, its tines caked with earth. There was a rusty trowel, a spade, and a stack of flowerpots. A packet of fertilizer stood in a corner, so old that it had hardened into a lump. I prodded it with my foot. "Nathan always meant to take this to the council dump."

While I cornered Lucas and ordered him to return Blanky, Rose ferreted around in the shed. She emerged with the fork and a trug with a splintered handle, into which she had teased a handful of the fertilizer. "Now . . ." She catalogued the wandering lines of the lawn, the tangle of weed and grass, the un-pruned clematis. She shaded her eyes with a hand, and I knew she was peering into the past. "If I'm truthful, I didn't *want* you to be a gardener, Minty. Certainly not in my garden." Her eyes betrayed a sudden amusement. "But, I needn't have worried." She picked up the package. "Where shall I plant this rose?"

"I don't want it."

Her fingers curled round it protectively. "But Nathan sent

it. He must have been thinking of us both. It belongs here, and it matters where it's planted."

"What's the point?" I gestured at the garden. "It's not likely to flourish."

Rose hacked off the top of the package with the secateurs. "I take it you'll be living here for the time being?"

"You know as well as I do that I have to be here. Anyway, the twins' school is very close." I peered at her. "I assume you have talked to Theo all about the will?"

"Yes, I have." She was not going to pursue the subject. "If you're staying here you should think about the garden."

Felix's little fingers pressed into mine. "Rose, I don't think it is your business."

That silenced her. No doubt Rose was grateful for her little extra acquired immunity—for she had had time to get used to being without Nathan. But I had not and I was not under control. She did not challenge my rudeness, but smiled at Felix, who had raised his head. His tears had ceased, and he was studying Rose with unabashed curiosity.

Rose hunkered down to Felix's level. "We haven't really said hallo, Felix." She held out her hand. "I knew your daddy."

Felix dropped my hand. "Daddy . . ." he echoed, and favored Rose with one of his devastating wide-eyed looks that I knew of old could reduce their recipients to weak-kneed adoration. Rose's eyebrows flew up, and in the instant I could see that she had been ravished.

She swallowed. "He's so beautiful, and innocent," she murmured, and her eyes filled. "And so like . . . him. But, then, what else would you expect?"

Felix moved closer to Rose. "Why are you crying? Mummy, why's the lady crying?"

I gave him a little shove. "Go and find Lucas, Felix. I think he's in your special camp."

Felix required no further urging. He scampered around the shed and disappeared. Rose had turned away. She wiped her eyes on her sleeve, and sniffed.

"They're a little difficult at the moment. I'm feeling my way."

She did not answer. Hovering on the borderline between irritation and murderousness, I said. "Just shove the damn thing in, Rose, and go away."

"Okay. I don't want to be here any more than you want me." She began to pace up and down. "Here," she pronounced eventually. "If I plant it here you will be able to see it from the kitchen window."

The fertilizer had leaked from the trug and left a white trail over the lawn. Rose rubbed it in with her shoe and began to dig. Last night there had been drizzle, and the damp soil yielded easily to the fork.

I watched her. "When did Nathan ask for help with the garden?"

"I can't remember."

"Lots of little chats about it, then?"

A garden must have good bones, Rose would have said. Or something similar. And no doubt, Nathan had hung on her words.

"Nathan and I kept in touch. Obviously."

Did exchanging gardening notes constitute adultery? Yes, in a way—in a far more telling way than the actual *slip-slap* of flesh on flesh, and elbow talk in the panting aftermath.

Rose sieved the stones that had worked their way to the surface and evened out the perimeter of the hole she had dug. Her body was toned, and her waist defined. "This is crazy," I said at last.

She continued to dig. "No, it's not."

"I really don't want it."

Rose pulled herself upright and leaned on the fork handle. "You *should* want it."

I closed my eyes. "Were you seeing a lot of Nathan?"

Her head whipped around. "I wasn't *seeing* Nathan."

"Excuse me?"

The roots of the rose were dry and unpromising. Rose eased it into the hole, teased the roots apart, and dribbled soil onto them. "It really should have soaked for a while, but no matter." She tamped down the soil with her foot. "Perhaps you should know, Minty, but it's not possible to dismiss a marriage just like that. And believe me, I wanted to." She looked up. "Hold this steady, will you?"

I obliged. Under my fingers the rose was thorny and unyielding. "How stupid did you want me to feel, Rose? Because I felt very stupid when I realized how often Nathan was in touch with you."

"Well, now you know what I felt." Rose did not sound that interested. She slapped her gloved hands together, which made a dull, hollow sound. She began to say something, checked herself, then stepped back to survey her handiwork. "I wonder what he was thinking of when he ordered this one? It's a repeat flowerer."

I swung round on my heel and walked back into the house. Behind me, I heard the rattle of the shed door and Rose's footsteps on the patio, then her "Good-bye, twins, I hope to see you again." *She is not having my children,* I thought, bleak and unfair and sorrowing.

Rose came into the kitchen and placed the wrapping on the table. "I don't know where you put the rubbish."

"Leave it."

"Fine." There was a short pause. "I must go because I have an article to write. Deadlines." The professional female was speaking to the professional female. You see and hear the exchange everywhere. Two women lunching: one or other taps her watch and murmurs, "The meeting" or "You should see the house." Or "I want to sleep for a decade." Rose and I used to talk to each other like that.

"Go then," I said.

She shook dirt the gloves into the sink. "About the children, Minty . . ."

"*Don't* bring them into it. We're doing fine. We're coping." *Felix's little figure sitting at the foot of the stairs.* "We're doing our best. I don't need help."

Again, Rose glanced at her watch, and there was a degree of hesitancy. "Keep watering the rose for a few days . . ."

"Rose, you are not involved. Okay?"

She said softly. "Don't take it out on Nathan . . ."

"Nathan is dead," I hissed through my teeth. *"Dead."*

Across the road Mrs. Austen, who had given up hope of any further street theater from us, was loading her car with plastic bags of rubbish. A lorry was depositing a builder's skip on the opposite side of the road.

Provoked beyond endurance, I cried, "Did you plan this with Nathan in one of your cozy chats? Did he say to you, 'Minty needs help. She's not up to looking after the twins'? Which was his way of telling you I was not up to scratch."

"That's your interpretation, not mine," Rose said quietly. "I'm only a guardian if you're not around. It was a precaution, that's all."

"I wish you'd vanish," I said. "But you won't."

Rose swung round so abruptly that she dislodged a cup from the dresser, which fell to the floor. Neither of us moved to pick it up. It rolled away and came to rest by the table. "I don't know what you spend your time imagining, Minty." Her voice was flat. "But just *think* for a minute. I have tried to get rid of Nathan. After he went off with you . . . after you took him, I had to remake my life, and it was tough. I have no wish to be dragged back into his. Or yours. I don't want *anything* to do with your children."

"Then go away."

"But equally, I have no intention of vanishing, as you put it, for your convenience. I will do as I wish, when I think fit."

Angry, jangled, and edging closer to despair, I lay awake for much of the night. The first time Rose brought me back to Number 7 and introduced me to Nathan it had been a warm night. *Perfect, Minty, for dinner in the garden. Do come.* Before the introductions were completed, my disloyalty to her had already taken shape. It hadn't been difficult to effect. As the three of us discussed the nature of long-lived friendships, I looked at Nathan and widened my eyes just a fraction. That fraction was sufficient.

He said to me afterward, "I don't know what came over me, Minty. I have sometimes been tempted before, but I've never *done* anything."

In the end, we had married thinking the other had wanted the opposite of what they really did. In a rush of blood to the brain, Nathan had abandoned Rose and their life in Number 7 Lakey Street because he had developed a yen for something that was unpredictable, spontaneous, and glamorous. He wanted to try another way of living before it was too late. "Your flat is perfect," he had said, flinging himself down on the (necessarily) small double bed. "We are free of all those tedious domestic complications."

I did not tell him that he was not seeing straight. That would have embarrassed him. No one wishes to be told that they are trying fruitlessly to turn the clock back.

"You do understand?" he asked.

I stroked his face. "We're as free as birds."

I did not confess to entertaining an attractive mental picture of a woman moving around the kitchen at Number 7 . . . or a woman presiding over the dinner table . . . clean socks in the drawers, milk in the fridge, soap in the bathrooms in a house where there was plenty of space. That woman was me.

The clock said five-fifteen A.M. I ran my hand over my body, and felt my rib cage and hip bones outlined more sharply than before. My eyes stung, my head was thick and heavy. There was no more sleep to be had that night. I got out of bed, went downstairs, and let myself out into the garden.

It was chilly, and I shivered. A spot or two of rain fell onto my face as I picked my way over the lawn.

I should have been honest with Nathan and told him, *We won't be free. It isn't like that.*

His death—his untimely, stupid death—deserved to be marked by more than small eruptions of anger between Rose and me. Nathan was owed a banquet, a cinematic farewell, a clash of cymbals. I owed him an august sorrow that would cleanse spite, guilt, and disappointment.

I knew this. I knew it very well. Yet I found myself staring down at the rose. I reached over and grasped it by the stem. A thorn drove itself into the base of my thumb, and a pinprick of blood appeared. With a little gasp of pain, I pulled the rose from the earth.

Chapter Eighteen

Two months later, at three o'clock precisely, Barry, Chris, and I disgorged out of a taxi at BBC's Television center in Wood Lane. "Right," said Barry, after he had paid the (very large) taxi fare. "Now to battle."

I murmured, "All for one and one for all."

Barry murmured, "Glad you haven't lost your sense of humor, Minty."

The center had been built in the 1950s and was a maze of studios, stacked scenery, and coffee bars in odd corners. Ed Golightly's office was situated in the basement of E Block, opposite Scenery Block A. We were ushered through a half-empty production office and in a room which was furnished with a black leather sofa and chairs and overlooked the Hammersmith and City Line.

Ed was short and red-haired, a condition to which he drew attention by constantly running his hand through it. He had the world-weary expression of a man who had devoted his life to the tough business of pushing through arts programs onto the air.

He was rifling through the Paradox dossier entitled *Pointe of Departure* that I had prepared and sent in to him two weeks earlier. He did not look up. "Sit." Then, at last, "Right." He had the grace to add apologetically, "I've just gotten around to reading this."

I heard Barry click his tongue against his teeth but Chris said, "Take your time, Ed."

"Would you like me to run through?" I offered. "The idea and format is simple. A well-known ballerina will try her hand at tango, break dancing, belly dancing, and rock and roll . . ."

Ed leaned back on his chair. "Any particular ballerina in mind . . . ?"

Barry took over. "Nora Pavane. She's excited about the idea. Legs that do things you wouldn't believe."

"Very bankable. Very personable. Can talk to anyone," Chris said.

Ed grimaced. "I have a problem, a big one. As an arts editor, if I submit any idea to controller two with the word 'dance' in the title, he'll utter profanities. Or laugh. That's the way it is. Now if I said Nora had agreed to have live cosmetic surgery, no problem . . ."

Chris asked, "Do you have any budget at all?"

Ed was guarded. "A little."

At this point, I suggested, "Why don't we get Nora to meet the controller? Is there a do coming up where we could arrange it? I'm sure if he met her, he'd be charmed."

Ed seemed marginally more galvanized by the project and rifled through his diary. "He's giving a lecture at the Royal Television Society . . ."

Barry cut in. "Easy then, Ed. I know the director of the RTS. He used to work for me on the *Late, Late Show*. I'll e-mail him and get an invite for Nora. She can sit next to the controller at the dinner." He grinned at Chris and me. "That's it then, guys."

On the way home, I picked up my winter coat from the cleaners and a couple of bottles of fruit juice from the shop on the corner of Lakey Street. The wire coat hanger cut into my fingers as I walked along the street. The day had been warm and sunny. In Mrs. Austen's window box, a bright blue lobelia was blooming. It had been a successful day and I should have been feeling happy about it. Yet if anyone had wished to ask me—if Nathan had been there to congratulate me on a successful pitch—I would have replied, *You know, I don't care that much.*

Eve was washing up in the kitchen. "The boys are outside," she said. "It is so nice out there." She stacked the plates and said, "I go now," and disappeared up to her room. Her radio snapped on.

I squinted out the back door. The boys were running about in their pajamas and did not notice me. I listened to my phone messages. Poppy's breathy voice filled the kitchen. Could I ring her office? She would be there until late. Next up was Sue Frost. Had I decided about bereavement counseling? I ran myself a glass of water and drank it. If being married invaded one's privacy, it was even more so as a widow. Everyone wanted to help themselves to a bit of my predicament. Mrs. Jenkins was constantly on the phone advising me on how to handle the twins. Paige and Gisela frequently offered contradictory advice. Mrs. Austen asked me point blank if I had enough money to live on. Kate Winsom insisted that I sign up for a course of colonic irrigation. "It's so cleansing. At a time like this you can't afford to house toxins." Others demanded to know how I was managing. Without waiting for an answer, they proceeded to tell me how they would manage. I had begun to feel like a large fish in an aquarium where viewers are parked below the water level so they can enjoy uninterrupted views of the exposed underbellies. No one ever considered the shark's right to privacy. They should.

Obediently, I rang Poppy at the candle factory. "It's Minty." Since the funeral, we had met only twice, each time with the twins, and our conversations had remained within the bounds of politeness.

"Thanks for ringing," she said, more hesitant than usual. In the background, I could hear the subdued whine of a printer. "The thing is, Minty, I wanted to ask you how things were progressing with Dad's will."

Was it odd that Poppy had not talked to Theo herself? "We . . ."—I emphasized the "we"— . . . will have to wait a little longer. Theo is still waiting for probate to be granted."

She hesitated. "So we are no closer to sharing out the money?"

"Theo is doing his best."

"It takes such a *long* time." Poppy's urgent cry echoed down the phone. "Can't we hurry it up?"

"Is there some problem about the money? Theo explained it quite carefully, I thought. Have you got a complaint?"

"No, no, nothing like," she countered hastily. "I was just wondering, that's all. Theo did say that Sam and I were due our share, and I could . . . do with my mine. There are one or two things that I must . . . I would like to use it for."

"Can't Richard tide you over?"

"No." Her voice veered upward. "I mean yes. I *will* ask Richard. He's always so generous. But I don't rely on my husband." She gave a little laugh. "Well, as little as possible. Did I tell you he's been promoted again? So have I, in a modest way." The printer choked, interrupting her. "Oh God, I must go. I'm trying to print out a delivery note to go with a huge order of Christmas candles from Liberty's and the printer keeps jamming. Will you let me know as soon as possible?"

Through the open door, I caught sight of Felix sticking out his leg and Lucas go sprawling over it. I switched my gaze back to the kitchen. If Nathan was sitting at the table with me, he would say: *She's my daughter, and I must help.*

I took a deep breath. "I'm worried you're in trouble, Poppy. Would you like to talk things over sometime?"

"No . . ." and her panicky voice convinced me that I was right. "It's none of your business."

"Are you sure?"

Poppy turned hostile. "I am absolutely sure, thank you, Minty. Could we leave it now? Please."

"I'll ask Theo to get in touch with you."

I terminated the call and went to say hallo to the twins, who occupied me for the next couple of hours. But I was troubled by my conversation with Poppy.

Later, coming downstairs, my eye lit on a vase of dying irises in the hall. I carried them into the kitchen and emptied the water, which smelled disgusting. By mistake, I dropped one of the irises onto the floor and the pulpy stem left a stain on the tiles. I got down on my hands and scrubbed at it with a tissue, which disintegrated. Wearily, I got to my feet to fetch the dustpan and pain flickered in my knees. That made me smile. Nathan had married me because he thought I would make him young again. But instead I had grown older.

I scraped the rubbish into the bin and the lid banged shut.
A deep, unhealed loss held me in its tight grip.

I was woken by the sound of starlings on the stairs. I glanced
at the clock—five-thirty A.M. Groaning, I got out of bed. "And
just what are you two doing?" I demanded. The twins were
dressed and kitted up with their school rucksacks. "And what
are you carrying?"

"It's our food for the journey," Felix explained.

"Turn round." Felix did so, and I unzipped the rucksack.
Inside I found an apple and a couple of bourbon biscuits and
Blanky. The last was significant. Felix would never leave the
house without Blanky. "Did you pinch these from the tin?"

"It's for our journey," Lucas repeated.

"What journey?"

Felix tugged at my sleep suit. "A special journey, Mummy."

I sat down on the top stair. "You were running away
without telling me. I wouldn't have liked that, you know."

This worried Felix. "We're going to find Daddy," he said.

To hide the rush of sharp, hot tears, I dropped my head
into my hands. There were further starling rustles and a twin
inserted himself on either side of me. I put out my arms and
drew them close. "What am I going to do with you?" They
knew enough to know the question was rhetorical, and neither answered. "I've told you both about Daddy. He's gone to
another place where he will be perfectly at peace. But he can't
ever come back."

"Oh, yes he will," said Lucas. "When we dig him up."

I ached for their misery. I pressed them close. My sadness
was now complete, and I searched desolately for the best words,

the right thing to do. "Well . . ." I managed finally. "Why don't we think about it in bed?"

Fifteen minutes later, they were both asleep, but not before I had extracted a promise from them that they would never, ever leave the house without telling a grown-up. I lay awake, born aloft on a layer of biscuit crumbs because they had insisted on eating their provisions.

"Minty . . ." A voice called behind me as I was dashing out of Number 7 on the way to work.

It was Martin. He was in his office suit, with a briefcase and a matching overnight bag in the softest leather, the kind top executives favored. "I was hoping to catch you. I'm sorry I haven't been around, but I've been so busy. Paige tells me you're coping, but . . ." He placed a finger under my chin and tilted it up. "Bit pale, thinner, but that's to be expected."

I licked my dry lips. Almost, I had almost forgotten how to respond to human beings, let alone friends.

"I'm afraid I need to talk to you," he said.

That shook me out of my torpor. "Trouble?"

"Trouble," he conceded. "Have you got time?"

I glanced at my watch. "I'm due at a meeting in an hour." That would take up the morning. Lunchtime would be devoted to struggling uptown to buy new uniforms for the twins. In the afternoon, a final meeting was scheduled with Ed Golightly at the BBC and everyone was crossing fingers for the green light. With luck and a following wind, I would make it home to bathe the twins. "I have time."

"Coffee then?" Martin jerked a finger at the café on the corner.

We sat at a too-small table that lurched alarmingly if one

or other of us leaned on it. Martin blew into the cappuccino, and the resulting ruffle on the froth mirrored his frown. He looked worn out and angry. A dot of shaving cream nesting behind his left ear skewed his conformist, businesslike appearance.

"Martin. This looks bad."

"It is." He picked up his cup and put it down again. "Paige and I have split up," he admitted. "Or, rather, she has told me to go."

"*What?* She hasn't said anything to me."

Naturally, that was neither here nor there to Martin. He raised his eyes and looked directly into mine. "You know the expression blow in the solar plexus? It doesn't describe the half of it."

A picture of Nathan sitting in the blue chair, dead, swam into view. "Actually, I have some idea."

"Yes, of course you do. I was forgetting." He frowned and the hollows under his eyes looked alarming. This was a man who was hoping to be mistaken, who was grappling with a mystery he suspected he had no hope of solving.

"How long has it been brewing then?"

He shrugged. "Who knows what goes on in my wife's mind?"

I searched for a clue to Paige's decision. Had Martin beaten her up? Demanded that she become a sex slave? I tried the obvious line. "You can go a little mad after having a baby. I think I did. You feel so unsettled and unsure."

"*Paige?*" he said. "Never." Yet his bewilderment and hurt were so profound that I could almost touch them. "Paige feels that I don't pay enough attention to the children but apparently, I demand too much from her. She says she has enough children to look after and needs to concentrate on them. According to my wife, I get in the way."

Despite the sun warming my back, I felt chilled to the bone. "Martin, Paige *has* gone mad. Are you sure the doctor she's been going to is keeping an eye on her?"

"As far as I know, but I've been away quite a lot." He pushed aside his untouched coffee. "It's a battlefield at home, but Paige is sane and well. I've no doubt of that. Each time she gives birth she becomes . . . well, stronger and more implacable. Like Clytemnestra or whoever that dreadful woman was who killed her husband for fun."

"He had just slaughtered her daughter."

"Had he? Oh, well." He reached down for the handle of his bag. "It is perfectly correct that I don't devote every waking breath, or every sleeping one, for that matter, to the children. I leave that to Paige."

"What did you want me to do, Martin?" I put the question gently. "Do you wish me to do something? Although, I'm not sure what I could do except try to persuade Paige that's she wrong."

Martin shot me a look. "Try and persuade Paige to do anything, and you'll achieve the opposite. But could you keep an eye on her? She's not as strong as she thinks." He got wearily to his feet. "I have to go." Large and baffled, he hovered above me. "I know it's a lot to ask you, Minty, just at the moment, but if you could keep tabs on her. Sooner or later, she will come to her senses. Actually, I'm not sure I want to live with her at the moment, she's so awful." He yanked out the expanding handle of his suitcase with some force. "She should never have left the bank. That's where her energies are best deployed. Children have ruined her."

When I tackled Paige, she was unrepentant and not at all mad. "Martin does not fit in with the children," she said, as she hefted baby Charlie from one breast to the other. I noted the breast was looking less joyously abundant, and more floppy than it had been. "He's always coming home at the wrong time and wanting a meal or his shirts washed."

"Linda can do that, or some of it, surely?"

She thought about this for a while. There was an exultant expression in her eyes that I did not recognize. "He prevents me concentrating on the children."

I changed my mind. Paige was unhinged. "Have you been to the doctor lately?"

"No need." She addressed the fuzzy head of her suckling son. "Mummy's fine, isn't she? We're doing just fine."

"You should go for another checkup," I said.

There was a hum of machinery in the quiet, organized kitchen. Dishwasher. Washing machine. Upstairs my twins were being entertained grudgingly by Jackson and Lara. It was only four o'clock on a Saturday afternoon but the table was already laid for the children's six o'clock supper, and the over timer had been primed to spring into life at five-thirty.

Oddly at sea, I twisted my hands in my lap. "Obviously, I cannot occupy the high ground on broken marriages . . ."

"Obviously," said Paige rudely.

"But that's it, Paige. I can say something because I know."

"Know what?"

"How to convince yourself that what you are doing is okay."

Little Charlie thrust his head back and Paige's nipple emerged with a popping noise. "Oh, look," she exclaimed, "he's got a sore lip. Poor little boy." She nuzzled his cheek with lingering tenderness. "Mummy will make it better."

I did not often think about my mother and it is safe to say that while she was alive, my mother did not often think about me in a real, proper, motherly way. First, she was always too tired trying to earn a living after my father abandoned us. Second, she did not like me. Consequently, I lay many of life's ills at her door because, as the self-help manuals point out, it's your mother who sets the tone. When she was alive, I pretended she was dead. Then she was dead and, for a while, I pretended she wasn't.

"Listen to me . . ." Paige did not look up from Charlie. I got up and I snatched poor Charlie out of her arms. He felt bulky and compact and smelled of half-digested milk. He protested at this sudden change, but I didn't care. "You *will* listen to me. It's very easy to think oneself into rightness. 'Yes,' I used to say to myself. 'Rose is so complacent. She doesn't care about Nathan in the way he needs. She deserves to lose him. A person as careless as Rose doesn't deserve a husband like Nathan.' In the end, I felt it was almost my duty to take Nathan away."

"And you succeeded. So?"

"You're missing the point, Paige. You can reason yourself in and out of anything. That's the trouble with reason. It's flexible."

Paige stood up and held out her arms. "Give me my baby," she ordered. "He needs changing."

I clung to Charlie. "You can't honestly think that the children will be better off without Martin."

"Hark at who's talking."

"Felix and Lucas are suffering terribly."

Paige succeeded in prizing Charlie away from me. "I appreciate your concern, Minty," her face closed, "but I'd rather you didn't interfere in this one."

"Don't imagine because I've been away that I'm letting you out of my sight," Gisela said, "I want to know everything. You will hate me for being a busybody, but you'll also be grateful."

Gisela had been in the South of France for a month, and on her return, she phoned and arranged to take me out to lunch. The Vistemax car had picked me up from Paradox, a little perk that I made no effort to hide from Deb et al. Gisela was installed inside it. She was tan and fit and kissed me warmly. I kissed her back, for I had missed her.

"I hope you're demanding answers from Theo," she continued. "Unless you are stroppy, lawyers let things drift."

The car purred off in the direction of Kensington. I gave an edited rundown on the financial and legal situation, then asked, "Did anyone help you, Gisela, when you were struggling with all the details?"

She hesitated. "Sometimes. . . . Well, Marcus did. He's good on that sort of thing."

"Actually, the details aren't my main worry. It's the boys. They miss Nathan."

She glanced down at her hands, folded elegantly in her lap. "It's awful for you at the moment."

"Sometimes their sadness is almost too much to bear. They wanted to go looking for him the other day. They'd packed their bags."

A variety of expressions chased across Gisela's smooth complexion. Then she said briskly, "Bear it you must." She opened her bag and produced her diary. "Now, I need *your* advice. Or rather, I'd like to talk to you, so I'm going to offer you a bribe."

"I suppose it's about Marcus."

"In a way everything is always about Marcus. I've tried not to let it be, but it has proved impossible. He's sort of . . . always there."

"Because you want him to be," I pointed out.

"I suppose so."

The car slowed for a traffic light. The thought of the expensive food that Gisela was about to buy me made me feel a little nauseous. "Gisela, I warn you I'm not that hungry. My appetite seems to have deserted me."

"That's no surprise. Look at it this way. Many women would kill to be in that position. I want to whisk you off to Claire Manor for a couple of days' pampering. The treat's on me, you'll have to listen to my problems and you might forget yours."

I reached over and touched her elbow. "You are lovely. It would be . . ." Then I heard myself say, "But it's a bit soon for me to leave the twins. I don't think I could do it to them."

Steel crept into Gisela's limpid, sympathetic gaze. "Yes, you can, Minty."

I tried another, perfectly truthful, tack. "I can't afford it, Gisela."

"I'm paying, that's the point."

"I can't take any more time off from work, not one second. Paradox is waiting for an excuse to offload me, now that I'm a liability."

"Is that true?"

I thought of Chris Sharpe and his ambitions. "I think so. Or, rather, I don't wish to give them an opportunity to prove it."

"Of course. I see that absolutely. We'll go at a weekend."

As the car slid to a halt in front of the restaurant, she turned to me. "You are looking bad, Minty. Pale and sad. That isn't good for Paradox. You must give yourself two days off; it's the least you can do." She reached over, took my hand, and patted it. "It's a deal and I won't take no for an answer."

That night when I got ready for bed, I forced myself to conduct a mirror session. The eyes and the hair it reflected were lank and lusterless. Most of all, my eyes bothered me. They were lifeless.

Chapter Nineteen

I planned my assault on Barry carefully.

La Hacienda nightclub was two flights of steps underground and sparing on lights. Barry had taken Chris, Deb, Gabrielle Syriol, and me here to celebrate the green light for *Pointe of Departure*. Chris and Deb lounged on a sofa and Syriol was dancing solo in the gloom on a small square of dance floor. The sound level on Iggy Pop was deafening. Barry sucked at a bottle of Barcardi Breezer (reduced sugar).

I took a swig of tequila and the salt burned my lips. "Barry," I shouted. "Can I leave early a week from Friday? There's no meeting or anything, I've checked."

He removed the bottle from his mouth and shouted back. "Why?"

I edged closer and put my lips to his ear, hoping he would not get the wrong idea. "Weekend away."

"Must you?" he yelled.

I glanced round. The strobe light configured on the dance floor had turned Syriol a peculiar color. On an adjacent sofa, a couple was eating each other up. Deb was gazing into Chris's eyes, but his were fixed on Syriol. The gloom and the noise were uncomfortable, and I felt old.

"Yes, I must," I said. "But I'll be back first thing on Monday morning for the meeting with Ed."

"Mind you are," he said. "We have to keep pushing, to show that we mean business."

Eve was also agreeable. She was briefed and bribed with double pay, the meals planned. I rang Paige and begged her to act as backup. Still smarting from our previous conversation, she was not forthcoming. "Only in an emergency," she said. "Jackson has his maths coaching on Saturday mornings, and Lara has ballet all day. Sunday we're at my mother's."

The edifice of care was thus constructed. No expedition to the moon could have been planned in more detail. Meals, clothes, money. No contingencies could have been so closely considered.

I explained to the twins that I was going away for two days and two nights to a place where they made you pretty, and my promise to take them to see the dinosaurs at the Natural History Museum when I returned was written in blood.

But I was not doing it very well. Lucas jumped up and down on the spot. "Don't leave me. Don't leave me."

Patiently, I explained that Eve would be looking after them, and it was not for long. I listened to myself spell out—in soothing and placatory tones—that I would be away Friday and Saturday and be back to kiss them good night on the Sunday.

"But you're pretty already, Mummy." Felix reached for Blanky.

He had succeeded in pricking my conscience and I said,

more crossly than I intended, "I need a little rest, Felix. It's hard work looking after you two. Did you know that?"

Felix and Lucas took a simultaneous step back, exchanged some form of extraterrestrial communication—and without a word, filed out of the room.

"Twins," I called, "please come back."

They climbed the stairs, still ominously silent, and went into their bedroom. The door banged. An object was dragged across the floor and thumped against it. I went up to investigate. "Felix, let me in. . . . Lucas . . ." I rattled at the door. No answer.

I dropped to one knee, applied an eye to the keyhole, and saw the back of the painted chair wedged against the door. "Felix, Lucas . . ." I wished I sounded more certain, more like a parent in control.

For all the response I got, I might as well have been in outer space. The twins were out of my sight but there were cautious flurries of movement. The carpet pile pressed into my knee, my toes cramped as they always did in that position. In that position, I was a fool. In that position, the twins had the upper hand. As I got to my feet, a piece of paper shot under the door: "Go away, Mumy," in green crayon.

I leaned against the wall and crumpled slowly, wearily, to a sitting position. The misspelled "Mumy" was clear, accusatory, and reproaching. It cut like a knife.

This was usually the moment when I demanded, "Nathan, will you please sort this one out? The twins are naughty/revolting/obstinate/crying . . ." Looking back, I issued the challenge to him more often than I cared to admit. And imperfectly concealing his pleasure at my SOS for a firefighter, Nathan would slouch into the fray. "You all need your heads knocked together. Just be firm."

He had been fond of saying *Take no nonsense. Let them know who's leader of the pack.* Occasionally, I teased him for being pompous and—sometimes—I cried because I could not get the hang of family life. Here was the continuing conundrum. How on earth had an intelligent, capable woman like me got into such a muddle?

I looked up, fully expecting to hear Nathan's tread on the stairs, the hand on my shoulder, his voice in my ear. Then I heard myself murmur aloud, "Nathan will never have really gray hair."

But all that lay in the past.

Go away, Mummy.

At Claire Manor, I resorted to a sleeping pill and woke in an unfamiliar bed artfully draped in muslin, *à la Polonaise.* Across the room, the curtains fell expensively to the floor, and the cushion on the chair sported antique tassels.

It was the kind of room that was featured in magazines. It exuded discreet affluence and comfort, an exemplar of the bargain struck between fantasy and reality. No one could, or would, ever live in it.

Luxuriously and beautifully run as it was, Claire Manor was not an innocent place. In fact, its raison d'être was knowingness. In the bathrooms there was a battery of potions and creams which guests were invited to secret in their luggage. Their promises were wanton and enticing—if we used these potions, then dewy skin and renewed collagen were ours. They posed an interesting dilemma. There was no chance that they could deliver what they promised. But if the situation was left to nature there was absolutely no chance of achieving them either. The selection of books ranged on a shelf—*The Insightful Soul, Ten Steps to a Beautiful Body,* and *Managing Ourselves*—added to the cool, considered conspiracy.

Across the corridor that was covered in deep-pile carpet, Gisela occupied a room identical to mine—except that it was larger, had a complimentary fruit bowl, and the bathroom was draped with more towels.

No child ever set foot in Claire Manor. No child would be permitted to invade its pink, scented, draped, and hushed interiors.

I stretched out to experiment with toe aerobics, and tried to recapture the uplift of spirits I had experienced when Gisela and I had arrived in reception. "I can run amok," I confided to Gisela. "Eat pickled onions and order a BLT on room service at four in the morning." She had looked at me oddly. "Minty, this is a health farm. May I remind you that your body is a temple." In the cold light of morning, groggy with the sleeping pill, an all-too-vivid mental picture took shape. I bet Lucas and Felix were sitting up in bed and saying to Eve, "Mummy's gone too."

As we ate dinner (mung beans and onion ragout), Roger phoned Gisela twice for no good reason. Gisela listened, soothed, and apologized for the intrusion. "Roger gets agitated when I go away. He hates it." She poked at a bean. "This is a man who has run a couple of large companies and made millions . . ."

"And . . ." I prompted when she fell silent.

Gisela grasped her water glass. "That's what I want to talk to you about. But not tonight. Tomorrow."

The threat of the conversation-to-come loomed over me

as the last vestiges of sleep fell away. There was a knock at the door and a girl in a shell-pink uniform came in carrying a tray. She had thick fair hair pulled up into a ponytail and a stern expression. "Your breakfast." She placed a single cup of hot water with a slice of lemon beside the bed. "It's a beautiful day," she commented, as she pulled back the curtains and warm sunlight flooded in. "You've had your program explained to you . . ." She picked up the printout on the table and checked it. "Do you know where to go for your first appointment?" She pressed a hand on my foot under the bedclothes. It was a professional touch, designed to reassure and give the illusion of expertise. "Enjoy your day."

"My body is a temple," I muttered and sipped the hot water. On the breakfast satisfaction index, it had a ways to go.

At home, Felix would be staring glumly into his cereal bowl as he did every morning. Breakfast was not Felix's thing. "Not hungry." Lucas would have eaten his already, quickly and efficiently. They had grown cunning and wily, accomplices in deception. When he thought I wasn't looking, Felix slid his bowl to his brother. I watched for that. Nathan and I had discussed the prospect of Lucas becoming all-powerful over Felix. Nathan had scratched his head and said, without a trace of irony, "It's the law of the jungle. They will have to learn."

"That's strange," I said. "There's something odd here. Sometimes you're the toughie, and sometimes the softie."

"Times change," said Nathan.

They had. They had. Times had changed out of all recognition.

I picked up the phone and called Eve. "Everything all right?"

She sounded hoarse and tired. "I think."

"You think."

She coughed, a nasty sound. "It is alright."

Nine o'clock. Fitness class. I went through the motions. Squeeze pelvic floor (now they tell you). Control breathing. Contract sitting bones and concentrate on hip flexors. The language and commands issuing from the lips of a slender instructor in gray sweats were familiar. Their aim was unreachable perfection. That was how she made her living.

"Stretch. Flex. Bend." Along the way to this moment, I had picked up another language, now more familiar than this one, which was chock-full of commands like "Wash behind your ears" and "Just you get into the bath" and "I'll have no more nonsense." Its aim? To get through the day intact, and to end up with a pair of fed and washed boys.

Ten-thirty. I climbed (naked) into a contraption that resembled an iron boot and was encased in mud up to my neck. It was not an entirely pleasurable sensation. An hour later, I was hosed down by another honey blonde in a white uniform. She directed a stream of water onto my torso. I yelped. It was ice cold. The girl smiled encouragingly. "You're doing very well, Mrs. Lloyd." Her gaze slid over my stomach and hips.

I grabbed a towel and wrapped it round me. Used as I was to being naked at the gym, I had not until this moment appreciated how delightful and desirable modesty was.

After each procedure, the girls in charge—the white uniforms—wrote a report and slid it into the plastic folder that every client carried around.

One o'clock. Wearing dazzling white toweling dressing gowns, Gisela and I met for a lunch of French beans and walnuts in a lemon dressing. The dining room was sunny, with a view of an immaculate English garden in which delphiniums and poppies mingled with exotically shaped foliage.

"My report card?" Gisela seemed distracted. "Oh, it's fine. Except they seem to think that my diet is unbalanced, which I assured them it was *not*." She pulled herself together. "Have you rung home? All under control?"

"Eve sounded a bit strange, but so far, so good."

The dressing on the beans was extra extra tart and the inside of my mouth puckered at the first mouthful. I had never cared for lemons. A tall, tanned man at the adjacent table was gazing with unabashed horror at the plate of mung beans and tofu that had been placed in front of him. He looked across to me, and I found myself smiling in sympathy. He shook his head and smiled back.

Gisela was not enjoying her meal. Unusually, she was jumpy and unsettled. I forced down a mouthful. "I guess Marcus has issued an ultimatum."

She leaned back in her chair. "I can't argue that it's a surprise."

"He's called your bluff. Either Roger or him?"

Gisela picked up a spoon and attacked the (very) small slice of pawpaw balanced on a piece of melon. "It's very inconvenient of him to make a fuss at the moment."

"Poor Marcus."

The corners of Gisela's mouth went down. "He knew the situation."

That was irrefutable, and I pondered the logistics of Gisela's existence. Did she take Marcus as a lover all the time? Or only between husbands? Was there a code of practice for this sort of thing? The melon on my plate was frigidly cold and my teeth jumped as I bit into it. "What are you going to do?"

She tensed. "That's what I want to talk about."

"I'm touched that you wish to confide in me . . . and this is wonderful . . ."—gestured to the room—"but I wonder if I can be of any help."

"I'm surprised." She was taken aback. "You've been there. In your time you've been ruthless, and I wanted your clear head."

I absorbed this in silence. After a moment, I said, "But you knew that one fine day, you'd arrive at this point."

She sighed. "I tried not to think about it because I knew if I did, I'd lose my nerve. Even I thought how peculiar and far-fetched the setup was. Marcus accepted that I wasn't going to marry him until he began to make some money. He had other women too, and whenever I was free he was not, and vice versa. The timing was hopeless. But I always told him he was free to go, and he could have abandoned me years ago. It's only now that he's put his foot down. I never meant *not* to marry him. Things did not work out quite right."

"I don't hold any brief for Roger," I said, "but I suspect it would hurt him a lot if you left."

Gisela bit her lip. "Normally, I don't have this problem. My husbands usually die, and that's quite different."

"Quite different." The conversation was not exactly leaving a good taste in the mouth, and I applied myself to the frozen melon.

Gisela abandoned hers. "I've realized something rather dispiriting. I'm no longer a risk taker." I was about to say that I considered her to be quite the reverse when she added, "Marcus has been my life. If I say no to him I'm cutting him off forever, and I can't bear to think of that. Being married to Roger is more complicated than it ever was with Nicholas or Richmond. They left me alone, in a way that Roger doesn't."

"Are you sure he has no idea about Marcus?"

Gisela dropped her eyes to the table. "No."

The big hand of the clock over the buffet table had inched on to the hour. "Gisela, I've got an appointment with hot stones. We'll have to continue this conversation later."

Gisela consulted her file. "And I'm for the mud."

She hurried off, and as I threaded my way through the tables, the tan man looked up and said as I passed, "I ate the tofu."

"And you lived?" I murmured.

"Just."

Whoever dreamed up the hot-stones treatment knew a thing or two about the human psyche. The girl in the white coat explained that during the Middle Ages, patients were cupped with heated glasses to draw out their humors, and this was not a dissimilar process. Such a neat idea, and so suggestive. Bad temper, ill grace, and melancholy could be dispersed with a hot glass or a hot stone. So too could grief and regret, if you believed it.

I emerged with red patches imprinted on my skin and a pounding head—the toxins making their exit felt—and fell onto a massage couch.

An angel in white pressed confidently on my spine, a light, detached touch.

Behind my closed eyelids, the twins ran downstairs on a Saturday morning into the kitchen. "Daddy, what are we going to do today?"

And Nathan, biting into his toast, would say something

along the lines of, "Well, I think I'll test you on your spelling." Then, when the cry of outrage went up, "No? What a surprise. I thought you boys loved spelling. I'd better think of something else. Let me see, what about some dusting for Mummy? No . . . ?" Five minutes or so later, the twins having (unaccountably) rejected homework, housework, and gardening, Nathan played his fishes in. "Wait for it, yes, one of you is sending me a message. It says . . . I'm getting it . . . what *does* it say? Adventure playground and pizza . . . am I right?"

Very often I said, "Oh Nathan, just *tell* them."

The masseuse's fingers sought out the area of my sciatic nerve. That particular game had been played for the last time, and I was shaken by its loss. I would miss its absurdities, the crackle it imparted to a Saturday morning.

"You are very tense, Mrs. Lloyd," the girl remarked.

How many times a day did she repeat this mantra—so soothing in its understated sympathy? She was implying that those lying on her couch had the troubles of the world locked into their muscles and only she, the professional, possessed the power to help.

She cupped my head and manipulated my neck. "I think you are very stressed. I can tell from the way the muscles have clenched." The fingers dug and probed. "They are very . . . very . . ."—she paused for complete effect—"tight."

It was like being given a medal. My fatigue and stress were proof that I mattered in the outside world (all those other fatigued and stressed movers and shakers), and I merited a place on this couch. I needed her, and she required my depleted state as a reason for working. It was a tidy arrangement.

At the end of the session, she fussed over the removal of

the towels. "I'll leave you now." She stood in the doorway. "You must take care of yourself, Mrs. Lloyd."

She meant each word, and yet none of them. "Thank you."

I had just arranged myself satisfactorily beside the pool, which was a deep turquoise flanked by (fake) marble pillars when I felt a presence. It was the man from the dining room.

"Hallo."

My response was polite but not enthusiastic. "Hi."

"I could do with some company." He smiled invitingly. "I'm here on my own and finding it tough."

"Food killing you?"

He dropped into the seat beside me. "Whoever invented tofu deserves to be taken to the vet and put down."

I laughed. "You can order the nondiet diet, you know."

"I shall. Name's Alan Millett. I'm here because my family have thrown me out while they organize my birthday surprise. They don't know that I know."

"But you went along with it?"

"Why not? It's giving Sally, Joey, and Ben enormous pleasure. I agreed that I needed a bit of a break and allowed them to pack me off."

The plastic envelope fell to the ground and I bent over to pick it up. I found myself looking up at Alan Millett in the way I had looked at Nathan when Rose had taken me home to meet him. Alan Millett looked back at me. His was an open, honest regard. It said: I am a family man, and I love my family but . . . hey, you know what?

"You have interesting eyes," he said. "Has anyone ever told you so?"

Had my Pavlovian responses been blunted? Why did I not feel: this might be worth a punt? Why did I not instinctively arrange my features into invitation? I sat up straight. "Yes. My husband, in fact."

A woman at the other end of the pool stood up and peeled off her dressing gown to reveal a bright red swimsuit. She stepped lightly and confidently down the pool steps and launched herself, with a muffled gasp, toward the center.

Alan Millett tried again. "Would you like a drink? I think there is a choice of pounded wheat grass or something equally unspeakable."

"You really haven't taken to the culture."

"Not in the slightest," he said cheerfully.

"I'm with you, but please don't say anything. My friend has given me this as a present."

"That's funny," he said. "I'd have thought you'd have been all for it."

I watched the swimmer in red for a moment, then asked, "What's your birthday surprise?"

"A party, with a marquee and all the works. They must have thought I was blind. Strange markings on the lawn. A stash of candles. And most telling of all, my wife bought a bathroom scale. That means she's trying to squeeze into a new dress." He spoke affectionately.

"You'll enjoy it?"

"Sure. It's not every day you turn fifty. Why not celebrate?" He inclined slightly in my direction and raised an eyebrow. I knew that I had only to respond and opportunity would fall into my lap. Light, amusing, and with no strings. "I didn't catch your name," he added.

"I didn't say, but it's Minty."

"Unusual. And why are you here?"

"For all sorts of reasons." I got to my feet and tied my dressing-gown cord tightly round my middle. "Your family sounds very nice, and I hope your party is a success."

I left him staring thoughtfully into the pool's blue depths.

As I dressed for dinner in the luxurious room, I found myself talking to Nathan. "I was the target of a pickup today."

"And . . . ?"

"Not interested, Nathan. He was very nice, but it isn't the same."

The answer to that was indistinct.

I was frightened that I was beginning not to remember Nathan with any precision. My memories of him were already blurring and changing shape. *Was that true? Was it really like that? Did he really say that to me?*

Chapter Twenty

"Minty, you worried me last night." Gisela was blunt. "You looked terrible."

Rule number five: Apart from life or death situations, a friend's absolute duty is to lie.

"It's the toxins," I said. "They won't be told."

It was early on Sunday morning and we had escaped into the manicured manor grounds—ha-ha and borders, stone steps, and an expanse of lawn—for fresh air before the day's work. It was going to be hot, but we had caught the moment when the air and plants were fresh. It felt good to be alive.

Gisela pressed the case. "For obvious reasons, you are not at your best." She lowered her voice sympathetically, "But is anything in particular worrying you? You can tell me, you know."

"It comes and goes," I admitted. "I panic." Even to articulate the word caused the ever-more efficient black feelings to take residence in my chest. "I panic that I can't carry what I've got to carry."

Gisela, the adventurer and realist, understood perfectly. "You've got enough money, I take it? The payout?" The insider who would be privy to the exact sum of the Vistemax severance package (courtesy of pillow talk) but could not admit it, she spoke with extreme delicacy.

"Let's put it this way, I need my job for the time being."

She regarded me shrewdly. "Sometimes we get what we want."

"I didn't want Nathan *dead*."

"I meant, you wanted a serious job. And at least you know what you have to do. There's a lot to be said for that." She kidnapped my arm. "No feeling sorry for yourself. Understand? It's the resort of the stupid. And don't think, Minty."

Between not thinking and not feeling sorry for myself, there would not be much space. But Gisela had a point. Setting stern standards to curb internal wails was sensible and life-preserving.

She picked her way down the path that ran alongside a herbaceous border and stopped by a plant blooming in a bright blue cloud. "Marcus was right to say that enough was enough, but I wish he hadn't. Things were fine as they were."

The bees were banqueting on this plant, and I bent down and broke off a sprig. Its smell was sharp and vaguely familiar, and I tucked it into my pocket.

"Fine for you, perhaps but Marcus clearly has another point of view."

"That's what I mean about not thinking, Minty. It weakens one's position."

It struck me then that Gisela and Roger made a perfect pair. Had he but known it, Marcus, with his hopeless romantic notions about his *dame lointaine,* had lost out a long time ago. "Marcus has had a rough deal."

An unseen string jerked Gisela round to face me. "What I can't make Marcus understand is that living with a person you love is not necessarily the best thing."

I glanced back at the venerable gray-stone manor, every window polished, every blade of grass trimmed. It was expensive, exclusive, and out of reach for most. "So that's it," I said, tumbling to the whole picture at last. "You don't want to lose all this. It's too risky. Poor Marcus."

Lymphatic drainage consisted of someone's passing their fingers over my face and neck with fluttering movements. It was not unpleasant. In fact, it was quite the opposite, and I felt myself slip into drowsiness.

The fingers fluttered and stroked . . . birds wheeling south . . . the beating of a moth's wings at dusk . . . little slaps of the sea on the shore.

Definitely, I was trying not to think.

Little slaps of sea . . . like the sea at Priac Bay that Rose had described so well that day . . . the day Nathan had died in her flat . . . to which I had taken the boys.

It was a tiny bay, she had said. (She was right and the boys had loved it.) The coastal path ran along the cliff where there were always walkers tramping. Correct. Thrift grew in clumps, sea grass, and, at the right time of year, daisies. The sea can be many things, Rose said, but she loved it best when it was flat and it was possible to peer down through its turquoise shimmer to hidden rocks and seaweed. From the coast guard's cottage it was possible to look out over the rocks where, centuries ago, wreckers plundered stricken vessels. A path was cut into the cliff where the pack animals had waited as the looters scrambled up with their booty.

After a while, the fingers began a sweep across my neck. "You'll feel drowsy for the rest of the day," the girl informed me. "You must allow yourself to give in to it."

As I dressed, yesterday's headache stole back. I checked my watch. Eleven o'clock. The day stretched out in a beautifully solipsistic shape. It would be the last one like it for a long time. That much I was sure of.

I made my way out of the Beauty Suite (all pink swags and niches where potions were arranged in tiers to be worshipped), and my mobile rang. I waited until it had rung six or seven times before I answered it.

"Mrs. Lloyd . . ." Eve sounded hoarse and frantic. "I no well. I ill."

I sat down on one of the chairs in the corridor—left, no doubt, to aid those weakened by the pursuit of beauty. "What sort of ill, Eve?"

"I can't breathe . . ."

"Where are you?"

"In bed."

"The twins where are *they*?"

"At Mrs. Paige's." I heard her choke and the phone was tossed around. The choking sounded serious.

"Eve . . . Eve . . . can you hear me?" A nasty silence. "Listen, Eve. I'm coming home now."

Gisela understood and did not understand. "I suppose you must go." Her tone implied that she could not conceive why the au pair's illness could not be dealt with by someone else. "It's only until tonight."

"I know. I'm so sorry."

I was fully dressed, with my packed bag at my feet in reception. There were two flower arrangements in pastel colors,
a portrait of a girl on horseback in a tight green costume, and
three receptionists with immaculate complexions. "I can't thank
you enough for your generosity, but I need to go back. If Eve
is really ill, I must organize cover for work tomorrow."

Gisela tensed impatiently. "Oh, well." She was cross because her present to me had been spoiled and because she needed
to talk to me further.

"Let me know about Marcus."

She took a step back. "Of course."

I picked up my bag and heard myself say, "You will think
about Roger?" Although why I should care about the man who
sacked Nathan was a mystery.

She flung me a savage look. "Don't worry about him. He
gets exactly his side of the bargain."

On the way back in the train, I stared out of the window
at the speeding landscape and remembered the Nathan who,
having left Rose, came to me alight with fervor. "I've done it,
Minty." He kissed my arm all the way up its length. "I've left
Rose. And it's all going to be quite different."

The discrepancy between his excited words and what we
were alarmed me. This man had graying hair, a knee joint that
ached, and grown-up children. I fancied the Lexus, his credit
card, and the nice house.

But the curious thing was . . . the really, truly curious
thing . . . I had believed Nathan.

Eve was curled into a fetal position in her bed. The window
was closed, and the room was stuffy and smelled of illness.

There were a couple of glasses, a half-drunk mug of tea, and a packet of aspirin by the bed.

It took only one look to conclude that the situation had progressed way beyond aspirins. Within fifteen minutes, I had bundled her into the car and driven her to the nearest emergency room.

Three unpleasant hours later, during which we had witnessed a drunken fight, a screaming girl put into handcuffs, and a man covered with blood begging for help, a doctor announced "pneumonia" over the flushed, almost comatose, Eve, with a veiled suggestion that it was my fault. He explained that Eve required a couple of days in the hospital to stabilize her, then a period of careful nursing. Again, I caught a hint that it was up to me to make up for deficiencies in my duty of care.

I left the hospital, furious with him, with Eve, with myself, with everything.

Paige delivered the boys back to me. When I answered the door at Number 7, the twins, who had not been expecting me, let out a collective shriek and windmilled at high speed into my stomach. "Careful, you two."

"You smell funny," said Lucas, sniffing my arm, which, only this morning, had been so carefully anointed by the handmaidens at Claire Manor.

"Don't you like it? It has roses and thyme in it."

"Dis . . . gus . . . ting."

Paige brushed aside my profuse thanks and declined to come in. There was no mistaking the new coolness between us. "How is everything?" I probed gingerly, but she was not having any of it.

"Before you ask, I can't help out tomorrow."

"Ah."

Paige shook her head. "Can't be done. Linda has a day off, and I'm busy with the children. Sorry." She softened. "Why don't you try Kate Winsom or Mary Teight?"

She left with my thanks ringing in her ears. I hit the phone.

Kate Winsom's son was going to tea with another boy after school. "I'm so sorry I can't help, particularly as . . ." she left me to conjecture the precise nature of her regret at my widowhood. Mary Teight had arranged to take her daughter to the doctor. Millie's mother, Tessa, was contrite. "Oh, Minty, I'm so sorry but Millie is staying with her father tomorrow. Why don't you ring an agency?"

"I would," I pointed out, "but today is Sunday."

"Can't you take the day off?"

After Tessa my list of contacts ran out. I knew no one else except for Sue Frost, who did not count, and I had no intention of being counseled on child care. This state of affairs reinforced my sense of isolation.

While the twins ate baked beans on toast, I paced up and down the kitchen, recalling Chris Sharpe's hard, hazel gaze that would not soften a jot if I rang up and said that my child-care arrangements had crashed. From Barry's point of view that eventuality came under "liability" and "not on top of the job."

Gisela rang to check that I had made it back home and to tell me about the marvelous facial I had missed. "They used mud imported from the Dead Sea. . . . Have you sorted things out? What are you going to do?"

"I don't know," I replied truthfully.

She *tsked tsked*. "It can't be that difficult, surely?"

There spoke the childless woman. "Gisela, I'm sorry we

didn't have time to talk things over further. Have you made your decision?"

"I don't know," she said. "I really don't know."

"There's an awful lot of not knowing about," I said.

The twins retreated to the floor and began to wrestle like puppies, my return having made them feel safe enough to lapse into boisterousness. Even so, now and then, one or the other would bound up and touch base with my arm, knee, or face.

I fought not to panic. I fought not to hate Nathan for leaving me in the lurch. I fought to reclaim the clear, hard sight of my former life that would urge me to ring up an agency first thing in the morning and employ *anyone* who was available.

The boys' noise level rose. "Mum," Lucas shrieked, and I found myself warding off a serious head butt.

"You mustn't do that, Lucas, you might hurt someone."

I was not sure I could dump them on a strange agency person.

"Mum . . ." said Lucas, "Dad says . . ."

There was a sudden, wrenching silence. I knelt down and drew my boys close. Their heads nested into my shoulders, and their little bodies sank against mine. I murmured. "Yes, Lukey. What did Dad say . . . ?"

A strange agency person might take against Lucas's head butting. Or Felix's sudden silences. An agency person might handle them roughly, or feed them eggs, which they hated. An agency person would not understand that they ached for their father.

"Dad says . . ." echoed Felix, the eyelashes around his big eyes resembling wet feathers. I looked into their blue depths, which seemed to contain so much more knowledge than his years allowed. I turned to Lucas. "What does Dad say . . . ?"

Lucas stared at me, blankly. Then he shook his head. "Dunnow . . ." he muttered and launched himself across me to hit Felix. There was a shriek as Felix was felled.

I allowed them to fight. Fighting gave them relief, the consolation of thumps, and I looked at the clock on the wall. Never had the numerals on it appeared so black and precisely etched. Sunday . . . Sunday . . . Time was running out.

My mind clicked into overdrive. One scenario in particular sounded a reveille to the black feelings.

"Sorry," Barry would say when I rang to tell him I could not make the meeting on Monday. "I'm not sure this arrangement is working." I pictured him spreading his hands and the wristbands rippling. "We need someone we can rely on, Minty. It doesn't look like you at the moment."

The mark of a civilized man (the civilized woman was not included) is to be able to hold on to contrary propositions in the head at the same time. Nathan . . . was dead. His children lived.

An idea took shape. *Listen,* it insisted as I dismissed it. I studied my fingers. *Think about it.*

The decibels ascended to a dangerous level and I set about prizing the boys apart. Felix rolled over and bit my hand hard. I snatched it back. "*Don't* do that." He stiffened and rolled away. I crouched down beside him. "Felix, you never, *never* bite people. Have you listened to Mummy? I am trying to teach you something important."

There are many ways in which to tackle survival. "We will now discuss in a little more detail the struggle for existence," Charles Darwin wrote in *The Origin of Species*.

Once, after we had been married for a little while, in middle of making frantic love, Nathan halted. "I have never desired anyone like I desire you, Minty," he confessed in a thrillingly passionate way. He did not say, "I have never loved anyone like I love you," as he had done once before. I had noted the omission but concluded that desire would do fine.

It had and it hadn't. Desire was good and it got us through some bumpy times. The absence of mutual love was another matter—and I chose to ignore it.

Again I picked up the phone and with a tearful Felix clinging to my legs, dialed the innocent configuration of numbers. It was answered quickly.

"Is that Rose?"

"Minty."

"I know I am disturbing you . . ." The pause confirmed this diagnosis. "I want to ask . . . I *have* to ask you a favor." Rose was not going to help me out and another long pause ensued. "Please . . ." That "please" hurt, and I felt a flush creep up my cheeks.

"I'm not sure, Minty. What is it?"

"You have no reason to help me. Except for the boys. There's a problem."

"Why me?"

"Because Nathan thought you should be involved. I'm doing what he . . . suggested."

"The boys," she cut in. "Are they okay? Are they ill?"

Confessing my predicament punctured the angry boil, and I found myself sobbing hysterically down the phone. "I need someone to look after them tomorrow. I can't miss work, and Eve is ill in hospital. After tomorrow, I can arrange cover."

Sam delivered Rose to the doorstep of Number 7 at eight o'clock precisely. "He was staying with me and gave me a lift," she said.

Sam hovered on the door step. "Hallo, Minty. I can't stop."

"Congratulations again on the job," I had the presence of mind to say.

He frowned. "Bit of a poisoned chalice," he said. "I'm up here to sort out the final details."

"Has Jilly decided to go with you?"

"I'm working on it."

I thought of Poppy's request. "Is there anything I can do?"

"Actually, no. We'll sort something out." He smiled to take away the sting. "Nice of you to offer."

The ranks had been closed, and I took the hint. I did not feel I could do or say any more—which constituted a tick for failure and a cross for endeavor. Sam said good-bye, and I led Rose into the house.

She followed me into the kitchen and placed her handbag on the table. She was dressed in jeans, a skinny T-shirt, and a black cardigan that made her arms appear even more slender than they were. "I'm not sure what to say, Minty. I'm not sure why I'm here." She had her back to me. "But I think I'm doing this for Nathan."

The boys were summoned from their bedroom, which they were in the process of dismantling. Lucas was wearing his green trousers, and Felix his blue socks. "Boys. You remember Mrs. Lloyd."

"Just Rose." She held out a hand. "Hallo, Lucas? Good, I guessed right this time. Hallo, Felix."

A burst of wind rattled at the cat flap. *Clunk.* It was, as always, an eerie sound. A shadow passed over Rose's face.

"That's the cat's door," said Felix.

"Do you have a cat?" asked Rose.

"Mummy says no."

The twins maintained their distance and confined themselves to scrutinizing her. They conveyed boredom, rejection, and more than a little weariness. "This is Sam and Poppy's mummy," I explained again. "She's come to look after you today. You remember she knew Daddy."

Felix hunched his shoulders. "Why can't you look after us, Mummy?"

"Because I have to work. Otherwise the office will not be pleased with me."

"He sounds *just* like Sam," said Rose.

Again, the rattle of the cat flap. It reminded me of the ordinariness of life, the inexorability of each day with its small routines. Rose had declared how wonderful and diverse she had discovered the world to be. For me it was different. The *click clack* of the redundant cat flap only anchored me to the shifting, echoing landscape of loss, calamity, and grief through which I was journeying.

Rose busied herself with her bag. "I imagine I was the last resort?"

"If I'm absolutely truthful, yes."

That made her smile, and the atmosphere lightened. "You must have hated ringing me."

"Yes. And if you're truthful, you hated coming here."

"Well, that's clear, then." She produced a packet of colored markers and two pads of paper from her bag. "Felix and Lucas. Shall we see who can draw the best cat? Then I'll take you to school."

Felix had been busy working things out. "You are Poppy's mummy? Like Mummy is our mummy?"

Rose nodded. "Exactly the same."

Lucas seized a pad and a green pen. Felix held back. "These are my blue socks," he informed Rose and stuck out a leg. "Daddy liked them."

Rose looked steadily at the sock and the small foot inside it, and tears spilled down her cheeks.

I turned away.

As I left the house, I glanced into the kitchen. Rose was leaning against the table, one leg swinging and the twins were drawing. Rose was saying, "Did you know that your daddy loved swimming? Once he swam so far out to sea that we had to go and get the boat to rescue him."

In a manner of speaking, I was gazing into the heart of my darkness, however brightly lit it was.

"Good-bye, boys," I hitched my bag onto my shoulders. "Be good."

They barely glanced up. "Bye, Mummy."

At six o'clock on the dot I let myself noiselessly into the house. Rose was ensconced with a boy on either side on the sofa in the sitting room. She had her arms around them. "Then your Daddy got hold of the fishing line and pulled. He pulled and pulled . . ."

So intent were all three that they did not hear me come in. Rose lifted a hand and absently stroked Felix's hair. He snuggled farther into her.

"Do you know what was on that fishing line?"

"The biggest fish." Lucas held up his hands. "As big as this . . . ?"

"No."

"A dead man?" Felix's eyes widened in alarm.

"No."

"A whale?"

"I'll tell you," said Rose. "It was a suitcase with R. PEARSON painted on it. Inside it there were tins and tins of peas."

I scuffed a foot on the carpet and Rose turned. Our eyes locked and her arms tightened possessively around the twins. "Look who's here . . ."

"Yes," I said. "It's your mummy."

Rose stood in the hall with her bag over her shoulder. "Good-bye, boys. See you soon." She handed over the front-door key. "They were no trouble." One thing was absolutely settled with regard to the situation between Rose and me. I was in the wrong, the black-hearted villain of the piece, and Rose was the person to whom wrong had been done. Which left me—if one accepted the determinist argument—free to continue to err. "Nathan loved you," I said. "He always did."

Suddenly Rose laughed. "Oh my God, the tables *have* turned." She choked a little. "Don't you see how funny it is?" She held out a hand, a wooing gesture. "Don't you?"

I could not bring myself to take her hand. "I'll work on it."

Rose sobered up, and her face now registered sadness and regret. "I think Nathan did love me, despite everything."

"But you," I pushed it further. "Did you . . . ?"

Rose moved toward the door. "I've done you a favor today, Minty. Let's leave it at that." She placed a hand on the catch. "For the record, Nathan, having done it once, would never have left the twins. And he would never have regretted having them. Ever."

"That was not my question."

"But it's my answer," she said gently. She tugged at the door latch.

"Here, let me," I pulled the handle. "The lock is tricky."

"Oh, I know *that*," said Rose. "It always was."

Chapter Twenty-one

Before twenty-four hours had elapsed Poppy was on the phone. "Minty, I don't think it's a good idea to use my mother as a fallback nanny."

As it happened, I agreed with her. "Did Rose put it that way?"

"Not exactly, but she told me you rang up at the last minute and begged her to step in." She added, "I object."

"I had to find someone to look after the boys."

"You're their mother. Don't you understand how it would have *upset* her?"

I reminded myself that Poppy had no children. As a result, she did not have the faintest idea. Poppy had not lain naked and trussed and given birth amid what resembled a cocktail party. She did not lie awake at night entertaining that special brand of parental imagining: *Lucas might run out into the road when a lorry just happens to be coming down it at full speed.* She did not understand that adaptation was survival. Furthermore, Poppy had no idea how a pair of fair, tousled heads had a way of sneaking past every defense. "Your mother could have said no."

An impatient noise sped down the line. "Don't you know by now that Mum puts up with everything?"

"I'm not sure I agree, Poppy."

"She has some crazy idea that Dad would want her to look out for them. I've told her she shouldn't stand for it. Richard says you should make your own arrangements."

Despite my best intentions, I was stung by the last. Our occasional rueful exchanges had seemed to indicate that Richard and I understood each other. "Does he really?"

"Um. Well, we both agree."

It was a fair bet that Richard had said nothing of the sort. "Poppy . . ." I said. "I'm doing the best I can, but things are difficult at the moment, and the boys are more important than anything else."

"And?"

"I was afraid that I might lose my job if I didn't turn up." Even to say the words caused sweat to break out on my top lip.

"Can't you negotiate? There's legislation for this kind of contingency." Pause. "I wouldn't stand for it, Minty."

"I expect you would if you had to." My knees had turned shaky. "There is theory, and then there is practice."

"Oh, for goodness' sake."

I glanced round the kitchen. Without Eve, it was showing signs of neglect. There was dust on the windowsill, spilled coffee grounds by the rubbish bin, and a couple of dirty saucepans waiting for attention beside the sink.

"By the way, two things, Poppy. I don't think it would do good if I intervened in the Jilly-Sam situation. I got a polite brush-off from Sam."

"I bet you didn't try hard enough."

"Actually, I did. I put feelers out, and it was clear that I would not get anywhere. I'm afraid the ball's back in your court. You'll have to deal."

"Hmm. You sound like Sam. All bossy and older sibling. And the second thing?"

"I've spoken to Theo. I'm afraid the money won't be forthcoming just yet. He could not say exactly when it would be."

"Oh, my God," Poppy said. A note of desperation had crept into her voice. "Are you sure, absolutely sure?"

I did not have time, nor, to be truthful, the inclination, to take on Poppy's woes. This was the girl who had dressed up in black for my wedding, called her father—and by extension me—an old goat, and deliberately mucked up family Christmases. She and I did not have a relationship where, if one was in trouble, the other one said, "Hang on, I'm coming at once."

Against all reason, I took a deep breath. "Poppy, I suspect you have got yourself into trouble over the poker. Am I right?"

There was a choking sob. "I can't tell *you*."

"Actually, you can."

It took a little more urging and probing but eventually Poppy confessed. "Poker got a grip on me. I don't how. It's a mystery how quickly I became wrapped up in it. I lie awake at night and ask myself how. Then I borrowed money because I didn't win and I can't afford to pay it back. I couldn't pay off my credit card, so I borrowed it from one of those firms who promise the world and forget to tell you that the interest is unbelievable. A career in candles isn't big beans . . . well, it's a career in candles. Need I say more? I can't tell Richard, because he would be horrified. I can't tell Mum, and the bailiffs will come and I'll get credit blacklisted if I don't do something soon . . ."

At this point, I interrupted. "Poppy, listen to me. Have you stopped playing? That's the first step."

"Of course I have."

Poppy was a hopeless liar. "I don't believe you, Poppy."

The situation was still too delicate for the direct approach, and I had been clumsy. She turned savage. "It's none of your business. I can deal with it. If you can just arrange for the money, then it will be sorted."

A lifetime of self-help manuals came to my rescue. "Why don't you go and talk to someone?" I lowered my voice. "Poppy, I can find out who."

There was more choking. "I miss Dad. It's like having a hole in the head. *Why* did he have to die?" Silence, and then her bleak, disembodied voice at the other end of the line. "I wish I was dead."

I glanced at the clock. I had one hour precisely in hand, but it would be put to better use than in pressing the jacket that was next up on the list. "Hang on, Poppy." I felt the thrill of stepping into untrodden territory. "I can come over."

"No," she said. "Don't."

Eve was lying in the farthest bed from the entrance to the ward, which, I imagined, gave her a modicum of peace. The traffic in and out was staggering—trolleys, visitors, doctors in white coats.

She was propped up on pillows and her color matched the linen. "Hallo, Mrs. Lloyd."

"Eve, are you feeling better?" I placed a basket of fruit on her bedside table and drew up a chair. She was too exhausted to talk much, so I held her hand and stroked her fingers. The gesture seemed to please her for she smiled faintly and closed her eyes. After a while, I went in search of information.

The head nurse was ensconced at the nurses' station. She was neat, careworn, and so small she barely crowned the pile of papers in front of her. "Who?" she asked. It took her a couple of minutes to sift through the notes and get a fix on Eve. Then she informed me that Eve could leave the hospital the following day but required dedicated nursing and would not be properly on her feet for at least six weeks. She outlined a program of light meals, sponge baths, and pill taking whose implications instantly triggered a cold trickle down my spine.

I tackled the live-in agency stand-in who had arrived for the week and gave a rundown of Eve's nursing care. The girl—Australian, blond, smiling—shook her head and said politely, "I'm afraid agency rules prevent me from doing anything except look after the kids."

The telephone odyssey recommenced. "If you could look in once," I pleaded with Tessa/Kate/Paige. "Just to check up on Eve and make sure that's she taken her pills and eaten something."

Tessa said, "If she's really ill, you'd better get in an agency nurse."

"I already have an agency nanny, and she's costing the earth."

Kate was more sympathetic but less helpful. "You'd better stay at home, Minty. How would you feel if something happened to Eve?"

Paige said, "I'm not talking to you, Minty. Not only do you lecture me, but I've discovered that you're on Martin's side."

"How?"

"He let slip that he recruited you over a coffee."

"That was ages ago. Anyway, what should I have done? Ignored him?" There was a silence, and I added desperately, "Eve does need checking over, and the agency girl can't or won't."

"Okay." Paige was not enthusiastic. "I'll send Linda over. She can give Eve a meal."

That was the best I could wrest from the situation. It was bad but not terminal and I set about drawing up a list for Linda.

To begin with, Eve was very weak. Then she got better and stronger, but it was not straightforward. Some days she could get up for an hour or so. On others the lightest tasks were beyond her. Ignoring my dwindling cash reserves, I hired the agency nanny for another two weeks.

Paige was of the opinion that I should sack Eve. "You've got to survive," she argued. "You can't afford a weak link. It's either you or her."

Centuries' worth of social and ethical thinking that had crept snaillike toward compassion for, and nurture of, the weak flicked through my brain. "As a matter of interest, is that what you feel Martin is? A weak link?"

Paige gave the impression that she was talking to a recalcitrant child. "I haven't got time to nurture a liability. You haven't got time for a nonfunctional child carer."

Eve might have been ill but she was no fool. She could sense what was blowing in the wind. "Please don't lose me the job," she begged in genuine terror that I might cast her out into the street. For ten seconds or so, the idea of buying her a one-way ticket to Romania jumped the top of my list. I took her sickly face between my hands. "Don't be silly, Eve. The boys need you and they are very fond of you. *I* need you for the boys, so will you please concentrate on getting better?"

As I climbed the stairs to her room in the evenings, bearing a meal tray, I wondered what Nathan would make of me now.

At Paradox, I had taken to draping a jacket (which I changed every two days) over the back of my chair and leaving it there. This was to encourage anyone glancing into my office in the early morning or late evening to conclude that I was already/still at work. I typed out a list of so-called lunch meetings in twenty-point bold Garamond and stuck it onto the side of my computer screen. In actual fact, I was sacrificing a proportion of the family's weekly budget on taxis so that I could race back to Lakey Street to feed Eve. It was a killing schedule, but I had a discovered a quirk in my psyche. I did not mind putting myself out.

Barry and Chris had developed an unhealthy symbiosis. "Chris thinks my thoughts and walks my walks," Barry announced during an ideas meeting that Chris had dominated.

Deb went pale and stared hard at the coffee machine. "I'm looking for a new job," she had told me earlier, without enthusiasm.

Chris had not looked at Deb. He gathered up his papers and waggled his fingers. "See you later, guys."

Barry followed him, leaving Deb and me at the conference table. She cocked an eyebrow. "I feel I've fallen behind, Minty. And I can't put my finger on how it happened."

At the weekend, I took the boys to Gisela's for tea. Since I had been there last, she had redecorated the drawing room in pale gold and cream, with Venetian mirrors and authentic tapestry cushions.

"Felix, no," she said sharply when Felix picked up one of the cushions. "It's very old and valuable." Her attention veered to Lucas, who had discovered that the Aubusson rug concealed an exciting piece of parquet on which to slide.

I called the twins to heel but they were restless, uneasy, and disinclined to obey. This had been a pattern for the last few days and I was fighting to come to grips with it. Lucas happened to be standing closest to Gisela when he sneezed fulsomely. I hastened to pass him a tissue, which, after he had used it, he offered to Gisela with his sweetest smile. Gisela recoiled. "Why don't I ring for Angela, and she can give them tea in the kitchen?"

Roger put in a brief appearance on his way to a golf club gathering. He advanced into the room in a hearty manner and kissed my cheek. "So *good* to see you," he murmured, one eye on his wife. "I hope everything's under control." He looked healthy and wealthy, but not particularly rested or happy.

I was tempted to punish him with a catalog of what was not going well, but spared him. More than once over the past few weeks as I reflected on what had happened to Nathan, it had occurred to me that Roger—for all his power and success—was as likely to be done to, as often as he did by. Sooner or later, Roger's career would end.

After he had left, and Angela had brought in tea and chocolate cake and taken the boys away, Gisela asked after Paradox and the job. I put down my cup into my saucer. "I have a fight on my hands," I said. "I'm going to need every ounce of guile I possess."

Gisela cut a minute slice of chocolate cake and arranged it on her plate. "I appreciate how difficult it must be for you, Minty. I admire how you're handling everything."

It was nice of her to mention it, but I wondered if she meant it. "Have you heard from Marcus?"

At his name, she leaped to her feet. "No, I haven't."

I waited for more information, but Gisela had retreated into painful reflection. The scene on the tapestry cushion at my right elbow depicted hunters in the forest and a wounded white stag. The forest had been woven with a dreamy, mysterious quality and its floor was carpeted with little animals and flowers. "Are you angry, by any chance, Gisela?"

"I am and I'm not." Gisela took up a position by the long window and fingered the curtain tieback. "Okay. I'll say this. In the end, I felt I had no choice. I'm married to Roger and I can't just break a vow as easily as Marcus suggests."

This shone a new, fascinating light on the situation. "Gisela, since when have you minded about marriage *vows*?"

She tossed her head. "You've read me wrong, Minty. I always observed the contract. I did exactly what was expected and what I undertook to do. Marriage is a business, not some mystical revelation." She fiddled some more with the tieback. "In the end, it wasn't a choice. That what's upset me . . . a little. I did not have it in me to consider the alternative with Marcus to what I have now, with Roger. I could not see it."

"Ah."

"Does that make me dead?"

I hazarded a shrewd guess. "Is that what Marcus said?"

Gisela smiled bleakly. "Something along those lines. But it's done." She returned to her seat, and I watched her slip back into the hostess's skin, straightening her skirt and lifting the teapot. "More?"

Gisela's pact with the devil had not made her happy. "Are you sure?"

She put down the teapot. "You know what they say about addicts? If you take away the addiction and the fuss around it, then there is nothing left to fill the day."

"Charity work?"

It was as bad a joke as Nathan would have made. Gisela managed a wintry smile. "Then I would be truly dead." She pointed to the cushion. "French. Eighteenth century. Note the superb vegetable dyes."

"Noted." I had half an ear listening for the twins and whether they were creating mayhem with Angela.

Gisela traced the outline of the wounded stag on the cushion with a finger on which gleamed an important diamond ring. "I had become used to a setup where everything on the surface appeared straightforward but wasn't, and only I knew about it. There was an edge to my life like the hem on a garment. I could say to myself, 'I'm married to Nicholas or Richmond or Roger, but I have the option to pack my bags. . . .'" She laughed bitterly. "The trouble is, since I've told Marcus to go, I spend all my time thinking about him in a way I never did when he was on the scene."

"Oh, dear," I said. "That's bad. You've got guilt plus the grass-is-greener syndrome rolled into one."

Gisela was startled. "What do you mean?"

"It's a stubborn, pesky illness that won't go away."

"How do you know?"

"I am intimately acquainted with it," I said.

In the car on the way back, Felix piped up, "If you don't have a daddy, does that mean we are not a family?"

"No, Felix. You can be a family without a daddy."

"And you really are a mummy."

I stared at the snarled traffic. "I really am a mummy."

When we got back, Eve was in the kitchen. She looked a lot stronger, even if her clothes hung off her. "I make supper," she said, and when I tried to stop her, she held up her hand. "I do."

I helped her to cut cucumber and carrot sticks, and to heat the fish pie. She moved tiredly, painfully slowly, but with determination. Afterward, she insisted on clearing up. She raised her normally indifferent eyes to mine, and in them sparked gratitude. "You are nice, Minty."

During the bad nights, I had been getting rid of Nathan. It should have been a logical process—Nathan was no longer here to wear his shirts, socks, suits, shoes, and ties, and they were easy to sort and easy to pack. But their disposal defied logic. Sometimes I managed to clear a drawer, sometimes it was beyond me. It was a process that had to be secret because I did not wish the boys to witness it and because it hurt. So I accomplished it in fits and starts, by dark and stealthily during those nights.

It was a quarter to two when I got myself out of bed and opened the doors to Nathan's wardrobe. Already a light dust coated the contents. There were his ties, blue, red, and green. A scarf was jammed onto the shelf and I picked it up. It was an expensive one, and I caught the faintest echo of his aftershave. The sensation of a sharp instrument striking through my breast made me gasp. I sank back down on the bed, holding it between fingers from which the feeling had drained.

Nathan was dead.

After a while, I put it aside and took down his favorite gray suit and laid it on the bed. Into the jacket, I tucked his favorite blue office shirt. Round the collar went the tie, red silk. A pair of silk socks and polished shoes completed the ensemble.

There. This was the shell of Nathan. I could pretend he was there, leaning against the pillows, hands folded behind his head. *Minty, will you please pay attention . . .* Pillow punched. Shoes eased off and discarded. *Minty, what do you think?*

The bag for the charity shop was on the floor. If I removed the tie from the shell and placed it in the bag, then a part of Nathan was gone. If I took out the shirt, as I now did, and folded it carefully, then another bit of him had vanished. The shoes . . . the shoes? If I dropped them into the bag, then it would be impossible for Nathan ever again to walk into Number 7 and run up the stairs—*where are my boys?*

And with the suit went the businessman who formulated strategies and said: *our competitors are really strong, let us give them a hard time.*

"When I married Nathan," Rose confided to me at one of our lunches in the early days, "I was broken-hearted from a love affair that had gone wrong. But Nathan was so anxious to make me happy, how could I resist? He was a rock, and Hal was unreliable sand. What more could I ask?"

I was not so convinced by Rose's capacity to sort out the rocks from the sand. This was a woman who, she also confided to me, used to slip into St. Benedicta's church en route for home and light a candle under the Madonna. If that was not building a house on sand, I didn't know what was.

"Hal could never be what I wanted," Rose added. "We both knew it. But Nathan was."

Downstairs, one of the twins cried out. I swept the suit

into the bag and went to find out which one. Felix had had a bad dream. "Mummy, there was a big cat with big claws and he was trying to claw me . . ."

I drew his hot little body close and whispered, "It's all right, Felix. Mummy's here. I've chased the bad cat away. Look, it's gone."

It was not all right. Yet as I soothed my son with this lie, I took a curious pleasure and pride in its construction. Until the boys were big and bold enough to know better, it was my business to shield them from the worst.

Chapter Twenty-two

When I turned out the pocket of my black linen trousers, I discovered the sprig of the plant I had picked at Claire Manor. It was brittle and withered, with only faint traces of the vivid blue that had attracted me. Intrigued, I looked it up in one Nathan's books. It was called nepeta and its old nickname was Kattesminte. So powerful was its attraction to cats that infant seedlings had to be protected against them.

The phone rang as I was reading about catmint. "If you set it, the cats will get it/If you sow it, the cats won't know it."

"I know I'm not talking to you," said Paige.

"Okay," I said. "I'm not asking you how the baby is."

"He's developing into a bit of a screamer." Her voice wavered. "I've never been so exhausted." For Paige to admit anything of the sort was serious. "Three children, and I have to turn them into human beings without turning into a monster myself." Her voice veered up the scale. "It's so tough that I sometimes wonder."

It was almost unheard of for Paige to have doubts. "Paige, have you been in touch with Martin at all?"

"Tell you what, ask me about Lara's arabesques instead."

"Paige. Have you been in touch with Martin?"

"Minty. Don't interfere. Okay?"

I raised my eyes to the ceiling. "How are Lara's arabesques?"

"Funnily enough, very good. She has an excellent line, but she's let down a bit by her feet. Pats of butter, unfortunately. But we'll get to work on them."

I felt sorry for the ramshackle, terrorized Lara. From now on, her feet would not be her own. At the other end of the phone Paige sighed heavily, a sound filled with despair and uncertainty, and I weighed in. "You have got to think again about Martin."

"I *think* about him, Minty, all the time. And I am very fond of him. Very. But I haven't time to be married. Not with three children. Not if I'm to do things properly."

"Paige, have you eaten today?"

"Eaten? Not much. I'm far too busy. And before you ask, no, I'm not sleeping well. I know you think I've gone mad with postnatal depression and maybe I have, but at the best of times, Martin is a reluctant father. He doesn't enjoy it. He hates the house being full of children. Now, who's the one with a psychosis?"

"All the same, he needs to be there."

There was an ominous silence. "Minty, I'm not sure about lectures from you."

"Where is he living?"

"At his mother's. She's put him in the attic bedroom for the time being."

———

I rang Martin and arranged to meet him the following afternoon at the bank. "Minty, is this urgent? I have a big conven-
tion in Geneva and I'm traveling for the next couple of weeks.
But if you really need to see me I can fit you in at two-
thirty."

To his credit, Martin was on time, which did not give me
much opportunity to study the building's stunning glass atrium.
He stepped out of a lift, kissed my cheek, and steered me down
the corridor. "This had better be good."

"You asked me to keep an eye on Paige."

"Ah, my wife." For all the lightness of tone, Martin was
on the alert. He led me into the canteen, which was more like
a banqueting hall, did the equivalent of clicking his fingers,
and, lo and behold, we were presented with freshly made espres-
sos, hot milk, and a cantucci biscuit. Living with his mother
was doing him no harm physically for, unlike his wife, he was
immaculate, slim, and healthy complexioned.

I could never resist cantucci. I dipped mine into the espresso
and bit into it with the special pleasure reserved for the forbidden. "Martin, you must go home."

He frowned. "*She* threw me out. Remember?"

"*She's* just had a baby. We've agreed you're half mad when
you've had a baby. You stay half mad, I reckon, until they're
adults. Paige is half mad anyway." Martin snorted. "She won't
listen to me because I'm a sinner. Or, at least, she won't take
my advice." I stared longingly at Martin's cantucci and, obediently, he handed it over.

"The children, Martin . . . they'll be suffering from all this.
They may not show it, but they will be." I included my own
in the generalization, which made the declaration even more

impassioned. If Felix or Lucas hurt, I hurt. "Do you really hate them?"

"Is that what Paige says?" Martin frowned. "I knew before they arrived it would be tricky, but even I was surprised by how impossible it became. I warned Paige that she was becoming obsessed. But . . ."—he now gave me a steady look, the I-am-a-rock one in which Nathan had specialized—"I would never have left of my own accord."

I countered, "Paige has had a baby. She's weak, her hormones are all over the place, and she's not thinking straight."

To my acute distress, Martin's eyes filled. "Don't mind me," he muttered. "But could you stop right there."

I made a rapid reconnaissance of the room. No one had noticed Martin's tears. Had it been taken on board by beady-eyed rivals, it would have done him no good. A group of bankers in pinstriped suits plodded in. They were all as plump as pullets and spoke to each other in low, earnest tones. I jabbed a finger in their direction. "Doesn't look that much fun working here."

"It isn't." He shaded his eyes with a hand. "Nothing's much fun these days."

"You could put things right."

Martin pulled himself together. "As a matter of interest, Minty, why are you taking this view?" He meant: why should you, the wrecker, argue so strongly for family unity? I might have taken offense but I had grown used to my label. "I have two small boys," I said.

He directed a countenance so full of woe at me that I was forced to look down at my coffee cup. "Just walk back in, Martin. Tell Paige she's wrong and that you won't have a broken-backed family. Tell her it's for the children's sake."

"I did not agree to be hauled out of an important briefing meeting so you could tell me what is blindingly obvious."

"Nevertheless."

To my surprise he reached over and took my hands. "It was well done, Minty."

I let my hands rest in his. I knew perfectly well that whatever I said or advised would have very little influence on him, but I had said and would continue to say it. "On second thought, Martin, tell Paige it's for her sake too. *Do it.*"

I left him by the state-of-the-art elevators, which would whisk him back up to the nineteenth floor, and headed out of the door.

A postcard arrived in the post. "Dear Minty. I enjoyed seeing the boys and I wondered . . ." there was a space between "wondered" and "if I could see them again? I would love to take them to the zoo or to the cinema perhaps. Rose."

The card did not exude confidence. The writing was hesitant and the wording suggested that it had been written against Rose's better judgment. But in her sending and my receiving, an element shifted in the balance between us.

A week elapsed before I responded.

At Paradox, I chipped away at the final details for *Pointe of Departure* and toyed with the notion of developing a history of choreography but discarded it. Deb announced that she was off to work for Papillon and when I told her how sorry I was, she replied, "Oh, I don't have time to hang around anymore," in a nonchalant manner that imperfectly hid her unhappiness. The mention of time got me thinking about the abandoned middle-age project, and I retrieved it from my reject file and dusted it off.

I threw myself into administration. I wrote letters to the bank. I had several long conversations with Theo. I researched addiction counselors. I paid bills. I rearranged the furniture in the sitting room and my bedroom so that the house took on a different aspect. Nathan's study had been transformed into a cozy, feminine space. My papers were on the notice board. School rotas. Work schedules. Those lists.

My clothes occupied the total space available in/on the wardrobes/drawers/pegs. My bottles occupied the shelf in the bathroom. Upstairs in the attic a cardboard box contained Nathan's razor, a shaving brush made from badgers' hair, a hairbrush, and a new comb still in its plastic wrapping. There they would wait until I gave them to Felix and Lucas.

I lay awake and counted the ghosts. I had been wrong. There *is* some kind of justice for no one ever escapes anyone else. Nathan never got away from Rose. Rose never got away from Hal. Rose and I never got away from each other.

After Rose had been sacked as books editor, and I had taken over, I plotted how cleverly I would achieve a transformation and spice up the pages and transform them. *My* books pages would fizz with new ideas. Yet when Timon sacked me, he damned my efforts. "In the end, Minty, you hadn't done anything to write home about. Your pages were nothing new."

Rose told me that she suffered torment and anguish over Hal, her first lover. But the memories also held moments of such sweetness and ecstasy that she carried them with her always. I do not possess memories such as those, but Rose's were like fragrant sachets tucked into a drawer. I envied her.

My reply to Rose took me a long time to write, and the words were bottlenecked at the end of my pen. "Would you like to come to sports day at the boys' school?"

It was agreed. Rose wold come early to watch the opening events with Eve, and I would join them for those in which Felix and Lucas were competing—the sack race, egg and spoon, sprint, high jump. There was, in addition, a dire form of advanced torture called the parents' race, which Lucas informed me, I was expected to win.

Sports Day minus twelve hours. Felix and Lucas dragged me into the garden after their supper. They wanted to practice running and the three-legged race. I protested that they would get indigestion but Felix pulled at my arm and said, "Please."

Thus it was I found myself standing patiently—an adverb that had many nuances—with my watch in my hand as the boys pelted up and down the lawn until Lucas turned pale and announced he felt sick.

Sports Day minus five hours. The starlings were roosting outside the bedroom door again. It was five to six in the morning. Lucas snuck into the room and climbed onto the bed and nuzzled me. "Mummy, you must come."

"Why?" I squinted at him. He was in his dressing gown.

"Come and see," persisted the voice in my ear.

Somehow, I got out of bed and stumbled into the boys' room. There, neatly laid out on his bed, was Felix's sport kit. T-shirt, navy blue shorts, white plimsolls, and white socks. "Have I got it right, Mummy?" he asked.

Lucas said, "Look at me," and tore off his dressing gown. He was wearing his—but his T-shirt was back to front. He mimed a couple of air punches and dropped to one knee. "Ready, steady . . . go."

"Come here, Lukey. You've got your T-shirt on wrong."

Felix scrabbled under the bed and, with an air of triumph, produced my trainers, which he must have taken from my wardrobe, and laid them at my feet. "That's for your race, Mummy."

"Right . . ." I wrestled with Lucas and the T-shirt.

Felix was cataloguing his kit. "There are my shorts. These are my shoes . . ."

"Very good, boys," I said. "Brilliant." I sat down on Lucas's bed. "Do you know how early it is?"

Felix had finished his inventory and was hopping around with his pajama bottoms round his ankles. "You will come, Mummy, won't you?"

I rubbed my eyes. "*Of course,*" I said.

At Paradox, I worked solidly through the morning and I got ready to leave on time, armed with the file entitled *Statistical Analysis of Depression in Females, 40–65.* Then Syriol called, "Visitor for you, Minty."

A wan, appreciably thinner Poppy sat on one of the seats, leafing through *Television Weekly.* At my approach, she threw aside the magazine and leaped to her feet. "Hi. I'm sorry to do this to you, but have you any news from Theo?"

"No. It's taking a heck of time, but there's nothing I can do."

Poppy looked as though she might faint. "Oh, God, Minty." She had tied her hair back savagely. It did not suit her.

"Here," I said, "sit down."

"I keep thinking Dad would have so hated me for this. He was always so careful and taught me to be careful, and it's haunting me. I can't get this picture out of my head that he's thinking I've let him down." She wrapped a piece of skirt around her fingers, bandage style. "I hate to think he would be disappointed in me."

"You have got to talk to Richard, Poppy."

She shook her head. "I have to deal with it myself. It was a mistake, and just because I'm married to Richard it doesn't mean he has to know *everything* about me." She fingered her handbag strap. "My poker debt is a private matter."

"What about your mother? She would understand."

"You don't know Mum," Poppy said miserably. "She's not forgiving on some things. What I need is the money Dad left me, then I can pay off my debt and I won't bother you again."

"Theo's still wrestling with the Inland Revenue. There were a couple of problems that no one could iron out to do with the money your father inherited from your grandmother." I was curious. "Why did you do it, Poppy?"

She shrugged. "It was exciting. I thought I could beat the system. All the usual excuses." She observed a point on the wall. "So boring and predictable."

She was so agitated that I got up and went over to the water cooler and ran out a mugful. I pressed it into her hands. "You know, it's all perfectly manageable."

Barry walked down the corridor and raised an eyebrow. I made a nondescript gesture, and he disappeared. I glanced at my watch. Time was leapfrogging, and Lucas was due to run in the egg and spoon.

Poppy noticed the gesture. "I'm sorry to bother you, Minty. I know you're busy." The concession was so unexpected that I sat down beside her with a *thump*. "I don't understand, Minty, why I was caught. Then I think, I *wanted* to be caught by it. . . . Then I thought, I can give it up anytime. But I couldn't. I thought I was bigger than it was. Oh, what the hell . . . What the hell."

There was not much slack in my finances, but sufficient to

take a temporary knock. I reached for my handbag for my checkbook. "Look, why don't I lend you some for the moment. It will stave off some of the problem, and then you and I will go and see Theo. He is bound to confidentiality."

Poppy raised her head. "Would you do that?"

Her astonishment was—almost—offensive but funnily enough, I understood. "Yes."

"Okay. Thanks." Tears streamed down Poppy's cheeks. "I'm a mess, Minty. That's what I am. And what do I do about it?"

Egg-and-spoon race. Next up the sack race. Felix was in that one. I hauled my notebook out of my bag. "Actually, Poppy. I've done some research on counseling."

"Counseling." She was dismissive.

I stared at her. "Are you serious or not?"

Poppy did not answer. I grabbed her wrist, hauled her out of Paradox, hailed the first taxi, and ordered him to drive to an address in South Kensington. "I am taking you to a counselor who is highly recommended. When we get there, Poppy, you are going to make an appointment and I'm going to watch you do it."

By the time I arrived at the common, the races had been run, the rosettes pinned onto chests, and the picnics were in full swing.

There was the usual melee of parents, mostly mothers, with one or two progressive, unemployed, or browbeaten fathers. An area of the common had been roped off. It contained a table on which flapped a white cloth held down by several silver cups. Their status came under the heading of reprieved: the cups were the relic of an earlier era, and there had been much solemn debate among the staff as to whether competitive races should be allowed.

It was hot and sunny, and children in blue shorts and red jersey hoodies ran about like ants on speed. It took me two seconds to locate Rose in the crowd. She was sitting on a tartan rug with Felix with an open cool bag between them. Her full pink skirt was the color of a flower. Eve was sitting with another group a little way away, chatting with a friend. A similar tableau was repeated ad infinitum: tartan rugs, open cool bags from which disgorged potato chips, slices of cold pizza, and fruit juices, plus bottles of wine to save the adults' sanity.

Rose waved a cocktail sausage in the air and said something to Felix, who laughed so hard that he fell back onto the rug and kicked his legs in the air. He always threw himself backward when I made a joke, but I had not seen him laugh like that for a long time.

"Hallo," I collapsed onto the rug beside them. Rose was cool. "Hallo, Minty. Lucas is over there." She pointed to a knot clustered around the games mistress. "He did well."

Felix pulled at my jacket. "Hey, careful." I bent over to kiss him. He was hot and sweaty, and smelled of wine gums and orange juice, which was not particularly enticing, but it was dearer to me than anything I could think of at this precise moment. "How did you do?" I whispered.

He pressed his mouth to my ear, and the roar of his breath assaulted my ear drum. "I came in tenth, Mummy."

Rose gazed into the middle distance. A couple of teams were conducting an impromptu tug-of-war. "The boys kept asking where you were." She added. "Whatever it was I hope it was worth it."

"I do too," I echoed, fervently.

"Really, really worth it," she repeated. "Lucas was . . . a little tearful. He won the egg and spoon, you know."

I knew what Rose was thinking. Hell-bent on pursuing my career, I was prepared to sacrifice my sons' happiness and welfare. "Oh, come on, Rose, you know as well as I do what happens in the office. You told me that whenever Sam and Poppy had a carol service or sports day, or whatever, there was a last-minute panic or hold-up at Vistemax that made you late."

Rose had always been fair. "True."

I squinted to where Lucas was at the center of the games mistress's huddle. "What's going on?"

"A disputed second and third in the twenty-meter race." The suggestion was that I should know what was going on. "You know, he was so hoping you'd turn up in time to see him run. They both were." She paused and said, "But you were carrying on in your own sweet way, Minty."

"Sometimes you sound like Nathan," I remarked.

At that, she flinched and reflected for a moment. "But Nathan would have asked what could be more important than supporting your sons at sports day." She shaded her eyes and looked over at Lucas. "At least, that was the sort of thing he said to me."

"Rose, I did not want to be late."

Felix tilted back his head. "Are you talking about my daddy?" He blinked his blue eyes. "Did Daddy run in races?"

"I'm pretty sure he did, Felix." There was a proprietorial note in Rose's voice, to which I objected. Lucas came running over, the windmill in full sail. He was grubby and happy. He brushed past without seeing me, and flung himself against Rose. "I was very fast."

"Yes, you were. Felix and I are hoarse from shouting." She placed a finger on the rosette pinned to his shirt.

"Lukey . . ." I said, feeling the flame of jealousy. "Hallo. Let me see your rosette."

Lucas looked up at me. "You didn't come, Mummy." He frowned and turned back to Rose.

Rose read my thoughts. She could almost have said: *But you took Nathan*. Instead, she raised a cool pair of eyebrows and murmured to Lucas. "Have you said hallo to Mummy?"

I clasped Lucas to me hard. I do not know why I did not choose to defend myself and explain to Rose why I had been late. There was no reason to defend Poppy, except, perhaps, for a curious loyalty.

Rose stacked the plastic picnic plates and mugs. She swept up the potato chips packets and stowed them in the cool bag. "Have you eaten? There's a sandwich left."

"No, thank you." My voice shook.

Rose's self-command was perfect. She dusted a shard of potato chip from her finger. "Now that you have turned up, I think perhaps I should go." She picked up a canvas bag and hitched the handle over her shoulder.

A couple of yards away, a toddler was roaring for its mother, a posse of children was playing tag, darting between the spread rugs, and one of the teachers was telling off a sullen girl with scraggly braids. "It's a long time since I've been at a sports day." Rose pointed at the roaring toddler. "Presumably it has a mother? By the way . . ." she hesitated. "Minty, I don't know what you'd say to this, but Felix has been going on about a kitten. Would you allow me to get you one? I know a source."

"No," I said flatly. "No kittens. No cats."

"Okay. It's just that it might help Felix . . ."

"Perhaps we shouldn't repeat this," I said. "It's too difficult. I'm sorry I ever involved you with the boys."

"How silly, Minty." Suddenly an angry red patch appeared on Rose's neck, and she was transformed from the collected creature of a moment ago to someone who was seriously angry. "It can't do any harm, and I'm interested in them. I like them."

"Even so, Rose."

"Nathan was right."

"And what was he so right about? What did you both conclude during your cozy chats?"

Rose stared at me, and her features hardened into acute dislike. "Nothing." She hitched the strap of her bag farther up her shoulder and walked away.

Chapter Twenty-three

I worked late into the night on the resurrected middle age idea. "If we accept that time is an artificial construct," I wrote in my notes, "then what matters is experience. Experience is what tempers us and helps us to carry our mistakes. It also helps us to understand that death, which is waiting, informs life."

Was that correct? Did I believe it? As a theory, it sounded good and convincing, and the people to whom it applied were the cream of the crop: the rounded, complete, mature personalities. It would be nice to say that I was counted among them.

I pushed aside the notes. The idea required further work as it was still gestating. It needed time to grow its wings.

I rubbed my eyes and ran my fingers through my hair, which needed a cut—goodness knew when that would be possible.

What had Nathan been right about?

What had he and Rose agreed about me?

I was on the old switchback again.

I went to make some tea in the kitchen and, on the way, glanced up at the landing, where the ironing board was and where Rose, when she lived here, had used to have her desk. She was still in this house, Nathan too.

I put the kettle on, unlocked the back door, and went outside into the summer night.

What had Nathan and Rose decided between them?

I sat down on the bench and ran my fingernail along the table. There was lichen growing on it, and it needed scrubbing. I remembered Nathan sitting opposite me at this table. We had been married for three years and one day. Because it was such a warm evening, we were having supper of seafood pasta (I was eating the seafood without the pasta) outside and we had embarked on a negotiation as to where we should take a holiday.

"I want somewhere hot," I said as I always did, so my pitch held no surprises.

He dug his fork into the pasta, twirled it expertly, then lifted it to his mouth. "And I want to go to Cornwall," he said as he always did.

"I've looked up a place on Rhodes. Nice villa by the sea. The boys would like it."

"The boys are too young. When we took Sam and Poppy . . ." Nathan did not continue. He put down his fork and looked everywhere but at me.

That was the moment when a voice in me articulated clearly. "Do you realize you have taken on enough history to fill a library?"

I got up, went inside, and rattled in the cupboard for salt.

I was ashamed and devastated by the revelation, and also, curiously, calm because everything was now crystal clear.

Nathan would never let go of his past life, *could* never let go.

He followed me into the kitchen. "Minty, this has got to stop. I can't pretend I didn't have Poppy and Sam."

"No," I said.

Upstairs, one or other of the twins called out. As one, Nathan and I turned our heads in the direction of the child's cry. "You or me?" asked Nathan.

On that at least we were united.

Now, in the kitchen, I ran hot water into the sink, and plunged my chilled hands into it. Then I boiled the kettle and took a cup of chamomile tea up to bed.

I switched off the light and lay down. After a while, I put out my arm and let it rest in the space that Nathan should have occupied.

Rose did not reply to the messages I left on her answer phone. I allowed two days to elapse. After that, I took myself round to her flat after work.

She answered the door. She was dressed in a skirt I recognized from Prada, a leopard-print cardigan, and a necklace of large wooden beads. She looked wonderful and not very surprised. "I suspected you'd turn up, sooner or later."

She did not invite me in, so I summoned my best brand of gall. "You didn't answer my calls. I've come to sort things out."

Rose kept her hand on the door, and I said, "Rose, if we get this over and done with, then it will be over and done with."

Eventually she stepped aside. "Come in."

The sitting room was a mass of flowers. Rose explained, "I've just landed a one-off slot on a gardening series for television," she explained. "I'm doing small city gardens. People have been kind and sent flowers."

"Who with?"

"The Activities Channel, but it's being made by Papillon. It probably won't get a large audience, but you have to grab these opportunities. Anyway, it will be fun."

"Papillon? That must be Deb." I glanced at the label on a huge bunch of lilies which read: "Love from Hal." "How is Hal?" I asked.

"Fine. Busy."

"I often wondered if you'd marry him."

"As it happens, he has asked me." Rose pointed to the blue chair. "Sit down, Minty."

I avoided the blue chair where Nathan had died and sat on the sofa. "Why not marry Hal?"

"I like what I am, I'm fine as I am. I don't want to change anything," Rose replied, but her voice was not entirely steady. "Hal's the sort of person in a life who never leaves you and he hasn't. So . . ." she fell silent. "I don't know what to think. I may or may not. Probably not. I don't want the disruption. I've got used to thinking of myself as independent." A flash of uncertainty and doubt. "It's difficult at my age . . . so . . ." She switched the subject. "Say whatever you want to say, then go. Let's not waste each other's time."

My mouth and throat were dry, but I could not bring myself to ask her for a drink. "I want to know about you and Nathan."

"Nathan and I were married. We had two children. I had

a good job. Then I hired you and I brought you home to meet him over a spaghetti supper. You know the rest of the history."

"No," I said. "That's not what I am asking."

Rose was keeping something back. The light played on her honey hair and creamy skin. In the past, Nathan had touched that hair and skin. They had belonged to him.

Thirsty and burning with humiliation, I asked the question that had to be asked. "Rose, did you take Nathan back as a lover?"

Rose shifted in the chair. Slender but not too slender, toned and groomed—she was a world away from the frazzled working mother whom I first encountered in the Vistemax office. Yet she was vulnerable too. *It's difficult at my age.* And vulnerability has its own eroticism. Of course Nathan would have wanted her back.

She placed her hand on her chest, in the region of the heart. "It feels like a stone sitting on my chest, mourning Nathan. Like a gigantic attack of indigestion."

"I know," I said.

We could ask each other, Do you weep for him, like I do?

"*Do* you?"

"You're not answering the question."

"That's because I'm not going to."

I bit my lip. "*Tell* me, Rose. What was it you and Nathan decided?"

"He said you were ambitious."

"So was he at my age. So were you. You had a fight with him about going back to work."

The hand on her chest curled into a ball. "It's irrelevant now. Old, old ground and I don't wish to go over it."

"Old ground for you, perhaps." I closed my eyes for a second. "But Nathan didn't like it, and it was a source of friction."

"For God's sake, Minty. What do you want from me?"

"I suppose . . ." I said miserably. "I want to tell you that he wasn't really happy with me. And that he regretted leaving you." I hesitated and then forced out the words through gritted teeth. "Did he come back into your bed?" Rose made a noise between a laugh and a gasp, but I ploughed on. "Nathan had been there so many times before . . ." Yes, he had shared the everyday language of small noises and touch with Rose. He had listened to her breathing in the night, heard her clean her teeth, fill the kettle . . . "It wouldn't have been such a big step." Rose held up a hand to stop me, but I ignored it. "I could never share the long history you had with him. I could never compete. You were always there, ahead of me. Always."

"Stop it, Minty."

I had wit enough left to obey her.

Rose flashed a wry smile. "I want never gets." It was a saying we had used often in the office. Once. Years ago. Timon, the editor, had always wanted more books, fewer books, different ones. *I want never gets.* Except in that case, I want usually did get. She continued, "When Nathan first told me he was having an affair with you, I asked him why he'd told me. If someone is having an affair, they should be very clever and very secret. I still believe that."

"Nevertheless, I need to know."

Rose's smile had vanished. She leaned toward me to emphasize her point, and I smelled her jasmine scent. "I don't have to tell you anything, Minty." She spoke without malice, almost gently. "You lost the right to my confidences long ago.

I don't have to discuss anything with you and I certainly don't feel I have to help you sort things out."

She got up and disappeared through the door, returning with a bottle and glasses on a tray. "You'd better have some of this. Hal brought it from Italy."

As I accepted the glass, my blouse, which was cut tight into the torso, dug into the flesh under my arm. "The boys ask after you. Quite a lot, actually."

Quick as lightning, I picked up the flash of delight that lit her face. "The boys . . ." Her voice was soft, almost possessive. "They are sweet."

My instinct was to hiss: keep off my sons. I looked down at my hands and struggled for mastery. "Old friendships and old loyalties. Do you remember? You talked about them at that supper when I first met Nathan, about how hard it is to shake them off?"

She smiled grimly. "Believe me, I could shake you off, Minty, with no trouble at all. It would not take much."

She meant it, and I flushed, not with anger but despair. As the woman who had pinched her husband, I was culpable, pitiable, and all the other things that Rose cared to name. And yet, all those years ago, I had witnessed her rush into the office, too-pink lipstick smudged, her sweater ill fitting, swearing that Nathan/the children had been difficult/demanding/cross. I used to think she deserved the pity.

I drank my wine and looked around the room. In its calm, ordered magnolia and cream with blue touches here and there, it reflected what Rose had become. It was a room that was arranged entirely to the satisfaction of its occupant. "There are advantages to living alone," I remarked.

She understood what I meant. "Actually, yes."

We exchanged a glance. *Funnily enough, we do understand each other.* Rose put down her glass and said, "Nathan and I were married for a long time. We knew each other very well. Just as . . . just as . . . you and I do. It was easy to pick up conversations." She got up and walked over to the window. "My life with Nathan was private until you came along. If our marriage had bad patches and areas of blindness, it was ours and it worked, until you prized it apart. Then everyone took a good look, and it was open house." She turned round and stared at me, calm and steady. "You must admit that I don't owe you anything, Minty. No explanations. No loyalty."

I cried out, "Nathan came here because he wanted comfort and conversation. He didn't find them with me. Your bed would have been a natural progression."

She leaned her forehead against the curtain and sighed wearily. "Why don't you stop now and let it go."

"Because I'm angry with myself, Rose, but I'm also angry with Nathan."

"Oh, Minty, won't you leave him alone. Give him *some* peace."

"You're right, I should not be here."

"Quite," she said coldly. She poured a second glass of wine and hugged it to her chest. I made no move, and she said, "Aren't you going? Go."

What did the self-help manuals have to say on the subject of the second wife apologizing to the first? Those books that so encouraged people to believe they could get a grip on their lives and make changes, that concocted dazzling fantasies of resolution and forgiveness, and other castles in the air?

"I want to say sorry to you," I confessed. "I did not realize what I did until I had married Nathan and had the boys. Then it all looked different, particularly when I grasped how disappointed Nathan was at times. He used to look at me sometimes, and I could see how he hated what he'd done. It wasn't that he didn't care for me, but that he realized how much he cared for the things that he had discarded."

Nathan had used Rose badly. I had used Rose badly. And I already knew that the full import of one's transgressions do not really hit home until years after the event. The manuals don't mention that one. It was probably too complicated a subject for them to tackle.

"Poor Minty," said Rose, and her irony cut me to the quick. She remained hunched over her wine. "You were welcome to him," she admitted. "He had hurt me so much. Sometimes, I thought I would die of the hurt. But you know the aphorism: this too will pass? It's true—it does. Thank God. When he turned up here on the day he died, I didn't make him particularly welcome. Actually, I didn't want him here. I was busy. He could see that and was disappointed. But you know, I didn't feel I had any reason to put myself out. I had spent so *long* shaking free, and Nathan's problems were not mine. . . . I could no longer engage with him, not the way he wanted. . . . Actually, I blame myself for that."

"That was a shame," I managed. To be unwanted as you are dying is a terrible, terrible hard fact . . .

She gave a choking sound. "For God's sake, he left me, for you. Remember?" She turned an anguished face toward me. "Remember?"

"I think of it most of the time. Never more so than now."

Rose made a visible effort. "You have the twins to consider. Sam and Poppy suffered. You may think that they were too old, but they weren't and they did. I blame you and Nathan for that. There was nothing I could do to help them. You can't inflict your anger and regret on your children." She twirled her glass between her fingers. "I won't let you."

A tiny pulse beat in Rose's temple and, no doubt, one did in mine. I fixed on the blank television screen in the corner of the room. "I'm truly sorry about Poppy and Sam." For good measure, I threw in, "Poppy has taken it out on me. She's a fighter."

Rose bent down and picked up a mother-of-pearl button from the carpet. "That's Poppy for you. And Sam? He's struggling a bit at the moment. I am a little worried about him and Jilly. . . . I want to be around to help, but I'm busy, earning a living and getting on with my life, and they have to sort themselves out." Her voice was tender. "Much . . . much as I love them." The tenderness excluded me. She continued in a kinder voice, "Grief saps the confidence, Minty. I can tell you that. But it can be fine, in the end. Believe me." She gestured at the room. "When Nathan left, I felt I'd failed myself and the children, but I survived. It took blood and tears, but I did it." She balanced the button on the palm of her hand. "Nathan did what he wanted to do. I failed to see that he was changing as he grew older. And why shouldn't he have changed? It was his right. But I didn't see it then. So, it was not all your fault, you know."

Rose was letting me off the hook, a little. The wine had loosened my tongue. "Roger and Gisela Gard came to dinner once. Believe it or not, I was playing office politics. One of the twins was naughty, and it was Nathan who dealt with it. I saw Roger watching Nathan, I could almost hear him thinking, this is a man who's lost his stuffing and brimstone, and the thought flashed through my mind that it was better to be dead than a failure." I put down my wineglass. "The question is, did I wish Nathan's death on him, Rose? Did I?"

Rose swirled her wine round her glass. "When Nathan left, I thought how much easier it would have been as a widow, not as the dumped wife. For a start, no one could have said it was my fault, unless I'd fed him hamburger and chips every night. If he had died, the situation would have been easier to handle."

"Yes."

She put down her glass, and the gold ring gleamed. "I still would have lost my job to you, wouldn't I?"

"Probably," I conceded. "I wanted it and I reckoned loyalty in the office was an old-fashioned concept."

"And now?"

I thought of Chris Sharpe. "Much the same." I looked down at the carpet. "Was Nathan trying to humiliate me when he asked that you be made a guardian?"

"Perhaps he was thinking of what's best for the boys."

"Perhaps."

Rose took my hand. The touch of her flesh on mine was unexpected. "Minty, what you don't understand is . . . I had got away. Finally. At last. I had stopped dreaming about Nathan. I wasn't about to involve myself in his life again. I had cut him off."

I allowed my hand to rest in hers and told her what festered in my mind. "I never loved him, Rose, not truly. Not really truly. Not heart, soul, body and mind. He knew he was getting older and wanted different things, and I was not going to make it easy. If I'd loved him, I would have let him . . . oh, go to Cornwall, a million things." My fingers pressed Rose's. "I think he felt desperately alone."

Rose took away her hand. "I'm going to show you a letter, Minty." She went over to the desk in the corner, picked up a padded postage packet, pulled out an envelope, and handed it over.

I spread out two closely written sheets of writing paper. "My Dearest Rose . . ." *"Dearest" means closest to the heart.* "I have no right to ask what I am going to ask, but I have an idea it might be necessary. If you receive this letter, which I am lodging with Theo, then I will have judged correctly.

"I am writing to ask you to remember that you were once good friends with Minty. If you are reading this, it means she is on her own with the twins. Of course, I have no idea how long that might be for. When I came over to see you in the flat, I asked you if you would be a guardian if anything should happen to me, and to her, and the boys were still underage, and you said you would consider it. I can't think of anyone better to ask. It is a huge thing to lay on you, especially given our history, but I know you through and through, Rose, and there is no one I trust more . . ."

For a moment, I could not continue, "Oh, Nathan . . ."

"Are you okay?" asked Rose.

I nodded. "All I can say in mitigation for my actions toward you is that the complications of feelings and impulse take us to strange places. They certainly took me away from you, whom I loved, to Minty. But I loved Minty too and I want to say the following. There is so much in her to admire (you spotted it first when you became friends) and that still holds true. It has been difficult for her, and not as she expected. Thus, I ask you again, if she ever needs it and asks you for help with the boys, or even if she doesn't ask you, please will you do it?"

I put down the letter, picked up my bag, and got to my feet. "Why didn't you tell me about this? I know, I hurt you beyond words, but you *should* have told me."

Rose's response was short and simple. "Yes."

"It would have made everything easier to bear."

"Yes, I suppose it would. But I wasn't thinking about you, Minty."

So Rose had taken her revenge on me with her silence, and I could have expected no better and no less.

My head swam, and I wanted very badly to go home. I managed to say, "I never loved him properly. Truly, properly." I was weeping openly. "It's in the letter."

Rose folded it and put it back on the desk. "When he left me, I stopped loving Nathan the way *he* wanted. It was inevitable. There was no other way of surviving."

We looked at each other. In that exchange lay the past, which we had shared, mourned, and regretted. She picked up the padded envelope. "One more thing. He asked Theo to send this to me. I think it is a diary of sorts. I haven't read it, Minty. Or only a little bit. I couldn't. I think you should take it."

She placed the envelope in my hands, and I peered inside. It was the missing notebook.

That too had gone to Rose.

The hardest thing of all to govern is the heart, and I had finally understood that I could not blame Nathan for the struggle with his. If one's own nature and impulses are unfathomable, then to reach into other minds to make sense of the rage, passion, and loyalties that lie within them is impossible.

In our separate ways, Rose, Nathan, and I had cheated one another and, in doing so, cheated ourselves. "I must try harder, Rose. To make something out of this," I said.

"Yes," she said. "Yes, we must."

On my return home, the boys, who had been watching for me at the window, ran out to greet me. I scooped them up and hustled them inside. I closed the front door, leaned against it, and breathed in deeply.

Chapter Twenty-four

It was Friday, four weeks before Christmas. In the meeting room at Paradox I watched the clock inch past five-thirty. Barry was in full flow and was not going to stop. What he had to say was interesting but I wished he had said it earlier in the day.

Chris propped his head in one hand. During a pause, he looked up. He had spotted my sneaking regard for the clock. "Are you in a hurry, Minty?"

"Not at all," I replied coolly.

"We're coming to you in a minute, Minty," Barry said.

In a feeble attempt to recognize the season, Syriol had draped a string of fairy lights over the picture on the wall. It was by Shiftaka, and I had persuaded Barry that it would be a good investment when he had decided to plough a portion of Paradox's profits into an asset. (When I pointed out that his employees might be considered assets, Barry grinned and said he needed *fixed* assets.)

Shiftaka's painting depicted an abstract figure, half flesh, half skeleton, lying on a bed of glowing coals. The colors were violent reds, the blackest of blacks, and a white background that could only be described as dirty. The label read: KYOTO RIP. The jury was still out as to whether I consider Shiftaka a good painter or not, but I am working hard on my "uneducated" eye. Still, if Barry *thinks* Shiftaka is cutting edge, it was a bargain.

When I had taken Barry to view it at Marcus's gallery, Marcus had been sitting at the desk, head bent over the laptop. At our entrance, he looked up and I was shocked: he appeared considerably older than I remembered. He took a second or two to place me and when he did, there was an unmistakable flare of hope in his eyes, which was as quickly extinguished when it became obvious that I was not Gisela's envoy.

I introduced the two men and explained that Barry was looking for an investment. Marcus swung into professional mode—an ease of manner, patience, careful sizing up of a potential client—and I thought what a much nicer man he was than Roger.

While Barry patrolled between the two rooms, Marcus turned to me and asked, in his unexpectedly deep voice, "How's Gisela?"

"Fine, I think. I haven't seen much of her lately."

He chose not to indulge in small talk—another factor in his favor—and went straight to the point. "She didn't seem to understand that I didn't want a wife. I wanted her. Not someone who stockpiles jam and checks over the dinner menus. But when it came to a decision, I think she preferred it. Gisela had got used to being a professional wife."

"I think you're right."

Marcus's rightness, however, was of no help to him. "What can she possibly gain with Roger? The dullness of such an existence . . . and *I'm* the one who loved her, not Roger."

With regret, I noted the past tense. "It's not dull, Marcus," I pointed out. "It's different."

Barry stopped prowling and pointed at *Kyoto RIP*. "I'll take that one." He pushed his face close to Marcus's. "Now, you are sure I won't be throwing my money away?"

Marcus did not even blink. "Nothing is certain."

So that was how Shiftaka had come to grace the walls at Paradox.

"Minty," Barry finally came to an end. "Do you want to go ahead?"

I pulled my notes toward me. "Okay. Remember last year we discussed an idea for middle age. It didn't work. But this will. Three-part series on being a parent. *Baby Love*. The format? Each section to be an hour, featuring expert talking heads and personal experiences of parents. The programs will ask: what are the stresses and strains of becoming a parent? Can you ever prepare for it? How does it affect a man or a woman physically or emotionally? What sort of impact do children have on marriages, friendships? How can if affect you if you become a stepparent to older children? How do you cope if you feel you are a failure as a parent? How do you *manage* as a lone parent?"

Good question. How do you manage as a lone parent?

Chris raised an eyebrow. Then he cleared his throat and made a note.

I continued, "The trick will be to handle the material in a fresh, bold manner, and to not be afraid to tackle the difficult aspects of being a parent. The programs *have* to be honest and say things that most people only think. Children do change you. You don't always love them. Parents do fail as parents. It is lonely."

"Any upside?" asked Chris.

"Oh, yes," I replied. "Plenty." I felt my heart squeeze. "But I will leave that for the parents to describe. They do it best." I picked up the treatment I had prepared and handed it to Barry. "We want it fast, colorful, daring, and I think BBC 1 should be the target."

Chris frowned. Barry gazed thoughtfully at *Kyoto RIP*.

"Minty, thanks," Barry said. "Not quite convinced, but I'll think about it. We'll talk."

"Think massive audience," I said.

Chris came into my office as I was shifting my papers into order. He closed the door and leaned against it. "I wanted to chew the cud about a few things, Minty."

"Sure." I clicked off my computer screen. As I did so, I noticed that my wedding ring was much looser and a vein running down my hand stood out in bas-relief. Not a good sign. Film stars had hand lifts for less.

"You heard we got the Carlton deal for the documentary on the pope?" He snapped his fingers. "Should boost the quarterly figures."

"Is that what you wanted to talk to me about? I would love to talk about it but could we do it tomorrow? I have to get home."

Chris levered himself away from the door and perched against my desk. Suddenly, my small office was very cramped. The hazel eyes gleamed. "You've had a tough year, Minty."

His kindness was unexpected, and I was still having trouble with kindness. It tended to reduce me. "Yes. But I'm coming to terms with it and making my way."

I need not have wasted my energy: Chris's kindness was merely a vehicle for other considerations.

"Minty, it might be better if you were working for a bigger organization which would have more slack for someone in your predicament. A very *real* predicament."

There was no point in getting angry. If I was to survive at Paradox until such time as I wished to leave on my own terms, I could not be angry. "Are you suggesting or *telling* me?"

He smiled gently, and I could not decide whether it was genuine or not. "Friend to friend, in this business it doesn't help to have additional pressures. A company as tight as Paradox needs to know it's functioning optimally with no unnecessary drag. You need to know that when problems arise, there is no problem in dealing with them, if you see what I mean."

"Sweet of you, Chris," I murmured.

In the old days, I would have deployed sex—which Nathan fell for. I would have opened my eyes, looked up from beneath the lids, and have made sure my cleavage was in the correct line of sight. I might have said, "How nice of you to take an interest," which would have introduced a faint chime of promise, sufficient to push Chris off the track. I'm not saying that I have come to despise such tactics, or would *never* use them again, only that sex took time, and the boys would be waiting for me.

Instead I placed the last of my notes in my bag and fastened it. "Chris, perhaps it would be better not to pursue this conversation. If you are trying to suggest that as a working mother, I'm a liability, it could get you into trouble . . ."

No fool, he backed off at once. "I was only thinking of you," he said.

On the way home, I passed Paige's house. The front garden was looking ultrasmart because the gardener had recently completed the autumn spring clean. "You can't call it a spring clean," I had pointed out to Paige when I phoned her the previous day. I can call it what I like was her reply.

"Has Martin been to see you?"

Paige bristled. "I *wish* you wouldn't interfere."

"And?"

"He's here at the weekend. But I'm not taking him back, Minty. As I told you, I'm far too busy with the children to be married."

The scene when I finally got through the door of Number 7 was much as I had pictured it. Eve had collapsed into a chair in the kitchen, and a small riot was going on in the boys' bedroom. One of Eve's hands lay on the table, so white and thin that it alarmed me.

First, I tackled her. "Look," I addressed the slumped figure. "This is not good. It's been going on for months, and you haven't got really better. You need to go home and see your family."

She raised her face from her hands and I was startled by the light in her eyes. "Go back?" She gulped a lungful of air—as if she was already breathing in the scents of river and mountains of her home.

That decided it. "You must go home for two weeks, see your family, rest, then come back."

"I get coach." Eve hauled herself to her feet, and her smile was pure joy. "I telephone. Now."

"No, that's a two-day journey both ways. No, you must fly."

"The moneys."

A stack of quick-fire calculations snapped through my brain. Eve needed a break. She needed her mother. Four days in a coach was not a rest. I needed Eve, well and strong, as she herself wished to be. "I'll pay your airfare, and you must go as soon as we can arrange it."

As I went upstairs, preparing for riot duty, the rest of the calculation slotted into place. What with the hit taken on my finances with the loan to Poppy, Eve's airfare equaled a reduction in the Christmas present list. It definitely put paid to the haircut, and the cost of her replacement would, no doubt, see off any strictly unnecessary seasonal frivolity. But that, I supposed, is what unnecessary meant. You could do without it.

It was the day before Christmas Eve, the kind of day that paraded a weak sun as a joke. I eased the car into the parking slot and got out. It was very cold, and I zipped up my fleece, a powder blue, then turned up the collar. I could smell frosted leaf mold and the faintest whiff of frying fat coming from a van selling snacks parked farther up.

I was relishing the moment of freedom, and allowing my mind to drift, before I took up the slack in the reins and pulled them tight. Moments such as these kept me sane.

I was contemplating getting back into the warm car, when a smart silver coupé drew up and parked in the space beside mine. One of the passenger doors flung open and Lucas tumbled out. "Mum . . ." He was followed closely by Felix. *"Mum . . ."* Both of them were clutching picture books with an illustration of a dinosaur on the front. I knew this because Felix virtually pressed his into my face.

A figure emerged from the driver's seat, dressed in a tweed jacket, black trousers, and boots. "Hi," said Rose.

She locked the car and, boys in tow, we moved off in the direction of the pond.

"Lucas didn't eat much lunch," Rose reported. "He was too excited. There was an exhibition about *Tyrannosaurus rex*. The model ate model prey and snapped its jaws. Lucas was transfixed, and Felix . . . well, I am not sure that he liked it much."

"Was it crowded?"

"Was it *crowded*?"

We circumnavigated the pond once, and that was enough. It was scummy and the council's attempts to landscape it had only gone so far before the money had run out. It was too cold. By mutual consent, we retraced our steps to the cars. "What are you up to?" I asked Rose.

"After Christmas I'm off to see Hal at the farm. I haven't seen him for weeks." Her face registered anticipation and pleasure. "After that, Vietnam, I think. There's a piece I've got to do."

We stood by the cars. "Thank you so much for taking them today," I said. "I'm so grateful." I fished in my pocket for my car keys, which had become attached to half a boiled sweet I had given to Lucas the last time he had felt carsick. Rose extracted her keys from a brilliant green lizard-skin handbag and zapped the lock. "Next time, I'll take them to the zoo. When it gets warmer."

We leaned toward each other, an awkward second elapsed as we clashed cheeks and exchanged the lightest of kisses.

"Thanks," I said again.

"That's fine." She kissed Felix and Lucas on the tops of their heads. "Be good, boys, and remember what I told you."

When the twins had been strapped into their seats, Rose and I drove off in opposite directions. Before she disappeared, Rose tooted her horn.

I drove back through the streets, where people made their way home from work. It seemed that there were couples everywhere. Hand in hand. Talking. Sharing a bottle of water or chips. Some had their arms round each other. One man had his hand tucked into the pocket of his girlfriend's jacket. At the corner of Albert Bridge Road and Battersea Bridge Road, another couple was wrapped in each other's arms. As I drove past, I caught a glimpse of the girl's face. It was enraptured, alight, quivering with a new dawn.

My eyes smarted with tears.

I had not read a self-help manual in weeks. For one thing, I had hunted down the statistics. "The most likely customer for a book on any given topic," concluded one researcher, "was someone who had bought a similar tome within the past eighteen months." This begged the question: if self-help manuals are so good at solving the problem, why would you need to buy another on *the same subject*?

"What was it that Rose told you to remember?" I asked the boys eventually.

Lucas went, "Roar, roar. That's the dinosaur eating the horse."

"They weren't *horses*," said Felix. "Not then."

"Boys, what did Rose ask you to remember?"

In the rear mirror, I watched Felix's brow wrinkle with effort. "She said we looked more and more like Daddy every day," he said.

I flicked my finger over my cheek where the tears continued to run. Rule number six of the rules governing my life is taken from something Rose said. It states: you must hold on, for this too will pass.

Poppy had been a little sour about the family decision to hold Christmas lunch at Number 7. "Richard and I could almost be offended," she pointed out, "and our house is bigger."

She had been mollified, however, when it was arranged that Jilly and Frieda would drive up from Bath, Sam would fly in from the States, and they would stay with Poppy for a couple of days. Jilly was pregnant again and, in the latest bulletin, Sam announced that they had agreed she would remain in the UK until after the birth—"we couldn't afford to have a baby in the States"—then join Sam in Austin.

The boys and I chose the Christmas tree from the trader at the corner of Lakey Street and brought it home, with a selection of particularly nasty colored baubles and colored lights with which they had fallen in love. It had been no use protesting that silver balls and white lights were prettier. They simply did not see it. Any idea I might have cherished of a sophisticated, elegant tree disintegrated in the face of a determined pair of twins.

After all, and after everything, it was their tree.

We put it up in the hall. Felix and Lucas did their best to hold it steady while I crawled underneath to screw it into the stand. The three of us stood back to assess the effect. "Mummy," pronounced Felix seriously, "it's a bit crooked." I bit my lip. This had been Nathan's job, and he had been expert in the fine-tuning. I saw "Daddy" float through their minds, and I said, "You're so picky, Felix," but I crawled back underneath the pine-scented branches and thought: *You should see me now, Nathan.*

I planned everything down to the last detail. Presents . . . bath oil for the women, which I employed Syriol to wrap, who was keen to earn a bit extra, and a good bottle of wine each for the men. Food . . . the turkey, ready-made gravy, cranberry sauce, bread sauce, vegetables, and pudding was to be delivered from the supermarket. I reckoned I could manage to peel the brussels sprouts and potatoes with the boys' help.

A big smile plastered across her wan face, Eve had flown home on Christmas Eve with so much luggage—mostly sweaters and socks from Marks & Spencer—that I was convinced she would not get through check-in.

I had filled the stockings several days previously.

On Christmas Day, I had been up at dawn laying the table. Having thought long and hard about the *placements,* I decided that Sam should be at the head with his mother and Jilly on either side. Frieda was beside her mother. Richard was at the other end of the table with me. Poppy had volunteered to sit the twins on either side of her to keep an eye on them. You are to make decent conversation, I admonished them. "What's decent?" asked Felix.

Sam arrived early straight from the airport. He was tired, unshaven, and foul breathed. I sent him up to the spare bedroom, where he could wash and brush up in peace. The rest arrived half an hour later.

There was confusion as to whether the presents should be opened before or after lunch, but I put my foot down and announced that lunch would burn if we delayed. Sam carved, and Richard poured the wine. Poppy had provided the candles (red and glittering), which, to be honest, would not have been my first choice, and played cat's cradle with the twins while the food was served. With one arm round Frieda, Rose talked earnestly to Jilly.

No one paid me much attention, but that was fine, particularly as I was busy in the kitchen. That was how I wanted it. As we sat and ate, conversation flew back and forth across the table, little snippets of gossip, an old joke, a snatch of reminiscence. Only so much could have been expected from six-year-olds and before long the boys had decided that they were jumping beans and Richard had to swap places to try to help Poppy control them.

When I emerged from the kitchen with two puddings burning merrily, there was a smattering of applause. I sat down, exhausted, speechless, and not hungry. At that moment, Rose sent me a little smile.

We discussed jet lag. "I've been taking melatonin," Sam rubbed his face, "but it's not great."

"You should try arnica. The pills, I mean," Rose said.

"It might be better if you didn't quaff huge quantities of wine on board." Poppy leaned over to poke her brother. "Eh?"

"Who are you to lecture on behavior?" Sam grinned all the same. "I know where your secrets are buried." For a second, Poppy's eyes were dark with terror. Under the table, I felt for her hand. After a moment, Poppy's fingers tightened on mine. Sam continued, "Who snitched the chocolate bunny from Gavin in the fifth form? That's what I want to know."

After the pudding Sam got to his feet, wineglass in hand. "We need a toast," he said. "Absent friends."

"Dad . . . ," cried one of the twins and I swiveled round to see which.

There followed one of the heartbreaking, emotion-filled

silences that no one wanted to last. The twins wriggled, Frieda made a face, and the adults drank our toast. *Absent friends.*

At which point, Freida threw herself back in her chair and overbalanced. "Oh, for goodness' sake," said Jilly. "I told you not to do that." Then she remembered it was Christmas and wiped the frown off her face. "Come here, sweetheart, I'll kiss you better."

Sam produced a digital camera. "Okay. Best smiles," he ordered. "Mum can you move up a bit. Frieda, sit *still*. Lucas, can you get onto your mum's lap? Thank you."

We held our poses, there were several clicks, and Sam fiddled with the camera. "Have a look," he said and passed it round.

Rose was in the middle of the group, with Jilly beside her. Richard's eyes were red. Lucas had moved at the crucial moment and, consequently, was a little blurred. Felix was pointing at something. Poppy was gazing at Richard. And myself? I was positioned in the left-hand corner of the photo, looking tired, which was not surprising. "It's quite good of you, Minty," Poppy commented and handed the camera back to Sam.

Rose sat herself down beside me. "I've been thinking about the garden, as you asked. We could put the catmint over by the fence. It would fit well there and leave space for the boys to play. What do you think?"

A candle guttered, and I leaned forward to shield the flame. It was hot against my flesh, and I flinched. "Mum . . ." shrieked Felix. "Mum . . . can we have presents?"

The flame steadied, and I took my hand away.

WIVES
BEHAVING
BADLY

Elizabeth Buchan

An Introduction to
Wives Behaving Badly

Thousands of readers fell in love with and rooted for Rose Lloyd, the winning heroine of Elizabeth Buchan's bestselling novel *Revenge of the Middle-Aged Woman*. What could be more delicious, more satisfying, than hearing how it all turned out for "the other woman," Minty, who stole not only Rose's husband but her job as well?

In *Wives Behaving Badly*, we are privy to the good, bad, and ugly of Minty's story. She has now been married to Nathan for seven years and given birth to twin boys, Felix and Lucas. But things haven't turned out exactly as Minty had planned. She seems unable to shake the stigma of being the second wife. Despite redecorating the entire house, Minty finds that the memories of Rose are everywhere. And ironically, after a passionate start, she and Nathan now find themselves immersed in the very domestic boredom that Nathan left Rose to escape. Worst of all, Minty is plagued by nagging doubts—does Nathan really love her or does he still love Rose? Did she ever truly love Nathan or was it the promise of a comfortable life that won her over?

When Rose calls Minty one day with terrible news that suddenly changes her world, Minty must overcome her shock and face head on all that she ever questioned and doubted about her marriage and her life. Once conflicted about motherhood, Minty now finds herself fiercely devoted to her children. Where before she always put herself first, Minty now comes to the aid of her nanny, her stepdaughter, and her best friend. At this time of her own great need and sorrow, Minty is finally able to give of herself. She grows up, into the mother, friend, and person she never thought she could or even wanted to be. And perhaps her biggest step forward is her embracing of Rose. Once dear friends and then bitter adversaries, Rose and Minty find themselves bound together by the very thing that drove them apart: their love for Nathan.

With her signature wit and unflinching eye for the modern-day drama of everyday domestic and professional affairs, Elizabeth Buchan has once again created a brilliant and poignant story about women, family, friendship, and the bumpy journey we all take toward a life we hope is worth living.

A CONVERSATION WITH ELIZABETH BUCHAN

1. How and when did you decide to write this sequel to your hugely successful book Revenge of the Middle-Aged Woman? *And how did you decide to do it from Minty's point of view as opposed to perhaps the more obvious choice of using Rose's voice? How did you feel about Minty when writing* Revenge of the Middle-Aged Woman *and did your opinion change or evolve in any way as you wrote* Wives Behaving Badly?

The idea for *Wives Behaving Badly* came to me when I was asleep. I woke up one morning with Minty in my head. I had written two other novels in between but, at that moment, I knew I had to complete the circle of the story that began with Rose and the destruction of her marriage to Nathan. From the first, I felt— and my observations bore this out—that these kinds of situations are never straightforward, and so it proved to be as the novel began to roll onto the pages. Rose and Minty are linked in a complicated way. Neither can dismiss the other. When I wrote *Revenge of the Middle-Aged Woman* I was inside Rose's head. Now, I had to perform the ventriloquist's trick and climb inside Minty's. Not surprisingly perhaps, since I had to establish an intimate acquaintanceship with her, I found myself rather involved with Minty. She had done great damage (so had Nathan), but by the end of the novel a different Minty was emerging: battered and chastened but on a new path. I hope readers will understand her better and like her enough to enjoy her particular take on life.

2. Minty's pain and reaction to having her husband die rings very true. In her book The Year of Magical Thinking, *Joan Didion talks about how the shoes were the only possessions of her dead husband's that she could not bear to part with. Minty has the same trouble with Nathan's shoes. Did you do some research into dealing with the death of a spouse or did you go by instinct alone as to how that loss might feel?*

I am so thankful to say that I have no experience of a spouse's death but, like everyone, there have been people close to me who have died. Looking now at the text, I can see that I drew on the experience of my father's death, although I was not aware of this as I wrote it. Your question has made me think back and I remember in particular when it came to sorting out his clothes it was almost impossible for my mother and my sisters to throw away his ties and his army medals. They were so much a part of him. To discard them seemed like the final straw, the final blow. There is always some object, very often an unexpected one I suspect, that comes to embody the dead person and that object seems to hold the very essence of them.

3. Minty has many good women friends (Paige, for one) yet betrayed one of her best friends, Rose. To generalize, this seems to represent

Are men and women so different in this respect? If you look at the events in the average boardroom or council chamber there are many, many betrayals and bloodlettings by men. The difference is those betrayals are portrayed in a different guise. They come under the heading of "business" or "economic growth" but the human activity going on under those banners doesn't deviate very much from the activity that goes under the banner of "family" or "friendship." It is interesting how we respond to both. If something is deemed good for business then it gets a tick, even if that something is morally questionable. We are far less forgiving of, say, the other woman such as Minty. Having said that, what Minty does is unforgivable on many levels for she does betray a friendship and, as it turns out, destroys a family. Yet Minty is looking after herself—and do we do any different? There is a part of Minty in all of us—and the struggle to balance morality with the impulse to serve our self-interest is one that continues through life.

4. Work is often ignored in novels, yet you always highlight its significance in your characters' lives. Would you talk about why the role of work seems to interest you so much and why it is often overlooked in many novels?

When my mother was a young woman, most women had to give up their jobs when they married, and a woman was obliged to obtain her husband's permission to run a separate bank account. Women going out to work has transformed many aspects of modern Western society. But it brings enormous pressures; it takes a toll and it has affected the way the family works. The subject of work, and a mother's working in particular, must be a huge and an important one for the writer—perhaps I feel especially strongly about the need to explore this in fiction because I found that being a working mother was very difficult and exhausting! I don't think there are any easy solutions though.

5. You have called marriage an endlessly fertile theme for a writer. In an interview for The Good Wife Strikes Back, *you said you were interested in asking why marriage works and why it lasts. Do you think you've figured out a lot of these questions over the years and answered most of them, perhaps with this novel in particular?*

I think I can safely say that there is no one definitive answer. The health of marriage—and judging by the divorce figures this is a little rocky at present—is an indication of what is going on with people and the society they live in. Until recently, marriage was one of the building blocks of society. It was sanctified by the church and ratified by the state. Governments and experts talked about the family and made decisions and assumptions based on the old nuclear unit. That is all changing. There are many reasons why this is happening. In my novels, for example, I have explored the wife who stayed with the absent and erring husband, the abandoned wife, and in an earlier novel, *Consider the Lily*, I wrote about the initially loveless marriage and how it was transformed into something that worked. In each of these situations, there were hugely interesting psychological and social aspects to write about—as well as the story. For example, in *The Good Wife Strikes Back*, the wife decides to stay with her husband because she does not want to damage her daughter and she decides to take the risk. In *Everything She Thought She Wanted* the contemporary heroine has to try to balance marriage and motherhood with her work. In *Wives Behaving Badly*, I compare two other marriages to Minty and Nathan's. Some might conclude that the bargain Gisela has struck with Roger to be questionable—but the marriage works. More problematic is Paige and her marriage to Martin—but Paige is

6

undergoing a type of transition as she pushes herself back on track from having had three children after giving up a high-powered career. It is going to take time for Paige to pull her type of personality back together into reasonableness.

6. In writing about Nathan's death, you seem to have crossed into some darker territory than your previous novels covered. Do you agree? Would you discuss the arc of your writerly life and how relevant your stage of life is to what you are writing at the time?

I have written about death before. In my second novel, *Light of the Moon*, quite a few characters met their deaths, including the main hero, because it was a wartime story and, in the circumstances, sadly inevitable. In later books, there have been deaths but I have never before tackled the subject quite so close up. I had to think very hard to try to convey its enormity and yet how death is felt and experienced in small everyday ways. A friend of mine told me that the death of her husband hit her hardest when she had to change a light bulb. It is those telling tiny details that I chose to work with. With respect to the writerly life, the novels have reflected the stages in my life. When I was younger I chose to write novels with bigger backdrops—the French Revolution, the Second World War. It was very useful for the infant novelist to have a set watershed event against which to pose characters and demand courage, hardship, passion, daring, etc. from them. As I progressed I became very interested in the smaller, but no less significant, arena. It seemed to me that those important shifts in emotion and sensibility can happen when you are shelling the beans at home as it can when you ride out to battle. And when I stepped into the middle-age bracket, I felt I had no option but to write about it— because I discovered that it was an exciting place to be.

7. Did you plan on having Nathan die when you first started writing Wives Behaving Badly? *If so, did you think it was absolutely necessary in order to tell Minty's story, and if not, how did you decide on this dramatic turn of events?*

Yes, I knew Nathan would die. This was a ruthless decision but I needed Minty to have to face the situation on her own in order to make the emotional journey that I had planned for her. I also wanted to examine the dynamics of this triangle. I suspected, and it became increasingly clear as I wrote *Wives Behaving Badly*, that it was not Nathan who occupied the top of the triangle but Rose. Her power became greater because of her absence from the marriage. She was the hovering ghost. The Other that haunts us. When Nathan dies that shifts into another plane and changes shape. Rose becomes—with some difficulty and distress—a kind of ally and Minty discovers that it is her children who now haunt her— as every new parent discovers.

8. Whose story are you most interested in telling next?

I have become fascinated by the illuminated Books of Hours that were produced in medieval times. They were often stunningly beautiful and I want to write about a woman—her name is Nell—who has been commissioned by a wealthy collector to track down lost pages from the fabled De Gris Book of Hours, which was cut up during the nineteenth century. The page depicts the figure of Bathsheba bathing and, in the past, has sent many collectors almost mad because it is so beautiful and desirable. But there is something else about the story of this book. Nell feels there is a puzzle to the picture and she needs to find out precisely what. In doing so, she will discover things about herself, things that are surprising and will change the course of her life. I hope to have lots of detail about medieval life and painting, and also about the highly charged contemporary art world, which seethes with ambitions and egos and is driven by a combination of big money and a love of beauty.

QUESTIONS FOR DISCUSSION

1. Minty recalls a quote that says "cynics are the only true romantics." Do you agree? How might it apply to Minty? "I was marrying Nathan without any of the true and proper feelings, only nonfeelings," Minty adds (p. 5). What does she mean by this? Why do you think she married Nathan?

2. In the opening of Chapter One, Minty lists the rules that govern her life—a partly humorous, partly serious list. What do you think of them? Do you have your own set of rules? If so, discuss them. If not, why not?

3. Minty is shocked when she discovers Nathan's personal journal with the notation about most people having a "secret grief." What do you think Nathan's secret grief is? Do you agree that everyone has one? Do you think Nathan, consciously or unconsciously, wanted Minty to read his private notebook? Should she have read it? Are there limits to privacy in a marriage, and when do private thoughts turn into secrets that shouldn't be kept?

4. What do you think about Minty's attitude toward motherhood? For example, "There are not many good things about being pregnant" (p. 113), and earlier Minty felt *absolutely nothing* when her twins were born (p. 28). These are certainly not the typical sentiments one usually hears about becoming a mother. Do you think Minty is just more honest than most about the subject or does she truly lack the maternal instinct? Given her feelings, why did she get herself into her current predicament?

5. Why do you think it was Rose whom Nathan first told about being sacked by Vistemax? What do you think Nathan's feelings for Rose really were? Why do you think Elizabeth Buchan chose to have Nathan die in Rose's house?

6. Minty decides to take the boys to the place by the sea where Nathan and Rose used to go. Why does she decide, after many years of resisting, to do this now? What does she discover there about Nathan and about herself?

7. Despite their seeming dislike of each other, Rose and Minty keep ending up together. Why is that? Do you think they need each other in some way? By the end of the novel they have made amends. Can a friendship ever truly recover from a betrayal such as Minty's? Do you think Minty will agree to keep Rose as the twins' legal guardian in the will, should anything happen to her?

8. When the boys' nanny, Eve, becomes ill, it seems to signal another significant turning point in Minty's life. Discuss how Eve's illness sets in motion other events and how it leads to further change in Minty.

9. At one point in the novel, Minty thinks, "I should have been honest with Nathan and told him, *We won't be free. It isn't like that*" (p. 240). What does she mean? Would it have changed anything if she had told him?

10. At the beginning of the novel, how did you feel about Minty? Did you find her sympathetic? Did your feelings change at all by the end of the novel?

11. Elizabeth Buchan makes beautiful use of the garden as a metaphor for life in many of her novels. Discuss how she does so here in *Wives Behaving Badly*.

12. Minty is working on a project about being "middle-aged," and the subject is often referred to throughout the novel. How would you define/describe "middle age"? Is it different for men and women? Has the definition changed over the years? Would you attribute Nathan's actions to a midlife crisis?

13. Marriage is a central theme here and in Buchan's other novels. If you've read her other books, discuss the relationships in each and what Buchan seems to say about marriage, monogamy, and fidelity. In addition to being a perennial subject of literature, marriage has also become a political hot topic as its very definition is being debated. Why do you think it sparks such intense feelings? Discuss what you think makes a marriage successful as well as the things that can doom it to failure.

For more information about or to order other Penguin Readers Guides, please e-mail the Penguin Marketing Department at reading@us.penguingroup.com or write to us at:

> Penguin Books Marketing Dept.
> Readers Guides
> 375 Hudson Street
> New York, NY 10014-3657

Please allow 4–6 weeks for delivery.
To access Penguin Readers Guides online, visit the Penguin Group (USA) Web site at www.penguin.com.

FOR THE BEST IN PAPERBACKS, LOOK FOR THE

In every corner of the world, on every subject under the sun, Penguin represents quality and variety—the very best in publishing today.

For complete information about books available from Penguin—including Penguin Classics and Puffins—and how to order them, write to us at the appropriate address below. Please note that for copyright reasons the selection of books varies from country to country.

In the United States: Please write to *Penguin Group (USA), P.O. Box 12289 Dept. B, Newark, New Jersey 07101-5289* or call 1-800-788-6262.

In the United Kingdom: Please write to *Dept. EP, Penguin Books Ltd, Bath Road, Harmondsworth, West Drayton, Middlesex UB7 0DA.*

In Canada: Please write to *Penguin Books Canada Ltd, 90 Eglinton Avenue East, Suite 700, Toronto, Ontario M4P 2Y3.*

In Australia: Please write to *Penguin Books Australia Ltd, P.O. Box 257, Ringwood, Victoria 3134.*

In New Zealand: Please write to *Penguin Books (NZ) Ltd, Private Bag 102902, North Shore Mail Centre, Auckland 10.*

In India: Please write to *Penguin Books India Pvt Ltd, 11 Panchsheel Shopping Centre, Panchsheel Park, New Delhi 110 017.*

In the Netherlands: Please write to *Penguin Books Netherlands bv, Postbus 3507, NL-1001 AH Amsterdam.*

In Germany: Please write to *Penguin Books Deutschland GmbH, Metzlerstrasse 26, 60594 Frankfurt am Main.*

In Spain: Please write to *Penguin Books S. A., Bravo Murillo 19, 1° B, 28015 Madrid.*

In Italy: Please write to *Penguin Italia s.r.l., Via Benedetto Croce 2, 20094 Corsico, Milano.*

In France: Please write to *Penguin France, Le Carré Wilson, 62 rue Benjamin Baillaud, 31500 Toulouse.*

In Japan: Please write to *Penguin Books Japan Ltd, Kaneko Building, 2-3-25 Koraku, Bunkyo-Ku, Tokyo 112.*

In South Africa: Please write to *Penguin Books South Africa (Pty) Ltd, Private Bag X14, Parkview, 2122 Johannesburg.*